In the latest thriller in the #1 *New York Times* bestselling series, homicide detective Eve Dallas investigates a murder with a mysterious motive—and a terrifying weapon.

Pediatrician Kent Abner received the package on a beautiful April morning. Inside was a cheap trinket, a golden egg that could be opened into two halves. When he pried it apart, highly toxic airborne fumes entered his body—and killed him.

After Eve Dallas calls the hazmat team—and undergoes testing to reassure both her and her husband that she hasn't been exposed—it's time to look into Dr. Abner's past and relationships. Not every victim Eve encounters is an angel, but it seems that Abner came pretty close—though he did ruffle some feathers over the years by taking stands for the weak and defenseless. While the lab tries to identify the deadly toxin, Eve hunts for the sender. But when someone else dies in the same grisly manner, it becomes clear that she's dealing with either a madman—or someone who has a hidden and elusive connection to both victims.

TITLES BY J. D. ROBB

ANTHOLOGIES

Silent Night
(with Susan Plunkett, Dee Holmes, and Claire Cross)

Out of This World
(with Laurell K. Hamilton, Susan Krinard, and Maggie Shayne)

Remember When
(with Nora Roberts)

Bump in the Night
(with Mary Blayney, Ruth Ryan Langan, and Mary Kay McComas)

Dead of Night
(with Mary Blayney, Ruth Ryan Langan, and Mary Kay McComas)

Three in Death

Suite 606
(with Mary Blayney, Ruth Ryan Langan, and Mary Kay McComas)

In Death

The Lost
(with Patricia Gaffney, Mary Blayney, and Ruth Ryan Langan)

The Other Side
(with Mary Blayney, Patricia Gaffney, Ruth Ryan Langan, and Mary Kay McComas)

Time of Death

The Unquiet
(with Mary Blayney, Patricia Gaffney, Ruth Ryan Langan, and Mary Kay McComas)

Mirror, Mirror
(with Mary Blayney, Elaine Fox, Mary Kay McComas, and R. C. Ryan)

Down the Rabbit Hole
(with Mary Blayney, Elaine Fox, Mary Kay McComas, and R. C. Ryan)

GOLDEN
IN
DEATH

J. D. Robb

St. Martin's Paperbacks

This is a work of fiction. All of the characters, organizations, and events portrayed in this novel are either products of the author's imagination or are used fictitiously.

Published in the United States by St. Martin's Paperbacks, an imprint of St. Martin's Publishing Group.

GOLDEN IN DEATH

For information, address St. Martin's Publishing Group, 120 Broadway, New York, NY 10271.

www.stmartins.com

Library of Congress Catalog Card Number: 2019036358

ISBN: 978-1-250-20722-7

Our books may be purchased in bulk for promotional, educational, or business use. Please contact your local bookseller or the Macmillan Corporate and Premium Sales Department at 1-800-221-7945, ext. 5442, or by email at MacmillanSpecialMarkets@macmillan.com.

Printed in the United States of America

St. Martin's Press hardcover edition / February 2020
St. Martin's Paperbacks edition 2020

10 9 8 7 6 5 4 3 2 1

Time shall unfold what plaited cunning hides:
Who cover faults, at last shame them derides.

—William Shakespeare

'Tis education forms the common mind;
Just as the twig is bent the tree's inclined.

—Alexander Pope

1

Dr. Kent Abner began the day of his death comfortable and content.

Following the habit of his day off, he kissed his husband of thirty-seven years off to work, then settled down in his robe with another cup of coffee, a crossword challenge on his PPC, and Mozart's *The Magic Flute* on his entertainment unit.

His plans for later included a run through Hudson River Park, as April 2061 proved balmy and blooming. After, he could hit the gym and some weights, grab a shower, have a bite in the café.

On the way home, he thought he'd pick up fresh flowers, wander through the market, and get the olives Martin so enjoyed, maybe a nice selection of cheeses. Then he'd meander to the bakery for a baguette and whatever else appealed.

When Martin came home, they'd open a bottle of wine, sit and talk and have some bread and cheese. He'd leave the choice of eat in or eat out to Martin, with, hopefully, a romantic ending to the day—if Martin wasn't worn out.

They often joked Kent as a pediatrician handled the adorable babies and charming kids, while Martin as headmaster for a K–12 private academy juggled charming kids with hormonal and broody teens.

Still, it worked for them, Kent thought as he filled in 21-Down.

Toxic.

He spent an entertaining hour with the puzzle, tidied up the kitchen while music filled the air of their townhome in the West Village.

Kent changed into his running clothes, added a light hoodie. He packed his gym bag, deciding he'd drop it off in his locker before his run.

As he zipped it, the doorbell rang.

Humming to himself, he carried his bag out to the living room, set it on the coral sofa he and Martin had chosen when they'd redecorated six months before.

Out of habit, he checked the door monitor, saw the delivery girl he recognized with a small package.

He disengaged the locks, opened the door.

"Good morning!"

"Morning, Dr. Abner. Got a package for you."

"So I see. You just caught me." He took the package, offered her a smile as the Queen of the Night's vengeful second-act aria poured out to Bedford Street. "Beautiful day!"

"It sure is. You have a good one," she added before she walked down the steps to the sidewalk.

"You, too."

Kent closed the door, studying the package as he carried it back to the kitchen. Since it was addressed to him, he opened the drawer for the box cutter. The return label had a Midtown address and a shop name—All That Glitters—he didn't recognize.

A gift? he wondered as he cut the box.

Inside the box, under the packing, another box. Small, simple, he thought, smooth, dark faux wood closed with a small lock, the key attached with a thin chain.

Baffled, he set it down, unlocked the clasp.

Inside the box, nestled in thick black padding, sat a small—undeniably cheap—golden egg, closed tight with a tiny hook.

"All That Glitters," he muttered, flipped the hook. The lid stuck a bit as he started to lift it. He gave it a harder tug.

He didn't see the vapor, didn't taste it. But he felt the effects instantly as his throat seemed to snap shut, his lungs clog. His eyes burned, and his well-toned muscles began to tremble.

The egg dropped from his fingers as he stumbled blindly toward the window. Air, he needed air. He tripped, fell, tried to crawl away. His system revolted, expelling the light breakfast he'd had with his husband. Fighting through the tearing pain, he tried to drag himself across the floor.

He collapsed, convulsing as Mozart's Queen hit high F.

On a bright spring afternoon, Lieutenant Eve Dallas stood over the body of Dr. Kent Abner. That late-afternoon sunlight streamed through the windows he'd failed to open, spilled over the pools of body fluids, the shards of broken plastic.

The victim lay faceup—though the contusions on

his forehead, temple indicated to her he'd fallen face-first. His eyes, red, swollen, with the film death had painted over them, stared back at her.

She could see, clearly, the smears feet, hands, knees had swiped through expelled body fluids. Footprints outlined with blood, bile, puke tracked the kitchen floor.

Her crime scene, she thought, had been shot to shit.

"Let's hear it, Officer Ponce," she said to the first on scene.

"The vic's Kent Abner, a doctor, lives here with his husband. Had the day off. Husband—that's another doctor, but the Ph.D. type, Martin Rufty—comes home from work—headmaster at Theresa A. Gold Academy—at approximately sixteen hundred. Sees the body. He walked right in the body fluids, Lieutenant, turned the body over, actually tried to revive him before he called the MTs."

The uniform, a burly vet, shook his head at the scene. "Then they come in, and we've got them all over it before we're called in. Did what we could to secure it at that point. Vic's been gone for hours. MTs said he was cold and stiff. And how it looked like some kind of chemical poisoning."

"Where's the spouse?"

"We got him upstairs. My partner's with him. He's a mess."

"Okay. Stand by." Eve turned to her partner.

"Peabody, I'll take the body. Find the security feed, take a look."

"Got that." In her pink cowboy boots, Peabody stepped carefully as Eve opened her field kit, crouched down.

She'd already sealed up, turned on her recorder, and now took out her Identi-pad to verify the victim's ID.

"Victim is identified as Kent Abner of this address, age sixty-seven. Contusions and lacerations on the forehead, left temple, also on left knee. They look consistent with a fall. Got some burns on the thumbs, both hands. The body's in rigor. The eyes are red, swollen."

Carefully, she opened the victim's mouth. "So's the tongue. Looks like . . . bits of foam and saliva, vomit. Blood and mucus, dried now, from the nose."

She took out her gauges. "TOD, nine-forty-three. Peabody! Run the feed back to this morning. Check when the spouse left, if anyone came in after that."

"I've got a male—tweed jacket—mid-sixties, about six-three, one-eighty, carrying the briefcase on the floor in there, coming in a couple minutes after four. Uses a swipe and code. And he's letting the MTs in at sixteen-ten. Two uniforms arrive at sixteen-sixteen."

Peabody, her dark hair in a short, bouncy tail, peeked around a door. "I'll run it back."

Eve continued with the body. "No defensive or offensive wounds. Head and knee—possible blow, but more consistent with a fall. He's a well-built man, looks strong. He would've fought back if fighting back was an option. Did he eat something, drink something . . . ?"

"Same male—has to be the spouse—walking out at oh-seven-twenty. No activity prior. And . . . we've got a female in a Global Post and Packages uniform. She's ringing it at oh-nine-thirty-six. Vic answers—friendly, like they know each other. He takes the package in; she leaves."

Eve rose, walked to the counter. "Standard delivery box? Say, ten inches square?"

"That's the one. I'm zipping through—nothing after the delivery and before the spouse comes back."

Peabody stepped out.

"Box cutter's right here. He's dead seven minutes after he takes the package. He brings it in here," Eve said. "Opens it. Takes out this other box—cheap fake wood, little lock and key. Opens that. We've got broken bits of colored material and shards—shiny gold color maybe on the outside, white interior—on the floor. Maybe hard plastic. Something in the box. Open that and . . ."

"Fuck." She stepped back. "Call the hazmat unit."

"Oh, shit."

"The spouse isn't dead, or the MTs, or the first on scene. Whatever it was must be dissipated enough, but call them in, let them know we have an unknown toxic substance."

Eve eased around, read the return address on the box.

"All That Glitters." She ran it. "Bogus name and address on the shipping box."

"They're on their way," Peabody reported, "and advise us to evacuate the premises."

"Too late for that. Seven minutes, Peabody. Subtract the couple minutes to walk back here, get the box cutter, open everything. He was basically dead when he opened the box over seven hours ago." And still, she thought. "Get Uniform Carmichael and Officer Shelby over to Global Post and Packages, find out where this package was dropped off for shipping, who signed it in, if there's any security feed. Then contact the morgue team, and tell them we may have a hot one."

"Dallas, you touched him—"

"I was sealed," Eve reminded her. "His spouse, the MTs touched him, too. Whatever killed him, it's done its work. It's finished."

She stood a moment, a tall, lanky woman with a choppy cap of brown hair, brown cop's eyes, wearing a bronze leather jacket, good brown boots.

Basic precautions, she told herself.

"I'm going to scrub up, just to cover protocol. When I have, we'll talk to the spouse. We're going to want whatever he was wearing when he touched the vic bagged for the hazmat team."

She grabbed her field kit, started off to find a powder room or bathroom. "Contact the shipping company first. We need to talk to the delivery person."

Going to be late, she thought as she used the scrub in her kit in a stylish powder room with maroon walls.

According to the Marriage Rules—self-written and -enforced—she needed to let her own spouse know. Roarke understood the job's screwy hours, but you had to follow the rules.

Peabody stepped up to the door. "Carmichael and Shelby are on their way to GP&P, and I have the name of the delivery person for this route. Lydia Merchant. She clocked out at her usual time, but I have contact info on her."

"Let's run her in the meantime. Seems long odds she'd make the delivery if she decided to poison a customer, but people can be stupid."

Eve waited for the special team, tolerated the scan to make certain she hadn't contracted some toxicity from the body—wanted to balk when the lead tech insisted on drawing some blood to test on the spot. But figured not only better safe than sorry, but quicker to deal with it and move on.

Cleared, she and Peabody headed upstairs to talk to the spouse.

"Lydia Merchant, age twenty-seven," Peabody began on the walk upstairs. "Employed by GP&P for six years. Clean employment record, clear on criminal."

"We talk to her anyway."

Rufty's clothes had already been bagged and sealed. In gray sweatpants and a navy sweatshirt with TAG in gold across the chest, he sat, shocked and grieving, on a curvy love seat in a sitting area of a bedroom done in rusty reds and old gold.

He had a neat brown goatee streaked with blond to match a shaggy mop of hair. A tall, gangly man, he had a long, thin face, dark, currently watery brown eyes.

He wore, as the victim did, a white gold band on the third finger of his left hand. And his hands stayed clutched together as if they alone kept him from shattering into pieces.

Eve signaled to the uniform who sat with him.

"Start the canvass with your partner. Anyone who saw anything, I hear about it. If you touched the body or anything in or around the crime scene, the hazmat unit needs to clear you."

"Yes, sir." He glanced back at Rufty. "He wants to call their kids, but I've held him off. He for sure touched the body, sir."

"We'll get to that. Take the bagged clothes down with you, give them to hazmat. Have one of them come up to scan and clear him."

She moved to Rufty, sat on the deep red chair facing him. "Dr. Rufty, I'm Lieutenant Dallas. This is Detective Peabody. We're very sorry for your loss."

"I—I need to talk to the kids. Our children. I need—"

"We'll let you do that very soon. I know this is a difficult time for you, but we need to ask you some questions."

"I—I came home. I called out: 'Jesus, Kent, what a day. Let's have a really big drink.'" He covered his long, thin face with his long, thin hands. "And I walked back to the kitchen, and—Kent. Kent. He was on the floor. He was . . . I tried to . . . I couldn't. He was . . ."

Peabody leaned over, took his hand in hers. "We're very sorry, Dr. Rufty. There was nothing you could do."

"But . . ." He turned to her, and the look, Eve thought, said: Help me. Explain. Make it stop.

"I don't understand. He's so healthy. He's always nagging me to exercise more, eat better. He's so fit and strong. I don't understand. He was going for a run this morning. He always goes for a run on his day off, and on his lunch hour if he can squeeze it in during office hours. He was going to finish the crossword and go for a run."

"Dr. Rufty." Eve waited until those shattered brown eyes focused on her. "Were you expecting a package today? A delivery?"

"I—I don't know. I can't think of anything."

"Have you ever ordered from an outlet called All That Glitters?"

"I don't think so."

"You get deliveries from Global Post and Packages?"

"Yes. Yes, Lydia delivers. But I . . ." He pressed a hand to his temple. "I don't think we ordered anything. I don't remember."

"That's all right. Look at me, Dr. Rufty. Do you know of anyone who'd wish to harm your husband?"

"What?" He jerked. Fresh shock. "Hurt Kent? No, no. Everyone loved Kent. Everyone. I don't understand."

Eve countered the spikes in his voice with absolute calm. "Someone from his office, from his practice, from the neighborhood."

"No, no. Kent has such a lovely practice. All those babies and little kids. It's all so happy there. He worked so hard for his children, his patients. You can ask," he said, his voice spiking again. "You can ask all of them, all of the people who work there. They love Kent!"

"All right. You've been married a long time. Were there any problems?"

"No. No. We love each other. We have our children. We have grandchildren. I need to call our children."

When he started to weep, Peabody moved over to sit next to him. "I know this is hard. Did Kent mention anyone who worried him? Did he say anything about someone or an incident that upset him?"

"No. Nothing I remember. No. I don't understand. What happened? What happened? Did someone hurt Kent?"

"Dr. Rufty." With no choice, Eve gave it straight. "We believe Dr. Abner received a package this morning, and that package contained a toxin, which caused his death."

Tears fell still, but Rufty's body straightened. "What? What? Are you saying someone killed Kent? Someone sent something into the house, into our home that killed him?"

Eve rose at the knock on the door, let in the white-suited sweeper. "We need to take precautions. We need to ask you to submit to a scan, to allow us to test your blood, as you touched Dr. Abner. It's possible the package he opened this morning contained a toxic substance."

"It's not possible." He dismissed it outright, and with the ring of certainty. "No one would do that. No one who knew Kent would do that."

"We need to take precautions." Eve sat again, looked directly into Rufty's eyes. "We're going to do everything we can to find out what happened to your husband."

"You loved him," Peabody said gently. "You want

to do whatever needs to be done to find out what happened."

"Yes. Do whatever you have to do. Then please, God, please, let me call our children. I need to talk to our children."

Eve waited while Rufty was scanned, tested, cleared. Whatever had killed Kent Abner had dissipated before anyone else had come in contact with the body.

"You can contact your children," Eve told Rufty. "Is there somewhere you can go, stay for a few days? It would be best if you didn't stay here."

"I can stay with our daughter. She's closer. Our son lives in Connecticut, but Tori and her family live just a few blocks away. I can stay with Tori."

"We'll arrange to take you there, as soon as you're ready."

Rufty closed his eyes. When he opened them, the tears had burned away to reveal the steel. "I need to know what happened to my husband. To the father of my children. To the man I loved for forty years. If someone did this, someone hurt him, I need to know who. I need to know why."

"It's our job to get those answers for you, Dr. Rufty. If you think of anything," Eve added, "anything at all, you can contact me."

"He was such a good man. I need you to understand that. Such a good man. A loving man. He never hurt anyone in his life. Everyone loved Kent. They loved him."

Someone didn't, Eve thought.

"I believe him," Peabody said as they finally left the crime scene. "That guy was cut off at the knees, and he honestly didn't know anything or anyone that put Abner in the crosshairs."

"Agreed, but a spouse doesn't always know everything. We need to dig into Abner, his work, his habits, his hobbies. Any extramarital relationships."

As she nodded, Peabody glanced back at the pretty brownstone with tulips blooming in its little front garden. "It'd be worse if, you know, it was just bad luck of the draw. If this was random."

"A hell of a lot worse. The package was addressed specifically so we'll look specifically. Let's talk to the delivery person asap."

Peabody programmed the address on the in-dash. "You feel okay, right?"

"I'm fine. Didn't the vampires draw my blood and clear me?"

"Yeah, but I'll feel better when they ID the toxin." Peabody frowned out the window of the car. "He laid there for hours. The good of that is whatever it was dissipated, so we're all not dead. The bad is he laid there for hours."

"Yeah, and think about that. Have the delivery in the morning, knowing nobody's going to go in there until late afternoon. It makes it look like a specific kill. Just Abner."

As she pushed through traffic, Eve took a contact from Officer Shelby on her wrist unit. "What've you got, Shelby?"

"They tracked the package to a drop-off kiosk on West Houston, sir. It was logged in through the after-hours depository—that's self-serve—at twenty-two hundred hours."

"Security cam?"

"Yes, sir. And the cam had a glitch at twenty-one-fifty-eight until twenty-three-oh-two."

"An idiot would call that a coincidence."

"Yes, sir. Officer Carmichael, who is not an idiot, has requested EDD examine the security camera and feed at this depository. However, if the killer proves to be an idiot, she used her credit account, via her 'link, to pay for the overnight shipping. Said payment was charged to the account of a Brendina A. Coffman, age eighty-one, apartment 1A, 38 Bleecker Street."

"We'll check her out now. Good work, Shelby."

Peabody didn't have time to grab the chicken stick before Eve wheeled sharp around a corner to change direction.

"Get a warrant," Eve ordered Peabody. "We need to look at Coffman's credit history."

"Brendina Coffman." Peabody read off her PPC as Eve fought her way to Bleecker. "Married to Roscoe Coffman for fifty-eight years, lived at the current address for thirty-one years. A retired bookkeeper who worked for Loames and Gardner for—wow—fifty-nine years. No criminal in the last half century or so, but a couple of dings in her twenties. Disorderly conduct and simple assault. They have three offspring—male, female, male, ages fifty-six, fifty-three, and forty-eight. Six grandchildren from ages twenty-one to ten."

"Start running the rest of them," Eve ordered. "It's not going to be an idiot," she muttered. "We don't have that kind of luck. But run them."

"Okay, well, the oldest offspring is Rabbi Miles Coffman of Shalom Temple, married to Rebekka Greene Coffman for twenty-one years—and she teaches at the Hebrew school attached to the temple. They have three of the kids—twenty, eighteen, and sixteen, female, male, and male, respectively—nothing flagged on the kids, no criminal on the parents."

With no available parking in sight, Eve double-parked,

causing much annoyance on Bleecker. Ignoring it, she flipped up her On Duty light.

"Keep going," Eve said as she got out, studied the sturdy old residential building. A triple-decker of faded brick, no graffiti, clean windows, some of them open to the cool spring evening.

"Marion Coffman Black, married to Francis Xavior Black, twenty-three years—no, twenty-four as of today; happy anniversary—is currently employed, as she has been for twenty years, as bookkeeper in the same firm as her mother was. Couple dings in her twenties for illegal protests, nothing since. Son, twenty-one, a student at Notre Dame, daughter, age nineteen, also at Notre Dame."

"Hold that thought," Eve advised as they approached the gray door of the entrance to 1A.

Decent security, she noted, but nothing fancy. She pressed the buzzer.

The woman who answered looked pretty good for eighty-one. She had a bubble of ink-black hair Eve figured wouldn't move in a hurricane, lips freshly dyed stop-sign red, rosy cheeks, and eyes heavily shadowed and lashed.

She wore a deep blue cocktail dress with a high neck, long sleeves, and gave Eve and Peabody a frowning once-over from nut-brown eyes.

"We're not buying."

"Not selling," Eve said, and held up her badge.

Brendina's face went sheet white under the rosy. "Joshua!"

"No, ma'am." Peabody spoke quickly. "It's not about your son. Mrs. Coffman's son Joshua's on the job," Peabody told Eve. "It's not about Sergeant Coffman, ma'am."

"Okay. Okay. What is it then?"

"If we could come in for a moment," Eve began.

"We're leaving—if Roscoe ever finishes primping."

"We'll try not to take much of your time."

With a nod, Brendina stepped back to let them straight into a tidy living area. So tidy, Eve thought, dust motes must run in fear. The furniture was old, like owned since their marriage began, and polished to within an inch of its life. A half dozen fancy pillows smothered the sofa.

A small piano against one wall with family photos crowded over it.

The air smelled of lemon.

"Is that your needlepoint, ma'am?" A craftsman to the bone, Peabody admired the pillows. "It's beautiful work."

"My daughter-in-law got me into it, and now I can't stop. What is this about?"

"Mrs. Coffman, did you overnight a package to a Kent Abner, for delivery this morning?"

"Why would I? I don't know any Kent Abner."

"Your credit account was charged for the shipment."

"I don't see how when I didn't send it."

"Maybe you'd like to check on that, while we're here."

"Fine, fine. Roscoe, we're going to be late again. Been waiting for that man for decades. He never can get anywhere on time. It's our daughter's twenty-fourth wedding anniversary," she said as she walked to a— very tidy—little desk and sat down at the mini-comp on it. "Married a Catholic. I never figured it to last, but Frank's a good man, good father, and he's given her a happy life. So we're— Well, son of a bitch!"

And there you have it, Eve thought as Brendina turned.

"I've been charged for that shipment. That's a mistake—it says my account was charged at ten last night. I was sitting in bed watching *Junkpile* on-screen at ten—or trying, as Roscoe snores like a freight train. I keep good records, so I know what I spend and how I spend it. I was a bookkeeper for more years than either of you have been alive!"

"We don't doubt any of that, Mrs. Coffman."

But Brendina's ire hadn't yet peaked.

"Well, GP&P is going to hear from me, you better believe." She fisted her hands on her hips, her eyes shooting daggers at Eve as if she'd been responsible. "And they'd better make this good. I'd like to know how somebody got my information, if that's what happened, or if some careless finger at GP&P hit the wrong key."

"We believe it's the former, ma'am."

"I'll be changing my codes asap, you can be sure of that! And I'm going to have my boy look into this. He's a police officer."

"Yes, ma'am. You can have your son contact me, Lieutenant Dallas at Cop Central. In the meantime, can you tell me who would have access to your account?"

Brendina stabbed a finger in the air, then tapped it between her breasts. "Me, that's who. And Roscoe, but he has his own, and only has my codes in case something was to happen. Same as I have his. Roscoe!"

"Stop yelling, stop yelling. Heavens to Murgatroyd, Brendi, I'm coming, aren't I?"

When he came out, *dapper* was the word that sprang to Eve's mind. He wore a pale blue suit chalked with white stripes, a white shirt, and a bright red bow tie with a matching pocket square. His hair, candlestick silver, was slicked back and shined like moonlight on water. His silver moustache was perfectly trimmed and groomed.

His eyes matched his suit.

"You didn't say we had company." He beamed at them.

"Not company, cops."

"Friends of Joshua's?"

"No, sir," Eve said. "We're here about a package that was delivered this morning. The shipment was charged to your wife's account."

"What did you send, Brendi?"

"Nothing! Somebody got into my account."

He looked at her with affection, and mild surprise. "How'd they do that?"

"I don't know, do I?"

"Ms. Coffman, do you have your 'link?"

"Of course I have my 'link. I was just changing purses when you buzzed."

She marched into what Eve assumed was the bedroom, marched back out with a gargantuan shoulder bag in vivid purple and an oversize evening purse in glittery red—to match Roscoe's tie, Eve assumed.

"I was just taking out what I need for tonight," she said, and dug in.

Her annoyed expression changed to alarm. Now she marched to the coffee table, dumped the contents of the shoulder bag.

Eve decided if the woman ever faced an apocalypse with that bag in tow, she'd survive just fine.

"It's gone! Oh my God, my 'link's not here."

"Where is it, Brendi?"

"For God's sake, Roscoe!"

"Don't worry now. I'll help you look for it."

Brendina's expression softened. "No, honey, it's gone. Somebody must've taken it out of my bag."

"When's the last time you used it?" Eve asked.

"Just yesterday—we were all out shopping. My girls

and I—my daughters-in-law, my daughter. Marion wanted
new shoes for tonight, and she needed to pick up the wrist
unit she got for Frank—she had it engraved. And— God,
we were all over. Had a late lunch. I used it to call my
sister, to tell her we were changing our lunch reservation
to two-thirty because everything was taking so long. She
was meeting us, and she gets cranky if she has to wait."

"Where did you use it?"

"Ah . . ." She pressed a hand to her forehead. "On
Chambers and Broadway—I'm nearly certain. We'd
only just left the jewelry store, and it's right there."

"As far as you remember you didn't use your 'link
since that point?"

"No. I know I didn't. We went shopping some more,
met my sister for lunch. We had a long lunch, and Marion insisted Rachel—my sister—and I take a car home.
She called for one and paid for it—insisted. I came
home, took a nap. Long day. Roscoe and I had dinner,
watched some screen. I didn't go out today. I needed to
clean the house, then get ready for tonight.

"I only keep one account on my 'link: my shopping
and household account. But—"

"It's all right, Brendi." Roscoe put an arm around her.
"I'll help you. And it's time you had a new 'link."

Sighing, she leaned into him. "Let me use yours,
Roscoe, so I can deal with all this. We really are going
to be late."

"Peabody, why don't you leave the Coffmans our
cards? You can have your son contact us."

"Yes, fine, thank you. I really need to deal with this.
You can talk to Joshua. He's a police officer."

2

Back in the car, Peabody strapped in. "Maybe the killer's looking for an easy mark. An older woman, distracted with a lot of other women. Maybe follow them awhile. Crowded shopping area, bump and snatch."

"Most likely," Eve agreed. "And with her being older, he might think if she can't put her hands on her 'link at some point, she'll just think she misplaced it. Maybe she doesn't change codes right off. He only needs a few hours. Use it, toss it, move on."

She muscled her way back across town. "It's not going to connect to the family. Not that having a cop and a rabbi in there exempts them, but it's sloppy and stupid."

"Are you going to read Sergeant Coffman in?"

"Might as well. If there is any connection, he can dig into that angle. We'll talk to the delivery girl—who's not going to be connected, either, unless somebody has a grudge there, saw this as getting her in trouble."

"That would be stupid, too."

"Exactly, but we'll talk to her. She works that route. Maybe she knows someone in the neighborhood who wasn't a fan of Kent Abner's."

Lydia Merchant lived five floors up in a post-Urban building over a bodega that smelled like mystery tacos. Nobody had their windows open to the spring evening, and most had riot bars.

Despite the five floors, one glance at the pair of green-doored elevators—one with a sign stating OUT OF ORDER, with a handwritten AGAIN! in angry block letters—had Eve shoving open the stairwell door.

Peabody hissed out, "Loose pants," and climbed with her through various scents—somebody's Chinese take-out, someone's very rank body odor, someone's heavy dose of cheap cologne (possibly Mr. BO), and, oddly, what might have been fresh roses.

On the fifth floor, Eve scanned the apartment door. Strong security here, in the way of locks: three police locks rather than electronics.

Cheaper, she thought, but pretty effective.

She buzzed.

Moments later, through the static on the intercom, somebody demanded, "Who is it?"

"NYPSD."

"Yeah, right."

"NYPSD," Eve repeated, and held her badge up to the Judas hole.

"I'm calling in to check that before I open the door."

"Dallas, Lieutenant Eve; Peabody, Detective Delia, Cop Central."

"Yeah, right again."

Eve waited, waited. Actually heard a squeal from inside, then rising female voices before locks began to clunk. She heard the distinct metal slide of a riot bar before the door popped open.

The two women who stood gaping hit about the same age. One was tall, busty, blond, the other just hitting average height with a small build. A mixed-race brunette.

Both had big blue eyes.

"Holy shit," they said in unison. "You look just like Marlo Durn did in the vid," the blonde continued. "Or Marlo, I guess she looked like you. We saw it twice."

"Great." She should get used to it, Eve thought.

She'd never get used to it.

"Did somebody break in and kill somebody?" Lydia, the brunette, demanded. "Somebody's always breaking into this dump, or trying to."

"No. It's about a package you delivered this morning, Ms. Merchant."

"Really?" Big blue eyes got bigger. "Which one?"

"Can we come in?" Peabody added a quick smile.

"Oh, sure. You're prettier than the actress in the vid," the blonde told her. "I know she was killed and all that, but it's just true."

The roses from the stairway scent stood on the skinny bar that separated the crowded living area from a tiny kitchen. A bottle of wine stood open beside it.

"Have a seat, I guess. We were just going to have some wine. Can you have wine? We're celebrating."

"No, but thanks."

"We both got raises." The blonde, definitely bubbly, perched on the arm of the chair. "I got mine last week, and Lydia's finally came through today. We're moving out of this hellhole!"

"Congratulations. Ms. Merchant—"

"Just Lydia's okay. It's really so weird you're both

here, in our hellhole. I deliver a lot of packages. I work for GP&P, but I guess you know."

"You delivered one to Kent Abner this morning."

"Dr. Abner, sure. I deliver to him and to Dr. Rufty. They're really nice—always give me a tip for Christmas. Not everybody does. Was something wrong with the package? I handed it right to Dr. Abner at the door."

"Was there anything unusual in how the package came to you?"

"No. It's mostly droids and automation at my distribution center. They load my van, upload the schedule— overnights with A.M. deliveries or special deliveries first and so on. It was—had to be because it was this morning—an overnight A.M. I don't get what this is about."

"We believe the package contained an as-yet-unidentified toxic substance."

Lydia's blue eyes went momentarily blank, then filled with alarm. "You mean like poison or something? Like terrorism or something?"

"We have no reason to believe, at this time, we're dealing with any kind of terrorist attack." Not altogether true, Eve thought.

"How do you know there was toxic stuff? Did Dr. Abner get sick?"

"Dr. Abner's dead. He died shortly after receiving and opening the package."

"Dead? He's dead!" Those blue eyes filled. "But . . . Oh my God. Oh my God, Teela!"

Teela immediately slid off the arm, into the chair with Lydia, wrapped her arms around her. "Lydia touched it. Is she—"

"We believe the substance was released upon opening."

"I'm fine, I'm fine. Dr. Abner. He's such a nice man.

He and Dr. Rufty are so sweet together. You can tell
when people are sweet together. I really liked them. I
didn't know. I swear I didn't know anything was wrong
with the delivery. I never would have—"

"No one's accusing you," Peabody soothed. "Do you
know of anyone, in their neighborhood, at your work,
anywhere, who might have disliked Dr. Abner?"

"No. I know some of their neighbors because it's my
route. But nobody ever said anything mean, or much
at all. Sometimes if a neighbor isn't home and doesn't
have a delivery box, one of the others will take it for
them—you have to have a waiver on file for that. Some
of them do. The doctors will sometimes take deliveries for the people on either side of them, and they
do that for the doctors, too. It's a really nice, friendly
street. But today, the only package on that block was
for Dr. Abner.

"Oh God, is Dr. Rufty okay? I don't think he was
home. It looked like Dr. Abner was going out for a run.
I sometimes see him running when I'm on my route,
and see Dr. Rufty coming home if I have late-afternoon
deliveries."

"Dr. Rufty wasn't home at the time."

"I don't know what to do. Is there something I
should do? What should I do?" she asked Eve.

"If you think of anything, you can contact me or Detective Peabody."

"You have to find out what happened. He was a really
nice man. He looked so happy this morning. I remember
that. He just looked happy, and said how it was going to
be a beautiful day. You have to find out what happened."

"We're working on it."

Out on the sidewalk, Eve considered the next steps.
"The victim's office is closed by this time. You head

home, and on the way contact Abner's office manager or whoever's in charge."

"Seldine Abbakar's listed as office manager—I pulled up the website."

"Good. Contact her, set up a meeting with the full office staff for the morning, as early as you can make it. Just text me the time, and I'll meet you there. You can keep McNab on tap—we're going to need to go through the electronics."

"Medical records," Peabody began.

"That's why I'm going to start working on a warrant on the way home. Hell, they can cull out the patient records. If this is an angry patient, the office staff's going to have an idea who. The spouse would have had an idea who."

"Technically his patients are babies and kids up to the age of sixteen."

"I've seen a lot of pissed-off babies," Eve countered. "And don't get me started on kids and teens. And they'd have a parent or parents. Anyway, set it up. I'll get the board and book started at home, write it up."

"I get the easy part."

"This time. If you can't get the interviews before eight, we meet at the morgue, seven A.M., go from there."

"Always a fun way to start the day."

"Get the interviews," Eve repeated and, still ignoring the vehicles and drivers blasting and cursing, slid into her car.

She flipped down the On Duty light, zipped out in front of a guy who was already giving her the finger.

She programmed coffee on the in-dash, tagged APA Reo.

"Please no," Reo answered. "I'm on my way home,

stuck in stupid traffic. All I want is an alcoholic beverage and quiet."

"You can have both after you get me a warrant. I'm just heading home myself—so too bad for us."

Reo sighed, tossed her head so her fluffy blond hair shimmered and swayed. "I'm getting out of this cab and walking. Pull over," she ordered the driver, and Eve went to blue holding mode while she assumed Reo paid the fare.

When she came back on-screen it bobbled as she strode along. "It's the as-yet-unidentified-substance case, isn't it?"

"They better have that as identified soon, and yeah. Victim was a doctor—baby doctor—and I'm interviewing his staff first thing in the morning. I need the electronics."

"You're not going to get medical records in a walk, or by morning."

"Just get me the rest—they can hold off on the privacy stuff for now. I need to know if he had any record of someone threatening him, any correspondence that sends off an alarm. Or if anyone on staff had issues."

"I can work that. I heard you were exposed. You don't look exposed to a deadly toxin."

"Whatever it was, it was as dead as Abner by the time we got there."

"Well, that's a bright side. I'll get back to you on the warrant."

"Appreciate it."

"You still owe me a drink from the last one."

"I'll make good. Later."

Eve clicked off, drank coffee, pushed her way uptown.

And as she pushed, it occurred to her that only a week before she'd been sitting on a terrace in Italy, drinking wine under the stars after a day of basking in the sun.

Eating pasta, sleeping late, having a lot of sex.

And no one had been murdered in the general vicinity—at least that she knew of.

Life since Roarke, with Roarke, never quite ranked as ordinary. Routine, maybe, for them—which probably wouldn't meet most people's routine level.

But it worked—really worked, she thought. And one of the reasons it worked, so well, was knowing she'd come home—and there was a glittering word—with this fresh weight on her shoulders, and he'd be there.

He'd look at her the way he looked at her that always, still, probably forever, brought a skip to her heartbeat. He'd make her eat something, even if she didn't want to, which was both annoying and precious.

And he'd listen. No bitching about her being late, no guilt trips. He'd listen, offer to help and, with all of that, with all of him, bring her a peace of mind she'd never expected to have in her life.

So when she drove, at last, through the gates, she felt that quiet click. Coming home. Under the night sky, the house Roarke built stood and spread and towered with its fanciful turrets, its grand design. Dozens of windows, so much light to welcome her, glowed out against the dark.

When she pulled up, got out of the car, some of the weight shifted. Work to do, yes, but home.

Because she was late—really late—she didn't expect the looming Summerset.

But there he stood, tall and bony in black, his cadaverous face set, his dark eyes arrowing their stare at her face.

She reached into her bag of insults, but he spoke before she could pull one out.

"He's worried. He'll pretend otherwise, but he heard about your exposure to a toxic material."

"I told him I was fine. I'm fine."

When Summerset only continued to stare, she had a bad feeling the former Urban War medic intended to do his own exam. Big no.

"Have they identified the substance?"

"I don't know. I'm going up to check. I'm fine." Irritable now, she dragged off her jacket, tossed it on the newel post.

"Make sure he knows."

She started to snap she already had, but that seemed pointless. Instead she paused on her way up the stairs. "Do you think I'd come home if there was any chance, any, I carried something with me that could hurt him?"

"Absolutely not. Which is why, as it's after nine, he worries."

Damn it, damn it, of course he did. "I had to— Shit. Where is he?"

"Your office, of course. He knows you're home. He set an alert."

She jogged up. She'd followed the Marriage Rules, she thought. And still she felt as if she'd screwed up somehow.

He sat on the sofa in her office, the fire going low, the fat cat across his lap. He had a book in one hand, a glass of wine in the other.

And yes, he looked at her in that way—but she saw relief bloom over it.

"And there she is," he began, with that wonderful whisper of Ireland in his voice.

"I'm sorry."

Even as he put the book aside and rose, she walked to him, wrapped around him, held hard. "I'm sorry."

"For being late?" Now she heard surprise as she burrowed into him. "Come now, Lieutenant, that's part of the job, isn't it?"

"For not making a hundred percent sure you knew I was okay. For not making sure you weren't worried I wasn't."

"Ah." He brushed his lips over the top of her head, drew her back. "That's part of the job as well. My part. There will be worry, darling Eve. But now . . ." He skimmed his thumb over the shallow dent in her chin, leaned in to kiss her—long and warm. "You're home. So sit a moment with the cat, as Galahad's had some concerns of his own. I'll get you some wine."

No bitching, no guilt trips, just wine and welcome. And a fat cat. So she'd sit for a minute, because he didn't just bring trips to Italy, real coffee, superior sex, and all manner of things into her life.

He brought this, the balance.

She gave the cat some strokes, a belly scratch when he stirred himself to roll over. And took the wine.

"They cleared me right at the scene."

"So you told me." Still those wildly, gloriously blue eyes studied her face before he lifted her hand, kissed it. "Have they identified the toxin?"

"I need to check, but not since I checked an hour ago. The body wasn't discovered until after sixteen hundred when the spouse got home from work. They wouldn't have started the process until . . . probably an hour ago. Protocols to follow, and all that."

"You won't have eaten."

"We were pretty busy."

"I imagine. Let's have a meal now, and you can tell me about all this."

"'Let's'? Haven't you had dinner already?"

"I haven't, no." He gave her hand a squeeze. "There was worry."

"Wait." She tightened her grip on his hands. "I'm going to promise you that I won't lie or downplay something that happens, if I'm in trouble or something's really wrong. I'll be straight with you."

"All right then."

She studied that amazing face of his. "And you'll worry anyway."

"Yes, of course. But that's appreciated. Now, I made a bargain with myself—or fate—to your benefit. That when you came home to me, there would be pepperoni pizza."

She brightened right up. "Really?"

"Such is the depth of my love I'm not insisting you eat a side of good vegetables."

"If you asked me to, right now, I'd eat them. So, same goes."

"You could have them on the pizza."

She shot him a—sincere—horrified look. "You'd ruin a perfectly good pizza?"

"I don't know what I was thinking."

He rose, strolled into the kitchen, so she sat another moment indulging the cat before taking their glasses, the bottle of wine over to the table.

She looked out through the glass doors to the little balcony and beyond. And the scent of pizza hit her empty stomach like a fever dream.

"I know if there was only pizza, I'd get tired of it," she decided. "But it would probably take a couple decades."

She sat with him, grabbed a slice. "Pretty soon it'll be warm enough to open those doors when we eat. It'll be nice."

Her 'link signaled. "Sorry. Reo?"

"Warrant's coming through—restricted. No medical records at this time. Is that pizza? Damn it, now I want pizza."

"Get your own. Thanks for the quick work."

Eve put her 'link away.

"Your victim was a doctor, I hear," Roarke said.

"Pediatrician. Married for nearly forty years. His husband found him. Private school headmaster. They've got kids, grandkids."

She picked up her wine. "Messed up my crime scene. He tried to revive him. The victim had been dead since morning, and he didn't die pretty, but the husband tried to bring him back before he called for help."

"Would you blame him?"

"No." She looked up, into that face carved by clever angels on a particularly generous day, into those magic blue eyes. "Maybe I would have a few years ago. Not now. They loved each other. You could see it, all over the house, see it in the survivor's grief. You have to step back from it. It can still put a crack in your heart, but you've got to step back."

"How was it delivered? The toxin."

"Global Post and Packages, overnight A.M."

"A package? That's . . . bold. You have the delivery person?"

"She's not in it. She's clean, and she liked them. That came across. Their neighbors liked them. The canvass turned up nothing except some shock, some fear, some grief. Everything so far points to the victim being a nice man, a good neighbor, somebody who kept fit—he ran, lifted—and was apparently on his way out when the package came. So he took it inside, back in the kitchen, opened it."

"There had to be a container. Even bold wouldn't risk an uncontained toxic in a shipping box."

She polished off her first slice. "It's looking like two—a container in a container. A cheap fake wood box with interior padding was on the counter, so considering the rest of the house that was likely in the shipping box. And there were shards and pieces of some sort of small container. Looked like hard plastic—cheap, likely gold outside, white inside. Whatever killed him must have been in there. He opened that, whatever it was hit the air, or had something he ingested, something that went through his pores when he touched it. He had burns on his thumbs," she remembered, then shrugged. "I don't know yet."

"You'll see Morris, and your friends at the lab as well tomorrow."

"Yeah." Since it was right there, she decided on a second slice. "We called in the hazmat team—no trace in the air by that time. In or on me or the spouse—we both handled the body. It was enough to kill Abner within minutes, and dissipated before anyone else came into the house."

"Addressed—the package—to the victim, I take it?"

"Yeah. From a bogus place, bogus return address. Dropped off at an after-hours kiosk. Jammed the camera while he did that, so he's got a jammer or he's got enough skill to make one."

"At a kiosk?" He let out a quick laugh. "Darling, a ten-year-old could manage that. I'd be more interested in how it got through the scans."

"Yeah, they're looking at that. A container within a

container within a container." She shrugged again. "And likely a small amount of whatever it is. Just enough to kill one person."

She glanced over as Summerset came to the doorway. She frowned over another bite of pizza. "We didn't call the morgue, did we?"

"You'll excuse me." Summerset kept his dignified nose in the air. "Dr. Dimatto and Mr. Monroe are downstairs. They'd very much like to speak with the lieutenant."

"Ask them to come up," Roarke said before Eve could get to her feet. "The lieutenant's just having dinner. I'll get some more glasses," he added as Summerset melted away.

Dr. Dimatto, Eve thought. Dr. Abner.

Did Louise know the victim? Long odds, of course, given there were countless doctors in the city. But then again, Charles and Louise lived only a few blocks from the crime scene.

"They're going to know each other."

"Hmm?"

Roarke brought over two more wineglasses.

"Louise, the victim. That's why they're here. And how the hell do I handle this?"

She figured she'd find out when Louise—delicate blonde—and Charles—tall, dark, and handsome—came in.

The fiercely dedicated doctor and former licensed companion made a striking couple, and another one that seemed to work really well.

"I'm so sorry." Louise led with an apology. "For just coming over this way, interrupting your dinner. I—"

"It's pizza, nothing interrupts pizza. How did you know Kent Abner?" Eve asked.

"How did you know . . ." Louise closed her eyes. "He walked into my clinic the week I opened it. He volunteered twenty hours a month. Just like that. That's the sort of man, the sort of doctor he was."

Tears trembled, spilled. "I'm sorry," she said again. "I'm having a hard time with this. I needed to come. I just needed to talk to you."

"Sit down." Roarke pulled out his chair for her. "You sit, have some wine. Could you eat?"

"He likes feeding people," Eve said, hoping to stem the worst of the tears.

"No, thanks, no on the food. I'll have the wine."

Roarke gestured to Charles, and the two of them brought over more chairs. They sat; Roarke poured the wine.

"I won't fall apart. Or not much," Louise qualified.

"Good. Now tell me what you know about Kent Abner, personally, professionally, and anything else."

Louise nodded, then, struggling a little, looked at Charles.

"I'll start," Charles said.

3

"We got to be friends," Charles told them. "Good friends. I met them through Louise after Kent started volunteering at the clinic. They invited us over for drinks, and we all, well, hit it off."

"I don't remember seeing or meeting them at your wedding," Eve pointed out.

"They were in Africa. Martin took a month's sabbatical because Kent wanted to join a medical group there for a couple weeks. They had a working vacation, you could say, and it conflicted with the wedding. They actually had a little neighborhood party for us when we got back from our honeymoon."

"They're lovely people," Louise added. "Lovely together. Both devoted to their work, but not to the exclusion of the rest. They liked to entertain, loved their family, liked the theater, the arts. Kent would nag Martin about exercise—saying it wasn't just for the mind. And Martin would tease Kent because Kent knew nothing whatsoever—and didn't care whatsoever—about any kind of sport. Those would be the level of disagreements I witnessed, ever, between them. They were sweet together, Dallas, the way you hope you'll be sweet together after nearly four decades."

Charles reached over, laid a hand over hers. "We asked ourselves, since we were good friends, if there was anything, anyone, any reason for what happened. There's just nothing. Are you sure what happened wasn't some sort of accident or mistake?"

"Yes." And that, Eve thought, was that. "Since he worked at the clinic regularly, there would be records."

Dr. Dimatto came out, front and center. "Patients' records—"

Eve just waved that away. "Blah blah, and I can get to them if I need to. But for now, as the owner of the clinic, you can get to them. You can read through them. And you'd know if anything seemed off. Outside of patient records, there'd be correspondence, memos, interstaff dynamics."

"You can interview everyone who works or volunteers at the clinic. I can tell you, without hesitation, no one who does would wish harm to Kent. He was valued, respected, and liked."

"Okay. How about someone who liked him too much?"

"I don't . . . Oh." Brow furrowed, Louise sipped some wine. "I don't see that. We have some parents who'd request him specifically, who'd wait, barring emergency, for his hours. But I never noticed that kind of vibe. Some jokes, sure. Like Hella—she's one of the nurses who volunteers, and she's still stinging from her second divorce. I heard her tell Kent it was just her bad luck he had to be gay and married, and why couldn't she find a straight, single guy just like him."

"How did he respond?"

"He said he'd keep his eye open for her. You know, Dallas, he'd bring flowers in sometimes because he said they brightened things up for us and the patients. Or he'd bring in a box of pastries. He was considerate and generous, and I'm sick about what happened."

"We haven't contacted Martin," Charles said, "because we don't want to intrude. But we thought if we could, maybe tomorrow, contact their son or daughter. Just to see if there's anything . . . There's never really anything."

"Can you tell us what happened? At least something that makes sense?"

Eve studied Louise—dry-eyed now, but barely. She'd tell them what they'd hear on the morning reports—and maybe just a bit more. "I can tell you the package containing the substance was addressed to Dr. Kent Abner. I can tell you the person who delivered it was just doing her job, and isn't a suspect. She shares your view of the victim. She liked him, liked them both, and in a way was victimized by the killer. She'll carry the weight for a while.

"We'll know more when we ID the substance, how it got into his system but, from the timeline, it only took minutes."

"You're sure of that?" Louise pressed.

"Absolutely."

"I'm not an expert, but I know something about poisons, toxins, exposure. If I knew his symptoms—"

"That's for Morris."

But Louise, in professional mode, didn't shake off easily. "You don't know if it was something he touched, ingested, inhaled?"

"That's for Morris and the lab."

"Fast-acting, very fast," Louise murmured. "Not ingested."

"Why?"

"A fastidious man, a little bit of a health nut? I don't see Kent popping something that came in the mail into his mouth right off. Well, maybe if he knew who sent it, or if he was expecting . . ."

"Bogus name and address."

"Then he didn't know the sender, he wasn't expecting a package. I don't see him eating or drinking something from a package without checking it first. And you said minutes."

"About seven from delivery to death."

"God." But she breathed that out, went back to doctor mode. "By touch then, especially if there's a cut or puncture. Or inhalation." Gray eyes narrowing with a frown, she shook her head slowly.

"But Martin's all right, he wasn't affected? The report said he found the body."

"He's clear. We're all clear."

"So the toxicity dissipated. Were there windows open?"

"No, but yes, it dissipated or disbursed or faded. How were they financially?"

"Martin and Kent? I'd say very comfortable."

"And Kent's practice? Successful? Lucrative?"

"God, it must be dark in a cop's world." Louise sighed again. "You have to think maybe someone killed Kent for money. It certainly wouldn't be Martin, whom I'd assume would benefit most there. Or their kids. Lissa— that's Melissa Rendi—worked with him, as the practice needed two doctors. She strikes me as a good doctor, but she wouldn't gain monetarily that I know of."

"We've met their circle of friends, Dallas," Charles

continued. "I wouldn't say we know them all intimately, but there isn't anyone we do know who I can believe would hurt Kent. I know you said it was addressed to him, but could it still be random? Like, Jesus, a name pulled out of a hat."

"Yes."

But she didn't think so.

"Is there anything we can do to help? I could work with Morris if—"

"Not my call. And not a good idea."

"I'm a doctor. I'm a scientist. I can be objective."

"He was a friend, and he gave time to your clinic. Better if you keep a step, several of them, back from the investigation. I'll tell you what I can when I can," Eve added. "It's the best I can do."

"A man suffered a loss," Roarke said gently, "from what I've heard here, a great one, a deep one. I would think he would welcome the comfort of good friends at such a time."

"He's with his family," Louise murmured.

"Isn't it only blood, just DNA, that separates good friends, true friends, from family?"

Louise's eyes filled again. "Yes. Thanks. Yes. We'll contact him in the morning. I know you probably told us more than you wanted to," she said to Eve. "It won't leave this room, I promise you. I'm really grateful. You know my complicated relationship with my own family. Kent— well, Martin, too—they've been surrogate fathers to me. Roarke's right. It's just DNA."

When they left, Eve sat back. "She looked steadier when she walked out. What you said helped."

"It all helped. And, as tragic as it is for our friends, it's a help to you to know and trust two people who appear to have known your victim so well."

"It doesn't hurt."

"Now, how can I help you, Lieutenant?"

She smiled at him. "I thought about that when I was driving home. Not what you could do, but that you'd ask. That you'd make me eat something, probably get some wine into me. You'd listen and offer to help."

She angled her head. "Do you think we're sweet together?"

"It would entirely depend on what level of sweet, wouldn't it?"

"The right level, for us. I say we sometimes hit that. I need to set up the board and book. If you want, you can poke around in the financials—the vic, the spouse, the practice. It's not going to be the lever, but we need to cross it off."

"Poking about in other people's money? A sweet reward for me."

She did all she could do—lab and sweeper and ME reports still pending. And since Peabody had the interviews at the victim's office set for seven-thirty, she had her schedule for the morning in place.

Interview, morgue, lab—all before she got to Central. Hopefully, some of the answers she drew in that mix would start clearing a path.

Who targets a well-liked man, a valued doctor, a loving and loved husband and father for fast, ugly death?

She'd damn well find out.

But since she'd done all she could for the night, she decided both she and Roarke had earned one more sweet reward.

She walked to his adjoining office, where he sat at his command center studying something that might have been written in Greek (nerd qualified, in her opinion).

"Done, are you?" He glanced over. "As I found nothing helpful, I didn't interrupt."

"What did you find that's unhelpful?"

"They're comfortable—very—as Charles and Louise assumed. The victim's practice did quite well, and his spouse draws a fine salary with solid benefits. They've invested wisely, have a smart estate plan in place. It looks to me as if they planned to retire in about ten years. They enjoyed traveling, and traveled well, and lived within their means. They give a fair and generous portion of their income to charities of their choosing—and I have to say I feel they chose well.

"No hidden accounts, for either," he continued, "no nefarious gambling debts or strange purchases. They have trusts set up, as I said, for their children, grandchildren, some generous but not outlandish bequests for people who work for or with them, and have for some time. They've left a particular piece of art to Charles and Louise. Other specifics—like a set of cuff links, an antique shaving kit, and such—to people I assume are close friends and would appreciate the memento."

One hip cocked, Eve leaned on the doorjamb. "I didn't ask you to look at his will."

"Ah well, once I started, I wanted to do a thorough job. I think I would have liked Dr. Abner."

"You wouldn't be alone. I'm calling it for the night. You?"

"With you, as always, Lieutenant. I'm just dabbling here—not case related."

"It doesn't look related to anything human," she said as he disengaged the comp.

"It is, and isn't." He rose. "A Mars Colony thing."

"Mars." She shook her head as they walked out. "You really are trying to corner the universe."

"And wouldn't that be fun? We could spend a weekend on Mars."

"Not in this lifetime or any other. Italy worked fine."

He slid an arm around her. "It did, yes, and very well."

"Your hotel thing there. It's going to be pretty great. The way it looks old, like it hasn't changed in a thousand years, but it's going to have everything."

"That's the plan. Still cool enough for a fire at night," he said as they walked into the bedroom, and ordered it on.

The cat already stretched his bulk across the bed as if he owned it. Eve calculated he'd soon stalk away in disgust.

She sat, pulled off her boots. "You remember how I kept my word on the shuttle to Italy? Banged you like a drum?"

"I have a very good memory."

"Yeah, you do."

She rose, unhooked her weapon harness, peeled it off. "I think it's time for a repeat performance."

He'd paused in the act of taking off his shirt, smiled slowly. "Do you, now?"

"I do. Despite ugly death, or maybe due to same, I realized today you need to appreciate what you've got when you've got it. More, you should grab on to it."

She hooked a hand in his waistband, yanked him to her. "I'm grabbing."

She took his mouth, dived deep, added a quick little bite at the end. And smiled. "Being an investigator who recognizes evidence, I don't have to ask if you're up for it."

With a pivot, her foot moving behind his to shift the balance, she had him on his back on the bed.

The cat, as predicted, leaped off the bed and stalked away.

"Nice move."

After straddling him, she curved down to him. "I got more."

And took his mouth again to prove it.

She wanted heat, and speed, some quick and reckless abandon for both of them. The man who'd waited, worried; the cop who carried fresh weight.

Here she could show him what she couldn't always find words for. That her love was boundless, furious, blazing through her so fierce she would always, always fight to hold it, hold him.

With her body she could give them both a reprieve from whatever tomorrow asked of them.

She let herself fly into it, not soft and slow, but like an arrow loosed from a bow. Hot-tipped and keen. And when his hands, all too clever and skilled, roamed over her, she stopped them, gripped them tight in hers. And conquered him with only her mouth.

His lips, his throat, his chest. That heartbeat pounding, pounding as she feasted on warm flesh, on the quiver of strong muscles.

"You wait," she managed, ripe with her own power as she released his hands. "You wait." Undid the buttons to free him.

And gripping his hands again, used her mouth.

She destroyed him. Relentless, agile, she destroyed control, layer by layer. Not eroded, he thought, already half mad for her, but simply burned it away like a brushfire.

The heat, God, the heat was unbearable. Was glorious.

He fought to hold back, swore he felt the world, the whole of it, turn upside down. She took him to the searing edge, left him there all but shuddering, as she worked her way up his body again.

At the end, at his limit, he said her name. Like a prayer, a plea, a demand all in one.

He saw her eyes, just her eyes, tawny as a lion's with her own power. She said, "You wait."

He snapped, and answered, "No."

He rolled her over, pinned her. And freed, his hands had their way.

He ravished, as she had, burned away those layers, as she had. Now he feasted, that lean and limber body his to touch, taste, take. She cried out as she came, a sound that thrilled, pushed him to drive her up again, sweeping her from limp to desperate.

Now the world spun, stealing the air, blurring the vision until they clung to each other, wrecked and ready.

When their eyes met, he plunged into her. Fast, rough, with a violence they both craved in the moment, they drove each other to that burning edge, clawed at it to hold the mad pleasure.

And finally spilled over.

Breathless, they lay like survivors of the wreck, waiting for sense and sanity to seep back.

"You said . . ." She had to pause, pull in more air through still-laboring lungs, then picked her way through something resembling Irish. "What does it mean?"

She'd mangled it, Roarke thought, but he put it together. "Did I?"

"Yeah, right before we killed each other."

"Apt then. It's *Is mise mo chiall.* You're my madness."

She thought it over. "I'm going to say that's a good thing, under the circumstances."

Turning his head, he brushed his lips over her hair. "You unravel me, Eve, in thousands of ways."

"I needed to, I don't know, burn off the day."

"I'd say we succeeded there." He shifted, drew her in so she curled against him. "You'll sleep."

"Yeah." She closed her eyes, breathed him in, began to drift. "You have lights on all over the house when I come home at night, when I come home late."

"To help you find your way."

"It's nice," she murmured, and slipped into sleep.

The cat, concluding his spot was once again clear, leaped onto the bed to settle in the small of Eve's back.

Yes, Roarke thought, it was very nice.

She woke alone and early, considered trying for another ten, then gave it up. Too much to do, she reminded herself, and stumbled across the room to program coffee.

The first life-giving gulp got her system going. She gulped more as she headed for the shower.

Between the coffee, hot jets on full, a quick spin in the drying tube, she felt not only human again but ready to deal with the day. The robe on the back of the door—thin, soft cotton the color of apricots—had to be yet another new one. When she shrugged it on, it felt like she was wrapped up in a cloud.

The man never missed.

And there he was, back from whatever predawn meeting he'd scheduled, sitting on the sofa in a perfectly tailored suit the color of moonless midnight offset by a shirt nearly as magical a blue as his eyes. His tie married that blue with paler tones in thin stripes.

The cat sat with him, content to have his head scratched by those clever fingers while Roarke drank coffee and watched the morning stock reports scroll by on-screen.

"I thought to wake you, but you got an early start."

"A lot going on." Since he'd programmed a pot, she poured coffee from the table into her mug. "And I may have to browbeat Dickhead for results."

Dick Berenski, chief lab tech, had skills—and a thirst for a good bribe.

"What'll it be this time?" Roarke wondered as she moved by him into her closet. "Single malt scotch, box seats?"

"Browbeat," she repeated from the depths of her closet. "No bribe. If he even hints at one over this, I may have to arrest myself for felony assault."

"I'll stand your bail."

In the closet, she thought of the interviews, the morgue, the lab, and all that might ray out from them. Too many clothes, too many choices.

Why couldn't everything just be black or brown?

"If I were interviewing grieving employees and likely family as well," Roarke said conversationally from the bedroom, "I'd go with somber. But not full black," he added even as Eve reached for black pants. "I'd leave black to those in mourning."

Brown, she thought. Brown was somber. She started to reach for brown pants, pulled back again. Thought, Shit.

Gray, maybe gray because it was almost black. But not black.

And she didn't want to think about it anymore.

It took longer than it should have, and she dressed in the closet to avoid having Roarke exchange one or all of her choices for something else.

Something, no doubt, better. But still.

When she stepped out—gray pants, darker gray boots, a thin navy sweater, holding a gray jacket (she'd spotted the navy buttons, the navy leather cuffs on the sleeves, trim on the pockets), he already had breakfast under warming trays.

"A very somber and dignified choice," he told her. "And still authoritative and fashionable. Well done."

"Bite me." She tossed the jacket over a chair, strapped on her weapon harness. "It took twice as long as black. You're wearing a black suit," she pointed out.

"Indigo, actually, but close enough. It suits, we'll say, my day's agenda."

"What planet are you buying?"

"While not buying Mars, as yet," he said with a smile, "I do have some business regarding the colony. But prior, I'll attend the first staff meeting at An Didean later this morning. After which, we'll have a secondary meeting including some of the staff of Dochas, as we'll want them working together as needs be."

She glanced over. "You could, potentially, have minors who come to Dochas for shelter transferred to the school."

"That's a hope."

She sat beside him. "It's a good thing, an all-around good thing. You said when we were in Italy everything's on schedule."

"And so it is." He lifted the warmers.

No oatmeal, Eve noticed—happily. Though she had a feeling the little dish didn't contain fruit and crunchy stuff over ice cream, but yogurt. Still, the omelets and bacon could make up for it.

"And Rochelle, she's working out?"

"Brilliantly. She'll mourn her brother for some time yet." He touched Eve's hand. "But you gave her and her family closure. She told me during a brief conversation yesterday that she thinks of him when she's in the school, thinks what a difference it would have made in his life, and how proud he would be she's a part of it."

"She moved in with Crack."

"She did, yes." Amused at her tone—not disapproving so much as baffled—he quirked an eyebrow. "Problem?"

"No. Just getting used to it." She picked up the yogurt to get it out of the way.

It wasn't actually horrible.

"And while we're, more or less, on the subject of An Didean, I told you Jake and his bandmates have volunteered to guest instruct from time to time. Music and songwriting."

"Nadine's rock star's okay."

"He is, and our Nadine, in addition to taking one of our students, the inestimable Quilla, as intern, will also come in now and then to talk about journalism, screen writing, writing in general."

She'd be good at it, Eve thought. Nadine knew her stuff, in and out and sideways. "You're pulling in a star-studded crew."

The yogurt wasn't horrible, but the omelet was terrific.

"I like to think so. We'll have guest chefs, artists, scientists, business types—"

"Are you going to guest star?"

"From time to time. Vocalists, designers."

"Mavis and Leonardo."

"Among others. Engineers, architects, programmers, doctors. Lawyers."

She grunted at that.

He smiled, sipped coffee. "We want a well-rounded curriculum, as well as care, shelter, nutrition, safety. Part of that curriculum and exposure needs the law. All areas of it. Who better than Lieutenant Dallas to guest lecture on police work?"

"Uh-uh. That's nuts." She bit decisively into bacon. "I don't know how to teach."

He angled his head—then pointed a finger at the cat to halt Galahad's bacon belly crawl toward the table. "I'll just say: Peabody, Detective Delia."

"That wasn't teaching. That was training. She was already a cop. And she wasn't a kid."

Undeterred, smooth as velvet, Roarke laid out his case. "Some of them will be troubled, come from difficult homes, much as Rochelle's brother before he turned his all-too-short life around. Much as you and I did, for all that. Who better to show them what a cop is, should be, can be than one who believes in the value of protect and serve? And kicks ass doing it?"

The man could negotiate with God and come out ahead, she thought. "You said that last thing to try to flatter me into it."

"You'll think about it." He gave her thigh a friendly pat.

Since she didn't want to think about it, she polished off breakfast.

"I need to get started."

She got up to gather up her badge, restraints, pocketknife, 'link, communicator, some cash before putting on the jacket.

Rising, giving Galahad a warning look, Roarke went to her, gathered her in.

Distressed, she hugged back. "That feels like worry. Don't start the day with worry about me."

"It's not. You'll take care of my cop. It's . . . grabbing on to what matters, and to the moment." He tipped her face up, kissed her. Then once again. "Until tonight."

Then he patted her ass, and made the vague concern

inside her slide away again. "And don't be too hard on Dickhead."

"That'll be up to him." She started out, paused at the door. "If I get home first—it happens—I'll leave the lights on."

He flashed a smile, and she took it with her down the stairs and out to the car.

Then she was out of the gates, into the early traffic. Too early, by about a half hour, she judged, for the ad blimps to blast. Not too early for the maxibuses, the first enterprising cart operator to have coffee going and what passed for bagels at the ready or the commuter airtrams to rumble across the sky with their load of sleepy people.

And not too late, apparently, for a couple of street LCs to grab cart coffee and what passed for bagels after a long night's work.

A block later, she spotted a woman in a gold evening gown, a short, silver cape over her shoulders, strolling along the sidewalk in her skyscraper heels.

Possibly an LC, Eve thought, though definitely not street level. And undoubtedly another long night.

She saw a dog walker herding a bunch of tiny, weird-looking dogs with pink bows in their hair, a jogger in neon red sprinting toward an invisible finish line, a sidewalk sleeper still dozing in a doorway, a woman at an already open market busily filling the outside stall with flowers for sale, and through a third-story window, a woman in a tiger-print leotard spinning in pirouettes.

If you didn't love New York, she thought, you didn't belong there.

And because she loved it, because she belonged there, because she was a murder cop who believed in protect and serve, she turned her mind to murder.

4

Because she wanted impressions of the walk Abner routinely took to and from work, Eve hunted for parking near the residence. It took time, even on the quiet street, but she had some to spare. Once she'd pulled in curbside, she hiked the block and a half back to the house with its sealed door, checked the time, started from there.

Neither doctor owned a vehicle. She imagined in seriously bad weather, they took a cab or car service the few blocks to their respective workplaces.

But her information at this point indicated Abner walked routinely—sometimes leaving early enough to squeeze in a run, or a workout at his gym.

He liked to take his runs—again in all but seriously inclement weather—in Hudson River Park. So they'd check that area, too, see if they could find other runners who knew him, interacted with him.

But on most workdays he'd taken this route with its pretty brick or brownstone homes, its scatter of upscale boutiques, its restaurants, cafés. She passed a bakery, paused. She could see a line had already formed at the counter inside.

Worth a stop on the way back, Eve decided, as it was most likely where the victim picked up the baked goods Louise said he'd sometimes brought to the clinic.

He likely had a favorite flower place, too, she thought. Fresh flowers in the house, flowers to the clinic.

Just one of a number of places his killer might have seen him, interacted with him.

Had to know his routine, she thought as she turned a corner. Had to know or strongly believe he'd be home to take the package, that he'd be home alone. Or else why pay for the expedited morning shipping?

Not that it cost the killer anything, but why bother if when he opened it didn't so much matter?

She stopped outside the townhouse, another brownstone, that held the offices. One of the plaques, gold against the brown, said:

Dr. Kent Abner
Pediatrics

The rails up the short steps glowed deep, dark bronze. Two white pots flanked the white door and held sunny little daffodils, some purple flower she couldn't identify, and some greens that trailed over the pots.

The windows sparkled.

The result, from Eve's view, equaled classy, safe, welcoming.

Another layer of safe came from excellent security, including a door cam.

She turned, again to get a sense of the area where there would have been interaction, routine, certainly deliveries. And spotted Peabody on the opposite corner.

She wore her pink coat—surely with the winter lining zipped out for spring—her obviously beloved cowboy boots, navy pants that may or may not have been loose, and a scarf, silky rather than knit, that held flowers not unlike those in the white pots.

The sun bounced off the lenses of her sunshades, making Eve wish she'd remembered her own.

Peabody crossed over, hoofed down to Eve.

"Mag morning! It should always be spring."

"You're wearing flowers."

"Spring. I just ran this up last night." Peabody patted the scarf.

"Ran it up where?"

"On my sewing machine. I don't see the car."

"I parked back at the crime scene so I could walk Kent's usual route."

"Oh. Well, damn, I should've had that apple turnover. I bet McNab gets one on the way to Central, because nothing sticks to his skinny ass. He's on tap when and if you need him to deal with the electronics. Oh, look how pretty those mini irises are with the daffs and those sweet potato vines."

Puzzled, Eve stared down at the pots. "They're growing potatoes outside the office?"

"No, those are just decorative vines."

"How do you know these things?" Eve wondered as she started up the steps. "Wait, Free-Ager. Never mind." She pressed the buzzer.

The woman who answered had deep gold skin, dense black hair wound into a wide knot at the nape of her neck. Her eyes, richly brown, wide, thickly lashed, showed signs of recent weeping and considerable fatigue.

She wore a simple black suit, sensible black shoes.

"You are the police," she said in precise English with the faintest of accents.

"Lieutenant Dallas," Eve said, offering her badge. "Detective Peabody."

"Yes, Detective Peabody and I spoke. I am Seldine Abbakar, Dr. Abner's office manager. Please come in."

The reception/waiting area had walls of cheerful green holding cheerful art. Photos of babies, toddlers, older kids covered an entire wall. It offered thickly cushioned chairs in primary blue in the main area, with another section offering crayon-red tubs of toys.

An alcove had rods—regular height, and lower ones she supposed smaller humans used—to hang up coats.

No one currently manned the long L-shaped workstation with several comps and screens behind the reception counter.

"I asked everyone to come by seven-fifteen, to be sure," Seldine said. "We are all here, and I thought it best to have you speak to everyone in our conference room. You will excuse us. . . ."

She paused, pressed her carefully dyed lips together. "We are, all of us, shocked and saddened. Dr. Abner, he was very loved."

"We're sorry for your loss."

"Thank you. It's a great one."

"We appreciate you arranging this time."

"He would have wanted it so. It is your duty to find who did this terrible thing. I want more than I can tell you for you to do your duty. I will take you back."

"Before you do, how long did you work for Dr. Abner?" Eve knew—she'd run her. But she wanted to hear it from the source.

"I began here at twenty-two, after college. I came from Iran as a student, and studied here, applied to live

here. That was twenty years ago next month. Dr. Kent—
Excuse me, he invited me to use his given name, but I
could not. So he was Dr. Kent to me."

"Understood."

"Dr. Kent allowed me to learn more, and encouraged
me to rise. My own father died in Iran long ago. When
I married, it was Dr. Kent I asked to give me away. He
allowed me very generous leave when I had my children,
and because I wished to work and to have my children,
he . . . We have day care, here in the office. He loves—
loved children, you see."

A tear slid down her cheek, and she brushed it
away. "Excuse me, I am upset. He was a father to me.
Dr. Martin, his husband, was family to me. They were,
in all but blood, grandfathers to my children."

"I'm going to ask you this and get it out of the way.
Can you tell me where you were night before last at ten?"

"This is your duty. Yes, I can tell you. My sister-in-
law, my husband's sister, had a baby on that night, at
ten-sixteen. A boy, eight pounds, one ounce, who will
be called Jamar. I was with her, as she asked me to be,
through the labor and delivery, and we stayed, my husband and I, with her and the family until nearly midnight."

She let out a breath. "Dr. Kent was to be Jamar's
pediatrician, as he was for my children. I will give you
the names, the address of the birthing center so you can
know."

She knew pure and simple truth when she heard it,
but Eve nodded. "Thank you. We'll talk to the others
now."

Seldine opened a side door, led the way past a series
of exam rooms, a couple of stations. An office that had

Abner's name on the door. A second office that had the associate's name.

They went up a flight of steps—closed off with another door—and came into a kind of break room/lounge area, what was obviously the—currently empty—day care area, and into a room with a large table, a number of chairs, a couple of counters holding an AutoChef, coffee and tea setups.

Those around the table looked up as they entered. Eve saw a lot of weepy and reddened eyes. And more than one person clinging to the person beside them.

The air was thick with grief.

"This is Lieutenant Dallas and Detective Peabody. They have questions, and we honor Dr. Kent by answering them fully and honestly. Please sit, Lieutenant, Detective. You will have coffee?"

"Thanks. Black."

"Cream, two sugars," Peabody told her. And, following Eve's lead, started it off. "We understand all of you have had a terrible shock, and we're sorry for your loss. It's always hard to be asked, but by getting everyone's whereabouts at certain times, it helps us eliminate and move on to other questions."

"I'll start. I'm Melissa Rendi. Dr. Rendi, Dr. Abner's associate."

A mixed-race woman in her mid-thirties, she sat with a tissue clutched in her hand. "I came into the practice three years ago. Everyone else has been here longer, so I'll start, if that's okay."

"It's fine. Can you tell us where you were night before last at ten P.M.?"

"I— But I thought Kent was killed yesterday morning."

"That's correct," Eve said. "We also need this information."

"I was home, with my fiancée. Do you need her name?"

"Please."

"Alicia Gorden. We had dinner in—we'd both had a long day—and we're getting married next month, so we went over some of the RSVPs, and other wedding plans. We stayed in all evening."

"How about yesterday, about nine-thirty in the morning?"

"Here. It was Kent's day off. I had patients starting at eight."

"This is correct," Seldine said. "Dr. Lissa was in the office all morning, took her lunch break in the lounge at one, and had afternoon appointments beginning at two-fifteen. Is this helpful?"

"Very." Peabody added a quiet smile.

They went around the table. Receptionists, nurses, the physician assistant, the two day-care workers, the cleaning crew.

Rendi was right, they'd all worked for Abner from seven years to twenty.

They ran through whereabouts, alibis, tears.

They'd check the alibis, Eve thought, but wasn't hopeful anything would shake loose from them.

What she saw was a tight-knit office of people who got along well, and it all centered around Kent Abner, and his personality and professionalism.

"Did Dr. Abner have any problems or issues with anyone? A patient—the parents or guardian—someone who used to work here, another associate?"

"It's crazy to think anybody hurt him on purpose." The youngest of the staff at twenty-six, Olivia Tressle burst out with the objection. "It has to have been some horrible mistake, or just somebody crazy. A crazy person."

"Olivia," Seldine said gently. "This was not Lieutenant Dallas's question."

"I know, but . . . He was such a wonderful man. Such a good doctor. This is such a great place to work. It's all . . . it's all just wrong."

"She's right." One of the nurses spoke up now, a male, early forties. "It's just wrong. He was a really good man, and he had this way. The kids loved him. I tell you he had a way. Say a kid or baby would come in sick or fussy, he could find the key to smoothing it out. So the parents loved him. He even gave hours a month to a free clinic. During the holidays? Every kid who came in got a little gift—just a little gift, but it came out of his pocket, not the office. Every kid got a card on their birthday. He cared. It wasn't just a job to him, wasn't even just about healing. It was caring. When you find who did this . . . prison isn't bad enough."

They ran through all that until Rendi spoke again.

"I don't know if he told anyone else, but he had words with a doctor—I think it was Ponti or Ponto—at the ER at Unger Memorial."

"What about?"

"Kent went in because one of his patients had a fall, greenstick wrist fracture, and the parents contacted Kent because the kid was a little hysterical and wanted his Dr. Kent. Kent, being Kent, went in. And while he was there, this other doctor was, Kent told me, berating and humiliating a woman because her kid was dirty—or that's what the guy said. He was reaming her for not cleaning the kid up before bringing him in. It's a damn ER," Rendi said with feeling, "and Kent said the woman was obviously homeless or the next thing to it, and doing her best. Besides, you don't treat people that way."

"What happened?"

"Kent said he pulled rank—he has privileges there—and told the stupid ER doc to take a walk. He dealt with the kid and his mother, told them about Louise Dimatto's clinic—that's where Kent gave time. Then he unloaded on the guy, and the guy got back in his face about how it wasn't his business. How he should work a few doubles in the ER instead of his fancy private practice before he spouted off."

"When was this?" Eve asked her.

"It was months ago, I think like, October—no, November. It was November, before Thanksgiving. I'm sure of that. Like, a week before Thanksgiving because we had the turkeys up, and the Halloween stuff down. I want to say it can wear on you, ER shifts. I did some of my residency in ER. I don't mean to get this doctor in trouble, but it's one of the rare times I've seen Kent really angry."

"It's helpful to have any information. Anything else like this? Any time Dr. Abner had words with someone, or was angry with someone?"

"A few years ago he reported a parent for child abuse." Sarah Eisner, one of the other nurses, looked over at Seldine. "He was angry—who wouldn't be? The mother brought the little boy in for a routine, and he had all these bruises. She tried to say he was just clumsy, but she broke down, told Kent—I was in the exam room— her husband got angry and hit the boy."

"Yes, Thomas Thane. I remember. He was . . . three?"

"That's right," Sarah confirmed. "And when Kent managed to get through the fear, he told us about his father getting mad because he broke something. And it wasn't the first time."

"There would be a police report?"

"Yes," Seldine said. "Dr. Kent talked to the police. I know he spoke to the mother about taking the boy to a shelter, or getting counseling. But they didn't come back. I don't know what happened."

"We'll find out. Is this the only time Dr. Abner reported on an abused patient?"

"Only two others since I've worked for him. So three that I know of in twenty years."

"We'll need names, dates, any information. We will be taking Dr. Abner's electronics, and—"

"Oh, but the patient data."

Seldine looked at Rendi. "It is Dr. Kent. It is for him."

"I understand, but there are laws and privacy issues. We—"

"We have a warrant," Eve interrupted. "You can separate out private and confidential patient records, but we take the rest."

"I can do this," Seldine assured her. "It will be done by midday if you would give me that time."

"That's fine. We'll need to look at his office now. If there's any confidential patient information in there, you need to separate it now."

"I will do this. If you would help?" she asked Rendi.

"Sure." She rose. "I—I want you to know that I want you to find who did this. But I have a duty to our patients. Kent always put the patients first."

"Understood. Peabody, contact EDD, let them know they'll need to come in here at, say, thirteen hundred." She looked around the table at those who remained in the room. "You can contact me through Cop Central at any time if you think of anything else. Another person

Dr. Abner had words with or trouble with, another time there was something out of the ordinary."

"You get this son of a bitch," the male nurse said. "You get him. I swear when he goes on trial, I'm going to be there every damn day until they put him away. Kent and Martin are two of the best people I know. Things like this shouldn't happen to them. It shouldn't happen to anyone."

Eve left them in the conference room, walked back down to Abner's office.

She found Seldine in tears, and Rendi trying to comfort her.

"I am sorry." Seldine swiped at her face. "We . . . I found in his calendar . . . He had planned a party for me, next month. Twenty years, you see. He had—he had already ordered a cake. I loved him. He was a father to me."

"Please, can I take her out? I closed off the patient records. Can I take her upstairs for now?"

"Yes."

"Please." Seldine fought for composure. "If I can help in any other way, please tell me. And please, would you please tell Martin we are all here for him when he is ready? We send him love and comfort. Would you do that?"

"Yes."

"You've been very kind. Please be vigilant in your duty."

When they went out, Eve looked at Peabody. "The odds of finding anything in here are slim to none. But let's be fucking vigilant in our duty."

When they left, Eve drew in the noise, the chaos, the clashing colors of New York like breath, and found herself grateful she'd parked blocks away.

"Morgue next, then the lab. Meanwhile let's pin down

this Dr. Ponti or Ponto from Unger, and get the sheet on the abuse reports."

"On that." Peabody pulled out her PPC. "You know how just a couple weeks ago we're looking for who killed a rapist asshole fucker?"

"I recall."

"I think we've got what you could call his opposite in Kent Abner. And as hard as it was to push through a rapist asshole fucker's murder, this is harder."

"They're all hard. They're supposed to be. We're going to stop in this bakery just up here."

"Oh, come on, man. Apple turnover. Loose pants."

"Louise said Abner would sometimes bring pastries or flowers into the clinic. Let's check and see if there's anything there. We're going to need to hit the clinic, too, talk to the staff, go through his records."

"Yeah. Dr. Milo Ponti—resident at Unger, in ER. Early forties, married two years, no offspring. Wife's a surgical nurse at Unger. Went to Columbia Medical, lives Lower West. No criminal."

"We'll make him another stop. Bakery."

"We could split a turnover. If you split one, you're basically not even having one. Because it's half. When you cut calories in half, it's a good thing. In fact . . ." Peabody warmed to the theme. "It's an admirable thing."

"What if I don't want a turnover?"

"It's half, so it's not a turnover. It's practically a minus-over. Besides, who doesn't want all that yum, or half the yum?"

"Why is it a turnover anyway? Why isn't it just a hand pie?"

"You turn over the pastry," Peabody said as she opened the door to the bakery, "to keep the apple goodness inside. Oh, smell that."

Eve did, and decided she could choke down half a hand pie.

The first thing she noticed after the scents of glory was the black armband on the sleeve of the white tunic the counter girl wore.

Word had spread.

They hit the bakery, the gym, a local market. Peabody, showing great restraint, waited until they got back in the car before unwrapping her half of the turnover.

"You know," she said as she took the first tiny bite (make it last), "I hope when I die—say, a hundred years from now, in my sleep, after having wild, steaming sex with McNab—people who worked with me, or knew me, think half as much of me as the people who worked with or knew Abner think of him."

"At least one person didn't share those feelings."

Eve polished off her half in three careless bites as she drove toward the morgue.

"None of the people we talked to along his route, none of the people the uniforms talked to in the can- vass remember seeing anyone around the residence who didn't belong in the neighborhood—or at least no one who seemed off or made repeated visits."

"And nobody recognized the ID shots you showed them of Ponti or the parents Abner reported."

"They're still our best bets at the moment."

"We've got a doctor, and I lean there right now because it seems like a doctor would know more about poisons, and might be able to access something like this."

"Whatever this is," Eve muttered, "but that's a point."

"We have a city maintenance worker who figured he would knock his wife and kid around when he felt like it." Another tiny bite for Peabody. "Somebody in a uniform—people don't look twice."

"Another point. And we've got a junior executive who from his ID shot would blend right into the neighborhood. That one didn't do time—good lawyers—but he had to go through six months' mandatory counseling, the mother of the kid sued for full custody and limited, supervised visitations, and got it. That could piss you off."

Peabody took another tiny bite of turnover. "Five years ago, though, a long time to stew about it. And the last one's longer ago yet, fifteen years."

"And he spent two of those years in a cage. We talk to all of them."

But for now, she wanted to hear what Morris could tell her, and what the dead had told Morris.

Peabody managed to finish her turnover before they started down the white tunnel. Eve caught the scent of something stronger, deeper than the usual mix of industrial cleaner, disinfectant, and death.

And found the doors to Morris's theater locked with a RESTRICTED sign posted.

She pressed the buzzer, felt a hard knock of relief when she saw Morris through the porthole glass, heard the locks release.

"Your timing's impeccable," he told them. "I've just now cleared the room and the body."

His voice came tinny through the breathing apparatus on his full hazmat suit, but he gestured them in.

"Give me a minute to lose the gear."

"How long have you been at it?"

"We needed to close the body off—protocol— before we opened him. And keep him in a controlled area during the autopsy. I was able to start on him last evening."

Morris removed the headgear, placed it in a tub. "There

were several tests to run—protocol again—before I could take a look inside."

As he stripped off the rest, Eve noted rather than one of his excellent suits, he wore a T-shirt, sweatpants. He'd drawn his long, dark hair back in a tail.

"You've been here all night."

"Controlled area," he repeated. "I keep clothes on hand for such events. Protocol also requires a two-hour break for sleep. A slab's comfortable enough with a gel mattress."

He smiled at them, but his eyes looked tired.

"I'll be glad for a shower, some decent coffee, some breakfast."

"Peabody."

"On it."

"Oh, don't bother with that," Morris began, but Peabody was already out the door. "Well, I appreciate it."

"I've had plenty of all-nighters, but didn't grab a nap on a slab."

"It is my home away from home, after all."

Now Eve walked to the body—closed now with Morris's long, precise stitches. "What can you tell me?"

"The lab will tell you more, but the good doctor suffered a painful death—quick and painful—via a toxin I'm unable to confidently identify. There's no evidence he ingested it, or that it entered his bloodstream through injection or through touch. He inhaled it—it was airborne. And that, of course, added time to the control protocol."

Morris gestured to a counter where sealed, labeled containers held various internal pieces of Kent Abner.

"I believe you have a nerve agent. His nervous system was destroyed, as were his lungs, his kidneys, his liver, his intestines. He suffered a massive stroke, internal burns as well as the burns on both thumbs. His esophagus was scorched from the inside.

"He might have had seconds, ten, fifteen, of awareness, and as he was a medical doctor may have realized he'd been exposed to a toxin. But he wouldn't have had time to do anything but die. Minutes of agony—three or four, I'd say, given his height and weight. Perhaps five, as his muscle tone indicated superior fitness, but his internal organs were so compromised I can't tell you if they were healthy prior to the exposure."

"I'd say they were, from the evidence we have. He worked out regularly, was a runner. You said you can't confidently ID the poison. You've got a guess, an opinion."

"We want an expert on toxins and biologicals here, Dallas."

"And we have them. I'd like your take first."

He sighed. "I would have said sarin—which is extremely worrying. But my equipment and my observations don't give that a hundred percent. He was exposed in a closed home—doors, windows."

"It was hours before he was found."

"Even with that, there should have been trace—enough to set off the special team's alarms. And on the body itself. You, though sealed, handled the body, as did his unsealed spouse. But neither of you showed any sign of contamination.

"A sarin derivative, maybe. Though there's a possibility of sulfur trioxide. His eyes, his skin, the burns there." Morris shook his head. "The best I can conclude is a combination of agents and poisons, somehow released in vapor form, causing death within minutes, and clearing within hours—or less."

"Somebody would have to know what they were

doing, how to handle deadly toxins." Eve walked around the body. "To know how to keep it contained, to set it up to release when and how they wanted. Somebody who works with hazardous materials, handles poisons. A medical who knows how they work, a researcher, a chemist, lab rat, military."

"It's doubtful your average Joe or Jane would know how to access or create something like this, and know how to disburse it without exposing themselves—or others. A package through a delivery service, for God's sake. If it had leaked . . . I believe this was a small amount, and still, I would say it would have killed any living thing within twenty or thirty feet. And not yet knowing how long it would take to clear the air? Hundreds could have been exposed."

"He didn't want hundreds," Eve murmured. "Just Kent Abner."

Peabody came in carrying a surgical tray. On it coffee steamed beside a plate of bacon, eggs, hash browns.

"Food, too?"

"You said breakfast."

"This is . . . That's real bacon. Those are actual eggs. Food fit for gods."

"God of the dead." Pleased to help out, Peabody beamed at him. "Where do you want it?"

"Oh, just on the counter there."

When she spotted the jars, blanched, Morris actually chuckled. "I'll take it, and I can't thank you both enough. I'll be checking with the lab. I very much want to know what we're dealing with."

"We're heading there now. I'll make sure they send you a report."

Nodding, he took a stool at the counter, laid the tray

down. "Find this one quickly, my treasures. He may not be one and done."

As they walked out, Eve saw him spread the napkin Peabody had provided on his lap, and prepare to have some breakfast with the dead.

Home away from home, she thought.

5

After Eve filled in Peabody on Morris's opinion, her partner remained silent for several moments.

"I did okay in chemistry," Peabody began. "I wasn't like a whiz or anything, but I know what sarin is, and Jesus, Dallas."

"He didn't think straight sarin, which doesn't make sense. If you have it, why wouldn't you use it straight? Look up the other one he said. The sulfur trioxide."

"Sarin's banned—I know that, too. It can't be a snap to . . . Okay, sulfur trioxide's pretty damn bad, too. It can be colorless, can be liquid or solid—like crystalline. The fumes are toxic—he said fumes for Abner."

"Fumes, vapor—airborne."

"It's bad stuff, too. I'm sorry, but I don't understand a lot of the technical stuff, the chemistry stuff, but without medical intervention asap—and even with, if it's direct exposure—you're going to die pretty quick. You've maybe got a little more time than with sarin."

"It's not terrorism," Eve said as they started into the

lab. "Not in the traditional sense. At least not yet. If Abner was a test case . . . And that doesn't make sense. If you're testing it out, why go for a single person, someone alone in a house? Why not go for an office, a store, a public place? Get some impact. This was about Abner."

She spotted Berenski at his counter, his egg-shaped head bobbing as he used those spider fingers to stuff a doughnut in his mouth.

Son of a bitch!

She stalked over, resisted knocking him off his stool. "Sorry to interrupt all your hard work."

He swiveled around. "Kiss my ass. I've been here all night, got a couple hours down in my office. And I'm not the only one pulling all night on this."

She saw it clearly now that he faced her. The bloodshot eyes, the dark circles under them. And the strain.

Dickhead, he might be, but at the moment, he was all in on the job.

"Peabody, how about getting Berenski some coffee to go with the doughnut?"

"Yours?" He perked up. "The real? Make it two large. We think we've got it. I want to call Siler out. He's catching a couple z's, but he should talk this through. He's the expert on this around here."

Eve held up two fingers, then turned back to Berenski. "You start."

"We'll start with the egg."

"What egg?"

He swiveled again, brought up an image on-screen. Split-screened it. "You see there's the container—the egg. We put it together from the pieces on the floor of the crime scene. The other's what we've determined it looked like before it broke. You got a golden egg. Looks like cheap plastic, right? A piece of crap."

"Okay."

"And it is, except the inside of the piece of crap's been coated with a sealant, lead based."

"To beat a standard scan."

"Sure. And there's a seal—thin, airtight—around the edges. This here held the agent."

"Sealed in, airtight."

"Took awhile even with the comps to put it all together. Then we needed to identify the seal, the inside sealant. And see, it's got the hook-and-eye lock on it, the back hinge? Simple—probably came that way. But the seal, that was added on. You unhook it, and you'd need to give it a little tug. Nothing muscular, right, but a good tug to break the seal. And when you did?"

"That's the end of that."

"Morris said airborne."

"Yeah, it hit the air when the seal broke, and the air—the oxygen triggered the agent. Inside the seal, it's inert, get it?"

"So why wasn't whoever put it in there, then sealed it up, on Morris's slab?"

"Wait for Siler. Who was the DB?"

"A pediatrician."

"Shit. That doesn't make sense, and I lose twenty. I figured military. Siler went with CIA. Hey, I didn't lose twenty. Nobody put in on a kid doctor. Siler." He crooked one of those long fingers at a small man—maybe five-six—working his way through the labyrinth of the lab.

His white lab coat flapped around a pair of checked pants, a T-shirt that read SCIENCE RULES ALL. He had bright red hair that had never been found in nature springing out in every direction, a hooked nose, dark, sleepy eyes.

"Dallas," Berenski said by way of introduction. "Abdul Siler."

"Yo. CIA hit, right?"

Eve said, "No."

"Damn. I could've used the twenty."

"You're getting coffee that's worth more," Berenski told him. "Here comes Peabody with the black gold. Siler," he added, and took the coffees from Peabody.

Siler sniffed his, blinked his sleepy eyes, sipped. Closed the sleepy eyes and said, "Gooooood."

"I got started on the egg. You take it, but don't get all technical. They're cops. Science is like a foreign fucking language."

"Sure. So. We put the egg together—made in Mexico, according to the stamp. You'll probably find a couple dozen shops in New York have them in stock for under twenty bucks. Cheap, gaudy. You could use them to put candy in or whatever. Bigger than a chicken egg, but maybe for like an Easter egg hunt or whatever."

"That's their job, Siler."

"Right. The interior was coated with sealant, not unlike what you'd have in your field kit, but with a lead base. And a secondary seal, with an adhesive, was added around the edges of both sides of the egg to make it completely airtight. The fabricated wood box, which we assume held the egg, was also sealed, same method. The interior padding, that woulda been added to the box, woulda cushioned the egg."

"So whoever did it was careful."

"You bet. Mmmm." He drank more coffee. "Padding inside the shipping box, inside the wooden box to protect the egg in case the package got dropped. It would probably work unless it got slammed or crushed. But it didn't."

"What was inside the damn egg?" Eve demanded.

"That's the really frosty part."

"Keep it simple, Siler," Berenski warned.

"I want to say it wasn't simple—it was pretty damn brilliant, and took some serious skill. What you had in there, probably in crystalline form—before it hit the air and vaporized—was sulfur trioxide."

"Why is that brilliant?"

"Because that was mixed with sarin. With— What's the word I want? A soupçon of sarin. And that? That was mixed with an agent that kills them both—but it kills them about fifteen minutes after the whole shebang hits the air."

"So," Eve deduced, "the agent had a . . . like a shelf life once released."

"Exactamundo!" Siler gave her a happy look, a friendly slap on the arm she decided to let pass. "See, oxygen triggers the whole thing—releases the toxins that, merged together, are going to kill the shit out of you within like five minutes, and the clearing agent that's going to kill the toxins inside about fifteen. Biowarfare-wise, it's total mag because you can target specific, and anybody outside say, twenty feet's not going to feel a thing, and anybody coming along a few minutes later, same deal."

"Military?" Eve pressed.

"If it is, they'll deny it because it violates all sorts of conventions and treaties and interplanetary laws. That's why I went CIA—because, you know, covert. Because CIA. You're sure it's not?"

"Doubtful. How would you get those agents?"

"You gotta figure we've got bioweapons stashed away in some secret locations. Getting one out? I don't know, man. And they're unstable on top of it. It's going to take steel balls, and some crazy with it."

"How do you make it?"

"You'd need a seriously controlled lab, special containers, glassware, a fume hood. And yeah, a bunch of skill, a whacked-out brain. The whacked-out because if you screw up even a little, you're gone, gone, gone. I can get you all the substances and precursors that go into it. I was going to write it all up after I got some shutdown, but the coffee's got me revved, so I'll have it for you in a couple hours. You're going to need somebody who gets the science. You're looking for somebody who gets the science or can pay somebody who does."

"All right. Copy the ME on the report."

"The body was clean, right? Organs gone, eyes all burned, like that, but the agent was dead?"

"That's right."

Siler drank more coffee. "Brilliant."

Outside, on the sidewalk, Peabody stopped, turned her face up to the sky.

"What're you doing?"

"Blue sky, pretty day. I'm reminding myself the world isn't a completely fucked-up place. I did just okay in chemistry, like I said, but I know enough to get that somebody spent a lot of time, took a lot of risks to create something to kill a good man. Overkill, it seems to me."

"Yeah, it does." Eve jerked a thumb toward the car. "And back to specific. Just Abner—adding the kill agent in there proves that. He didn't want Rufty, for instance, running back home. Forgot something, whatever, and being exposed. He didn't want anybody to die but Kent Abner."

"Unger Memorial?"

"That's right. Maybe Dr. Ponti's brilliant."

Middle of the morning, Unger's ER was busy but not insane. Eve suspected a good portion of the people waiting had put off going to a doctor for whatever ailed them until they hit desperate.

She could relate.

Others looked like a mix of falls, bumps, fights, kitchen mishaps.

She went to the check-in counter, pulled the woman on the stool's attention away from her comp screen.

"We need to speak to Dr. Ponti."

"Dr. Ponti's with a patient. You'll need to sign in here, then—"

"We need to speak to Dr. Ponti," Eve repeated, and held up her badge. "Police business."

"He's still with a patient."

"Where?"

She checked her comp screen. "He's in Exam Three—and if you try to go in while he's with a patient, I'll call Security whether you have a badge or not."

"We'll wait. Outside of Exam Three."

With Peabody, she hunted it up, stationed herself outside the door.

"The other three on the list," Peabody began, studying her PPC. "There's nothing to indicate they'd have the knowledge or skill to create the toxin. Or have access to something like we're dealing with. Or, for that matter, the financial means to pay for somebody who did."

"Blackmail, force, like minds," Eve reeled off.

"Yeah. Still, it has to cost. I'll start going down levels on the financials."

"Do that. And military or paramilitary backgrounds or associates. Spouses, family members. Same with science and medical."

As she spoke, the door opened. "Change that dressing tomorrow. You should see your regular doctor within the week."

"Okay." The man with the bandaged arm and sour expression kept walking.

"And you're welcome," Ponti muttered.

"Dr. Ponti."

"Yes?"

"Lieutenant Dallas, Detective Peabody. NYPSD. We need to speak to you."

Though he looked pretty fresh—Eve figured the three-day scruff was a fashion statement—he gave them the weary eye. "If this is about the stabbing a couple nights ago, I gave the officers all the information I had."

"Something else. Would you like to talk here, or somewhere more private?"

He sighed, a man in his early forties with streaky blond hair to go with the scruff and good high-tops, pressed jeans, a pale blue shirt, and a white doctor's coat.

He wagged a thumb, started down the hall. "I can't take ten unless I get a buzz. What's this about?"

"Dr. Kent Abner."

"Who? Oh, right, right." Now he rolled his eyes, pushed a door open into a small lounge. He walked straight to the coffeepot. "What about him?"

"He's dead."

Ponti paused in pouring the coffee, and the eyes that had shown no interest whatsoever narrowed with it now. "Police dead? What happened?"

"It's odd you wouldn't have heard, as Dr. Abner had

privileges here. I would think some of the staff would mention it."

"I just came on at eight. I've been busy. This is my first break."

"Your wife's a surgical nurse here?"

"That's right." Interest turned to wariness. "What is this? What happened to Abner?"

"Poison."

He finished pouring the coffee, sat. "Not accidental, I take it."

"No. You and Dr. Abner had a disagreement."

"You could call it that, or you could call it him pushing his weight and opinion in where it didn't belong and undermining me with a patient, and with the chief resident."

"It pissed you off."

"Damn right it did. And if I poisoned everybody who pissed me off, the ER would be overflowing. Look, I was on the last leg of a double. I was tired, and maybe a little short-tempered. The woman brings in her kid—bronchitis—and he's filthy. He's got a couple of scrapes, infected from not being cleaned properly or treated. I'm telling her what needs to be done, and granted maybe I wasn't polite about it, then Abner's letting me have it and taking over. We had words, and my supervisor took his part of it. I got a wrist slap and a day off. That was months ago."

"Had you seen Dr. Abner since that incident?"

"I've seen him around. I stay out of his way. He comes in here from his private practice. I'm in the trenches. I didn't appreciate what he said or did, and said so. This brings the cops to my work?"

"That's right. Where were you night before last, about ten o'clock?"

"Out there, dealing with a teenager with three holes in him from a sticker. I was supposed to be off at ten, they brought the kid in at nine-forty-five. I triaged him for surgery, gave a statement to the cops. I didn't get out of here until at least ten-thirty."

"And then?"

"I went home, where my wife was waiting for me. We drove to the Hamptons. We have a friend with a beach house, and they'd told us we could have it for a couple nights. We both had the next day and night off, so we spent it there. Slept, had sex, ate, drank, slept some more. We drove home early this morning. Jesus."

"Did you see or speak to anyone while there?"

His temper rose, visibly—the heat in the eyes, the tightening of the jaw.

"No. The whole point was quiet, solitude, relax. We walked on the beach a few times, but we weren't being sociable. Look, I have to get back. This has nothing to do with me."

"Who owns the house?"

He hissed out a breath. "Charmaine and Oliver Inghram. Ollie and I went to med school together. He's private, too. Cosmetic surgery, so he can afford a beach house. We borrowed my brother-in-law's car, as we don't own one. He's a lawyer, and if you come back on me again, I'll be contacting him."

He stormed out, and Eve angled her head.

"Bad attitude, bad temper, resents not having a pot of money. He stays on the list—along with the wife."

"She could've made the drop," Peabody agreed. "Then they drive to the Hamptons for cover. It's not bad."

"Yeah. We'll keep looking at them. Now let's go talk to men who liked to smack little kids around."

"The fun never ends in Homicide."

They tracked down Ben Ringwold at his food truck in a primo spot a block off Fifth. Though not yet open for the lunch crowd, he answered the door at their knock.

Incredible scents poured out.

He wore a splattered white bib apron, had his hair shorn close to his scalp. His face was as splattered with freckles as his apron was with sauces.

"Sorry, ladies, we need about fifteen minutes."

The "we" included a second man, as black as Ringwold was white, working at the stove where all those spicy smells came from. The second man—also an ex-con, from Peabody's search—had a head full of dreads covered with a cook's cap.

Eve just held up her badge—and watched Ringwold's face tighten with stress.

"We have our licenses, our permits." He pointed back in the truck where they were displayed.

"We're not here about your license, Mr. Ringwold. We're here to talk to you about Dr. Kent Abner."

"Kent Abner?" He didn't pretend not to know the name. "What about him?"

"He's dead. He was poisoned yesterday morning."

"Poisoned? Jesus. Look, you better come in—it's tight, but if we have the door open, people are going to start lining up."

"What time in the morning?" Ringwold's partner, one Jacques Lamont, spoke with a musical accent that explained the name on the truck.

CAJUN BON TEMPS

"About nine-thirty," Eve said as she and Peabody crowded in.

Stains and splatters might have painted both aprons

like crazed art, but the cook and prep surfaces were shining clean.

"We already prepping by nine," Lamont said. "Getting our supplies for the day. You can check."

"How about ten o'clock the night before?"

"I was at a meeting. Addicts Anonymous, at Blessed Redeemer Church—we use the basement. From about eight to about nine, nine-thirty. Then I had coffee and some pie with the kid I'm sponsoring. We left about eleven, I guess, to head home."

"How long have you been clean?" Peabody asked him.

"Nine years, eight months, two weeks, and four days. I'm not going to give you the kid's name, but I'll give you the diner where we had coffee—and some pie. I'll give you the waitress's name. I'm a regular, Susan knows me. We were there until about eleven. It's only a couple blocks from my place, and I walked home, went to bed. It's the Bottomless Cup, on Franklin. Susan Franco waited on us."

"What about you, Mr. Lamont?"

"Nobody calls me mister." He rolled his enormous dark eyes at them as he stirred something in a huge pot. "Me? Night before last I'm with my girl, Consuela. Ten? We were naked and busy." Now he grinned, but there was worry in those big eyes. "I'm a cook. Who's gonna eat my food I go poison somebody?"

"It's about me, Jacques. Kent's the one who reported me for hurting Barry."

"Long ago, *cher*. Under the bridge now."

"Never all the way. I haven't seen Kent for a couple of years. He came by the truck, that's the last time I saw him. But it's been close to nine years since I made my peace with him. I didn't feel that way when I went inside, or when I got out, but I got to it. I used, a lot, back when I hurt my boy, his mother. I've done what I can to make peace with them, too, to make amends."

"And you done good," Jacques assured him.

"Still got a ways to go. Barry's still a little unsure—can't blame him—but we see each other every few weeks. Carly—his mom—she's forgiven me, and I'm grateful to her. I came to be grateful to Kent. It took me longer."

"My man goes to meetings like clockwork," Lamont said. "He got me going to them. Me, I wouldn't have Consuela I wasn't clean."

"How long for you?" Eve asked.

"Seven years. I went in for the junk, and stealing to buy the junk. My man here got out first, and he starts pushing at me to go to meetings. I want to get the truck, make some money. I'm a good cook, always was—my *grand-mère*, she taught me. I shamed her. Now she's not shamed no more."

"We've got a good thing going here, and we work hard to keep it that way," Ringwold put in. "We wouldn't have it if we hadn't cleaned up. Maybe I wouldn't have gotten clean if Kent hadn't reported me. Maybe, and it's kept me up at night more than once, I'd have done worse to Barry and Carly. I'm sorry about what happened to Kent. I know he was a good man—and he forgave me."

She believed them—the alibis were too easy to check, and they'd have a hell of a lot to lose to kill a man over a fifteen-year-old grudge.

But she got all the contact information.

"You taste this." Lamont scooped up some rice, coated it with red beans and sauce. "You see we don't kill nobody when we can serve the best Cajun food in New York City."

"I don't—"

But Lamont pushed the plate at Eve, pushed forks on Peabody.

"Better eat some," Ringwold said with a quick grin. "He's real proud of his red beans and rice. His grandmother's recipe."

Peabody went first, took a forkful. "Okay. Okay. This is really, seriously good."

Because she had to respect a couple of ex-cons and recovering addicts who tried to walk the line, Eve took a forkful. Peabody was right.

"You've got a good thing going here. Don't screw it up."

"No way we doing that! I make my own hot sauce— gives this a kick, right? We get enough going, I'm gonna bottle it up, we gonna sell it and make ourselves millionaires. *N'est-ce pas, cher?*"

"Bet your ass."

Since lines had formed before the partners opened the serving window, Eve figured they had a decent shot at it.

"They do have a good thing," Peabody said as they walked back to the car. "Hard to see them in this."

"We'll talk to the ex and the son, get a sense there, but no, they're not in this. Let's hit the exec, see how he plays."

6

Thomas T. Thane had a modest office in the advertising firm called Your Ad Here. At forty-two, apparently glued to the designation of junior exec, he carried an extra fifteen pounds and a sour expression.

The rundown in his online data made Your Ad Here his fifth employer since college. His division handled ad blimps—a fact that Eve had to push aside to maintain any semblance of objectivity.

He didn't help his own cause by being a dick right off the mark.

"Yeah, I heard about Abner. What's it to me? I don't like cops coming to my place of work. And unlike you, apparently, I'm busy."

"Then we won't waste any more of the valuable time you spend thinking up blather to blast out of blimps than absolutely necessary."

Okay, maybe she hadn't pushed it all the way aside.

He bared his teeth at Eve. "You can kiss my ass— and talk to my lawyer. Get out."

"Fine. We'll expect you and your legal representative in Interview at Cop Central at . . ." She glanced at her wrist unit. "One this afternoon. Reserve the room, Peabody."

"Bullshit!"

"Talk to us here, talk to us there." Eve shrugged. "We've got nothing better to do."

"I'm not going anywhere."

Now Eve just lifted her eyebrows. "Maybe you'd prefer us to obtain a warrant and escort you from the building in front of your employers and coworkers. It really isn't any skin off ours."

"What the hell do you want?"

"The answers to some very basic questions, such as your whereabouts at ten P.M. night before last."

"More bullshit." He made an ordeal of getting out his pocket calendar. "Bullshit from a couple of pussy cops."

Eve heard Peabody's distinct hiss, and simply gave Thane a flat-eyed stare. "Suspect demonstrates disrespect and animosity toward females, particularly females in authority."

"Kiss my ass," he repeated. "At ten night before last I was having drinks with friends."

"Location and names of friends, as picturing you with friends strains credulity."

"Fuck off, bitch."

"Lieutenant Bitch," Peabody snarled out before Eve could. "Location, names."

"After Hours, it's right across the damn street." He reeled off three names—all male.

"Same question for yesterday, nine to nine-thirty A.M."

"At my desk, right here. I had a meeting at nine-fifteen."

"The last time you saw or spoke to Dr. Kent Abner."

"I had nothing to say to that son of a bitch. He tried to ruin my life, cost me a job because he couldn't keep his big nose out of my business."

"That business being physically assaulting your three-year-old son and his mother?"

He kicked back in his chair, actually put one fancy shoe on his desk as a show of disrespect. "More bullshit. I had to discipline the kid because his mother wouldn't, just let him run wild. Added to it, he was clumsy, always falling down."

"Would that be the mother or child who was clumsy?" Peabody wondered. "Seeing as they both had injuries."

"I don't have to talk to you about that. I did the community service, the ridiculous probation period, completed the asshole anger management."

"Which seems to have worked so well," Eve commented.

He lifted his hands, spread his fingers. "I don't even know where the bitch and the brat are, and don't care. Both were more trouble than they were worth. Now I've got work to do."

"It sounds as if you had hard feelings for Dr. Abner."

"I figure he got what he deserved, and so what? Then again, he's a good part of the reason I don't have the bitch and the brat, both whiners, dragging me down." He showed his teeth again in a big, exaggerated smile. "Maybe I should send flowers."

Eve edged closer, watched Thane's fists ball as he dropped his foot back to the floor, straightened in his chair. And something else. She saw the flicker of cowardice in his eyes.

"Just how many bitches and brats do you figure you've slapped, punched, shoved in your worthless life?"

"You'd better get the hell out before I file harassment charges."

"You think this is harassment?" Just a little closer, close enough to see a thin line of fear sweat pop out above his upper lip as those fists balled tighter. "Not even close. But it could be, and soon. Watch yourself, Thane, and think twice before you use those fists on another woman or minor. Because the next time you do, it won't be community service, probation, and anger management. I'll make sure you go inside. It'll be my mission."

"Ours," Peabody corrected. "And we're really good at fulfilling missions."

"I'm calling my lawyer."

"You do that."

Now Eve showed her teeth in a big, exaggerated smile before they walked out.

"I was waiting for you to kick his ass," Peabody muttered as they worked their way around the cubes to the elevator. "I was actually hoping you would."

"This way was better, and less paperwork. Now he's shaken, pissed off, and worried."

Peabody sucked in a breath, huffed it out as they rode down. "You have good men in your life, in your work, you mostly forget that type's around. Damn it, I just thought of something. When he said kiss my ass, I should've said how he couldn't get a woman to perform that act unless he paid for it."

Because she could all but see the steam puffing out of her partner's ears, Eve gave Peabody's shoulder a pat. "There's always next time."

"He could've done it." As they crossed the small, empty lobby, went back outside, Peabody glanced back. "He's got the temperament to want serious payback. He may not know where his ex and kid are, but you can make book if he saw them, he'd want to hurt them. He knew where Abner was."

"Agreed. And we can look at his attitude two ways: Why antagonize the cops, bring more attention to yourself if you're guilty? Or make sure you do so they consider the blatant stupidity and think you couldn't be guilty. Check out the names and location for the time of the drop."

"Thane and three guys." Peabody pulled out her PPC as they got into the car. "Probably their weekly meeting of Misogynists United. We're talking to the maintenance guy next?"

"He's up. Then I want to go by and talk to Rufty again, their children if they're with him."

Curtis Feingold had a craphole apartment in a craphole building on Avenue C. As the exterior had been thoroughly tagged—much of it anatomically impossible drawings or badly misspelled insults and/or sexual suggestions—and more than one window had boards instead of glass, Eve figured he didn't maintain much.

The interior only cemented that opinion, with its grungy closet of a lobby, its out-of-order elevator (also tagged), and the broken door on the stairwell.

Fortunately, Feingold's craphole squatted on ground level. Eve pressed the buzzer, but didn't hear it sound. And since she could hear, clearly, voices raised in an argument inside, and somebody's poorly played horn from across the hall, she judged it busted.

She hammered the door with the side of her fist.

"Fuck you want?" came the response through the closed door.

"NYPSD. Open the door, Mr. Feingold."

"Screw you."

"We can and will return with a warrant—and a representative of the Division of Building Standards and Codes, as this building appears to be in violation of too many of both to count."

The door opened an inch on its security chain. A bleary eye peered out—and the sour smell of booze flooded through the crack. "Screw you," he repeated. "Don't have to talk to no cops."

"Would you prefer a conversation or a few hours in the tank while the BSC reps inspect this building?"

"Not my fucking building," he muttered, but released the chain.

In a white T-shirt that may have been clean in some forgotten past and a pair of brown pants that strained against his belly, he had the doughy look of a man who'd gone to fat but had once been big and muscular. His hair, sparse, thin, and dirty, barely covered his scalp. His eyes, bloodshot and angry, ticked from Eve to Peabody and back.

His breath was enormous.

"Fuck you want?"

"To speak to you about Dr. Kent Abner."

"Doctors're bullshit artists. Don't believe in them."

The apartment would have been called an efficiency, but there was nothing efficient about it. The screen—the source of the argument between a group of people on some sort of talk show—took up one short wall. The rest stood naked and dingy, as did the pair of windows facing the street.

The bed sort of sprawled in the middle of the room, covered with a jumble of sheets. Take-out cartons and empty bottles appeared to comprise the decor.

"Dr. Abner was murdered yesterday."

"So the fuck what?"

"Dr. Abner was your daughter's pediatrician and the one who filed the complaint, testified against you, which resulted in you doing two years for child abuse."

"That fucker's dead? Calls for a drink."

He walked over to the bottle and glass on the table beside the bed, poured himself some cloudy brown liquid.

"Where were you at ten P.M. night before last?"

"Right here. Got nowhere I wanna go, nobody I wanna see."

"So you saw and spoke to no one?"

"So the fuck what? You thinking I killed the asshole? What the fuck does that get me? System's rigged against somebody like me ain't got money to grease palms. Old lady took off with the kid, and good riddance there. Who the fuck needs them?"

"Yesterday morning, about nine-thirty. Where were you?"

"Right the fuck here. I got 3B bitching about roaches, and 2A screaming about seeing a damn mouse, and what does 2C do but skip out without paying the rent. Somebody's always beating on the door, bitching about something."

"You are in charge of building maintenance," Peabody pointed out.

He just snorted, drank. "Place is a shithole. Always going to be a shithole. So the fuck what? People don't like it, they can sidewalk sleep."

"When's the last time you saw or spoke to Dr. Abner?"

"In court when the fucker tried to make me out to be some kind of maniac because I gave that sniveling kid a few smacks. Kid's *my* flesh and blood, ain't she? I can do what I like with my own flesh and blood. But the system's rigged, so they tossed me inside. You're telling me somebody gave that fucker some good smacks, maybe beat him to hell for being all holier-than-thou? I say good for them."

He poured another glass, plopped down on the nasty-looking bed in front of the arguing screen. "We done?"

"For now."

"Don't let the door hit you on the ass on the way out. Fucking cops," he muttered, and drank.

"Gee," Peabody said when they walked outside. "He seemed so nice!"

Eve had to laugh. "A pillar of his community. Contact BSC."

"Really?"

"Really. He could kill," Eve said flatly. "His five-year-old daughter had a concussion, three broken fingers, and a dislocated shoulder because he thinks he can do what he wants to his own flesh and blood."

It burned in her, burned because she'd seen hints of Richard Troy—who'd thought he could do what he wanted to his own flesh and blood—in Feingold.

"In a drunk," Eve continued, "he could pound somebody to death, pick up a sticker, slice them. But he's far too stupid to think of something as elaborate as shipping nerve agents. That doesn't mean he deserves to squat in that filthy hole of his getting free rent from some slumlord who doesn't give a shit how people live."

"This makes me feel better," Peabody decided as she pulled out her 'link.

The building in SoHo might have been a universe away from the one on Avenue C. Well maintained, it boasted a street-level restaurant where customers sat at sidewalk tables and waitstaff in fitted vests over white shirts hustled out with drinks and plates. The entrance door, painted a quiet beige, boasted solid security. Rather than mastering in, Eve pressed the buzzer for Victoria Abner-Rufty and Gregory Brickman's loft.

A male voice—not computerized—answered.

"Lieutenant Dallas and Detective Peabody."

"Yes, come right up."

The door released.

Though she found the entranceway well maintained, Eve still took the stairs.

A man stood at the open door of the second-level unit. He looked exhausted. A well-built, mixed-race man in his late thirties worked up a polite smile that didn't reach his quiet brown eyes.

"Greg Brickman." He offered his hand to both of them. "I'm Tori's husband—Kent's son-in-law. Please come in. Thanks for calling ahead," he added. "It's given Marty a little time to compose himself. He's back in the kitchen with Tori. Ah, Marcus and Landa— that's Tori's brother and his wife—they're upstairs. They're working on the . . . the arrangements. We, ah, sent all the kids out to the park with the nanny. I hope that's all right. We just felt it would be better if . . . if they were out while you talk to Marty."

"That's fine, Mr. Brickman."

"Greg. It's a horrible time. We're, none of us, doing very well. If you'd wait, I'll go get Marty."

The living area, comfortable, cheerful, had its wide window overlooking the street and the artistic hustle of the area. Like her fathers' home, the daughter's displayed a lot of family pictures, some good art, a sense of color and style without being too fussy about it.

Greg brought his father-in-law out along with a

woman who had her dead father's athletic build, a messy tail of brown hair, a grief-stricken face devoid of enhancements.

"This is my daughter, Victoria." Rufty clung to her hand. "I don't . . . Marcus?"

"He and Landa are upstairs. Do you want me to get them?" Greg asked.

"I don't know. I can't seem to think more than a minute ahead."

"I'll get them."

"Come on, Daddy, let's sit." Tori led him to the sofa, sat close by his side. "Do you have any news for us? I'm sorry," she interrupted herself. "Please sit down. I should offer you something. Daddy, why don't I make you some tea."

"We're fine. We're sorry to intrude at this difficult time," Eve began.

"You were kind yesterday. I remember you were kind. Everyone's been kind. Seldine said you told her she could call, she could come. She's family. We're grateful."

"Dr. Rufty," Peabody said, "I'm sure you know, but I'd like to say that everyone we talked to in Dr. Abner's office spoke so highly of him, and with such warmth."

"Thank you for that."

Greg came back with another man and a woman. The son took his build from his other father. Tall, gangly, with Rufty's eyes blurry with fatigue, he moved to Rufty's other side as his wife took a chair.

"This is my son, Marcus, and his wife, Landa."

"Have you found who did this to my father?" Marcus demanded.

"We're pursuing several lines of inquiry, and the investigation is active and ongoing."

"That's just cop talk."

"It is cop talk," Eve agreed. "It's also true."

"They aren't the ones to be angry with, Marcus," his wife murmured.

He opened his mouth, shut it again. Then took a moment to breathe. "You're right. I apologize."

"Not necessary. We have some follow-up questions, Dr. Rufty. Did your husband talk to you about a Ben Ringwold?"

"I . . . I'm not sure."

"Fifteen years ago, Dr. Abner reported Ben Ringwold for child abuse."

"Wait, yes, of course—"

"Is that who killed my father?" Tori asked.

"No, no, no." Rufty spoke quickly, rubbing her hand in his. "I remember Ben very well now. He came to see Kent—several years ago now. He was doing the Twelve Steps. He came to apologize, and in fact, thanked Kent for helping to stop him."

Nodding slowly, Rufty brought it all back. "He'd made peace with his ex-wife, had reached out to his son. Step Nine—he was doing what he could to make amends, and came to Kent. The three of us talked for some time, I remember."

He smiled a little. "Ben said he'd started a business. A food truck. We went there once. Kent was so pleased. He said how it renewed his faith in people to see someone turn his life around. You don't suspect him of hurting Kent?"

"No, not at this time. He has a solid alibi, and appears to have done just what your husband said. He's turned his life around. He may contact you, Dr. Rufty, to offer his condolences. Did your husband speak of a Thomas Thane?"

"I'm not sure."

"I know that name." Marcus spoke up. "I know that name. Dad reported him. He beat his wife and child. We had a discussion about it after he got off—community service or some *bullshit* like that."

"Did your father indicate Mr. Thane had made any threats?"

"No."

"How about Curtis Feingold?"

"Yes, yes, I know that one." Rufty nodded. "I remember because his wife was a teacher, and I helped her get a position at a school in Yonkers. I have some colleagues there. He—Feingold—was an abusive drunk. I know he went to prison."

"Dr. Milo Ponti?"

"Yes, yes. We all know that name. We had a family dinner, and Kent was late because he'd checked on a patient in the ER at Unger. He gave this Ponti a talking-to because he'd berated a woman who'd brought her young boy in. Kent couldn't abide seeing someone in pain or distress not being treated with compassion. But you don't kill a man for giving you a talking-to."

"We're looking at every angle."

When she gave Peabody the nod, Peabody took out her PPC, brought up the reproduction of the egg. "Have you ever seen anything like this?"

Rufty frowned over it. "A golden egg—like the goose? I suppose I have, in trinket shops, in drawings, that sort of thing. What does it mean?"

"We were able to reconstruct this from the broken pieces on your kitchen floor," Eve told him. "In doing so, our forensic specialists were able to determine the inside of this . . . trinket had been painted with an airtight sealant, and a sealant had also been added to the edges of the open halves. When Dr. Abner opened this container, the toxin inside was released into the air. This caused his death."

"But—but—that's diabolical, isn't it?" Rufty went very pale as his daughter put her arm tight around him. "We don't know anyone like that. It had to have been meant for someone else."

"Sir, the package was addressed specifically to your husband. I'm asking you now if Dr. Abner spoke of anyone in the last few weeks that concerned him, that he'd had an altercation with, or words with."

"No one. I swear to you. I'd tell you. Why wouldn't I tell you?"

As his voice rose, shook, tears blurred his eyes, his daughter, trembling, held him tighter. "Daddy, don't be upset. We want to know who hurt Dad. We have to know."

"But she said how everyone loved him." He pointed at Peabody. "She understands that. And now someone . . ." He squeezed his eyes shut as Landa rose and slipped from the room. "All right, all right. Someone . . . this took planning and resources and knowledge and—and terrible cruelty. We don't know anyone who could do this."

He leaned toward Eve now, his eyes full of grief and pleas. "Understand, please understand, Kent and I lived a good life together, tried to do good work, to be good people. We raised our children to be good people, to do good work. To care. Please understand."

"I do, Dr. Rufty. I do understand. Nothing your husband did caused this."

Landa came back with a glass. "You drink this now, you take this soother. No argument. I'm a doctor, too, and, my darling, you drink the soother, or I get my medical bag."

"He was so proud of you. He loved you like a daughter."

"I know." Landa pressed the soother on Rufty, kissed his cheek. "You drink this now, then you come upstairs with me and lie down awhile. I'll stay with you."

"But they have questions."

"No, that's all for now." Eve rose. "Again, we're sorry for your loss. Those are cop words, but they're also true."

It's never just the dead, Eve thought as they got back in the car. Death—but most especially murder—ripped so many lives to shreds. And no matter how they were put back together, they were never, never the same.

For some killers, she thought, that miserable truth was a kind of bonus point.

They swung by Louise's clinic, and found the waiting area packed. An enormously pregnant woman sat beside a woman with a squalling baby. The pregnant woman seemed delighted to coo over the type of being she'd soon have to deal with around the clock.

A trio of marginally older kids banged or squabbled over a collection of toys in a corner. Adults sat in chairs with watery eyes, hacking coughs, bandaged limbs, or simply the blind-eye expression of those waiting their turn in what reality deemed wouldn't come quickly.

Eve walked to the check-in counter, started to take out her badge.

"Lieutenant, Detective, Dr. Dimatto's expecting you. Go right through the side door. Sharleen will take you back to the doctor's office. She's with a patient," the receptionist told Eve. "But she'll be with you shortly."

"Great. Thanks."

Once through the door, a perky little redhead in a flowered tunic guided them past exam rooms, a lab station, and into Louise's tidy office.

"She shouldn't be too long," Sharleen began.

"We can start with you," Eve said, and made Sharleen blink.

"Oh. Okay. Um. Dr. Dimatto said we need to give you our cooperation."

"Makes it easier all around. You knew Dr. Abner?"

"Sure. I've worked here about eight months now. Dr. Abner was one of our regular volunteer docs. He was just great with kids. I'm studying to be a pediatric nurse, so he let me assist him whenever he could."

She paused, lost a few layers of perky. "I really liked him a lot. It's hard to understand . . . It just isn't sinking in, I guess."

"Do you know of anyone he had problems with?"

"I just don't. Like I said, he was really good with kids, and they liked him. Your kid likes the doc, you're going to like the doc. And he never played big shot or sticky benefactor with the staff, if you know what I mean. He was just . . . just one of us."

"Did you ever see him or interact with him outside of work?"

"No. Wait, that's not true, I guess." She held up a finger with the nail painted bright purple. "A couple months ago he had a late shift, and I was working. He walked me home after—insisted. I only live a couple blocks from here, but he didn't want me walking home alone. It was late, and it was icy. He walked me home, so that was outside work."

She sighed and the perky dissolved into distress. "He was nice that way."

"All right. Sharleen, why don't you see if anyone else is free to talk to us. You could send them back."

"Sure. Okay."

They got cooperation, anecdotes, regret from another two on staff before Louise came in.

"Sorry you had to wait." With her traditional white coat flapping around a black shirt and pants, she headed straight to the mini-AC on a shelf behind her desk.

"It isn't your blend, but it's several steps up from the usual office-slash-waiting-room coffee. You want?"

"We're good."

"Sorry about your friend, Louise," Peabody added.

"Thanks. Me, too." She gulped down coffee, breathed out. "I want to say straight off I'm really glad it's the two of you investigating. We're pretty slammed today, but you can use the office for interviews, and I'll have the staff come in on rotation."

"We've already started," Eve told her, and got a raised eyebrow.

"Is that so?"

"It is. We also have a warrant for anything relating to the victim that isn't privacy protected."

"Figured you would." Louise walked to her desk, opened a drawer, took out a disc. "We came in last night after Charles and I talked to you. This is everything. It's not much, Dallas. He was an invaluable asset to the clinic, but it was still only a handful of hours a week."

Eve took the disc, passed it off to Peabody.

"And I should tell you, I spoke to the staff first thing—and contacted staff who are either off today or on the late shifts. I know you have to talk to them, be thorough—I want you to be thorough, but you're not going to get anything."

"Maybe while we're here, I should examine a couple of your patients. Come up with a diagnosis or two."

"Ha ha." Visibly tired, Louise sat on the edge of her desk. "You're probably not going to be any happier when I tell you I talked to a few people I know who know or have worked with Ponti."

"Jesus Christ, Louise."

"Before you unload on me, understand medicals are more likely to speak frankly to another medical."

"And if Ponti turns out to be a killer, and gets wind you're asking about him? Killers are more likely to go after nosy civilians than cops."

Louise only shrugged. "Maybe, if I'd come up with anything other than the opinion he's an arrogant asshole with considerable skill, particularly in emergency medicine. He's not well liked, doesn't appear to care. He didn't appreciate Kent's setdown, or the fact Kent had him written up. He hit back with the claim Kent was a rich, entitled elitist who wouldn't last a full shift in the ER. Bitched about it for a few days with anyone who'd listen, then moved on to the next drama."

"He likes drama?"

"Word is he has a scene, an altercation, a disagreement—some sort of drama—every week or two. Which I have to say isn't that unusual in an inner-city ER."

Eve waited a beat. "How about his wife?"

"Surgical nurse. Cilla Roe. She's more liked, supposedly rock steady in the OR and out of it, apparently the contrasting smooth to Ponti's rough edges."

"Fine. Now stay out of it. I mean it, Louise."

"She does mean it," Peabody added. "And I'm going to say exactly the same."

"Could you do nothing if one of your friends was murdered?"

"You're not doing nothing," Peabody said before Eve could speak. "You're trusting us to stand for your friend, to get justice for him. You need to trust us."

"I do. Absolutely. There's a section on the disc listing the names of people I spoke with about Ponti, what they said, how to contact them if you need or want to follow up."

"Great. Now back off. All the way off. That goes for Charles, too. And stay away from Ponti."

Louise pushed off the desk. "Do you think he killed Kent?"

"I don't know who killed Kent at this point in the investigation, but I know Ponti's an arrogant asshole, and one with a temper. So steer clear."

"All right, all right. I've got patients waiting. I'll tell the staff to rotate back here. Oh, and the others, including volunteers, are on the disc, too, with contact information."

"See if you can find a spot, Peabody," Eve said when Louise walked out. "Start with the staff and volunteers on the disc, and I'll take the rest here. Let's get through this."

"I know a spot. How about the medicals she talked to about Ponti?"

"They'll wait."

Eve glanced at the AC, decided she could wait for real coffee, then took the chair behind Louise's desk to deal with the rest of the interviews.

Because Louise was right. They weren't going to get anything new or revelatory here. But they had to tie it off.

7

When Eve finally walked into the bullpen at Central, she went straight to her office and coffee.

Peabody could handle the rest of the interviews via 'link, note if any required a face-to-face follow-up. Eve needed to set up her board, her book, write up her report.

As always, the routine helped—the physical act of arranging the board, reviewing as she did the faces, the images, the data.

Creating the murder book, writing a report put it all down in a clear, cohesive manner.

Facts, statements, evidence.

Suspects.

She ran thin there, admittedly. Topping the short list, Ponti and Thane.

With another cup of coffee, she put her boots on the desk, studied the board. Those faces, images, the time-line, the alibis.

Ponti, a medical, had to have a better than basic

knowledge of chemistry, would likely have access to a lab. So that gave him a leg up on Thane.

Still, wasn't it possible Thane had a connection to someone with knowledge and access?

Both had grudges against the victim—and grudges could simmer for a long, long time.

And both had tempers—and that was a strike against. Something cold in the killing. Not a hot-temper hit, but a cold one, and a remote one. No satisfying strike, no physical altercation, no looking into the victim's eyes as life drained.

She swiveled to study the lab report again.

Not just rudimentary or even average knowledge. A real skill necessary, and patience, precision. Every step and stage covered. Nothing impulsive or of the moment.

She heard the footsteps approaching—not Peabody's familiar clomp, but strong, authoritative strides.

She swung her boots off the desk and rose as Commander Whitney came to her open door.

"Sir."

"Lieutenant."

His stride suited the authority he carried on broad shoulders. An imposing man, he filled the room as he crossed over to study her board. He might ride a desk, but his eyes reflected the street cop he'd been. The gray threaded through his close-cropped hair added a kind of weighty dignity. The lines on his wide, dark face showed he carried that weight.

"I'm on my way to a meeting with Chief Tibble and the mayor now that I have your report."

"I apologize for the delay, Commander. Detective Peabody and I have been in the field."

Whitney waved that away with one finger as he stood at her board. "While procedure and policy demanded we report this death and its circumstance to Homeland, the lab results indicate this wasn't an act of terrorism."

"No, sir. Not only was this act very victim specific, the killer took steps to be certain the poison was contained to a very restricted area, and that it would dissipate quickly."

"There are still concerns this single victim may have been a test case for a mass kill."

"If that were the case, Commander, why go to the trouble of the additives that ensured the substance would dissipate, would kill only the specified target? The lab tech stated to control the substance to that limit of time and space took skill, effort, and resources."

"Agreed. Which is why Homeland has passed on moving into the investigation. For now," he added, as warning. "Their agent in charge will receive copies of all data, all reports."

He turned back to face her. "You're leaning toward the other doctor. Toward Ponti."

"He checks some boxes. He has an alibi for the drop, but—"

"His wife is part of his alibi."

"Yes, sir. And though she has a reputation for being less volatile than Ponti, she's another medical, another who would have some knowledge of chemicals, have access to a lab. Who might harbor a grudge against Abner, for her husband."

"You also have two ex-cons the victim helped put away."

"Yes, sir. Ringwold's alibi's solid. He appears to have rehabilitated, made amends with his ex-wife and son, has built a stable business. He credits Abner with forcing him to begin to confront his addictions. He reads very believable. The second . . . He's too damn stupid, sir. He's a lazy drunk. Mean enough to kill, no question, but not smart enough for this."

"And the ad exec? Some of your boxes checked there, too."

"A mean streak, a grudge holder. And one I think wouldn't confront a man like Abner. A strong, fit man like Abner. Not one-on-one. But find a way to pay him back, from a distance? Yes, sir. That would be his style."

She looked back at the board. "The killer's a coward. He's smart, precise, methodical, but a coward. Poison's a weapon of the weak," she said, thinking out loud. "A weapon often used by women because they are, most usually, physically weaker than men. And in this case, the poison used was used remotely. So the killer doesn't need to see the results, doesn't have to see his target die. There's no passion here."

"An interesting term for it, Dallas. *Passion.*"

"It's . . . like pushing a button to end a life. All the work, the thought, the effort went into creating the weapon. But there's enough emotional distance here so the killer didn't have to see the weapon work. There's no explosion, no screams, no blood, no panic, no pleas. He—or she—shipped the package, walked away, and waited for the media reports."

"An assassination."

Because it never hurt to have your commanding officer follow your line of thinking, Eve nodded. "It has that lack of heat, yes, sir. But the victim wasn't a man of political power, or great wealth and influence. He was a good doctor, by all accounts, a good husband, father, and friend."

Now her eyebrows drew together. "If we go back to test case, Commander, and he was somehow a random target, a surrogate for some sort of actual assassination, why alert Homeland? There's a brain behind this, and a brain would know releasing a nerve agent would do just that. Why not test it out on some sidewalk sleeper no one would miss, then dispose of the body? Abner generates media because he was a well-respected doctor."

"You have a point, and I'll bring that point up in my meeting. The mayor may be relieved with that point. Keep me updated, Lieutenant."

"Yes, sir, I will."

When he left, Eve sat again, put her boots up again, and frowned at the board.

Assassination. It fit the kill in her mind. A true assassin killed without passion, without heat, without regret. But where was the purpose? If she eliminated politics, power, money, religion, what remained?

Jealousy. Revenge.

Either or both, she thought. And either or both would be cold, calculated, and cruel.

Jealousy. Revenge. Both could fester for a very long time. Maybe something deep in Abner's past had clawed its way into the now.

Calling up his data, she began a methodical search back, beginning with his parents.

What was that saying? The sins of the fathers something something. Well, some believed it.

Father, mother, stepmother, brother, half sister. All living, though none in the New York area. The half sister carried a little trouble along the way. Teenage shoplifting, truancy, underage drinking, possession of illegals. Married at eighteen—Jesus, who did that? Divorced at nineteen (surprise!). But no violent crimes, no major bumps. Just what looked like a long, rough patch that smoothed out in the mid-twenties.

Now a moderately successful writer of children's books, married, two offspring, and settled in St. Louis.

She combed through his family, moved into his college years, med school years. And heard Peabody coming down the hall.

Her partner carried a fizzy and a tube of Pepsi.

"I thought you might want to switch it up from coffee about now."

"Yeah, probably. Thanks."

Peabody sat—gingerly—on the ass-biting visitor's chair. "I got what you'd expect from the interviews with Louise's staff and volunteers. People liked Abner. One of the med-van crew even admitted to having a little crush on him. Harmless," Peabody added when Eve's eyes narrowed. "He's in a long-term relationship, was, in fact, throwing a birthday party for his partner at the time of the drop-off. It came off sort of like how I have this little crush on Roarke. You know."

"Do I?"

Peabody shrugged, grinned, slurped some fizzy. "Abner tried to work in one run a month in the mobile, and none of that crew remembered any issues, any problems."

"Somebody had one with him." Eve cracked the tube. "Assassination."

Now Peabody's eyes narrowed. "You think it was a professional hit?"

"No. A pro would've killed him low-key. Gutted him on one of his runs, slit his throat on his way home one night. But assassination in that it's target specific for a specific purpose, and contained to that target and purpose. Cold-bloodedly, precisely."

"But what's the purpose? We've got nothing on motive."

"There's always a motive, even when it's ludicrous,

petty, stupid, or just plain crazy. I'm looking at his history. Family, education, prior relationships, business dealings. Something's in there."

"Or." Peabody shot up a finger. "Random specific."

"What the hell is that?"

"If we follow the crazy, we have somebody, skilled, knowledgeable, who either by accident or on purpose develops this poisonous agent, and decides he wants to try it out. So now he works on a delivery system, then he has to pick a subject for the rest of the experiment. Maybe he knew Abner, maybe he just saw him on the street, decided he'd do. Maybe they struck up a conversation in a bar or Abner's a friend of a friend's cousin, but he decided on Abner."

"Cold-bloodedly," Eve added.

"Yeah. Like a mad scientist, and Abner's just a lab rat to him, right? He has to continue his research, note down the subject's habits, schedule, familiarize himself with the neighborhood rhythm. It's all part of the experiment. He ships the package, waits for the results."

"Wouldn't you want to see the results? Note how long it took the subject to die? How his system reacted?"

"Yeah, there's a flaw," Peabody admitted. "But mad scientist, and being a mad scientist doesn't mean you wouldn't have some basic sense of self-preservation. Plus . . . how do we know he didn't? The body wasn't discovered for hours. Lots of windows in the house. Position yourself somewhere, stroll that way after the delivery. Mini pair of binocs. Or scientist—maybe you rig up a heat sensor. You can't actually see the subject, but you can watch his heat mirror on your screen, time it. Like that."

Eve sat back, rolled it over, scanned the board. "It could play. It's a solid theory, Peabody."

"It feels like if the motive is actually the result, that equals random specific. There's a problem with it."

"Which is?"

"Well, remember when you did science stuff, lab stuff in school?"

"I try not to."

On a laugh, Peabody drank more fizzy. "I liked the lab stuff a little. Cooking and baking are like kitchen science. Or magic, depending. Anyway, some lab experiments need to be repeated with the exact same factors to prove the hypothesis or whatever."

"If we go with your mad scientist theory, Peabody, he was always going to do it again. It worked. You don't quit while you're ahead."

"You're supposed to quit while you're ahead."

"Why?" Eve demanded. "If you quit, you can't run a streak, and a streak rules." Pushing up, chugging Pepsi, Eve scanned the board, then paced to her skinny window to look out at the city. "Set factors—if we go with the mad scientist—a male of Abner's race, age, height, weight, health, and fitness level. It's the physical elements that would be important."

She watched the people below, going busily on their way.

"Troll gyms," she speculated, "running parks and paths. It would take some time, but what's the hurry?"

She turned back. "Combine them. Mad scientist experiment, target-specific assassination. Abner's the target—the subject—because he fits the requirements for the experiment, for whatever reason. And because the killer knows him. Doesn't have anything against him, at least not particularly. But he can get to Abner, knows his habits—maybe he has to dig into them a little deeper, maybe not. He needs someone, and Abner fits the bill. If it's really random, why not pick someone who wouldn't be missed, someone you could bring into a lab—a controlled area—record the results?"

"Maybe he doesn't have a place private or controlled enough."

"Right, no kill zone available." Possible, Eve thought. Possible. "But unless we have deaths that match—and we're going to check into that asap—Abner was the first target. Cold blood, scientific, why not select some-one you know? Add the possibility of some resentment playing in. Good-looking, successful, respected—even revered—doctor. Long marriage, kids, nice home. Everybody likes Kent. Could piss you off a little. Why not use him?"

"Add really healthy and fit. Wouldn't you want a healthy subject? Yeah, yeah, if you select someone you don't really know, you can't be sure he doesn't have a secret drinking problem or illegals addiction, some con-genital condition."

Eve could see it, pulled it along. "You'd want prime. But let's check poisonings, unexplained deaths, misad-ventures. Sidewalk sleepers, street LCs, runaways, Jane and John Does. We'll go back a year."

"Gonna be a bunch."

"Yeah. Round them up, shoot me half. It's an angle," Eve decided. "Let's work it."

"Here or home?"

"Why would . . ." The question had Eve checking the time. "Shit, how does that happen? Round them up here, work them at home. I've got paperwork crap I haven't dealt with in two days. Head out once you do the run."

"On it." Peabody started out, glanced back. "I feel like maybe this isn't just an angle. Maybe it's *the* angle."

Maybe, Eve thought. And maybe if they worked it right, no one else had to die.

By the time she got home, her mind stunned by forty minutes of brutal paperwork and two quick roundups with her detectives on active cases, an ugly drive home, as April decided to rain again, Eve decided she wanted ten solid minutes of quiet.

And she wanted them in water that wasn't rain.

A few laps in the pool would do the trick before she tackled her share of the list of dead.

She walked inside, where Summerset loomed, bony in black, and Galahad padded his tubby self over to greet her.

"Barely late," Summerset commented. "No visible blood or bruises. Has death taken a holiday?"

"I wouldn't risk it, so you don't want to go out there," Eve said as she shed her jacket. "There's some lightning with the rain, and with that steel rod up your ass, you're a prime target."

Satisfied, she tossed her jacket over the newel post, and headed up. The cat jogged up with her, then settled on the bed to watch while she took off her weapon harness, emptied her pockets.

Moving to the intercom, she checked to see if Roarke had beaten her home.

Roarke is in the dojo.

She decided on some martial arts instead of the swim, and changed into yoga pants, a sports bra.

She took the elevator down, slipped into the dojo to see Roarke in a classic black gi, working with the hologram of the master. His movements managed to be both flowing and powerful as he executed the complex kata.

A battle dance, Eve thought, precise, disciplined. She could hear the crack of the gi with the elbow jab, the side kick. And see, in the quiet light he'd chosen, the faint sheen of sweat on his face.

The master might have stood quiet as the light, his hands folded, his face inscrutable, but he pushed you to work, and work hard.

She still considered the gift of the dojo, the lessons both live and holographic, the best Christmas present ever.

When the kata ended, and Roarke shot out his fists in salute, the master nodded.

"Your form and focus are good, show improvement. There is room for more improvement. You require more time and practice to reach your true potential."

"You're not wrong." Roarke walked over, grabbed a towel to mop his face. "But I'm grateful, Master, for the time I have under your instruction. Program end."

He started to reach for his water bottle, spotted Eve.

"Not bad," she said as she moved into the dojo. "How long were you at it?"

"I gave it thirty, as my cop wasn't yet home."

"Now she is, and you should be pretty warmed up." She planted her feet, fisted her hands, saluted.

"Seriously?"

With a smirk, she repeated the salute.

"Bloody hell." He gulped down some water, set the bottle aside. And, moving back to her, returned the salute.

They both crouched into a fighting stance.

She went straight at him, spinning into a chest-high kick, coupled with a backfist. He blocked, would have

swept her legs out from under her if she hadn't been quick
and agile.

Their forearms slammed together on the next block,
but she whipped in a fist that stopped a breath from his
face.

"My point," she said as they stepped back.

They circled.

He feinted; she blocked, and barely avoided his follow-up. He went under her fist, pivoted, slapped away
the jump kick, shifted his weight. And his foot from a
side kick stopped just short of her midsection.

"And that would be my point."

Circling, striking, she crouched into a snake pose,
lured him in. Flipped back, used the pump of her arms
to shoot her legs up.

"Must you always go for the face?"

She smiled. "It's so pretty I can't resist. My point."

After five sweaty minutes, though she nearly took
him down on the move, he scored with a backfist.

She could hear his breath laboring a bit, as hers was,
over the soothing tinkle of the waterfall.

When he moved, she saw his guard drop slightly,
sprang into a flying kick. Her point.

But he was also agile and quick, reengaged. She
blocked, pivoted. And she spun back to find his fist a
breath from her face.

"My point."

Before she could step back, he grabbed her.

"And I'm calling a draw."

"Maybe I'm not done yet."

"I didn't say anything about being done, did I now?"

She knew that look, answered with one of her own.
"Seriously?"

And with a smirk, he took her mouth.

Well, what the hell, she decided, and tugged at the knot of his black belt. Before she could finish, he hauled her up and over his shoulder.

"What?"

Carting her over, he dumped her on a mat. "Might as well have a soft landing," he said as he dropped down to pin her.

"I'm not looking for soft."

Still a little winded, he laughed, then yanked off her sports bra. "I am."

He took her breasts with his hands, his mouth, and let himself revel in the taste, the feel of her skin, damp from the fight.

Evenly matched, he thought as she tugged his hair free of the leather strap he'd used to tie it out of the way. As she fisted her hands in it, arched up.

The sparring had been foreplay; they both knew it. Quick and agile both, they stripped each other.

He slipped inside her, into the wet and the heat.

They moved together, watched each other as damp flesh met, as hard and soft joined. Slow and easy now, the fight done. Just pleasure, all pleasure with the sound of water gently striking water, the sound of breath mixing, of hearts beating.

He felt her rise up, heard her sigh deep as she slid over. Pressing his lips to her throat where her pulse beat for him, he went with her.

Loose, warm, and oh so very soft, she lay under him with her hand stroking his back.

"That worked," she murmured.

"I should hope so."

"Well, yeah, that always works. I meant the whole deal. A good, sweaty fight, some good sex. I had paperwork brain, and now it's all cleared up."

"Cleared my own of a similar thing with the session." Lightly, he nipped at her jaw. "But I liked parts two and three much better."

"How about a few laps for part four?"

"I wouldn't mind a swim." He eased back to study her face. "You didn't close it."

"No, but we're working an angle. It feels like it might be pretty solid."

"Well, we'll have that swim, then we'll go up, have a drink and some food. And you'll tell me."

Yeah, she thought, she would. Because that always worked, too.

When she sat with him over that meal, she gave him a rundown of her day.

"Difficult, isn't it," he commented, "to sit with the newly grieving and ask them questions about the one they've lost."

"It's part of the job."

He just looked at her.

"A really hard part of the job," she conceded. "The upside of it in this case is, unless I'm missing something, the spouse, the family, they're clear."

"You don't miss much."

"The same with his staff, with the staff and volunteers at Louise's clinic. There's just nothing there."

"Which takes you to your random-specific assassination by a mad scientist."

"Yeah." She poked at the pork on her plate. "Which sounds really weird when you say it out loud, but it feels like a good angle."

"You make a good case for it," he countered. "From all you've said, it's more logical if the killer knew him, even casually. Your mad scientist theory—"

"Peabody started that one rolling."

"Well, it fits as well, doesn't it? You can't just pop into the corner chemist—pharmacy," he corrected, "and pick up a handy nerve agent. There's the black market, of course, or someone deep enough in the military who might be able to access something like. But you spoke of additives and sealants and so on. It sounds homegrown."

"It does. And it doesn't feel military or professional. Too many complications and variables for either. It's cold-blooded, but . . . it still feels personal. People are always finding ugly ways to kill each other, but if the kill was it, you'd just jab a sticker in him or beat him with a brick. The method matters."

"What's the gain?"

There she stuck. Just stuck.

"That's just it. The spouse gets the bulk, and there's no evidence they had any marital issues. No side piece on either side, no ripples, and no financial problems. The other bequests just don't work. Nothing to show Abner knew something he shouldn't have. There's no gain I can see. Add a person could die pretty satisfied knowing he leaves behind family, friends, employees, the lot who really loved him. Everything, absolutely everything, points to a man who led a really good life."

"But you still have the other doctor he dressed down, and the man he reported for child abuse on your list."

"Yeah, and they'll stay there until I'm convinced otherwise."

He topped off his wine, but Eve shook her head before he could do the same with hers. "No, I've got a lot of DBs to get through."

"Which would have most reaching for the wine. What can I do?"

"I need to handle the DBs. It may be I won't know what I'm looking for until I see it."

"Why don't I dig down a little in the snarly doctor's and the child beater's financials? Hiring a mad scientist or accumulating the proper chemicals would cost, wouldn't it? Then there might be some sign of educational skills that play in that don't show on a standard."

Frowning, Eve sat back. "Don't you have a country or two to buy?"

"I can do both. Oh, by the way, I bought Nowhere."

"What's that? Some galaxy inside a black hole? Wait." The light clicked on. "You mean that dive bar that played into the Pettigrew case?"

"Yes, though now I covet a galaxy inside a black hole."

"It's a dump. That bar's a dump."

"A bit dodgy, yes, and quite a bargain due to just that. There's potential there with some vision and a bit of wherewithal to turn it into a nice little neighborhood pub."

"The neighborhood is a bit—what is it?—dodgy, too."

"A bit. And a dodgy neighborhood needs a good pub."

She thought of the Penny Pig in Dublin, and the young street thief who'd enjoyed a pint in a pub.

"If you say so."

"I do, yes. So I'll look into the two on your list, which is its own entertainment, and play around here and there with a face-lift for Nowhere."

"Are you keeping the name?"

"Absolutely. Who doesn't want to go to Nowhere for a pint?"

She had to shake her head, because, despite herself, she could see he was right. And would likely make a killing.

"Did you sell that pit in wherever Nebraska you turned into a postcard?"

Now he smiled, sipped some wine. "It's in your name, remember? Since the work's complete, we're entertaining offers. I'm letting a little bidding war play out, then I'll have some paperwork for you to sign."

"It was a bet, and I lost the bet. Why do I get the money?"

"It's your punishment."

She rolled her eyes, rose, started to clear the plates, since he'd put the meal together. "I have work."

"And I have entertainment." He took his wine, went into his adjoining office.

8

Eve spent the next three hours picking through the deaths of the desperate and disenfranchised. They ranged in age from seventeen to ninety-four. Street LCs, unlicensed sex workers, addicts, runaways, the homeless, the nameless.

And none of them offered any element of similarity with her victim.

She read Peabody's results as they came in, found the same.

She started to reach for coffee, realized she'd had her fill. Instead she rose, walked to the glass doors of the little terrace.

The rain had long since stopped, and she could see a few stars, a stingy slice of moon, the lights of the city that never stopped moving.

Kent Abner had been the first. She'd run the probability and the results matched her own gut.

She didn't hear Roarke come in—the man moved like a damn cat (Galahad excepted)—but sensed him before his hands came to her shoulders to knead at the tension.

"There's nothing there," she told him. "Peabody hasn't quite finished her share, but there's not going to be anything there, either. You've got your stabbings, bludgeonings, strangulations, your ODs, suicides and accidentals, but nothing remotely like Abner."

"Then you've tied off that thread."

"Yeah." But she didn't feel much better about it. "How about you?"

"Ponti's got some debt—it costs to get a medical degree. He and his wife make ends meet. I'd say they're reasonably careful about what they spend. Nothing tucked away in a dark corner. No major income or outgo. As for knowledge and skill that applies here, he was a middling student. Not stellar, but good enough. She, on the other hand, excelled. Educationally her work in chemistry—organic, inorganic, pharmaceuticals, biology, her lab work—all exceptional. She did a well-received paper on chemical poisonings in her senior year of high school."

Intrigued, Eve turned to face him, said, "Huh."

"From what I can surmise, nursing was her long-term goal, and OR work became her focus in college. She appears to excel there as well."

"So she's smart, goal-oriented, would have to be controlled to work in the OR. She has the knowledge. And Abner got her new husband written up."

"You'll have a conversation with this Cilla Roe, I take it."

"Oh yeah, we'll have a conversation. She was, according to Ponti, home waiting for him at the time of the drop. Poison's generally a woman's weapon."

"Sexist."

"Statistics," she countered. "Yeah, we'll have a conversation."

"Tomorrow. You've done what you can for tonight, and so have I. Let's put the cat to bed."

Eve glanced back at her sleep chair, where Galahad sprawled. As if sensing the end of the workday, he opened his bicolored eyes. Yawned hugely, stretched every tubby inch.

Then he leaped down, trotted out of the room.

"He'll be on the bed before we get there. What a life."

"Let's follow suit." Roarke slid an arm around her.

When she woke, the cat had deserted the bed for Roarke's lap in the sitting area. With the usual morning gibberish muted on-screen, Roarke played with one of his tablets.

She grunted at him, followed morning routine. Coffee, always coffee. Shower. Brain engaged.

Clothes. Sometimes she actually missed the days when she just put on a damn uniform.

But not very much.

Afraid black might still be out, she went for brown trousers and a navy shirt, grabbed a jacket and boots.

When she came out, Galahad had been banished across the room. Roarke had plates covered on the table, and continued to work on his tablet. She caught a glimpse of the screen, and what was clearly a bar backed with a brick wall and a number of shelves. Backless stools in front of the bar, booths, a few high tops, a good-size screen, lights with dark green shades.

It came off simple, uncluttered, and somehow warm.

"Is that Nowhere?"

"It could be."

She sat next to him, took a closer look. While she watched, he tapped something and added toe-kick lights to the bar, changed the floor to match the shades.

"How did you do that?"

"Which that?"

"All of it."

"There are programs, darling. I've designed a few myself." He leaned over to kiss her. "What do you think?"

"It looks like a bar. A decent bar." She lifted the cover from her plate, spotted waffles. "Score!"

She immediately smothered them in butter and syrup.

He couldn't hold back the wince. "Well now, that should keep you going."

"Good," she said over the first bite. "Because I need to have that conversation with Cilla Roe. They could have planned this out together. Revenge is always a good one. And I want to go back to the scene, take a good look at the eyeline from the windows. Maybe one of them, if it's one of them, kept an eye on the place to make sure the plan worked."

Happily, she shoveled in more waffle, then stabbed a plump raspberry.

"If not one or both of them, maybe the anonymous mad scientist wanted to document the results of the experiment. It's worth a look. I want to check on Abner's memorial. Wouldn't part of the experiment be the collateral damage? The killer may want to be there. Someone who knew him wouldn't be out of place."

Fascinated, Roarke tapped a finger on the side of her head. "Your brain's been busy in sleep."

"I guess." She glanced at the tablet he'd set aside. "Yours, too."

"But mine's a great deal more fun."

"Murder cops make their own fun." She ate more waffle.

When she finished, she rose to strap on her weapon harness, then reached for the rest of her belt and pocket business.

Roarke lifted an eyebrow as she reached for a handful of credits and cash. "Is that all the money you have?"

She shrugged. "It's enough."

"It's barely enough to buy a cart dog and a bag of crisps." He stood, pulled a clip out of his pocket, peeled off some bills.

"I don't want your money."

He eyed her, saw the flickers of temper; ignored them. "And that would be something you make clear at every opportunity. Regardless, you're not leaving the house with less in your pocket than a careless teenager might have."

"It's my pocket."

Just as irked, he simply stuffed the bills in that pocket. "And now it holds sufficient to see a professional through a workday. Don't be more of an arse about it than necessary."

She might have yanked the bills out, tossed them back at him. But that would make her feel like an arse.

Ass, damn it.

Instead she marched over, pulled open a drawer, and dug out a memo cube. "Dallas, Lieutenant Eve, owes Moneybags Roarke . . . How much is it?"

Unsure now if he was amused or annoyed, he angled his head. "Five hundred. That's USD for the record."

"Five hundred dollars. American." She tossed the cube on a table. Then shrugged the jacket over her harness. "I've gotta go."

"See that you take care of my irritable cop."

"Yeah, yeah." She headed out. "And the cat's got syrup all over his face."

She kept going, but heard Roarke's "Bloody hell," and smirked her way down. She swung on the leather jacket waiting on the newel post and kept going.

Outside it surprised her to see those yellow trumpet things had opened and waved, yellow as the butter on her waffles, in the light breeze.

How did they do that, just pop open when you weren't looking?

She hopped in the car, noted other things were popping out, too. White things, pink things, purple things. How did they know it was safe? How did they know the temps wouldn't drop and kill them all dead?

Maybe they didn't care.

Since annoyance had her leaving early, she opted to drive to the crime scene first. And drummed her fingers on the wheel as she navigated.

She'd meant to hit a machine for more cash. She'd forgotten, that's all. That didn't make her careless. It made her busy.

Plus, the way he'd just shoved the damn money in her damn pocket was just so . . . Roarke. And now she had too much money in her pocket, and had to stop and get more in case she spent some to pay him back, so she'd have *more* too much in her pocket.

It made her tired.

So she put it out of her mind, contacted the hospital to get Cilla Roe's schedule. When she learned the surgical nurse had the morning off, she texted Peabody the address with orders to meet her there.

And pulled up near the Abner-Rufty townhouse.

She'd yet to order the scene cleared, so crime scene

tape still slashed across the door. Since the sweepers had filed their report, she'd handle that today.

But for now she studied the angles, moved down the sidewalk, strode back up again.

Wasn't going to play, she decided.

She moved to the entrance, cut the tape, mastered in.

The smell of death and sweepers' dust hadn't cleared, either. Ignoring both, she checked the windows, considered, moved to the back and the kitchen area.

And studying the congealed blood, the vomit, the assorted bodily fluids defiling the kitchen floor, she thought of Rufty coming home to this.

Avoiding the worst, she circled, checked the windows, the angles, the eyelines.

Didn't play. Just didn't.

She didn't reseal the door when she left, but decided she'd wait to officially clear it. Abner's family needed to hire a crime scene cleaner before any of them went back in there.

She waded through traffic to Roe's building. A solid fifteen-minute walk to the hospital, she calculated as she hunted for parking.

She had a brisk five-minute walk of her own when she finally found a slot. And spotted Peabody as her partner emerged from a subway station.

Eve's eyes narrowed. Peabody had left her hair down, sort of curly, and mixed in the dark, little tips and streaks of red glowed.

"What did you do to your hair?"

"I got Trina'd." Peabody's happy face glowed like the streaks and tips. "She was over at Mavis's last night, and I just went for it. It's fun."

"You're a cop. You're a murder cop."

"I'm loving it," she said, completely unabashed. "And McNab got all *mmm* after, so—"

"I don't want to hear it." Eve slapped a hand on her twitching eye. "Jesus Christ on an airboard, I don't want to hear it. Pull your shiny-faced self together. We're going up to interview a possible murder suspect."

"Oh, I can interview a possible murder suspect even with mag hair." As they mastered in the entrance doors, Peabody gave her mag hair a little finger flick.

"Don't *do* that. Don't go tossing it around."

"It's so soft!" Even as Eve ignored the elevator and started up the stairs, Peabody's glow didn't dim. "Trina put some genius product on it, gave me a sample to take home, too. My hair's thick, but a little coarse, and now—"

Eve stopped, gave Peabody the stony eye. "Another word about it, and I swear to the god of all cops I'll knock you out and shave your head bald with my penknife."

"Harsh."

"Don't test me."

Peabody cleared her throat and gamely took the second flight of stairs. Somebody, she thought, had gotten out on the cranky side of the bed. "So Ponti's new wife . . ."

"Did a research paper on poisons, aced her way through chemistry."

"Well, that's interesting."

"I'll add it to the book once we talk to her. Ponti's alibi holds—he was at the hospital. She wasn't, but supposedly was waiting for him."

They started up the third flight, so Peabody began her inner mantra of *Loose pants, loose pants.* "Probably not in tune with the mad scientist theory, or only part. But yeah, she could've been pissed since Abner dissed her husband. They could have worked it out together."

"I went by the murder scene. No way the killer or an accomplice could or would have hung around to see Abner die. First, you'd have to know just where he'd open the egg in the house to position yourself, and how would you? And even then, there's just not a good eye-line unless he was right in the front window."

"Yeah, I guess that was a long shot."

"I'm going to clear the scene so the family can get back in. Before I do, you could contact the son—I think that's the way to go—and give him the name of some of the mop-up crews."

"Sure, I'll take care of that."

When they reached the fourth floor, with doors opening and closing below, elevators humming as people rode down to start their day, Eve crossed over to the Ponti-Roe apartment.

Decent security, she thought, like the building was decent. She remembered Ponti's comments about Abner—rich, private practice—the fact he'd borrowed a beach house from a friend.

Envy often provided the springboard to violence.

She pressed the buzzer. After thirty seconds, pressed it again and held it longer.

"All right, all right!" someone shouted from inside. "Who is it?"

"NYPSD."

"What? Let me see a badge—you can just hold it up to the peep."

After Eve accommodated, she heard locks bang open.

Cilla Roe had short, russet-colored hair currently sticking up in every possible direction. She had a sleep crease in her right cheek and shadows under bleary brown eyes.

She wore a pair of striped pajama pants and a faded T-shirt. Her bare feet sported pale blue polish on the toes.

"What's this about?"

"Dr. Kent Abner."

"My husband's already at work. He had an early shift. And didn't you talk to him already?"

"We're here to talk to you."

"Me?" She rubbed her tired eyes. "I didn't even know Dr. Abner."

"But you were aware of his conflict with your husband."

"That?" Now the tired eyes rolled. "Does that really come up to the level of conflict?"

"Would you like to have this conversation in the doorway, Ms. Roe?"

On a little hiss, Roe stepped back, gestured them in. "If I'm going to have a damn conversation on four hours' sleep, I need coffee. You?"

"We're good."

Roe walked across the small living area and into a tiny galley kitchen. After hitting a button on the AutoChef, she waited, then pulled out an oversize mug of coffee.

"Let's sit down and get this done. I really want to go back to bed."

She took the single chair, leaving the short sofa for Eve and Peabody.

"Okay, yes, I know about the incident with Milo and Dr. Abner. I'm going to say Milo has about as much tact and diplomacy as I've had sleep in the last twenty-four. Which is little. He's a good emergency doctor, keeps his head and will work like a maniac to try to save a patient. But he doesn't have a good filter, and says what pops into his head. I like knowing he says what he thinks—but I'm not a patient."

She drank some coffee, sighed in a way Eve understood. "He told me you checked where he was on the night before Dr. Abner was killed—something about a package, a shipment, the time. I'm sure you've confirmed he was still on duty. He ran late with his shift. I was waiting for him because we were going to the beach for a couple days of very welcome R & R."

"Was anyone here with you while you waited?"

"With me? No, we were going out of town as soon as he got home."

"Did you see or speak to anyone between nine and eleven P.M.?"

"Why would . . ." Very slowly, Roe lowered her cup. "Oh my God, do you think I— Why would I kill a man I'd never met? Why would I kill anyone? Milo was tactless—I told him so myself when he told me what happened. He got slapped back for it. You don't kill someone over that."

"You know quite a bit about poison," Eve continued.

"I'm a nurse."

"Before you were, you showed an interest. You did a paper on poisons and nerve agents in high school."

Roe leaned back in the chair. "How do you know that? You've—you've looked into me, back to—to *high school*? It was a good subject for a paper, and I had an interest. I've always had an interest in chemistry, in fact, had thought to go into biochemical research before I fell in love with nursing, and surgery. I—I work to save lives. I'd never take one."

"So you didn't speak to or see anyone from nine to eleven that night?"

"No, I . . . When Milo texted he'd be late, I laid down right there on the couch, took a nap. Do I need a lawyer?"

"That would be up to you. You work in a hospital where Dr. Abner had privileges. You never met him?"

"No. A lot of doctors have privileges at Unger. I haven't met every damn one of them. He wasn't a surgeon. I work in the surgical wing. I'm not saying I never saw him, I don't know. He may have checked on a patient on the surgical level. I may even have assisted a pediatric surgeon who worked with him. But I didn't know him."

"He got your husband written up," Peabody pointed out.

"It's not the first time Milo's been reprimanded, and—trust me—it won't be the last. Listen, I work with doctors every day. A hell of a lot of them are arrogant and tactless. Most of them learn to filter it with patients—not all, but most. Milo either will or won't. I don't care. What do you think? The two of us plotted together to kill Dr. Abner over a reprimand? That's crazy. We're healers."

"Medicals kill, too, Ms. Roe." Eve rose. "We appreciate the time."

"That's it? You're just going to turn me inside out, then leave?"

"Unless you have more to tell us, that's all for now."

She sat where she was, staring after them, as they walked out.

"Felt believable," Peabody commented.

"Yeah. She also stayed steady as a rock. Yeah, we gave her a good jolt, but her hands? Rock steady. Could be she's just a damn good nurse and doesn't lose it. Or cold-blooded."

"Felt like the first to me."

"Felt like it," Eve agreed. "Next thing? I don't think she could've cooked up the agent in that apartment. Thin walls, too small, not enough ventilation. Which means if she's in it, they had to use a lab. You'd have to swipe into the lab sections of the hospital. So let's check, see if either of them spent any time there. Why don't you go ahead and contact the vic's son while we head toward the hospital. And find out if they've set a time and date for a memorial."

They spent a solid hour at the hospital, untangling the red tape, then verifying the IDs of those who swiped into the multiple lab areas inside or attached to the hospital.

And came up blank on Ponti and Roe.

"They could've had somebody swipe them in," Peabody suggested, but Eve shook her head.

"Adding another accomplice? No. This is a dead end. Time to suck that up and move on."

While they drove to Central, Elise Duran accepted a package from Allied Shipping. She had a busy morning, nearly put it aside for later, since she wasn't expecting anything.

But curiosity had her taking it into her well-organized home office to open.

Because she rarely watched screen, she had music on to keep her company and hummed along, even ticked her hips to the steady beat while she went through her mental list.

As a creature of schedules and order, she had a list on her tablet as well, and had crossed most of that off. This morning that included the breakfast dishes—she always sent her men off with a good breakfast—giving her kitchen a good scrub and polish, fussing with the dining room table, the spring flowers she'd arranged the evening before, the stack of pretty plates and napkins.

She still needed to put the refreshments together for her book club. She just loved hosting the book club, sitting and chatting with her group of like-minded literary friends. That included her mother and, to Elise's mind, nobody knew more about books than Catherine Fitzwalter.

After all, her mom had owned and run First Page Books for fifty-three years. Elise had grown up surrounded by books—something she considered an enormous perk. She worked there three days a week, and of course helped run the in-store book club.

But she so looked forward to the monthly meeting in her own home. There was something special in hosting a group, at home, sitting and talking about a book.

Not that they didn't often disagree about the book under discussion, but that was part of the fun, and the interest.

And it was a lovely excuse to have some wine with the light lunch and snacks she'd serve.

The house was perfect, of course, despite the clutter her husband and their two teenage sons generated. She'd already seen to that. Of course, she'd yet to fix herself up, but there was plenty of time.

She never failed to be on time.

She set the box—some shipment from a place called Golden Goose—on her neat little desk. She cut the packing tape, drew out the, well, unattractive box inside. Who'd send her such a cheap box?

When she opened that, she felt more baffled. A tacky golden egg? Nothing remotely her style. A gag gift maybe?

All right then, she appreciated a good joke, too.

She unlatched the egg, tugged it open.

She never had time to understand the joke was on her.

* * *

Eve walked into the bullpen at Central, and saw Jenkinson's tie. She figured it would burn your corneas if you viewed it from space. It was as if an evil rainbow infused with acid had exploded. Swirls and streams of ferocious color covered every inch.

She swore they moved, as if alive.

She wondered whether, if he dropped any crumbs from the cruller he munched on, those swirls would absorb them. And grow.

Risking temporary blindness, she walked over to his desk.

"You said you got those ties off the street. Where?"

Jenkinson brushed crumbs off the tie. Eve imagined the swirls covering his hand, pulling him in, inch by struggling inch.

"A stand on Canal. He's doing the street fair on Sixth on Sunday. You looking to get one for Roarke?"

"Sure, if I want him to have me committed. One day, one fine day, I'm going to do a drive-by of that stand, buy all the ties, and have them destroyed—it may take a vat of acid—for the public good."

"Aw, LT. They got pizzazz."

"I don't think that word means what you think it means. Don't even think about showing me your socks." She pointed at Reineke, Jenkinson's partner. "Don't even think about it."

And escaped to her office.

Coffee first, before she sat down to update her book and write up her notes, then a report. She updated her board with Roe's ID shot, and, studying it, rolled around the idea that a woman would murder, or participate in murder—a complex and canny one—because her husband took a slap at work.

Nothing, absolutely nothing in her background suggested it.

Ponti, a hothead, might strike back, but she imagined he'd do so impulsively, potentially with some violence.

But she couldn't quite see the two of them plotting this out.

"She's got your number, too," Eve murmured. "Knows you're kind of a dick, but doesn't seem to mind it."

Thomas T. Thane, she thought. More than kind of a dick. Easier to see him planning it out, figuring a way to pay back the man who'd screwed up his life—as that's how he'd see it.

Back to the mad scientist. Could Thane have hooked up with someone like that? Not impossible, and maybe—at the moment—the sharpest angle to pursue.

And pursuing it, she sat down to dig deeper into Thane. A college buddy, a client, a lover. Someone with the skill who'd work with him to kill. Or the opposite. Someone eager to kill, and Thane provided the target.

As she scoured through Thane's past, her communicator signaled.

"Dallas."

Dallas, Lieutenant Eve, report to 255 Wooster. Hazardous Forensic Team already dispatched due to potential poisonous fumes. Victim deceased. MTs, first on scene, and nine-one-one caller quarantined on scene until cleared. Hazmat protocol required until clearance.

"Copy that." Eve was already up, grabbing her jacket. "Dallas out."

She strode into the bullpen. "Peabody, with me. Now. We've got another one."

9

By the time Eve and Peabody arrived, the special team had cleared the scene, released the MTs.

The hazmat team leader, CI Michaela Junta, met Eve at the door. Music, some sort of bouncy rock, played on the house speakers.

"Air's clear and so's the body. You'll establish TOD, but I can tell you the nine-one-one caller, the victim's mother, stated the vic's husband and two sons would've left for work or school at about eight hundred hours. We've cleared her, and the two responding officers back in the kitchen area with her, also cleared."

Junta blew out a breath. "The mother's fighting to hold it together. It's the same basic setup as the Abner killing, but they used a different delivery service. Allied this time out. The egg hit carpet, so it didn't break. The agent dissipated, had to have done so, before the mother arrived."

"You got the time on that?"

"She said she came in about eleven. Nine-one-one logged at eleven-sixteen. You probably saw there's a security cam on the door, so you'll check the feed there. We'll stay out of your way until you give us the go."

"Appreciate it. Peabody, find the hub, check the feed. I'll take the body. Oh, and, Peabody, cut the music."

"This way." Junta led Eve through a tasteful living area where tall shelves held books—the real deal—photos, little trinkets, and into a home office/sitting room, with more of the same. There was a deep cushioned chair with tiny purple flowers against a cream background, and a footstool that matched. Beside it was a desk, with a mini-comp and desk screen. And the shipping box. A sharp-edged letter opener with a smooth white handle lay beside it. The fake wood box, identical to the one delivered to Abner, sat beside both.

The body lay on the floor, with what had expelled from it staining the cream-colored carpet.

The golden egg lay a couple of feet away, likely rolling or bouncing there after the victim dropped it.

"You know, you get jaded," Junta began. "You've got to get some hard or you couldn't face this, do what you have to do, every day. But I'm a mom, too, and I can't imagine walking in and finding my daughter like this."

Junta let out another breath. "So. We'll stand by."

Eve sealed up, then stayed where she was another moment to scan the scene. Fabric shades on the window—raised—but the window closed.

In her mind's eye, she saw the victim taking the package at the front door, walking into what appeared to be her home office space. She placed the package on the desk, got the opener. Dug through the packing for the box. Set it down, opened it, took out the egg.

And opening that, released the agent and went down. From the placement and position of the body, she hadn't tried to get to the window as Abner had. But then, he'd been a doctor, likely had a few seconds to understand what was happening.

This one never saw it coming.

Eve moved to her, avoided what she could of the fluids, did the official ID. And noted the same burns on the thumbs.

"Victim is identified as Elise Duran of this address. Age forty-four, Caucasian. Married to Jay Duran, age forty-six. Two sons, Eli, sixteen, Simon, fourteen."

She took out her gauges. "TOD is established at ten-oh-two. The mother entered at approximately eleven—security feed to verify—so the agent dissipated within that time frame, as specialty team has tested and cleared the mother.

"No visible signs of physical trauma, no signs of struggle. She opened the egg, which we have intact, released the agent. Succumbed. ME to verify."

Did you know Kent Abner? Eve wondered. Two kids, maybe he was their doctor.

What's the connection?

She called for a dead wagon, flagged the body for Morris, added a note on COD.

"Dallas." Peabody came to the doorway. "I got the feed. The package arrived at nine-fifty-four—male delivery guy in an Allied uniform. No other activity, in or out, until a woman—late sixties, early seventies—rang the bell at eleven-oh-three. She waited, then took a swipe out of her purse, used it. She had a bag—Village Bakery and Sweets, and a second bag from First Page Books. She carried them in. Next activity, the MTs—she let them in—at eleven-eighteen."

"Okay. It's the same, has to be the same. Another bogus name and address on the shipping box, same cheap box inside that, same cheap gold egg inside that.

"Same result. Contact Allied, get the name of the delivery guy for this route. Let's find out where it was dropped off. It's going to be a drop-off kiosk again. Why change pattern?"

"She had teenagers. Maybe Abner was their doctor."

"Yeah, same thought. We'll check that. Let's talk to the mother. She's Catherine Fitzwalter. We'll run them both, and the spouse, but let's talk to her first."

She stepped out, gave Junta the go. "Morgue's notified," she added. "You can let them in if we're still back with the wit."

"It's a really nice house," Peabody said, keeping her voice low. "Ult clean and tidy and all, but it's not fussy or rigid. She had to be expecting guests because she's got fancy plates and napkins set out on the dining room table."

Eve saw that for herself as they passed into the open kitchen area. Ult clean and tidy there, too. With two bakery boxes on the kitchen island. A cup of coffee—half-full—beside them.

Eve signaled to the two uniforms. "Give me what you've got," she ordered when they crossed to her.

"We responded to the nine-one-one from the MTs already on scene, arrived on scene at eleven-twenty-one. Ms. Fitzwalter let us in. The MTs were already with the DB. We, like the MTs, had the alert on the egg, the potential hazard, so we moved the wit and MTs back here, contacted Dispatch for the hazmat team."

"Ms. Fitzwalter's pretty shaky, sir," the second officer put in. "I know her, seeing as I grew up near her bookstore. It's like an institution in the West Village. I knew the vic, Lieutenant. She worked in the store."

"You were friends with the victim?"

"Friendly. We didn't grow up together, seeing as

she's got ten or twelve years on me, but I'd see her in there, have a word now and then. It's a good store, been around for like fifty years, family run. Like I said, it's an institution."

"Okay. You start the knock-on-doors. And when we're done here, you can do the same in the bookstore area, since you know it."

"Yes, sir. Can I—since I know her, can I give Ms. Fitzwalter my condolences again before we start?"

"Go ahead."

She watched the woman, face sheet pale, eyes glazed with tears, unclutch her hands and reach for one of the officer's. He bent to her, murmuring while she clung to his hand, nodded.

Eve waited until the uniforms left before she approached. "Ms. Fitzwalter, I'm Lieutenant Dallas. This is Detective Peabody. We're very sorry for your loss."

"Thank you. I can't— She's my baby. She's my girl."

"Ms. Fitzwalter, can I get you something? Some water?"

She raised her ravaged eyes to Peabody. "No, no, I don't think I could swallow anything."

Eve slid onto the padded bench of the breakfast nook to face her, made room for Peabody.

"Ms. Fitzwalter, I know this is difficult, but we need to ask you some questions."

"I know. I know how it works. I've read countless police procedurals in my time. I never thought . . . Who would do this? Elise never hurt anyone in her life. This is going to shatter her father, and Jay, the boys. I don't know how to tell them."

"We'll help you," Peabody told her.

"I know who you are. I read Nadine Furst's book. I've recommended it more times than I can say." She leaned forward, a pretty woman with a lovely swing of auburn hair. "Is it true, what she wrote about you? That you care, that you won't stop until you have answers? That you'll do everything, everything that can be done to find who did this?"

Eve decided simple was best. "Yes."

Catherine breathed out, lowered her head. "I need to know. We'll all need to know. Nothing can bring my girl back, but we need to know. You want to know if I know anyone who would want to hurt her."

She lifted her head again. "I swear I don't. No one's threatened her. She'd have told me. We talked about everything, anything. She and Jay have a good marriage, a fun, loving one, are raising good young men. Have they had spats? Of course. But they've been married twenty years.

"I want to tell you about her."

"All right."

"She's a good daughter—not that she didn't give her father and me some headaches along the way. She met Jay in college, and neither one of them ever looked back, or at anyone else. They shared a love of books. We raised her with books. When Rob and I retire—if ever—she was going to take over the store. She loved her family, loved her home. She loved tending it, making it a happy place, a good place. Like her dad, she was organized, almost terrifyingly."

The faintest smile came and went. "She ran on lists, had her schedules. You could count on her to be where she said she'd be when she said she'd be there. She loved hosting friends, and fussing so they'd—"

She stopped, let out a gasp. "Oh God, oh my God. The book club. They'll be here at one. We hold a book club here once a month, that's why I'm here. I—I—I picked up the desserts."

"Peabody."

"It's all right." Peabody slid out. "I'll take care of it."

When Peabody left, Eve drew Catherine's attention back. "You came early."

"Yes, yes. I had the desserts, and I was going to help her finish setting up, just spend some time with her. She didn't answer. I thought she might be in the shower. She'd want to fix herself up before everyone got here. I know my girl, and she'd have been cleaning and fussing first. So I used my swipe and came in."

"Can you take me through it?"

"I called out, then came right back here. I took out the bakery boxes, and I'd brought some pretty bookmarks, so I got a cup of coffee and one of her little vases to arrange them in. I set them on the table. I decided to go upstairs, see if she was nearly ready, but she wasn't upstairs. I wasn't concerned, just puzzled. I thought maybe she'd decided to run out for something, so I . . . I took out my 'link to tag her. I heard it ring from her office, so I went there. And I saw her. I saw my baby."

"Take your time."

"I think I could use that water now after all."

Eve rose, found a glass, filled it.

"I don't know if I blacked out or fell, or . . . I came back to myself on the floor, just sitting on the floor in the doorway of her office. I kept hearing this awful noise, like an animal in pain. It was me. It was me."

Covering her face with her hands, Catherine rocked. "I wanted to go to her, to my baby, but I knew I shouldn't. Preserve the scene—that's the term, isn't it?"

"Yes, ma'am. You did the right thing."

"They came very quickly. It seemed like years, but I know they came quickly, the MTs, and the police. Officer Krasinsky—Mike—I've known him since he was a boy. He's in the store many times. It helped to have someone who knew us."

"Do you know, or did your daughter know, Dr. Kent Abner?"

"I don't think so." Catherine drank more water, pushed her hands through her hair, pressed her fingers to her eyes. "I heard, there was a story about his death on Channel Seventy-five this morning. This is . . . the same?"

"It's possible. Have there been any problems at your bookstore? Employees you or your daughter had to reprimand, even let go?"

"We're like a family."

"Customers who've caused problems?"

"We're pretty good at handling complaints. We have customers who've shopped with us for fifty years, who span generations. We're not a huge business, you understand, but a steady one, a neighborhood fixture. Elise worked there three times a week—more if we needed. She focused on raising her boys, running the house, but she couldn't stay away from her second home. That's what First Page was for her. For us. No one who knew her would have wished her harm. I swear I'd tell you, without hesitation, if I knew of anyone. Even a sliver of doubt about anyone. She's my only child."

Catherine managed to drink more water. "The world's still going on outside this house. But for me, everything stopped. Do you know what I mean?"

"I do."

"I need Rob. I need my husband. I need to tell him."

"Where would he be now?"

"At the store."

"Why don't we send Officer Krasinsky and his partner to the store, and have your husband taken home?
We'll take you home. We'll . . ." She started to say notify, amended. "We'll talk with your son-in-law, and
have him and your grandsons brought to you."

"Yes, yes, then we'll be together. We need to be together now." She swiped at her eyes, then reached out
and gripped Eve's hand with her still damp one. "Nadine Furst wrote truth. You care. It shows. It matters."

Peabody had started back as Eve walked toward the
front of the house. "I've got Krasinsky and his partner
taking the father and the bookstore, and pulled a couple
more uniforms in to finish the canvass."

"Good." Eve rubbed at the tension in the back of her
neck. "We need an escort to take Ms. Fitzwalter home,
and let's have her taken around the back. She doesn't
need to see what's going on out here."

"I'll call for transpo. Look, why don't I walk her
around when they get here? So it's not another face, but
one she's already seen."

"Yeah, do that. Go, I don't know, sit with her until. I'm
going to start upstairs."

"Should I have EDD come in, scan the electronics?"

"Yeah. Allied?"

"Tracked the package. You were right, another
drop-off, twenty-three hundred. The charge? To an account of a ninety-three-year-old woman who reported
her 'link missing less than an hour ago."

"We'll talk to her, see if she can pinpoint when it
might've been lifted. Go back with the mother."

On the bedroom level, Eve found another home
office. The husband's, no doubt, she thought as she
stepped inside. Larger than the one on the main level,

and not nearly as tidy. Clean, she noted, but with a desk cluttered in the way someone busy and handling several tasks might clutter. Books again, the real deal again, but not all perfectly arranged. Since they were stacked, leaned, piled with no particular system, Eve concluded the victim hadn't fussed in here.

A guitar stood on a stand in the corner. The single pillow on the couch looked like one you'd actually put your head on when you stretched out.

Moving to the desk, she poked at books, discs, a couple of legal pads where he'd made actual handwritten notes.

She lifted one, frowned at his scrawling handwriting—worse than hers—but decided she'd found either attempts at poetry or song lyrics.

She unearthed more handwritten notes, realized they related to classroom projects.

Discuss how Shakespeare used music to add drama or levity to his works. Can you select current music to contemporize a particular scene or play? Provide examples.
    Possible spring project for Shakespeare Club?

She found other notes relating to books, authors—some she'd heard of, some she hadn't, but saw the defining pattern.

She took his chair, gave the computer a shot, and found her luck was in. Not password protected.

She found a family calendar listing schedules for his wife, his sons, family events. The older kid played basketball, the younger hooked with the drama club. So games, practice, rehearsal, performances.

She dug a little deeper, barely glanced up when Peabody came in.

"She's on her way home, and Officer Krasinsky notified the father, and they're on their way there, too. How do you want to notify the spouse?"

"We'll do it. He's a lit professor at Columbia." Eve sat back. "Maybe it's a big stretch to connect that to the headmaster of a private academy, but it's the only link we have. We'll come back for the rest of the house," she decided as she rose. "He's in class now, according to his schedule. We'll go to him."

"It's a pretty big stretch," Peabody agreed, quickening her pace as Eve jogged downstairs. "And the academics weren't the targets. There might be a connection with Thane. It could be the vic knew his wife, maybe helped her get clear."

"Worth looking into. Hold on."

Eve hunted up Junta to let her know they had to do a notification so she should seal the scene.

"We'll look into that," Eve continued as they went outside, where numerous people gave the sweeper van and black-and-whites the wondering eye. "Meanwhile, do a run on Professor Jay Duran before we get to him. And find out which building at the college we'll find him in."

"I bet it's the same as where Mr. Mira teaches."

"Huh. Hadn't thought of that." Eve used the dash 'link, contacted Mira's office. Hit the guard dog. "Listen, don't screw with me. I need to ask her one damn question, so put me through."

"She's preparing for a session" came the admin's stiff reply.

"I've got a woman's body fluids on my boots, and I

swear to every god there is, those boots will kick your ass if you don't put me through. One damn question."

"Please hold."

Eve bet, just bet, the woman left her on the blue holding screen longer than necessary.

"Dallas," Peabody began.

"Wait," she ordered as Mira came on.

"Eve. What can I do for you?"

"Do you know a Professor Jay Duran? He's at Columbia."

"The name's familiar." Mira frowned, brushed a hand through a wave of her mink-colored hair. "Why?"

"Somebody just sent a golden egg of poison to his wife. She's gone."

"A second one." Now Mira sat back, her quiet blue eyes going sharp. "We should talk, but for now I can only say the name's familiar. I could ask Dennis."

"That would be helpful. We're heading to Columbia now. Duran teaches literature."

"Then Dennis almost certainly knows him. I'll get back to you."

"Dallas," Peabody repeated with enough urgency this time to have Eve look over.

"What?"

"Duran's been at Columbia for seven years—eight this coming fall. But for nearly ten years prior, he taught language arts, literature, and creative writing at the Theresa A. Gold Academy."

"Son of a bitch." Eve rapped her fist against the wheel. "Son of a bitch! No way the universe just pulled that one out of its ass. Contact Rufty. If he can't come to us, we'll go to him. We need to talk about who might have had a hard-on for him, for Duran, or the school in general."

"Neither of the vics worked at the academy. He's going after spouses. I mean, Jesus."

"You kill somebody, they're dead. You kill what they love, they live. And live with that pain every day."

"It fits, doesn't it?" Peabody said and tried to ignore the manic way Eve wove in and out of traffic. "Cold-blooded, cruel, without passion. And if it does connect to the school, Duran hasn't been associated with it for nearly eight years."

"Didn't somebody say how revenge tastes better when you eat it cold?"

"I think it's like it's a dish best served cold."

"Well you don't eat the dish. You eat what's on it."

Couldn't argue with that, Peabody thought, but surreptitiously looked up the quote when Eve's 'link signaled.

"Dallas."

"I've just spoken with Dennis. Yes, he knows Jay Duran very well. I've met him and his wife. It's just that I've met so many of Dennis's colleagues through the years I couldn't quite place him."

"Thanks for checking. We're nearly there."

"Eve, I'm going to open up my schedule so we can discuss this as soon as you're able. Just let my admin know, and we'll work you in."

"I will. Thanks."

Eve navigated through the grand dignity of Columbia's campus, found a visitor's spot.

"Jeez, what a beautiful day." Peabody lifted her face to the sky. "And you forget how abso-mag this campus is, right in the city. Look at the daffs, the tulips!"

With her scarf trailing behind her like a happy flag, the red tips of her hair glowing in the sunlight, Peabody strolled along College Walk. Eve refrained from pointing out that cheerful flag could be used to strangle her in hand-to-hand.

Students milled or sat on the ground, on benches in groups, obviously as optimistic about the day as Peabody.

Eve thought about the man inside the dignified, beautifully preserved building whose day she was about to destroy. Whose life she'd indelibly mar.

She went inside, more milling, and a kind of humming hush punctuated now and then by rushing feet. She badged in, signed in, and as habit, took the stairs.

"He's on the second floor," Eve began. "And try to lose the springtime glitter in your eyes before we . . ." She saw him the minute they reached the second floor.

"Mr. Mira." And her heart, as it did whenever she saw him, went to mush.

He wore a tweedy jacket and a tie that had gone askew sometime during the morning. His eyes, green and kind, reflected sorrow.

"Eve." He took her hand, patted it, then Peabody's. "What a terrible thing. A tragic thing. I can't begin . . ." He glanced back toward a door. "She was a lovely woman. I met her many times at faculty events. I've enjoyed browsing and shopping in the family bookstore. And Jay. I wonder if you'd allow me to go in, bring him out. I thought it might help him to have a friend, a colleague when you tell him. I could take you to his office, then bring him to you so he doesn't . . . It's more private."

"All right. Do you know him well?"

"We're what I'd call work friends, but good ones in that area. We've had many discussions on literature since he came on board."

He led them down the hall. "Is it possible for me to

stay when you tell him? He was, from my view, very devoted to his wife, his family. They have two sons."

"That's kind of you, Mr. Mira."

He shook his head at Peabody. "It's just human."

He opened a door into what was more of a closet than an office. It made Eve's at Central look spacious, luxurious.

The two side walls were shelves, and the shelves were loaded with books, folders, some clear boxes holding discs and cubes.

The desk held more of everything.

Another guitar found a home in the corner behind the desk.

"Jay played in a band in high school. In college, too," Dennis explained. "He likes to say that's how he got his wife to look twice at him. The poor man."

Now he glanced around the room. "I'm afraid there won't be enough chairs. I can have another brought in, but don't quite know where we'd put it."

"It's not a problem."

"I suppose we'll figure it out. I should go get him. We shouldn't put it off. I'll . . . just tell him he's needed in his office. His TA can take the rest of his class."

Dennis gave a last distracted look around, then went out and quietly closed the door.

"The sweetest man alive," Peabody murmured as she took the two steps necessary to reach Jay's desk. "A lot of work, a lot of clutter—but he made room for a family picture on his desk."

She turned around. "What about the kids, Dallas?"

Eve shoved a hand through her hair. "See who's free in the bullpen. They should check, find a teacher who's good with both of them. Two teachers if necessary. And get them all somewhere private to notify them. It'd be worse if cops went in, just took them out of class, over to the grandparents. That would be worse."

"I think you're right. I'll go out and set it up. Should I wait until we notify Duran?"

"No, get it going. Something might leak, someone might say something."

Alone, Eve wondered how anyone managed to work in a room without a window. Then she wondered, with all of those books . . . Maybe they were his window.

She heard the door open, made her face blank.

He was a good-looking man with pale gold hair, pale blue eyes. Taller than Mr. Mira, younger, he dressed more casually with a shirt untucked, no tie, worn sneakers.

But he had an air—Eve caught it immediately—like Dennis, of kindness, intellect, and just a little vagueness.

"Hello." He gave her an apologetic smile. "I'm afraid I've completely forgotten an appointment."

"We didn't have one, Mr. Duran. I'm Lieutenant Dallas, with the NYPSD."

"I—*Eve* Dallas? Of course, I saw the vid with my family. I read the book. It was just marvelous. It's a thrill to . . ." Something clicked and his delighted smile vanished. "What's happened?"

"I regret to inform you, your wife has been killed. I'm sorry for your loss."

"What?"

Anger tinged disbelief. Eve recognized it, as it often came first in notifications.

"That's ridiculous. Is this a prank? It's not funny, not a bit. Elise is home. She has a book club meeting. You've made a mistake."

"I'm sorry, Mr. Duran. It's not a prank or a mistake. I've just come from your home."

"It's not possible. I just . . . Dennis."

When Jay's legs buckled, Eve started to move to him, but Dennis, for all his flustery ways, supported the younger man, eased him into one of the two folding chairs.

"Elise."

"Hold on to me," Dennis said when Jay began to shake. "Hold on to me," he repeated. And put his arms around the younger man when he began to weep.

10

Eve waited while Dennis comforted, and while he dug a handkerchief out of his pocket. Of course he had a handkerchief.

Of course he did.

Peabody came back in with a vending cup of tea, and Eve thought: Of course she'd think of that.

Of course she would.

And when Duran wiped his face, took, with trembling hands, the tea Peabody offered, she waited.

"You're—you're absolutely sure? There can't be a mistake?"

"We're sure, Mr. Duran."

"But how? How? Was there a break-in? It's a good neighborhood. Elise is careful."

"No, sir, not a break-in. Did you know Dr. Kent Abner?"

"I—I don't know. I don't think." He brought a hand to his temple, rubbed, rubbed. "Who is he? Did he hurt Elise?"

"No. Dr. Abner was killed two days ago. Both he and your wife were sent a package. It contained a toxic agent."

"A what? In a package? I don't understand. Who would send us a package that had a . . . I don't understand." Tea sloshed over the cup as he lurched to his feet. "Our boys. I have to get to our boys."

"Your sons are safe," Eve assured him. "We're having them picked up at school, taken to your in-laws."

"Detectives Baxter and Trueheart are already on their way to their school," Peabody told him.

"I know them, Jay." Gently, Dennis took the handkerchief, mopped at the spilled tea on Duran's hand. "They're very good men, and will take good care of your boys."

"I don't— What will I say to them? They've lost their mother. They've lost their mother, Dennis."

"You'll be strong for them." Dennis eased Duran back down.

"I'm sorry we have to ask you questions at such a difficult time," Eve began. "You worked at the Theresa A. Gold Academy."

"What? TAG? Yes, several years ago. I taught there before I got my doctorate."

"You know Dr. Rufty, the headmaster."

"I . . . Yes. He was coming in as I was going out, more or less. We were both there for one semester. I don't understand."

"Kent Abner was his husband."

"I— Oh, of course. I met him. I think. It was several years ago. But Elise didn't teach there, or know them. I think she might have met Dr. Rufty once, but I . . . I don't know. What does it mean? You don't think Dr. Rufty did this? That doesn't make sense."

"No, sir, Dr. Rufty isn't a suspect. Like you, he lost his spouse. And like you, he has a connection to the school, so we need to consider that connection. Do you know anyone also associated with the school, someone there when you were, who might have issues with you? Someone you had problems with, or who had problems with you?"

"No, no, God, it was seven—no, eight—eight years ago when I left TAG. When Dr. Rufty—Martin. That's right, Martin. When he took over as headmaster, we'd been going through some problems, yes, but . . ."

"What kind of problems?"

"I— God, it's hard to think. Some sniping, you could say, among the staff, and bullying with the students had become a serious issue. So had cheating—organized cheating. We'd lost a sense of camaraderie and, well, tone. In my opinion.

"But I don't understand how—"

"If you'd just indulge me, Professor Duran." Eve tried to find a spot between gentle and firm. "Tell me about the issues. Cheating, bullying? There must have been disciplinary action."

"Not really, no. The previous headmaster . . . She fostered a kind of competition, and a hierarchy. She inevitably took the side of the parents who complained or objected if their child needed to be disciplined for infractions or bad behavior. It didn't foster . . . Many of us felt she robbed us of authority, and put the emphasis on wealthier students, with parents willing to make donations."

"Did you have any altercations with her?"

"I don't know if I'd call it altercations, but I complained, stated my case. Many of us did. And so did many of the parents who felt their children weren't getting a fair shake, or were being bullied. We—several of us—grouped together, complained directly to the board because . . . There was a cheating ring, though we couldn't provide clear-cut evidence. Some students were pressured or threatened into cheating. Even physically assaulted, and the headmaster . . . Well, she looked the other way."

Peabody searched on her PPC. "That would be Dr. Lotte Grange?"

"That's right. But she left the school, took another position in . . . I can't remember." Rubbing his face with his hands, he looked like a man caught in some awful dream. "Somewhere else."

"Lester Hensen Prep School, in East Washington."

"That sounds right. I had issues with her, absolutely, but that was years ago. She'd have no reason to hurt Elise. And Martin came in after her. She'd already resigned. He—he changed the tone. He— Even though he knew I was leaving after the term, he met with me, talked with me about the students, about the changes he intended to make. I—I would have been happy staying with him at the helm, but teaching at college level was what I wanted."

"Anyone you remember unhappy with him at the helm, unhappy with the changes?"

"I suppose so, but—"

"You talk, fellow teachers," Eve pressed. "In the break room, the lounge."

"Yes, sure, but I feel like most were happy with the change, maybe relieved to see Grange go. Yes, we lost some students when Martin implemented disciplinary action for bullying, for copying. But we gained students—and even more important, it became a better place to work and to learn.

"I need to go to my children. I need to go to Elise."

"Peabody, will you arrange for Mr. Duran's transportation to his in-laws?"

"Right away."

"I'll contact you, or the medical examiner will contact you, when you're clear to see your wife."

"Is Elise with Dr. Morris?" Dennis asked.

"Yes."

"I know him, too, Jay, and I can promise you no one will treat Elise with more care and respect. I can tell you no one will work harder or more skillfully than Lieutenant Dallas and Detective Peabody to find the person who did this. In the meantime, you go to your boys, and I'll take care of everything here."

"God, the students. I left—"

"You're not to worry. I'll take care of everything here. You take whatever time you need, and you contact me if there's anything you need from me, anything I can do."

"Dennis." Jay squeezed his eyes shut. "She was the glue. Our boys . . ." He opened his eyes again, looked at Eve. "They're good boys, growing into fine young men. We built a good home, a good life together. But she was the glue. And I . . . Did I kiss her goodbye this morning? I think so, I think I did. But I don't think I told her I loved her. I don't think I did. Why didn't I?"

"Mr. Duran, from everything you've told me, there's no question in my mind, she knew you loved her. Please, if you think of anything, however insignificant it might seem, contact me."

Peabody stepped back in. "Mr. Duran, your transportation's coming. Why don't I walk you out to it?"

"Yes, thank you. Yes." He got to his feet, took a moment to gather himself.

Dennis rose, hugged him. Not the one-armed, pat-on-the-back man hug, but a full one.

"Anything you need, Jay. Anytime you need it."

Duran nodded, went with Peabody.

Dennis lowered to the chair again. "I know how often you do this, how often you have to tell someone the life they had five minutes before is gone. You're such a strong, brave girl, Eve."

"It's the job, Mr. Mira."

He shook his head. "A strong, brave girl. I hope I didn't overstep."

"No. You did everything right."

"You'll talk to Charlie about this?"

It always took her a moment to think of the elegant Mira as Charlie. "Yes, when I get back to Central."

"Between you, you'll figure this out. She's another strong, brave girl." He rose, and as he had with Duran, hugged her. And when he did, she felt every ounce of tension just slide out of her.

"Now, I'll go take care of things here for that poor man."

"Thanks for your help here."

He patted her cheek, had her heart melting. "We all do what we can."

And what some did, she thought when he left, was take lives, and destroy others.

Peabody met her by the car.

"Mr. Mira really helped. Duran told me when he came to Columbia, Mr. Mira was the first to take him out for coffee."

"That's how he's built. It's going to come from the school, Peabody," she said as they got into the car.

"That's the springboard. We need to track down this Lotte Grange."

"I'll get on that. When I talked to Rufty, he said he could come in if you needed him to. He's finalizing the arrangements for a memorial. He's having it in the park in the morning, where Abner liked to run."

"Set it up." While she did, Eve contacted Mira's office. For a change she got no grief from the admin, who told her the doctor would be available when she got back to Central.

"He needs an hour," Peabody told Eve.

"That works. Targeting spouses," Eve continued. "Or loved ones, as it's possible not everybody on his payback list is married. Would a chemistry teacher at a private school have enough skill to pull this off?"

"It seems way above pay grade, but who knows? And it looks like we're talking close to eight years of research and development time. Still, it didn't sound like Duran caused any big waves while he was there."

"People, especially homicidal people, have different perspectives. He did something, said something, was something that put him on that list. He's not going to remember it right off, not while he's in this first stage of shock. He may later."

"And Rufty, being brought in—it really sounds like to clean up a mess, or at least that's how Duran saw it— is going to have a wider overview. If he sat down and talked with an instructor who was leaving, he sat down and talked with everybody. He may have nudged some-body out. Or somebody saw his coming in as pushing Grange out. Still . . ."

"Yeah, she landed another position, another big school with rich kids and influential parents," Eve finished. "So what's the beef? We'll find out."

Just as she started the turn into the garage at Central, Eve had to hit the brakes to avoid mowing down a naked guy. He ran like the wind, his hair flying, his dong swinging merrily, with a handful of uniforms in hot pursuit.

Pedestrians scrambled clear as he loped along like a gazelle.

"Well." Eve watched another moment. "Even in New York that's something you don't see every day."

"He's really fast," Peabody observed. "We could probably cut him off with the car."

"Probably." Instead she just drove into the garage. "The uniforms need to get the lead out. Of what?" she wondered when she pulled into her slot. "Just what do you get the lead out of? Why would anybody haul lead around anyway? Language is ridiculous."

"I always thought it was your ass—not literally," Peabody added before they went down that road. "Just like you're slow because you've got the lead ass."

"What kind of ass do you have if you're fast?" Eve countered as they walked to the elevator. "What's the opposite of lead? Feathers? Hey, you're a real feather ass. Nobody says that."

They got into the elevator. "But they could," she continued, "because people just make shit up, then other people say it, and then it's a thing. I'm heading straight to Mira," Eve continued while Peabody was still processing. "Start digging into Grange so we have solid data before we talk to Rufty."

She rode up a handful of floors, then started to jump off to take the glides.

"Helium," Peabody called out. "Maybe because it's light it's sort of the opposite of lead."

"Well, those cops weren't helium asses, not the way they were running."

Eve continued on and, unlike her partner, who would ponder it for some time, she forgot the entire conversation.

Mira's admin gave her the hard eye, but cleared the way.

Mira sat behind her desk in a suit of pale lavender with a little flouncy thing at the waist. She signaled Eve to wait while she finished her 'link call.

"No, of course. Don't worry about that. I know, honey, I do. We'll eat whenever you get home, and talk about it. You did, but it's nice to hear it again. And I love you, too. I'll see you at home. Bye now."

She clicked off, sighed. "Dennis."

"I kind of figured."

"He's taking Jay Duran's Shakespeare Club meeting at five," she said as she rose and crossed to her AutoChef on purple heels. Their open fronts revealed toes with nails painted the exact shade of the suit.

How did anyone think of that? Eve wondered.

"This has hit him very hard."

"He was great with Duran," Eve told her. "He helped, a lot."

"I barely remember Elise." The air filled with the scent of flowers as Mira took cups of tea from the AC. "I didn't even have a clear picture until I brought up her data."

"You didn't really socialize."

"No." She handed Eve a cup, took a seat in one of her blue scoop chairs. "I don't get to many of Dennis's faculty functions. Work interferes. But I did meet her a few times. There are two teenage sons."

"Yeah. I had Baxter and Trueheart get them out of school, take them to their grandparents. The victim's mother found her."

"What a terrible day for them. I've read the data on the murders, the forensics, the timelines. Tell me what you know."

"The school—the Gold Academy—has to be the link. Duran had accepted the job at Columbia when Rufty came on as headmaster, but they worked there together for a semester. According to Duran, the previous headmaster had let a lot of things slide. More interested in courting parents with deep pockets than handling staff issues or problems with bullying, cheating, disciplinary problems. A group of teachers—including Duran—made a formal complaint to the board."

Mira sipped tea. "Was action taken?"

"I can't confirm that as yet, but the previous headmaster—Lotte Grange—transferred to a high-toned prep school in East Washington, and Rufty came on board at the Gold Academy. Duran states that Rufty changed the tone, took action, made changes. For the better, in Duran's opinion. I figure somebody didn't share that opinion."

"And you theorize someone is killing the spouses of those he had grudges against at Gold?"

"It's what plays. Duran claims he didn't have any serious problems or enemies, but—"

"What's a momentary annoyance or past issue for one is a deep and abiding insult to another," Mira finished. "And Rufty?"

"I'm meeting with him again shortly. I'll take him back to that first semester. With Duran in this, it has to go back to that timeline. Before, no Rufty, after, no Duran. Potentially we could have someone who developed a hard-on for Duran before Rufty came along, and got going on Rufty after Duran left. But I start with that timeline."

"Yes, I'd agree. What do you know about Grange?"

"Peabody's digging into that now."

Mira nodded, sipped her tea. "To kill the innocent in order to strike at the ones he's determined are guilty. He wants them to suffer, to mourn and grieve and live with great loss. He may perceive they caused him to suffer, grieve, and live with loss. There may be a personal as well as professional tie with Grange, or someone else who was pushed out—student or staff—during that timeline."

"And if that timeline's right, he's had about eight years to stew over it, to plan it, to create or access the agent."

"It's not impulse," Mira agreed, "but calculated. Highly organized and intelligent, and at the same time dispassionate. The kill is dispassionate," Mira corrected. "A painful death, yes, but quick—and calculated so no one else is harmed. That element must have taken extra time, more work, so it matters that only the person addressed is killed."

"He knows when to send the package," Eve added, "so it arrives when the target's alone. Or is scheduled to be alone."

"Again, a calculated risk." Considering that, Mira tapped a finger on the side of her pretty teacup. "Accidents happen in shipping, mistakes are made, plans change. But it's a carefully calculated risk, and what would he lose if something happened, someone else opened the package, or it was damaged? Nothing really.

"He has knowledge and skill," she went on. "He's certainly worked with toxic chemicals."

"Or is working with someone who has."

Mira angled her head. "Yes, very possible. He or they must have a lab where he can create the agent.

He's loved," Mira added. "Or believes he's loved. Whether or not he's experienced it himself, he understands the pain of loss. He uses it."

"He may have lost a spouse?"

"Possibly, or a child, or a parent, someone he loved or believes he loved. Even the removal of the person he loved—a breakup, moving away. But I see him as an observer. Someone who watches, documents—scientifically—more than participates. Again, if your timeline is correct, he's patient. He knows good work and positive results take time. Or she, of course. Poison's often a female weapon. Most of us, present company definitely excepted, lack the physical strength and skill to confront an opponent physically."

"He—or she—is also a coward."

"Yes." Mira offered the smallest smile. "Not only because you'd find them so, but in none of the statements is there any mention of any sort of physical confrontation or argument. No threats, no rivals or enemies. This rage, however cold, has been bottled up, hidden, and hidden well. When you find him, those who know him will be shocked."

"Yeah, the typical, he seemed like a nice, normal guy."

"And a fastidious one, that will factor in. The way he packed the shipment, so carefully. The strapping tape perfectly straight. You'll find his residence, his work area immaculate."

Now Mira sat back, recrossed her legs. "I'd pondered over the egg—until you found the connection."

"Gold egg, Gold Academy. That didn't just happen. It's a message."

"Yes, a reference back to what lit the very long fuse. And there's killing the goose that laid the golden egg, you can't make an omelet without breaking eggs, all that glitters isn't gold, and so on. It's a cheap trinket, like the box—but he painted the interior painstakingly, added the sealant."

"Both the box and the egg were dirt cheap, and available from half a million places online. We'll never trace them, but we will track them back to him once we have him."

"It's the economy of it. He didn't want to waste money on them. The chemicals had to have cost considerable, and the equipment unless he's able to access it from a workplace."

"Nothing we've found so far, but there are thousands of medical and research and educational labs in New York and New Jersey."

Sipping tea, Mira considered. "The economy tells me he values money, respects it. He spent it where necessary."

"But he sends them a cheap trinket because why waste good money."

"Very good," Mira said approvingly. "He lives alone. If he's working on the agent in his workplace, he has some autonomy. If he's working at home, he'd want privacy. He's driven, Eve. There's no time or room in his life for real relationships. He's not one to confront or debate directly, but to retreat where he can work toward his revenge. He may have done so many times before, in less lethal ways. Undermining a colleague or rival while carefully staying out of the fray."

"And observing, documenting. Keeping an account."

"Yes. He'll have everything documented. He's a scientist, whether by trade or inclination. Everything he's done and will do, all the data he's accumulated on his targets and his victims—as they are separate things—will be documented."

"So far his targets and victims have families. Grown children with children in the first hit, younger children in the second."

"It may be satisfying for him to shatter a family. If he had one, he no longer does. Why should they have one, intact and happy? Somewhere, at some time, in some way, they caused him grief. And now he gives them grief."

"Back to the school. Rufty first—he was in charge, he made the changes." Eve checked the time. "My interview with him's coming up."

She rose, paused. "Could he be on the young side? Say, somebody who was a student when Rufty took over? Maybe got booted out, or disciplined, or failed some classes after Rufty came on?"

"I nearly said doubtful, as the planning, the time gap shows maturity, patience. But think of the egg—and the name used for the return address. They're a kind of ugly joke, aren't they? I'd say the high intelligence and lack of genuine emotion or empathy are more solid factors than age."

"I think of Rayleen Straffo. She was a crafty little killer, and hadn't hit her teens. I'll talk to Rufty about students, too. Thanks for the time."

"When you find him, he'll have a cover, perhaps even seem to cooperate. But he'll be planning on how to strike back."

"I'll keep that in mind."

She took the glides back to give herself time to think, and found herself amused as some cops heading in the same direction discussed the Crazy Naked Guy.

"Son of a bitch made it twenty blocks, just sailing along, dick swinging. Patrinki says he's barely winded when they finally caught him. Claimed he was exercising his constitutional right. Freedom of religion, 'cause he was just giving his thanks to the god of spring. And clothes were a whatsit—societal construct or some shit."

"It takes all kinds," his companion commented.

Eve got off the glide at Homicide, walked into the bullpen. She tried to avoid looking at Jenkinson's tie, saw Carmichael and Santiago debating, hotly, some point of a case, Peabody deep in her research and guzzling a fizzy.

Yeah, it took all kinds, she thought, and went into her office to prep for the interview.

She booked a conference room. She didn't want Rufty to sit in the box, wanted more private than the lounge.

She updated her board and book, sat contemplating both before calling Peabody in.

"Give me what you've got on Grange."

"Mixed-race female, age seventy-two, two marriages, two divorces, no offspring. Currently headmaster at Lester Hensen Preparatory School, East Washington."

Peabody sent a hopeful look toward the AutoChef, got a nod.

"Thanks. You?"

"Yeah, fine. Keep going."

"Okay. Going by her data, she's stuck with private schools since she started—forty-nine years ago—in Baltimore, Maryland, worked her way to assistant dean of faculty, transferred to a school in Columbus, got the divorce, moved up to assistant headmaster there, transferred here as assistant headmaster, got married again, moved up to headmaster, got divorced, transferred as headmaster to East Washington. She averages about ten years at a school."

Peabody passed the coffee to Eve. "No particular interest or skill in science shows up. To me, it reads like she used teaching as a stepping-stone to administration and the hierarchy."

"The second divorce. When and who filed for it?"

"Ah . . ." Peabody pulled out her PPC. "The spouse—Reginald P. Greenwald—this was also his second. He filed in . . . January of 2053."

"The same year she transferred to East Washington. Reginald P. Greenwald. Sounds like a rich name."

"And you'd be correct. Second son of Horace W. Greenwald and CEO of All Fresh, which was started last century by Philip A. Greenwald—grandfather. They make home and commercial cleaning supplies and tools."

"Cleaning supplies." Eve felt a little buzz. "You'd need chemists on staff."

"Uh-huh. Sure you would. Labs for research and development, testing new products. You could buy a mad scientist with your take of a multibillion-dollar company. But why kill the spouses of a headmaster—who came in after your ex transferred—and a teacher who was about to transfer?"

"That's a question we'll ask Greenwald."

"Should I see if I can get him to come in?"

"No. He'll bring a bunch of shiny lawyers—that would be SOP. We'll do a drop-in, after we talk to Rufty." She glanced at the time. "Which is any minute. I booked a conference room."

"Yeah, that'll be easier for him than an interview room. Why don't I go make sure the AC's stocked. He drank tea, right?"

"Yeah. Go ahead. Tag me when he gets here."

She started to dig into All Fresh, confirmed they had research and development labs in New York, with "top scientists, chemists, herbalists, and innovators."

The wife gets reported by teachers—Duran being one—replaced by Rufty. Then gets dumped. How pissed off would you be?

As she began to play with a new theory, Peabody tagged her.

In the conference room, Rufty sat with his son-in-law. Peabody brought them both a cup of tea as Eve walked in.

"Thank you for coming in," Eve began.

"We hoped you'd have some news."

"We hope you'll be able to help us with some questions about the school, the staff, from when you came on as headmaster."

"I . . . Yes, of course, if it's helpful, but I don't see how it could be."

"Dr. Rufty, do you remember Jay Duran? He taught at the academy when you came on."

"I . . . We don't have a Duran in the faculty."

Eve drew out an ID shot. "Do you remember him?"

"Yes, yes, of course. I'm sorry, I didn't place the name at first. It was several years ago, and he was only there through the end of the term. I don't understand." His face went gray. "Is he— Did he kill Kent?"

"No." Not listening to the media, Eve thought. "Elise Duran, Professor Duran's wife, was sent a package this morning. She was killed."

"Oh dear God." He turned to his son-in-law, groped for his hand.

"It's the same?" Greg moved his chair closer to Rufty, put an arm around him. "The same as Kent?"

"Yes. Professor Duran indicated that there were a number of issues and problems at the school, with the previous headmaster, before you took over."

"I don't understand. What would any of that have to do with Kent, with Jay's—yes, I remember him now—with his wife? Wait." He held up a trembling hand as color washed in and out of his face. "Not them. Me. Because of me? Am I responsible?"

"Dr. Rufty, the person responsible is the person who sent the package, and anyone who, potentially, helped him. You're not. Jay Duran is not."

"But if I—"

"Would you blame Professor Duran for the death of his wife?"

"I— No." He swiped at tears, made a visible effort to steady himself. "No, I would not. I don't see how this could go back all those years. And Jay, he was only there a short time after I came on. He'd already accepted a position with . . . I can't remember."

"Columbia."

"Yes. Yes, Columbia. He was a fine teacher, I remember that. Very dedicated. Did he have children? I think he had children."

"He has two teenage sons."

"Oh, that poor family. They're going through what we are," he said to Greg. "They're feeling what we're feeling."

"Then we have to help them." Greg rubbed a hand up and down Rufty's arm.

11

Rufty gathered himself. "Whatever I can do."

"You came on as headmaster after the winter break, in '53. When did you accept the job?"

"That would have been around Thanksgiving the previous year. Dr. Grange was taking another position, and my impression was she'd made the decision quickly, and resigned, effective at the end of the year."

"Do you know why she resigned so abruptly?"

"My assumption was she'd been offered the position at Lester Hensen. It's a very prestigious institution."

"Dr. Rufty."

Eve's tone had him closing his eyes. "I'm sorry. It's simply ingrained not to speak ill or gossip about a colleague. There had been a number of complaints, by parents, by staff. And it seemed her marriage was ending." He sent a painful glance toward Greg.

"Whatever there is, Marty."

"There were rumors and accusations she'd had an affair with another member of the faculty, and possibly had inappropriate relationships with some students' fathers. Others claimed she'd turned a blind eye to accusations of bullying, intimidation, cheating, illegals, and alcohol."

"Did she?"

"Yes, I believe she did. When I spoke with the staff, there were many who told the same or very similar stories. Still, much of it was gossip, and hard feelings, and I could only form impressions. I met with Dr. Grange, of course, during the transition. She and I had different approaches and, to be frank, she seemed quite done with the school and ready to move on. She did list several names of teachers and administrators she found problematic."

"Was Duran on the list?"

"He was. However, when I looked at his records, when I met with him, I found him to be, as I said, a dedicated educator. And in the months we worked together, I only saw him as just that, and a man who worked very hard to reach his students. Others she listed were among those who had filed complaints."

"Was there anyone in that transition period, the early period, you had issues with, or who had issues with you?"

"Of course. It was a changing of the guard, and many changes in policy and tone. Her emphasis in many ways had been on bringing in large donations, giving naming rights, bolstering prestige."

Rufty waved a hand in the air. "That sounds critical, and frankly, it is. But those are important aspects to heading a private school. Still, I found serious lapses in discipline, an unfortunate bias toward some students whose parents provided those donations."

"Which Duran and others complained, formally, about," Eve prompted.

"Yes. There was an unstated policy that if a student was bullied, he or she should stand up for him- or herself, and not look to the school to handle the problem. If a student failed a test, that student was given an automatic makeup, or if the parents complained, the grade was curved up. Cheating was, unfortunately, rampant. Several students had formed a kind of business out of it. There were some teachers actively threatened. Drinking and illegals not only outside but on school grounds."

"How did you handle it?"

"I had meetings with everyone on staff. Some were very reluctant to speak out, as they'd been labeled troublemakers or, as I said, threatened. Some, like Jay, were already leaving or planned to, and it was easier for them."

"Can I say something?" Greg asked. "From an outside perspective?"

"Sure," Eve said. "Go ahead."

"It was pretty clear to us—the family—Marty had been given the position at TAG not only because of his reputation, his qualifications, but because of his, well, his philosophies. They—the board—needed someone to clean up the mess."

He turned to Rufty. "You dealt with a lot those first few weeks, Marty. I remember once, a family dinner, and you looked so tired and stressed. You said how when you needed to get a ship back on course after a storm, you couldn't take your hands off the wheel."

"How do you remember these things?" Rufty asked.

"Did you keep your hands on the wheel, Dr. Rufty?" Eve asked.

"Greg's not wrong about why I was offered the position and, honestly, why I accepted it. I knew it would be a challenge, and I wanted that. Clearly, what I intended to do, what I would do, wouldn't be popular with some."

"What did you do?"

"I instituted firm policies with specific disciplinary actions regarding bullying, cheating, drinking, and so on." Pausing, he linked his hands, set them on the conference table. "Some students were suspended for violations within days. As a result, I had several very unpleasant meetings with outraged parents. Some pulled their children out of the academy."

"So, as Greg said, a difficult transition."

"Yes. Yes, it was. I don't know what I'd have done without Kent those first few weeks. I honestly thought I'd be fired at any moment, as some promised donations were pulled, some students left, a few teachers who'd gotten used to a more . . . lax environment were unhappy."

"You never told us that." Greg shot Rufty a look of surprise. "That you worried about being fired."

Smiling a little, Rufty patted Greg's arm. "Children don't have to know everything. There were others, on staff, in the student body, and, yes, on the board, who were relieved, even pleased with the new rules, with the new tone. That balanced the scale. By spring it had largely evened out."

"You met the challenge," Peabody said. "You righted the ship."

He smiled again. "I like to think so, yes."

"Were there threats against you?" Eve asked.

"Oh, some parents throwing their weight around, a handful of problem students who tried to do the same."

"Did you expel anyone?"

"It didn't come to that, though I did suggest to some of the more outraged parents that perhaps their child and the academy didn't make a good fit."

"Fire anyone?"

"Again, I suggested to some that if they were un-happy with my vision and methods, they might find a better fit elsewhere. I felt I needed to give everyone time to adjust, so rather than expulsion or termination in those first weeks, I issued warnings in private meetings.

"It was eight years ago," he murmured, and even the hint of a smile died away. "I can't think of anyone who could remain so angry or resentful toward me they'd do this. Or Jay. He did nothing. He wasn't in charge of the school, only his own students."

"Why don't we do a cross-check? Take a look at his students, see which ones were problematic, or who might have been pulled out, whose parents were un-happy?"

When he looked at Eve, she saw relief. Something to do, she thought, something concrete and beyond grief.

"I can go into my records. I can do that. I'll be glad to do that if it helps."

"It would. You have chemistry labs, instructors."

"Of course. We have a lab for the upper grades, an-other for the middle grades. Another for more advanced students. Oh my God, you don't think . . ."

"We want to check everything," Eve said. "If you could give me the names of the advanced students, the teachers. And in your records the same from when you came on."

"Yes. Yes. We're going now to finalize the details for Kent's memorial. As soon as we're done, I can go to the school, pull the old records."

"We can do that if you give us your permission. We'll get a warrant to cover it, and I can have EDD access those records. Then if we could talk to you again once we've gone through them."

"Let her do that, Marty."

"All right. Whatever's best. I just don't remember as clearly as I should."

"You have a lot on your mind right now," Peabody soothed. "If you remember anything more, you can contact either one of us. Maybe you made some personal notes that you didn't add to the official records."

"I did at the time, of course. But I . . ." Rufty rubbed a hand on his temple as if to erase a block. "On my old tablet. When I replaced it, I deleted everything. I thought to donate it, but you said, didn't you, Greg, that nothing's ever completely gone if you know how to look for it?"

"You gave it to Ava—my daughter," he told Peabody. "Does she still have it?"

"Yes, I'm sure she does. Somewhere."

"If you could find it, EDD could try to recover the deleted data. It might be helpful."

"I'll make sure she finds it. Should I bring it in to you?"

"Why don't you let us know when you have it," Eve said. "We'll send someone to pick it up."

"If you're able to retrieve the data," Rufty put in, "and need any help interpreting my notes, I'll be glad to go over them with you."

"We appreciate your help."

"You're looking out for the love of my life. I'll do everything I can. I want to say your Dr. Morris was very kind." His eyes filled again. "Everyone's been very kind. I wonder if it would be appropriate for me to contact Jay, to offer my condolences. And it's possible we could jog each other's memory of that term. Maybe tomorrow, after . . ."

"He spoke highly of you. I think he'd appreciate it."

"Then I will. Tomorrow, after we say our goodbyes."

When Peabody walked them out, Eve arranged for the warrant, then pulled out her notebook.

She wanted the names of the graduating class of Gold Academy from '53. The names of students, and their parents, who were pulled out during Rufty's first term. The instructors and administrators on staff at that time—those who stayed, those who left. Any and all students who were suspended or otherwise disciplined during that same timeline.

Had to be that time frame, she thought, or else why hit Duran? It had to stem from the changing of the guard.

The board of trustees, she mused. Did they pressure Grange to transfer?

She continued to make notes as Peabody came back. "We need the chemistry instructors, and let's focus first on advanced students."

"We'd be going young, just a few years out of college now, or maybe in grad school. What, like twenty-five?"

"Around your age. You too young to be a cop, Peabody?"

"Hell no."

"And so." Considering, Eve leaned back in her chair. "When I was still a beat cop, I had to chase down this street thief, and when I caught him, he pulled out a sticker, tried to slice me. He was ten. Anyway, we have the older type on the list, too. Greenwald—Grange's ex."

"He should be home in about an hour," Peabody said. "His residence is on Riverside Drive. He has the entire top floor."

"Pays to be clean. Check if Feeney can spare McNab, maybe Callendar. We're going back to school."

Eve went back to her office, and figuring a trip to the school, then a drop-by with Greenwald, potentially a pickup on the tablet, grabbed a file bag, gathered what she thought she might need to wind up the day with work at home.

"They'll meet us at the car," Peabody told her when she walked back into the bullpen. "It turns out Callendar knows somebody who went to Gold. He graduated after Rufty came on, so it might be another source."

"A handy one."

"Oh, and they got word on the naked running guy."

"I've been on the edge of my seat about that all day."

"Turns out," Peabody continued, undeterred, as they got on the elevator, "he really is a runner. A marathoner. He had a whacked-out reaction to meds—prescribed for an injury—in combo with some homeopathic stuff he took. Stripped down and started running."

"What do you bet he gets a sportswear or running shoes contract—maybe both—by the end of the day?"

Peabody pursed her lips. "That would be really smart. You should say something to Roarke."

"If I thought of it, he thought of it before it actually happened. Like: Whatever Sportswear. The next thing to running naked."

Surprised, Peabody let out a laugh. "Hey! That's really pretty good."

"It writes itself."

In the garage, she crossed over to her slot, where McNab and Callendar already waited.

And here they had geekwear in Callendar's purple (to match the streaks in her hair?) shirt, polka-dot baggies worn with rainbow suspenders, and purple hightops.

McNab paired a shirt of plutonium green with orange baggies thinly striped in the same green, orange air-boots, and a green knee-length floppy coat that all but glowed.

She supposed in geek world they were coordinated.

They each carried a shoulder bag she assumed held e-tools that wouldn't fit in the multitude of pockets in the baggies.

Callendar said, "Yo. Hey, girl, you're rocking the red!"

Grinning, Peabody gave her hair a little shake. "Right?"

Eve rolled her eyes, McNab and Peabody exchanged a quick little finger wiggle, and everybody piled in the car.

"Can it be fizzy time?" Callendar asked from the back seat.

"Whatever." Eve pulled out. "The warrant should be in by the time we get there. We need records from '53 and '54, student body, staff, administration. Probability's high someone who worked or attended during that time period is our prime suspect. Possibility of a parent or a student, a close connection to one of the staff."

As the car filled with the scent of sugar-infused bubble drinks, Eve ran it through.

"According to statements we have so far, the previous headmaster ran a loose ship, let things slide, and focused on bringing in the moolah."

"I can checkmark that," Callendar said between slurps. "I'm friends with a dude who went there. We go back, and I know he had to dodge and sprint to keep from getting his ass kicked—didn't dodge and sprint fast enough one time and got banged up bad. He'd have graduated in like '53 or '54. His parents went in, more than once, and wanted to pull him out, but he really wanted to finish there. He works for Roarke now."

Eve shot a glance in the rearview. "Is that so?"

"Yeah. He's a game developer, and he's been working for Roarke World for a couple years. I can round him up if you want to jaw."

"I want to jaw."

"Solid. I'll fix it. We hung out a lot back then because, you know, gaming. He's wicked smart, and totally nerdy. Might as well flash a Kick My Ass sign to the assholes, you know? They wanted him to hack in for tests, or do their work, like that. I was taking martial arts, showed him some moves. It helped a little."

"And the school—the administration—let it slide?"

"From what I know, yeah. He was there on scholarship, and got a full ride to MIT, so yeah, wicked smart."

"Grange, former headmaster, either decided to take another job in the middle of the school year or was nudged out. Rufty, spouse of the first vic, came on and clamped down. Some weren't happy about it. Second vic's the spouse of a teacher who complained about Grange, and who transferred to Columbia. But he and Rufty got along fine during the term they worked together. Rufty states there were rumors that Grange had an affair—either with staff or daddies. Her husband filed for a divorce about the same time. We'll be jawing with him, too."

McNab gulped down his own fizzy. "Are you looking at her—Grange?"

"She's in East Washington. We'll check her travel, though it's a doable drive. But nothing in her background shows an affinity for chemistry. Her ex—that would be second ex—is the CEO of All Fresh, and that's a lot of chemistry."

The Theresa A. Gold Academy rose five weathered brick stories. Security cams winked over its double entrance doors.

Eve pulled into a loading zone, flipped on her On Duty light.

"School'll be out for the day." McNab stood on the sidewalk, studied the building. "That'll make it easier."

"Have you ever been in a school after hours?" Callendar asked.

"I guess, yeah."

"Creepy." And she grinned. "I can dig on creepy."

"They board," Eve added. "Top floors are dormitories. They have some administrative staff round the clock."

She approached the door, tried it, found it locked. She considered mastering in just for the hell of it, but hit the buzzer instead.

Welcome to the Theresa A. Gold Academy. Regular school hours are eight A.M. to three P.M., Monday through Friday, with specialty classes from nine A.M. to two P.M. on Saturday. Lectures and performances are listed on the website. If you are here for an after-hours appointment or visit, please state your name and the party with whom you wish to meet.

Eve thought: Blah, blah, blah. "Lieutenant Dallas, NYPSD. We're here on police business. You can inform whoever's currently in charge." She glanced at her PPC as the warrant came through. "We have a duly executed warrant to enter and search."

Please wait one moment while Assistant Headmaster Myata is informed.

It didn't take much longer for the doors to release

and open. A small, trim Asian woman with a wedge of raven-black hair held out a hand as delicate as a bird's wing.

"Lieutenant Dallas. I'm Kim Myata, assistant headmaster. Headmaster Rufty contacted me to let me know to expect you. Please come in."

The impressive entrance bore a large gold seal centered in the white marble floor. Two security stations flanked it. The ceiling soared up five floors with a stained-glass dome.

One wall held an enormous glass case displaying a multitude of awards. On another a life-size portrait of the benefactor and founder loomed.

To Eve's eye Theresa A. Gold, dead for a half century, looked pretty damn formidable.

Despite the grandeur, white marble, gilt frames, glittery gold behind glass, it still smelled like school.

Sweat, fear, hormones, secreted candy.

Eve had never been fond.

"We're all grieving with the headmaster," Myata continued. "We are ready to help and cooperate with your investigation into this tragedy. I hope I haven't overstepped by accessing the records Headmaster Rufty informed me you needed."

"We can take it from there. Are they in his office?"

"Yes. I've kept his office locked until he contacted me regarding this. I have his passcodes, as he has mine. Dr. Rufty also informs me his daughter found a tablet you wish to have. She is bringing it here for you."

"We can have it picked up."

"I believe she's already on her way."

"Fine. EDD can take it when she gets here."

"I'll see to it. Is it possible to have a copy of the warrant, in case there are legal issues?"

"Peabody."

"I'll print it out for you."

"Thank you. Please come this way. Most of the day students are gone for the day," she continued as she led them to the left and the glass-walled administration department. "We do have a few students doing projects, with supervision. The boarding students are restricted to the fourth and fifth floors unless they have permission to leave the premises or work on a project."

She swiped a card.

There was a long counter, currently unmanned, several seats in a waiting area, and a pair of workstations. "The headmaster's office is this way."

Eve imagined students called it the Walk of Shame, the Gauntlet, or some other colorful term, that trudge down a hallway, past doors, into the depths and the quiet.

Again, Myata used a swipe on the door with the plaque that read: HEADMASTER MARTIN B. RUFTY.

He had a generous space, a window with the privacy shields engaged, a desk facing the door holding a multi-line data and communication center, a couple of framed photos—family—interesting glass paperweights anchoring actual paper. Shelves of books, a huge corkboard holding announcements and playbills—theater, concerts, lectures, science fairs, career day, and so on.

He had live plants that appeared to be thriving, a small refreshment center, and a tiny sitting area that looked cozy rather than intimidating.

"If there is anything more I can do . . ." Myata broke off, and her eyes filled. "Pardon me. I was very fond of Dr. Abner."

"Were you here when Dr. Rufty came on as headmaster?"

"No. I was honored to join this administration two years ago. Dr. Rufty is an excellent headmaster, an excellent educator. We have suspended classes tomorrow in honor of Dr. Abner, and will take the students who wish to attend to his memorial."

"I'm sure Dr. Rufty will find that very comforting," Peabody told her.

"I hope he will. I have left the records you need on his unit. I understand you may look for others. Or need to take the unit. He has given his permission for this. Is there more I can do, Lieutenant?"

"Actually, yeah. I'm going to let EDD take this. Why don't you give me a tour?"

"Of course. I would be happy to show you our school. We're very proud of it."

"Great." Eve sent a silent signal to Peabody. "My partner could take a look at some of the classroom areas. I'd like to see the labs."

"Of course. Which labs would you like to see?"

"Chemistry. Let's start there."

"These would be on the third floor. There are elevators—"

"We'll take the stairs," Eve interrupted. "Get a better sense of the place."

"In addition to our administration offices," Myata began as she led the way, "we have our physical education center and an auditorium on the main level. We also have classrooms for grades kindergarten through six and a cafeteria."

They started up steps worn by decades of feet. "On this level, classrooms for grades seven through twelve, our computer labs, a second cafeteria, a teachers' lounge, study hall, our library—both digital and traditional—and our music room."

And all with the big, echoing feel of a building after business hours. Student artwork adorned the walls as well as school announcements, posters for the spring musical, the spring dance, the spring concert. Slender lockers painted alternately in what she deduced were the school colors—navy and gold—had swipe locks.

"I've heard of the school you and your husband will open—soon, I think."

"Looks like next month. It's really his deal."

Myata smiled. "It's a good and generous thing, to provide a safe place to learn, to socialize, to become. I teach math skills on the main level, to second and third graders. It's very rewarding."

"I thought you were administration."

"Yes." They started up to three. "It's our policy, one the headmaster implemented, that those in administration also teach at least one class every term. Dr. Rufty himself teaches U.S. history and cochairs our debate team. How can we administrate if we don't also educate?"

Righting the ship, Eve thought. Hands on the wheel.

"You admire him."

"Very much. Here on this floor we have more classrooms, science labs, computer science labs, our visual arts area, a small library-slash-reading room reserved for upperclassmen."

She paused. "We even introduce the lower grades to chemistry, in the classroom. Very basic introductions to experimentation and reactions. Like . . . baking soda and lemon juice. Such things that are very safe, very simple, and can be done with little hands."

"I'm more interested in the labs, the advanced programs."

"Because of how Dr. Abner was killed." Obviously

struggling with distress, Myata nodded. "You have to look for answers. I can only say no one in this school would wish Dr. Rufty harm, and by harming his husband, they would harm him."

"No issues, no problems, no disagreements?"

She smiled again, just a little. "It's academia, Lieutenant. There will be drama and spats. We deal with children, more drama, more spats. But the tone comes from the head, doesn't it? In here, the headmaster. We're encouraged to listen to each other, to resolve our disagreements, and to always put the students first. It's a good place.

"But you wish to see the chemistry labs, and I see Mr. Rosalind's doors are open."

They moved down the hallway, paused outside the open doors. Eve saw a tall black man in shirt and tie, wearing gloves and an eye shield, standing at the work counter next to a kid of about sixteen with a lot of tangled red hair and freckles.

Like Myata, Rosalind wore a black armband.

"Next step, Mac."

"Um."

"Follow the protocol." He nodded when the kid picked up a bottle. "And what is that?"

"It's, um, hydrogen peroxide. Um. Thirty percent hydrogen peroxide?"

"That's right, and what're you doing with it?"

"I'm, um, you know, gonna pour it into the other bottle."

"How much of it?"

The kid bit his lip, looked over at the screen. "Fifty milliliters." With the care of a boy making a boomer, Mac poured the solution into an opaque bottle, breathed out.

"Now?"

"It says to cap it—with this?"

"That's right."

"He's so patient," Myata murmured as Rosalind nudged the boy to what looked to Eve like a tea bag.

"Talk us through it, Mac."

"Okay, um, I'm opening the tea bag, and taking the stuff—"

"What stuff?"

"The, you know, tea stuff."

"Leaves."

"Tea leaves out of it. Then I need to put the, um, the po—po—"

"Read it on screen."

"Yeah, um, the potassium iodide into the empty bag."

"How much?"

"Um, a quarter tablespoon."

"Measure it out."

Eve figured she'd have wanted to stun herself by this time, but Rosalind stood, at his ease, as the boy painstakingly measured, added.

"Now I gotta, um, tie it closed, but there has to be enough of the string thing to hang over the lip of the bottle. Right?"

"Exactly right. Do that."

He might have been tying a couple of poisonous snakes together, but Mac finally managed it.

"Do I go ahead and open the bottle now?"

"That's right. Make sure you point the bottle away—safety first, right, Mac?"

With his teeth digging into his bottom lip, the kid angled the bottle away, uncapped it. Spotting the women at the door, Rosalind winked.

"Final step, Mac."

"I gotta put the tea bag with the potassium iodide in the bottle with the peroxide."

"Slowly."

Glaciers moved faster, Eve figured.

When the bag finally hit the peroxide, a big cloud puffed out of the bottle. The kid grinned as if he'd just split an atom or something, and his teacher grinned with him.

"That's so mega, Mr. Rosalind."

"Yeah, it's frosty all right. Now, I want you to write out the experiment, what you used, what steps you took. Then explain what reaction took place. Go ahead and take your tablet into the lounge and get started. Mac, gloves and goggles," he added as the boy grabbed his tablet.

"Oh yeah." He stripped them off, put them in labeled bins. "Thanks, Mr. Rosalind. Hey, Ms. Myata."

Myata stepped in as Mac rushed out. "Is Mac still having trouble with his labs?"

"He gets flustered, and does better one-on-one. I don't see a budding scientist in him, but he'll do all right with the course. Hello." He walked over, offered Eve his hand. "Ty Rosalind."

"Lieutenant Dallas."

"Ah." His smiling greeting faded. "Kent. We're all still reeling."

"You were friendly with Dr. Abner?"

"I was, yes. I talked him into speaking with some of my advanced students who planned to go into medicine. He always made the time."

"How long have you taught here, Mr. Rosalind?"

"Thirty-seven years. And one more if we count my year as a teaching assistant."

"So you were on staff when Lotte Grange was headmaster."

"Yes. Martin is the fourth headmaster I've worked with."

Martin, she noted, not the formal Headmaster Rufty.

"Dr. Rufty implemented a lot of changes when he took over."

"Yes, he did. I'm sorry, would you like to sit down? Kim, I've got some tea bags with leaves still in them."

"Oh, thank you, but perhaps I should leave you to talk. I can wait in the teachers' lounge until you're ready to go back down, Lieutenant."

"I can find my way back, thanks. You've been very helpful."

"If you need me for anything else, I'm available. I'll see you in the morning," she said to Rosalind.

"Interested in one of those tea bags?" he said to Eve.

"Not even a little."

But she walked in and took a good look around.

12

A good, organized space with a desk in the far front of the room, an old-fashioned blackboard behind it. Numerous counters and workstations, screens, comps, stools instead of chairs.

Beakers, vials, bottles, portable heaters for experiments.

"You're well equipped in here, Mr. Rosalind."

"We are. This is one of three chem labs. We have a smaller one on this level for advanced chemistry. Students need to qualify to take that course."

"Do you teach that, too?"

"I do."

"Who orders the chemicals, the equipment?"

"As senior in the department, I requisition administration. You think someone from the school did this to Kent? The reports weren't specific, but made it clear a chemical agent was used. I'm going to sit if you don't mind. I've been on my feet most of the day."

He lowered to a stool, sighed. "Without knowing

what was used, I couldn't tell you if such a thing could have been created here."

"You stock toxic chemicals?"

"We would certainly have the ability to create them. Even with something as entertaining as the cloud effect—the oxygen release—I had Mac do, you see we take precautions. And all the chemicals, even something as basic as this hydrogen peroxide, would be locked up before I leave. The lab is also locked when not in use."

"Why don't you tell me where you were the night before Dr. Abner was killed. Just to tie that off."

"The night before. That's easy. My wife and I were at my son's for dinner, and to celebrate our oldest grandchild's birthday. She's fifteen. Actually, Meris is a student here." He smiled. "And barely got through Introduction to Chemistry. She's more interested in theater—and is starring in the spring musical. She had rehearsal after classes, just as she does today, so I actually waited, took her home, met my wife there. I don't think we left until about ten-thirty."

"And then?"

"Well, we walked home, Lilliana and I. It was a nice night, and it's only a handful of blocks. Plus." He patted his stomach. "Birthday cake. I graded some papers in bed while Lilliana read. It was probably lights-out by eleven-thirty."

"Okay."

"I consider Kent and Martin friends. Considered Kent a friend." He looked toward the windows, toward the sky of tender spring blue. "Kent and I often ran together on weekends if we could mesh our schedules."

Now Eve sat. "Tell me about Lotte Grange."

He sighed again. "Thirty-seven years, four headmasters, so many students I've watched come in as hardly more than babies and leave as young men and women. It's still satisfying to me to help someone like Mac, who's so easily distracted, so unsure of himself, find some moment of triumph and fascination with science."

"I could see that for myself. But that's not about Grange."

"In a way it is. Every headmaster sets a tone, leaves a mark, has a vision. She was ambitious, and why shouldn't she be, and initially I thought her ability to court deep pockets could only benefit the school. She wasn't an educator, or was no longer interested in being one, and that sets a tone, doesn't it?"

"You tell me," Eve countered.

"Yes. She was solid as assistant headmaster—not like our Kim, who's a treasure, but solid. And initially, when she took over, she seemed steady enough. But it didn't take long before that changed, in my opinion."

"In what way?"

"The focus on those deep pockets took over. If a student had those pockets behind him or her, it became clear there would be little to no consequences for poor behavior, for missed work, poor grades. Factions often form under such a tone. Action—or inaction—and reaction. Some students—often ones like Mac—were cornered, humiliated, ganged up on with impunity. Or a pretense of disciplinary action."

He angled his head. "You don't seem surprised by this. You know all this already."

"Did you know Jay Duran when he taught here?"

"Of course. Different areas, but we teachers know each other. You've spoken to Jay? He's at Columbia now, or was when I last spoke to him."

"When was that?"

"In December. Some of us still get together for a little holiday cheer."

He doesn't know, Eve thought. "Mr. Duran's wife was killed this morning."

"What?" He pushed off the stool, shock lurching him to his feet. "But— How? Wait. No. The same? The same?"

"Yes."

Standing, he pressed his hands to the sides of his head. "This is horrible."

"Who was here, student or staff, during the end of Grange's tenure and the start of Rufty's who resented the change, who had an aptitude for what you teach?"

"My God, I don't know. I can't think who . . . Jay's wife—I can't think of her name now—she had nothing to do with the school."

"Mr. Duran complained about Grange, complained about the cheating, the bullying, and so on."

"So did I, so did many of us. What does that . . ."

Sharp mind, Eve saw as it clicked for him.

"My wife, my family."

"I'd advise you to tell your wife, your family not to open any packages. You can report any delivery to me." She dug out a card, set it on the counter. "We'll have it scanned."

"I don't understand how anyone could . . . I'd know if anyone used my labs. I'd know if anyone accessed the chemicals, the equipment. There were some issues, in the last year or so of Grange's rule, and in the first few weeks of Martin's."

"Such as?"

"Accessing swipe cards or cloning them, using the lab and supplies to make stink bombs, smoke bombs, flash bombs."

"Do you have names?"

"I couldn't identify them. I didn't have evidence to point fingers. Suspicions, and I wanted to have meetings with the students I thought might have been a part of it, or who might know who did. Grange vetoed it. I couldn't be sure, so she wouldn't have students, and their parents, embarrassed."

"Protecting the bottom line?" Eve suggested.

"I believe that absolutely," Rosalind said without hesitation. "Martin took a different route. When it continued after he came on, he held a full assembly, gave notice. Any student involved would face automatic suspension. Any student covering for one involved would lose privileges—no sports, no school activities."

"Did it stop?"

"Not right away, no. But a case in point. Before Grange left, one of the students was physically assaulted because he refused to cheat. His parents brought him in, and Grange dismissed it because the boy was afraid to name names. But they came back in after Martin took over. He had a private meeting with them, and with other parents and students with complaints. At the end of the day, eleven students were suspended. There was hell to pay from parents. Martin kept it contained, but we all knew, hell to pay. Several of those students didn't come back."

"Names?"

"God, I'm not clicking right on them—my mind is spinning. We'd have records."

"I'm getting them now. Do you recall if any of those students had an aptitude for chemistry?"

"The boy who'd been attacked—Miguel . . . I've lost the last name. But he ended up in my advanced class. He was here on scholarship, and went to—damn it—I think

MIT, earned several scholarships. Kendel Hayward—
spoiled young woman, and one who liked to humiliate
others. She came back, seemed to settle down."

"Was she involved in the beatdown?"

"I don't think so. The gossip was it was two boys—
maybe three?—who wanted him to cheat for them. She
likely ran with them though," Rosalind mused. "She ran
with a rough crowd. My impression was Kendel's parents gave her an ultimatum. She did satisfactory work in
my class, before and after. But after, she stopped mouth-
ing off. There were others. Damn it, I'm sorry. Kendel
was tight with one of the boys. Maybe more than one."

"You've been helpful. I can get the rest from the records. But if you do think of names or specifics, contact
me."

"I will. I have to get in touch with my wife. If anything happened . . . Jay and I weren't the only ones who
pushed back."

"Understood." She started for the door, stopped.
"Think of staff, too. Teachers, administrators, support
staff, anyone who might have been warned or disciplined by Dr. Rufty, anyone who left during the first
term, or didn't come back in the fall."

"All right. I'll do my best."

Eve headed down, wandering a bit as she went.

She found Peabody doing the same on the main level.

"I went up to the dorm floors, had a poke around,"
she told Eve. "Since I heard you talking with the guy in
the lab, I just poked around on the second level, then
down here. I walked into the auditorium. They're in
rehearsals for the musical. They're really good."

"Impressions otherwise?"

"Well-oiled machine."

"I've got the same. EDD?"

"Should be done or about. Since we had the warrant, they wanted to pull records from the guidance office, the assistant headmaster—before this one. He retired at seventy-eight in Rufty's fourth year, and moved to Louisiana, where his granddaughter teaches."

As Peabody spoke, Myata escorted EDD out of administration.

"Do you have all you need for now?" she asked Eve. "Detectives?"

"We've got copies of all the applicable records," Callendar said. "And the tablet, Dr. Rufty's old tablet."

"If there's anything else, please contact me."

When they stepped outside, Eve laid out the plan. "We can't be sure, at this point, who on staff when Rufty came on might have been on the team undermining Grange. And every one of them might be a target. So we're going to notify all of them—that's across the board—and issue warnings about receiving and opening deliveries. Peabody, you take the first half, I'll handle the rest."

"It'd go faster if we split it four ways." McNab looked at Callendar, got the nod.

"All right. Peabody, divide it up. I want a list of all, but mark who's handling who. I'll drop you off at Central. I'll head uptown, handle the rich guy interview."

"I can go with, take the subway back."

"I'd rather you get on this. Look, send the list to my units—including the in-dash. I'll start with the first ten while I'm en route. I don't think anybody's going to get a damn golden egg tonight, but we cover it."

"Got your copies here, too." McNab handed her a small file bag. "We did separate discs for faculty, for students, for admin, and for support staff."

"Good work. Let's get started."

* * *

Once Eve dropped off the trio and their fizzies (for which they apparently had a bottomless capacity), she headed uptown. Considering the time, the thickness of the traffic, and the potential interview, she calculated her get-home time as late.

She used her wrist unit to send a quick text to Roarke.

Still working. I'll be late.

She'd battled her way nearly to Midtown when his reply came through.

As will I.

Okay, she thought, that evens it out.

Maybe, considering the day behind her, the day still ahead, she had a wistful moment when she had to veer away from home and toward Riverside Drive.

In the smoky light of dusk, Greenwald's building was a gilded tower with a swirl of exterior people glides circling the first few floors, glittery glass elevators sliding and slithering along the north and south sides.

She pulled up at the curb of the entrance with its massive, three-story glass wall, and prepared to go toe-to-toe with the liveried doorman who hustled over.

Instead he opened her door before she could, smiled in greeting. "Good evening, Lieutenant. How can I help you?"

Okay, so Roarke owned the building.

"Reginald Greenwald."

"Of course. I believe Mr. Greenwald is currently at home. Carl at the desk will clear you up. Enjoy your visit to the Hudson Tower."

"Right."

He made it to the door ahead of her, hit a sensor that had eight square feet of glass sliding open. She had to admit it was impressive, as was the two-level lobby with its upscale shops, cafés, food marts, bars. She crossed the floor with its mosaic inlays depicting a sweeping river of serene blue, passed a central island of flowers white as snow circling a small blue pool with bright gold fish swimming.

She noted a wide curve of stairs leading to the second level, a bank of interior elevators, also glass—and a lot of discreet security, both live and electronic.

She stepped up to the desk where Carl, a distinguished fiftyish in his spiffy black uniform, beamed smiles.

"Lieutenant, welcome to Hudson Tower. You're here to visit Mr. Greenwald."

So the doorman gave the desk guy a heads-up. Efficient, she thought. But that was how Roarke ran things.

"That's right."

"Mr. Greenwald is currently in residence. Shall I announce you?"

"No. Just clear me up."

"Of course." Carl didn't miss a beat. "Mr. Greenwald has the fifty-sixth floor. Let me escort you to the proper elevator to reach that level."

He came around the counter, led her to a small, second lobby where glass tubes angling from a mirrored wall held strangely beautiful flowers of pale, pale pink and lavender.

Carl used a swipe to access one of the three elevators.

"Greenwald," he ordered. "Main entrance." Then he smiled at Eve again. "Enjoy your visit. Please let me know if you need anything else."

"Sure. Thanks."

The doors closed silently on an elevator that was, thankfully, not glass. Or not transparent glass, as the walls had a glassy sheen of quiet gold.

She appreciated the fact it rode smooth, and didn't stop until it reached the top floor.

Greenwald residence, the comp announced as the doors opened.

Here the carpet ran thick and silvery gray. She saw the car had opened in a central location, a few feet from double white doors—with enough security to protect a major stash of gold bullion.

She walked to the door, pressed the bell.

Mr. Greenwald does not accept unannounced visitors. Please return to the main lobby to request admittance.

"I'm not a visitor." She held up her badge for scanning. "I'm a cop, and this is police business."

One moment please.

She continued to hold up the badge as the scanning light ran it, as the door cam recorded her. And as, she imagined, the security comp notified Greenwald he had NYPSD at the door.

Your identification has been verified, Lieutenant Dallas. Please wait.

Eve waited until the door opened.

The woman hit mid-twenties. She had milk pale, flawless skin, a sleek fall of hair the color of warm honey, eyes of Arctic blue, a wide mouth dyed as pale a pink as the flowers fifty-five floors below.

"Please to come in. Thank you for waiting."

The careful English held an Eastern European accent. The diamond studs at her ears flashed fire as she stepped back into an entranceway flanked by statues of arty naked women who looked very stern.

"I am Iryna, Mr. Greenwald's personal assistant." She gestured with one graceful hand toward the living area. It had three conversation areas, all quiet, dignified colors with tables and chests of clear or mirrored glass. Heavy drapes fell over what Eve assumed would be glass doors leading out to a terrace. The art, interspersed with fancy mirrors, ran to more dignity in still lifes of vases or bowls of fruit.

It had the feel of a space rarely used.

"If you would please to sit. Mr. Greenwald will be shortly with you. Shall you have refreshment?"

"No, thanks." Personal assistant, my ass, Eve thought. Unless they were talking very personal. "Do you live here? On the floor?"

"Yes. I am available to Mr. Greenwald at all times."

I bet.

"How long have you worked for him?"

"It is now three years."

"About the same amount of time you've been in the country?"

"Yes. I should—"

"Do you know Mr. Greenwald's ex-wife? Lotte Grange?"

"I am sorry. I do not." Relief washed over her face as Greenwald walked in. "Lieutenant Dallas, Mr. Greenwald."

"Yes, Iryna, that's fine."

The little pat he gave her said, clearly, her assistance was very personal. It was meant to.

He held a lowball glass in one hand, offered Eve the other. "Roarke's cop."

He had a boom of a voice, almost jocular, that suited his waving mane of pewter hair, the amused dark eyes, the perfectly trimmed goatee.

A well-built man of about six-two, he'd dressed for an at-home evening in trousers and a sweater a few shades lighter than his hair.

He took a seat on a high-backed sofa in quiet gray, gestured for her to sit, then sat back at his ease. As if amused, he patted the cushion beside him for Iryna.

She sat primly, and obviously ill at ease.

"And what brings Roarke's cop to my door?"

"I'm the NYPSD's cop, Mr. Greenwald, and murder brings me to your door."

Iryna let out a little mouse squeak; Greenwald lifted his eyebrows. "Whose?"

"Kent Abner, Elise Duran."

"I'm afraid I don't know either of those unfortunate people."

"Both individuals were killed with a home-brewed chemical agent. You deal in chemicals."

His brows went higher, then lowered again as he took a casual sip of his drink. "I deal in cleaning supplies. I hardly think you're visiting everyone in the city who has some association with chemicals."

"Both victims also had a connection with your ex-wife."

"Which?" He smiled a bit. "I have two."

"Lotte Grange."

"Lotte? Well, this is interesting. Is she a suspect?"

"You and Dr. Grange were married when she served as headmaster at the Theresa A. Gold Academy."

"For a few years, yes. We've been divorced longer than we were married."

"When is the last time you saw or spoke to her?"

"That would be the day our divorce was finalized, with our lawyers present. As far as I know she lives in East Washington. The simple fact is, my marriage to Lotte was a small blip in my life. While we didn't part in a friendly manner, I stopped giving her a thought once that blip ended."

"You ended it."

"Yes, I did. Iryna, my sweet, why don't you freshen this for me?"

"Of course." She popped right up, took the glass, hurried away on heels that showed off excellent young legs.

"Can you tell me where you were last night and the night of April twenty-seventh? Between ten and eleven P.M.?"

"My." The eyebrows arched again, but the eyes beneath them hardened, just a little. "So official. I'm tempted to contact my lawyer, but at the moment, I'm still entertained. Last night *we* entertained. A dinner party here, for six guests. We sat down to the meal at eight. I believe the last guest left sometime after eleven. On the twenty-seventh . . ."

For this he took a small book out of his trouser pocket. "Ah yes. We were in Chicago, the second night of a two-day business trip."

"'We'?"

"Iryna and I." He smiled. "She's invaluable to me."

"I'm sure. Do you ever visit your company labs, Mr. Greenwald?"

"On occasion. I try to make an appearance now and then in all departments. It's good for interpersonal relations. After all, my grandfather founded the company. And before you ask, I do know a little of chemistry, just as I know a little about organic solutions. Why do you suppose I'd kill people I don't know?"

"Kent Abner was the spouse of Martin Rufty. Dr. Rufty replaced your ex-wife as headmaster."

"Rufty, of course. Of course." Interest lit on his face again. "I never actually met him, but I leaned toward liking him, as Lotte didn't like him at all."

"Is that so?"

"My sense is that he was very critical of her." He took the glass Iryna brought in, patted the cushion beside him again. "Lotte didn't—I assume still doesn't—take criticism well. Of course, at the time Lotte and I had our own . . . issues."

"What were they?"

"Perhaps I should not be here," Iryna began.

"Don't be silly." And Greenwald laid a hand, possessively, on her thigh. "Lotte and I married on a whim. A sexual whim. She was, again I assume still is, a highly sexual creature. I enjoy sexual creatures. She was also striking physically, intelligent, ambitious. Money wasn't a particular issue, as she had her own. I had more, considerably more, and that appealed to her."

Lifting his glass, he half toasted, then sipped. "We had an arrangement. If either of us opted to engage in sex outside the marriage, we would be discreet, and we would clear such activities with the other party before going forward."

"And she broke the agreement."

"She did. I received an envelope with, we'll say, compromising photos of Lotte."

"With who?"

"I can't tell you. The man's face was turned away, or conveniently obscured. When I confronted her, she shrugged it off. What difference did it make? All the difference, for me. She broke the agreement. Clearly, we would end the marriage, but we agreed to do so, well, discreetly."

He drank again. "She put out feelers for another position. She lived here for a few months, but we lived separately, you understand. She wanted a generous settlement; I wasn't inclined to give her one. We argued about that, but something was off. She was shrill, edgy, and it finally came out one of the instructors had walked in on her with another instructor. Compromising. Apparently it was quite a scene."

"Names?"

"I don't have them." He lifted his hand from Iryna's thigh, waved the question off. Placed his hand back on the thigh, just a bit higher.

"I didn't care. She wanted the position in East Washington, and a cushy landing. She pointed out that I had had affairs, and our agreement wasn't in writing. She'd take me to court, play the injured wife, and see to it my family name carried the scar. And she would have. It was worth a few million to end it, and be rid of her."

"What about the two instructors?"

"As I said, she wanted that position. Little stopped her when she set her sights. She told them both she'd go to the police, and go to the board, file sexual assault charges. So they should keep their mouths shut, and she'd be gone in a matter of weeks."

He shrugged, drank. "As far as I know they did, as she moved to East Washington just before the first of the year. I filed for divorce, as we agreed, included a settlement. She came back to finalize it, and I haven't seen or spoken to her since."

"Do you still have the photographs?"

He looked both surprised by the question and amused. "Why would I? I kept them, in case, until the divorce finalized. Then I destroyed them. A blip," he reminded her with another half toast. "And as we had a very satisfying private life during that blip, worth the cost."

He drank. "Added to it, the priceless lesson she taught me. Marriage is for fools. Why legalize and complicate what you can simply enjoy?"

Turning, he kissed Iryna's cheek. "Isn't that right, my sweet?"

"Yes, Mr. Greenwald."

He laughed, gave her thigh a quick squeeze. "Isn't she adorable?"

"Just precious. Iryna, where were you last night?"

She folded her lips, looked at Greenwald.

"Go ahead."

"We have—had—a dinner party. Cocktails and hors d'oeuvres from seven to eight. At eight there was dinner and more conversation. At ten coffee and brandy."

"Okay." Eve pushed to her feet. "Thanks for your time."

"I will escort you to the door."

As they approached it, Eve murmured to Iryna, "If you're not happy here, I can help you."

Iryna sent her a look of genuine surprise. "No, I am very happy. Mr. Greenwald is very kind, and very generous." She opened the door for Eve. "He does not hurt me. I know what it is like when men do. He does not, and would not, as he has no violence, so I am happy."

"All right. If anything changes, you can contact me."

Eve walked to the elevator and wondered what Iryna had experienced to be happy with a man old enough to be her grandfather simply because he didn't hurt her.

13

She drove through the gates after dark, and there they were. All those welcoming lights.

She had to stop, just lower her head to the steering wheel. Until that moment, she hadn't realized how much the day had dragged at her. All the death, all the grief, all the ugliness.

So she pushed it back, swallowed it down, and drove the rest of the way home.

She got her file bag—her day wasn't nearly over. She'd reached the names on her list, issued the warnings, struck fear into more than one person, more than one family.

But better fear than death.

She walked inside, where Summerset waited. He took a look at her.

"I'd say look what the cat dragged in, but he's been here all day."

Rather than punching back, she tossed her jacket

over the newel post. "Don't open any packages. Even if you're expecting them."

He stepped forward as she started up the stairs. "All deliveries are scanned."

"Don't open any, scanned or not. Just don't."

"Very well." He frowned after her as she continued up with the cat on her heels.

She went straight to her office, got coffee, checked first to make sure all the names from Gold had been notified.

Didn't mean someone might not ignore the warning, or just forget, but at least they had notification.

She updated her board, then sat down with her notes.

Roarke walked in the house mildly annoyed by a delay—another delay—on a project in Maine. Five straight days of rain might be good for the flowers, but it meant the exterior work on a rehab in progress shut down.

He couldn't control the bloody weather, but at times like this he yearned to find a way.

When he came in, he told himself to put it aside and focus on what he could control. But it burned a bit.

"As the cat's not with you," he said to Summerset, "the lieutenant must be home."

"She is, and something's troubling her. She looked tired, and . . . sad. You should deal with it. And she told me, very specifically, not to open any deliveries."

"There was another murder this morning." Roarke glanced up the stairs as he spoke.

"Yes, I heard. I can't see how it would apply to deliveries here."

"If she's worried about it, she has a reason. I'll find out what it is."

"You look a bit tired yourself," Summerset added as Roarke started up the stairs.

"Bloody rain."

"It hasn't rained today."

"In Maine it has."

He continued up, and because he couldn't quite shake off the irritation, detoured to the bedroom to strip off the suit—and the workday—changed into a light sweater and jeans.

When he went into her office, she sat at her command center. Rather than his usual spot on her sleep chair, the cat sat on a leg of her workstation, staring at her.

"You're starting to wig me, pal. Go take a nap or something."

She continued to work; Galahad didn't budge.

And Roarke could see the headache behind her eyes as clearly as a flashing sign. Likely the result of fatigue and skipping any resemblance to an actual meal through her day.

Annoyed all over again, he pulled a case out of his pocket as he strode to her command center. Both she and the cat turned heads to look at him.

The cat's look said, as clearly as Summerset's words: Deal with this.

"Take the blocker. You won't work well with that headache."

She started to refuse—he saw that—just as he saw her change her mind. When she took it without protest or excuse, he decided he did, indeed, have something to deal with.

At least it got his mind off his stalled project.

He glanced at her board, saw the stills of the second victim, the crime scene.

"The report said she had two teenage sons."

"Yeah."

"You don't suspect the husband."

She shook her head. "He teaches at Columbia. Dennis Mira knows him. He helped with the notification. The guy was shattered, just broken to pieces. Mr. Mira helped."

"Dennis is made of kindness and compassion."

She often thought if everybody in New York had just a little bit of Dennis Mira in them, she'd be out of a job.

"Before Duran—the spouse—taught at Columbia, he taught at Gold."

"Ah. You have your link."

"Yeah. A woman had to die to give it to me, but I've got the link."

"Eve."

She shook her head again, more vigorously. "It's not on me, I know it's not on me. But she's still dead. Jesus, Roarke, her mother found her."

Saying nothing, he stepped behind her, laid his hands on her shoulders, brushed a kiss over the top of her head. "What can I do?"

She spun in the chair, wrapped her arms around him, pressed her face against him.

"There now." It broke his heart. "Come away from this for a while."

"I need to—" She paused, gathered herself. "I need to say something about this morning."

Set to comfort, he went momentarily blank. "This morning?"

"You've already let it go. You were pissed, but you've already let it go. I was pissed, too."

Remembering, he shrugged. "Hardly the first or the last time for either of us."

"No, but—" She let him go, stood to face him. "I know people get pissed over money. Hell, they bash brains in over it."

"I don't see either of us going that far."

"I know it's stupid for us to get pissed over it. It's supposed to be the lack of it, or the carelessness with it, the greed for it, whatever. Not the fact that there's so damn much of it."

He traced a fingertip down the dent in her chin. "I don't plan for that to change."

"Oh, I got that. The thing is, I don't want to get used to you peeling off a bunch of money for me whenever I'm running a little short. I wouldn't have run short if I'd gotten by a machine. And goddamn it, I forgot to hit one today, which makes your stupid point."

"I still have your IOU."

"I don't want to get used to it," she repeated. "Start depending on it. I've gotten used to so much, depend on so much. You, this place, the life we have. The clothes in my closet, the damn coffee I drink."

"Why should that worry you?"

"It doesn't—or only a little sometimes—which is *my* point. It was stupid to get pissed because you lent me some money, but I don't want to start thinking, hey, no problem. Roarke'll cover it. I don't want that for either of us. It's important to me."

"I'll understand that if you understand it's important to me you don't walk out of the house with empty pockets."

"They weren't all the way empty. Anyway, that's just part of what I need to say. Duran, he's shattered, and he's trying to remember if he kissed her goodbye that morning. Did he say he loved her, did he kiss her goodbye, because she's gone. And I thought, I was pissed, and I walked out. I didn't kiss you goodbye. I didn't tell you I love you. And damn it, who knows better than I do that everything can change, can break, and you never get that chance again?"

"My darling Eve." He kissed her forehead, her cheeks, her lips.

"It'll happen again. It may be you who's pissed and walks out. So I want to say when it does happen, either way, to remember this right here." She cupped his face in her hands, kissed him. "Just remember."

"And you." He kissed her back. Then held her. "How do you feel about spaghetti and meatballs?"

Everything in her drained, then filled again as she rested her forehead to his. "Man, you know what button to push."

"I do, yes. So we'll sit, have some pasta, some wine, and you'll tell me about this link, and what it means."

"I'll get the food, you get the wine."

So they sat and ate while she took him through her day.

"There's a calculated cruelty, isn't there, to murdering the spouse of someone you have a grudge against." He broke some bread, handed her a share. "How does that apply to you telling Summerset not to open deliveries?"

"I not only spent time at the school, asking questions, having EDD access records, I made it clear to anyone paying attention—and if he's not, he's an idiot—we've made the connection. What better way to take a slap at the primary than to try for her spouse?"

She rolled some pasta. "It's low odds, but why risk it?"

"Understood. So you'll look hard at Grange, and the transition period, the change of headmasters."

"If the school's the connection, and it is, she's the strongest link. From everything I've looked at, she didn't give a rat's ass about the students or the instructors. It was all about prestige, about the big donations." She forked up a bite of meatball, gestured with it. "So two for you. What do you know about Grange's ex, Reginald Greenwald of All Fresh?"

"Ah. I believe I've met him a time or two. Considering that, I may have met Grange as well. The business is more than solid, and the family has a reputation for running it well. I don't recall hearing anything particular or peculiar. Do you think he's involved?"

"They have a lot of labs, a lot of chemists and chemicals. He's not only CEO, but the grandson of the founder, so who'd question him if he spent time in the labs?" She shrugged, ate some more. "But I don't see it, at least not with what I have. No love lost between him and Grange. They had an arrangement."

"Did they?"

"So he says. They married mostly for sex and because they suited each other's ambitions and images. If either of them wanted sex outside the marriage, all good, as long as they kept it private. She didn't. Not only did somebody send him photos of her, with her sex buddy's face obscured, but she dipped into the staff pool, and got caught."

"Careless of her."

"There's speculation she diddled a student."

"More than careless there. But . . . She and Greenwald are, as I recall, contemporaries. Wouldn't that make her roughly a half century older than the students?"

"Greenwald had a twenty-four-year-old live-in Ukrainian tootsie pretending to be his personal assistant. And you want to be careful there, ace, as the age difference falls in the same range."

"But she would be an adult, not a student," Roarke pointed out, "and there the difference widens a great deal."

"Won't argue with true."

"You ran her?"

"I did. He sponsored her, brought her over three years ago, so well after the divorce. I gave her an out, told her I could help her. She said she was very content—and she meant it. That he was kind to her, didn't hurt her. And she knew what it was like to be hurt by someone in power. So . . . their business."

"An unsavory gray area, but—not a minor, not a student. If Grange did indeed go there, she'd not only lose her position, and any remote chance of landing another, but face criminal charges."

"Yeah, she would. I'm thinking of mentioning that to her when I take a trip down to East Washington."

"You'd go to her?"

"I could start the process of having her come here for interview, but she could stall, and the first two kills were within two days. I'd rather not risk it."

"I'll arrange a shuttle. And if that's something you get used to," he said before she spoke, "it's to save time and frustration—potentially lives—in the work. So it's all to the good."

"The public shuttle's not that bad," she began, and tolerated his bland stare. "But yeah, it would save time. I'm figuring to go down after Kent Abner's memorial in the morning.

"Second question. What do you know about Miguel Rodriges?"

"I'm not entirely sure I know anything. Who is he?"

"I'll make it easier, since you basically employ the population of Uruguay. It happens he's an old pal of Callendar's, so she gave me the first tip. When I got the second from a teacher at Gold, I got his name from her to take a look.

"He went to Gold on scholarship," she continued as she wound more pasta around her fork, "got a full ride to MIT, and now works as a game programmer in one of your R&D departments."

"What is the population of Uruguay?"

"I don't know, but you probably employ it, so you don't know everyone who draws a paycheck."

"Not offhand, but everyone who does is thoroughly screened. Is he a suspect?"

"No. Callendar said how Rodriges got bullied, and beat up on when at Gold. I had a talk with the head chemistry teacher—who's worked at Gold for decades, so through Grange. Among other things he told me this Rodriges was a target of some of the troublemaking rich kids, got beat up when he couldn't avoid them—and wouldn't cheat so they could get decent grades. His parents met with Grange, who fluffed them off."

She ate, grabbed her water glass. "But then they came back when Rufty took over, and he not only didn't fluff, suspensions happened."

"A different kettle," Roarke commented.

"Opposites, really, so whatever the opposite of a kettle is. The chem teacher gave me a name, and I've got more from Rufty's notes. I'm going to check them out. I want to talk to Rodriges, too, get a picture."

"Easy enough to arrange. I'd like to refresh myself on him."

"The chem teacher, who struck me as solid, liked him. That came across. A serious brain, apparently, and since he got tuned up rather than cheat, I'd say that adds ethics and guts. Figures you'd snap him up."

"Only the best," he said as he reached across for her hand. "I'll look him up, talk to his supervisor. I can have him come to you whenever you like."

"Save me time. The memorial's at eight. They wanted to have it on his favorite running route. I can grab the shuttle by nine. Why don't I tag you when we're heading back? It might take a push to box Grange into an interview."

"I'd say having Whitney contact the board of trustees or the school's president—however it works—would cement that very well."

"Huh. I bet it would. Kind of a hard-ass way in, but . . ."

"Play to your strengths, darling."

"I'm going to take that as a compliment." She studied the very last bite of the very last meatball. "I wonder what genius came up with the concept of a ball of meat. There should be statues honoring him."

"I think there's likely more than meat in the ball."

"Don't tell me that." She ate the last bite. "I don't want to know that. Besides, you don't know any more about what goes into cooking stuff than I do. So we're sticking with a ball of meat."

"Probably best all around. And since you got dinner, I suppose I deal with the dishes."

As she went back to her command center, with coffee, it occurred to her that nobody who didn't actually know Roarke—who cut paychecks to the population of Uruguay—would ever imagine him hauling dishes into the kitchen.

You didn't know somebody until you knew them, she thought. Which made her consider Lotte Grange.

Her impressions included cold, sexual, ambitious, possibly greedy. But there had to be a solid brain and some definite skills in there, too. Nobody got to the headmaster position in tony schools by sexing their way up the chain. At least not for long.

Since Roarke's idea—he usually had good ones—of using Whitney's clout to secure the interview made sense, she sent him a request.

Then she did a run on Kendel Hayward—cheater, bully, high school bad girl. Eve knew her type—it wasn't exclusive to fancy private academies. It ran rough in public and state schools, too.

It seemed Hayward graduated, did a couple years, general studies, at the University of Maryland, dropped out to work with her mother in event planning.

And now lived and worked in—happy coincidence—East Washington. Her engagement to a congressional aide, who appeared to have money, a family name, and aspirations, had been announced the previous summer.

She'd plan on a twofer, Eve thought, and make the trip down even more worthwhile.

And she culled through Rufty's notes from back in the day, scanned troublesome students who'd been suspended or been pulled by parents.

She paused at one, as Rufty mentioned a friendship with Hayward. Marshall Cosner. Transferred from Gold to complete his last semester at Bridgeport Academy in Vermont—where his maternal grandparents lived. He'd gone on to study law, making him the fourth generation in his family to do so. But he hadn't, as his ancestors had, gotten into Harvard.

Cosner currently clerked at his family's law firm—in New York—and had not yet completed his law degree.

From the looks of it, he had a ways to go. Part of

the problem, she thought, might be time off for rehab in a very pricey and exclusive facility. After two illegals busts, with no time served.

Another stint in rehab, physical this time, after he busted himself and his vehicle up while under the influence.

Some addicts liked to cook their own, she considered. Maybe Cosner had learned more chemistry on the street than in the classroom.

She studied a handful of names, paused again on Rufty's personal notes.

She took a hard look at Stephen Whitt. Hayward's high school boyfriend, Cosner's good pal, and according to Rufty, a ringleader of troublemakers.

Like Cosner, he transferred during Rufty's first weeks, but in his case to—interesting—Lester Hensen Prep. She sat back, let that roll around. He'd transferred to the same school where Grange took over as headmaster.

He graduated in the top 10 percent of his class, went on to study international finance at Northwestern, another family tradition. He worked at his family's small, exclusive firm on Wall Street while he worked in tandem on his master's degree.

No criminal that showed which, given his history, she found suspicious.

She wondered if the trio from Gold kept in touch, then glanced over as Roarke came back.

"Miguel Rodriges," he began. "He's worked in my system for about two years, and has taken advantage of our program for continuing education. He's working on his doctorate through MIT online, and should have it by year-end.

"His supervisor considers him a strong asset, a

young man with interesting ideas, a flawless work ethic, and serious skills. We recruited him straight out of grad school. He requested the New York location, though we had offered him Madrid, because his family lives here."

He sat on the edge of her command center. "Again, according to his supervisor, he's destined to move up. He's bilingual, steady, currently in mad love with another young engineer, but he's too shy to ask her out."

"You got that?"

"We wanted to be thorough. In any case, you've only to let me know when you want to talk to him and we'll have him come into Central."

"I've been working that out. One of the mean girls who ganged up on your guy now lives in East Washington, so we'll talk to her while we're there. Then I've got two more names that pop for me out of Rufty's notes, both in New York. And one of them transferred to Grange's school after Rufty came on board."

"Isn't that interesting?"

"Yeah, I think it is. Did he follow Grange, did Grange make a pitch to the parents and their deep pockets? How'd he feel about being shipped off? Another one got shipped off to Vermont, boarding prep school, with his grandparents on watch. Wouldn't be as much fun. Vermont and the mean girl skimmed by on the education scale. The other got into Northwestern, and is now part of the family finance firm. International finance."

"What's the firm?"

"The Whitt Group."

"I know it, and Brent Whitt, who's likely your suspect's father."

"More of a person of interest at this point, but yeah, that's the father."

"The father, grandfather, and an uncle—along with,

now, the son and I believe a cousin—form the core of the group. Very exclusive. Their minimum investment to take on a client is, to my recollection, fifty million."

Eve sat back. "Are you with them?"

"I'm not, no." He lifted her coffee, sampled, put it down again, as it was stone cold. "After all, there was a time I could barely scrape together a few thousand to invest."

"And seeing that what you had would be from a fence."

He only smiled. "And that, of course. In any case, I prefer a more broad-based approach for my investment teams. Added to it, I didn't have—why not stick with it—chemistry with Brent Whitt when he and his team brought me a proposal."

"What was it that put you off?"

"Well, I'll tell you. I'm having a whiskey—and if you're going to drink coffee, at least heat it up." He walked over, opened a section of the wall where he chose a bottle, a short glass. "He's a smug, entitled sort, one who's always been wealthy and privileged and one who enjoys riding on it."

After pouring three fingers, he walked back to her. "It was his great-grandfather who made the first bundle, and with his son turned the bundle into a substantial fortune. So when Brent came along, he had a silver spoon well up his arse."

She knew the tone, however subtle. "You really don't like him."

"I don't, nor his type. He flaunts, and pontificates, condescends to his own team, who would have done the lion's share of the work on a very extensive proposal. My impression was—no," he corrected, took a sip of whiskey, "he very clearly demonstrated his firm very much wanted to acquire my portfolio, even though the source was far from ideal."

"You, the Dublin street rat who made good, being the source."

"Precisely."

"When was this?"

"I couldn't tell you exactly. A few years ago. Five, six."

"So before the youngest family member came on board. Just wondering if he'd been part of the team, if you'd met him."

"I doubt it. As I remember, the youngest who attended was female, mid-twenties, I'd say. The cousin of your person of interest, whom Whitt treated like an underling."

"How about his wife—or ex-wife?"

"I can't recall her, but then we'd have had no reason to meet. I heard, as one hears, there was some acrimony. But divorce rarely doesn't have acrimony. And she took a rather substantial settlement and relocated to Paris."

He frowned into his whiskey. "Or it might have been Florence."

"A long way from her only son," Eve commented.

"Now that you mention it. In any case, I should say that the Whitt Group, and Brent among them, know what they're doing. They have a fine reputation, a sterling list of clients."

"But not you."

"I'm more than satisfied with the firm I work with."

"Okay, since you know one of the families, let's try another." She had to check her notes. "Lowell Cosner and Marilyn Dupont—both lawyers with Cosner, Dupont, and Smithers."

"I've met them. So have you."

"I have?"

"At a couple of charity functions. She's very active in good causes. I believe she has her own foundation. Another wealthy family—they'd be second or third generation. Corporate law, estate law, tax law, and so on, though they also handle criminal and domestic. I know her—that would be Marilyn—slightly better, as she's appealed to me directly for donations and sponsorships. It must be her parents in Vermont."

He held up a finger, took another sip. She could see him flipping back through his extensive memory files. "I recall hearing bits of gossip about a son, and some trouble there. Illegals, and something . . . an accident that landed him in the hospital."

"You got it right. He did the rehab route, which didn't take enough to keep him from juicing up and wrecking his car. Single car accident, so he only busted up himself. No law degree yet, and he's currently doing drone work for the firm.

"Let's go with the last. Benson Hayward, Louisa Raines."

"Ah, Louisa Raines—top-tier party planner, socialite. Wealthy family again. The Raineses own a chain of those warehouse stores. I believe Hayward was another Wall Street type."

"They're divorced, about six years now. He gave up Wall Street and headed south. He runs a dive shop in Jamaica. That's the island, not Queens."

"I assumed, as there's little call for dive shops in Queens."

"Nothing about the daughter?"

"I think I read or heard something about an engagement to former Senator Bilby's grandson. The Bilbys would be another prominent family, deep in politics.

Patience Bilby-Scott, the senator's daughter and the fiancé's mother, is currently serving as secretary of education. Odds are high she'll make a run for president
next election."

"You sure know how to fill in some blanks."

"We do what we can. And what do those filled blanks
tell you?"

"It tells me none of these families are going to want
the offspring involved in a murder investigation, so I'm
going to be pushing back on a bunch of lawyers."

She picked up her fresh coffee, put her boots on the
desk while she studied the board.

"It also tells me you think Whitt is a dick. I suspect
his offspring was a cheating bully in high school, and
it got covered up. I wouldn't be shocked if it turns out
he had some cheating bully in him when he started in
college. And the fact his record's pristine leads me to
believe more got covered up."

"I love you for your cynical mind."

"Who wouldn't? It tells me the Cosner kid liked getting a buzz on more than studying, and probably didn't
have the guts to bully and cheat once he lost his cohorts.
He's a loser.

"And for Hayward, it tells me she had at least one
parent who made her stick it out, then at least pretend
to work for a living. That could be a pisser when all that
money's just there, and now you're hooked up with a
rich boy whose mom might be president one day. You've
got an image to maintain."

She drank some coffee. "All of them do."

"It doesn't seem like motive for murder."

She gave him a bland stare. "Didn't spend much time
in high school, did you?"

"We don't have high school, so to speak, in Ireland."

"Whatever it's called there."

"I went when I couldn't get out of it." Smiling, he sipped more whiskey. "There are a lot of ways out of it."

"Not in state school, so I can tell you grudges and resentments formed in high school root deep. And plenty of people—you have to know some—never fully leave high school, either because they were the big deal, or because they were less than nobody."

He glanced back at her board. "You're right about that, aren't you? So, persons of interest or suspects?"

"We'll keep them as POIs for now. But that rounds back to me being very interested in talking to Rodriges. It'll be tomorrow afternoon. I'll tag you when I have a better handle on the when."

"Good enough. I'm going to finish up a bit of work while you set up your tomorrow. Then, since apparently we had a fight this morning, we need to make up."

"I thought we already did."

"You're the one with the Marriage Rules." He toasted her before he finished off the whiskey. "There must be a notation on makeup sex."

"Maybe."

"If not, write it down," he advised, and strolled into his office.

14

She woke in slow, easy layers, and decided that makeup sex definitely promoted a solid night's sleep.

Roarke and Galahad watched the morning financial reports across the room. Over her head, the sky window showed a bold blue sky.

A pretty good deal all around.

She rolled out, headed straight for coffee. Because makeup sex meant she hadn't had the energy to get up for a sleep shirt, she drank the first sips naked.

"That's a fine sight in the morning," Roarke commented.

"I figure naked's a fine sight for you any hour of any day."

"You wouldn't be wrong."

She studied him in his perfect suit, perfect tie. "Since I can't go through the day naked, you pick out what I need to wear."

Fingers still lazily scratching the cat, he studied her in turn. "Are you quite well, Lieutenant?"

"I'm going to start the day with a memorial, go down to East Washington and take on a nasty-assed headmaster, shift over to deal with a pampered mean girl before coming back, working on a couple of bullies. And very likely a whole bunch of high-priced lawyers."

She walked toward the bathroom for a shower. "You'll figure it out quicker."

While the shower woke her the rest of the way, she rolled through her day's schedule. She'd meet Peabody at the memorial to kick it off. Would the killer make an appearance or resist that moment of satisfaction?

A former student, a parent, a teacher, another administrator.

He or she would be in that pool. Nothing else made sense.

She tossed on a robe, walked back into the bedroom to find Roarke had, as predicted, figured it out faster.

But still.

She frowned at the jacket and slim-cut pants set out on the bed. "What color is that?"

"I believe it's called fog."

"But it has, like, a shine."

"Sheen," he corrected. "A faint sheen. That's called power. And for today, a suit rather than separates adds another step of power. The monochromatic shirt and boots give you a sleek, unbroken look. You'll wince and wear these little sapphire studs—subtle, understated—to polish it off."

She did wince. "Maybe it's too fancy."

"It's not at all fancy, but again, powerful. And with a simple, elegant cut that will serve as an excellent contrast when you begin kicking asses."

"Hmm." She hadn't thought of that part, and found it appealing.

"Have your breakfast first. I've gone for a full Irish, as you'll have a long day."

She liked a full Irish, especially with another cup of coffee.

"You know, dealing with this whole school thing, getting a sense of how Grange ran it, how Rufty's running it, it's got me thinking about what you're doing with An Didean."

"What we're doing."

"I haven't done jack compared—"

"Not at all true," he interrupted. "You had input, and you gave me very important ideas on what not to do based on your experience. On what should be done."

"Well, anyway. Other than the scholarship kids, or kids from parents who saved like maniacs, Gold's a school for the privileged. Maybe more diverse economically since Rufty, but a private academy's primarily for rich kids whose parents want the status and the potential leg up into Ivy League. Nothing wrong with that, but . . ."

She thought about it as she ate. "An Didean's for kids who've probably already had some hard knocks, kids who wouldn't have a chance at the scope of the education and experience. Not just the, you know, math and science and language, all that, but the music, the arts, the nice rooms, the counseling. *Scope's* the word. It's a big scope. It's not going to take for some of them. That's not my cynical mind," she added. "It's just reality."

"I know it."

"But it will for most of them, and for a lot of the most it's going to change their reality. And I'm going to have that in mind when I talk to some of these spoiled rich kids today."

"I've met some rich kids in my time, some trust-fund

babies. Not all of them are gits or greedy bastards. Some do good works, and even if some of the some do it for image or tax breaks, the results are the same."

She considered as she munched on bacon. "Bella's going to grow up a rich kid, but with parents like Mavis and Leonardo, she'll never be a dick about it."

"She won't," Roarke agreed. "Nor will the one they have coming along."

She polished off the full Irish. "That's why I'm also going to look at the parents of the rich kids."

"The apple and the tree?"

"What about them?" she asked as she got up to dress.

"How the apple doesn't fall far from the tree."

"If you want an apple, you'd pick it before it fell." She shimmied into her underwear. "Otherwise it'll just lie there and rot."

"Not if you pick it up. That's why they call them windfalls."

She frowned at him as she buttoned on her shirt. "They call apples windfalls?"

"It's the concept of something falling at your feet, often unexpectedly."

"Somebody tossed off a roof can fall unexpectedly at your feet. How's that a windfall?"

He watched her pull on her pants. "We'll clarify by something worthwhile falling at your feet."

"The body might have a solid-gold wrist unit and pockets full of cash, so pretty worthwhile."

"Only you," he murmured. "And I obviously haven't yet had enough coffee to sort this out."

"Anyway." She strapped on her weapon harness, which Roarke thought added another brilliant contrast to the sleek and elegant cut of the shirt and pants. "One line, a parent might still be pissed about the way their precious got spanked when Rufty came on. Second line, parents who protect fuckhead kids from fuckhead behavior often promote fuckhead adults."

"That's one way to look at it."

"I've seen it go both ways. A good, solid, caring family produces a vicious killer. Vicious, violent people produce . . ." She looked over at him as she slipped into the jacket. "Cops and gazillionaires. So you could say the apple that falls from the tree might be full of worms, or it can end up making a damn good pie."

"Which ends up, quite remarkably, making an absolute truth."

She shrugged. "I could write a book of sayings that should actually *be* sayings if people didn't keep killing each other."

Sitting on the side of the bed, she pulled on her boots.

"Earrings," Roarke reminded her before she could rush out and pretend she'd forgotten about them.

"Okay, okay." She had to walk to the mirror to put them on, and wondered, as she often did, how she'd let Mavis talk her into getting holes poked in her ears.

Then she frowned at her reflection because, damn it, she could see exactly what Roarke meant. She looked competent and powerful, but not in-your-face. So when she got in somebody's face—and she suspected she would—surprise!

Of course, if she had to get physical, which happened, she'd mess up a really good suit.

"Okay, it works."

"It does, absolutely. It needs just one more thing," he added as he rose to go into his own closet.

"I'm not going to wear any more glitters." She already

had the fat diamond he'd given her on a chain under her shirt—but that was sentiment. Plus the wedding ring, which was, well, sentiment and a Marriage Rule.

The earrings were enough.

But he came out not with some shiny bracelet, but a jacket—coat. Which was it? Longer than the one she wore in spring and fall, and the exact same shade of gray as the suit.

She could smell the leather before he crossed to her.

"I've already got a . . ."

Her knee-jerk protest died because, hell, she could smell the leather. He knew she had a weakness for leather.

"You don't, but now do, have a magic topper. It's lined and treated, as your jacket and coat are."

A topper. Figured there'd be an actual word for it.

It wasn't fancy—he'd have known she'd balk at fancy. Just a simple smoke-colored deal, with pockets slit into the sides, that would probably hit about mid-thigh. The dark silver buttons—not shiny—bore the same Celtic design as her wedding ring.

So he had her on all fronts. Leather, simple, sentiment.

"Come, let's have a look." He held it up for her arms. "The pockets are nice and deep—and reinforced. And the length gives you another option."

With his hands on her shoulders, he turned her toward the mirror, stood behind her, studying the image. "Yes, it works quite well."

It felt frigging amazing. Soft as butter, light as air, but strong.

"It's great. Really great." Turning, she caught his face in her hands, kissed him. "Thanks."

"You're welcome."

She grabbed the rest of what she needed from the dresser, assigned things to various pockets. "How's Summerset going to know which jacket thing to put back on the post in the morning?"

"Consider it more magic."

"I guess I will." She walked back to him, kissed him again. "That was the goodbye kiss."

"So noted. Take care of my cop."

"She's got a magic topper."

She went out, detoured to the office for her file bag, jogged down the steps, where no jacket lay over the newel post.

Magic, she thought, in the form of Roarke buzzing Summerset.

And that was pretty decent magic.

When she got to the park, the memorial area had been staged. Numerous enlarged photos of the deceased stood on simple white easels.

Abner in his doctor's coat, in running gear, with his husband, with their family. Nothing formal, Eve noted, but warm and casual. Moments in a life.

Flowers made a riot of color in white baskets. Nothing formal there, either, or funereal. Cheerful, she'd have said.

Two tables stood under white cloths. People busily loaded food on one, drinks on the other. A number of runners, already into their morning routine, slowed, even stopped.

Eve kept her eye on them, on those who began to gather—some in running gear, some in mourning black, others in business suits.

She spotted Seldine and those she assumed were her husband, her children, with some of the family. She recognized other faces from Abner's office.

Buses glided up. She recognized Myata, the chemistry teacher, other adults lining students up as they got out.

By the time Peabody arrived, Eve estimated nearly two hundred already gathered to pay their respects.

"Wow, I didn't really expect there'd be so many who—" Peabody drew in a long, passionate breath. Whispered, reverently, "The topper."

"Shut up," Eve hissed. "Don't pet it. I mean it."

"Pet it? I want to lick it."

"Do and they'll be holding two memorials this morning."

"It's so—just so much so. Ooooh, and the suit! The boots! Holy crap, it's all—"

She broke off when Eve whipped her head around.

"Whew, nobody dressed like you are should be able to burn the flesh off somebody's bones with that look." Then she grinned. "It's the point!"

"Shut up about it or I'll crush your still smoking bones with my boot. Jesus, still more coming."

She'd stayed well back, hoping to scan faces, to judge body language. But now moved into and through the crowd. A lot of kids, she thought, from babies in those pushcart things or in backpacks to toddlers and up to teens.

She wove through to stand with Louise and Charles.

"I'm glad you came." Louise took Eve's hand to squeeze, then Peabody's. "It's a hard day, but the way they're doing it . . ."

"It shows not only that he was loved," Charles finished, "but that he loved. He cared. Delia." Charles bent down to kiss her cheek, then with the ease of a friend, flipped a finger in her hair. "I love the red."

"I'm having fun with it. How are you doing, Louise?"

"Hanging in. They asked me to give the eulogy."

Louise leaned into Charles as she spoke. "They were afraid none of the family would be able to get through it without breaking down. But I—"

"You won't," Eve interrupted. "You won't break down because you know what they need from you."

"That's what Charles said. I want you to know Martin has absolute faith in you."

"Oh hell."

"No, it's important for you to know. He understands we're friends, but he didn't have to tell me, and he did. He believes you and Peabody will do everything you can do. He said with all his years of working with educators, he can recognize whether someone has a passion for the work, the importance of it, or if it's just a job. And he recognized it's not just a job for either of you."

Louise put an arm around Eve for a quick hug before Eve could evade it. Then did the same with Peabody.

"It matters to him. It comforts him. And right now, when I'm about to speak about a really good friend, it comforts me."

"She won't ask," Charles put in, "so I will. Is there any more? Do you know any more you can tell us?"

"We have a full agenda today on the job that, no, isn't just a job. We have a lead, and we'll build on it. You know a lot of these people, so if you see anyone who doesn't fit in, or who just gives you a wrong feel, let us know."

She looked around again. "For now, we're going to move around, get a sense, pay our respects."

"We're going back to the house with the family, Kent's office staff, some of the close friends after. We'll pay attention," Charles assured her.

"I'll be speaking in a few minutes. I guess I'll have a pretty good view from up there." Louise gestured to a slim podium set between baskets of flowers. "I'll try my best."

With Peabody, Eve moved through the crowd, kept her eyes and ears open, until they paused near Rufty.

"Lieutenant, Detective. It's so kind of you to come."

Though red-rimmed, his eyes stayed dry.

"I saw you speaking with Louise and Charles. They've been such strong shoulders the last few days."

"We wanted to pay our respects, and to offer you and your family the condolences of the NYPSD."

"Thank you. Thank you very much. It's—it's time for Louise to speak. Our son started to write the eulogy, but, well, he couldn't. None of us felt we could manage it."

"It's time to sit, Daddy." His daughter took his arm. "Excuse us."

"Let's move back, Peabody. You go left, I'll go right. Find a vantage point."

Eve found her own, watching, watching as Louise began to speak, as people stopped chatting or moving around to listen.

She had a mini mic clipped to her black jacket so her voice carried. Eve didn't pay attention to the words as she studied faces, groups, but heard the tone.

Strong and soothing, and that hit the mark.

She didn't break down, and though Eve stayed for another ten minutes, no one gave her a buzz.

She signaled Peabody to meet her at the car.

"Louise did so good," Peabody said as she got into the car. "She was really loving and told sweet stories, and funny ones just when you needed one." Then she sighed. "There were so many people, and so many types. The killer could have been there, just blended in.

"It was worth a shot," she added.

"It might be worth another to go to Duran's memorial, see if we spot any faces who were here."

"Yeah. There'd maybe be some overlap, but yeah. Can I now?" Peabody asked as Eve drove toward the shuttle station. "Nobody can see."

"You can touch it, once."

"Once isn't a pet! Three times is a pet, that's minimum."

"That's not a thing. That's definitely not a thing."

But Peabody had already reached out. Stroked. "So smooth! Now you've got the black coat that says I'll kick your ass and the three asses with you, and the jacket that says I can handle whatever I need to without breaking a sweat. Now this? This says I may be classy, but you don't want to mess with me."

"Is that what it says?"

"Loud and clear. On somebody else, it would just say classy, but you put it on the cop, that's the punch."

"That's not bad. And that's three."

"I didn't think you were counting. I love my pink coat, and that color wouldn't work on me. But I can still lust for it."

"Keep your lusts to yourself. I don't plan to soft-pedal it with Grange."

"I guess that makes me good cop."

"I'm looking for you to judge her reactions and play it from there. She's used to giving orders, and being the top dog. I'm betting she's not going to much like either of us before we get started."

"Got it, and that's okay, because from everything we've learned about her so far, I don't like her before we get started. Thinking of all that, I can start off pretending to be a little awed and intimidated."

"Thanks to EDD and Rufty's reports and notes, we've

got a slew of names to hit her with. Including banging one of her teachers on school premises."

"Do you really think she . . . with a student?"

"Hard to say. Let's hope it's not so hard after we talk to her. We're doing this on her turf, so she'll think she has the advantage. She doesn't. We go from her to Kendel Hayward. We're not notifying her or asking her for an interview."

Showing her teeth, Peabody rubbed her hands together. "We ambush."

"Close enough. She's got a lot to lose if she's in any way involved. She's got a lot to lose if she knows or suspects anything and doesn't come clean. That's what we make clear."

"I don't need to pretend to be awed or intimidated."

"We pressure—from both sides—until we get a sense."

"Something could break loose. It's too bad we're going to East Washington after the cherry blossoms have peaked. I bet it's really mag."

They both spent the short trip drinking coffee and going over notes. With Peabody taking occasional happy glances out the window, and Eve avoiding same.

On the other end, a shuttle employee stood beside a car with its codes.

"It's already programmed for you, Lieutenant. When you're finished, you can leave the codes at the desk, and the car out here. We'll take care of it."

"Okay, thanks."

It was a DLE, she saw that straight off. This one in serious black with a few bits of shiny chrome—and a temp tag.

"It looks good in black." Peabody walked to the passenger side. "Still really unassuming and ordinary. And

I bet it has all the juicy bells and jazzy whistles. I didn't think the DLE was on the market yet."

Eve got in, felt the seat perfectly conform to her specifications—and as Peabody got in and sighed, Eve knew the passenger seat did the same for her partner.

"It's Roarke," Eve said simply, and engaged the codes.

Good morning, Lieutenant. Your AutoChef is fully stocked, and your personal settings already programmed. Feel free to change anything that does not suit. If you wish to proceed directly to Lester Hensen Preparatory, those directions are also pre-programmed for your convenience.

Of course they were, she thought, because Roarke. "How about Party Elegance?"

Yes, this destination is also pre-programmed, as is Kendel Hayward's residence. Simply request your chosen destination, and the GPS will engage.

"He doesn't miss a trick," Eve murmured. "Lester Hensen Prep."

Acknowledged. GPS engaged. Map displayed. Please have a safe and enjoyable drive to your selected destination.

She decided after three minutes of driving in East Washington that she seriously needed the computer prompts. Why did everything circle around? What was wrong with straight roads? Had they never heard of a damn grid?

"It's so pretty," Peabody said beside her as she opened the window for the breeze. "All the trees, the monuments, the flowers. It's solid spring here—just enough south of New York to be solidly spring. The grass is so green."

"Jesus, Peabody, the traffic's worse than New York."

It wasn't really, but she didn't *know* this traffic. And felt only sweet relief when she drove along the high iron fence that enclosed Lester Hensen Prep.

She turned in the entrance, blocked by a gate with a gatehouse and an actual gatekeeper. A droid, she noted once he stepped out.

"How can I help you?"

Eve held up her badge. "Lieutenant Dallas, Detective Peabody. We have an appointment, police business, with Headmaster Grange."

He scanned her badge, checked his log. "Please bear left at the split, proceed to visitor parking, administration. You will be met and escorted to Headmaster Grange's offices."

"Great."

The gates opened; Eve drove through.

15

The campus boasted, Eve had to admit, a lot of green. Sweeps of lawn, trees already in tender leaf. In the distance, she could see a number of kids in shiny red and white tanks and shorts running around a wide oval.

Likely track practice, she mused. She'd done some running in state school, a good outlet for her, as she could run and imagine herself going and going and going until she was free.

The buildings—brick, dignified, columned—had been built to look old, as if they'd weathered a couple of centuries. But her research tagged them as post-Urban construction.

From what she remembered of her history classes, the Urban Wars had done a number on what had been Washington, D.C. After all, it had been, and continued to be, the center of political power. Granting it statehood about the time she'd been born hadn't changed that.

She made her way to the correct parking area, took a good look at the main building with LESTER HENSEN

PREPARATORY SCHOOL carved over the massive double doors.

A fountain, separating the lot from the road that circled the building, arced water into the air. On its island, red and white flowers spelled out L H P.

"Formidable" was Peabody's impression.

"Yeah, that works."

"Well, a lot of lawyers, judges, political types matriculate here."

"That's not a plus from my viewpoint."

Peabody laughed as they got out of opposite sides of the car in a breeze appreciably warmer than the one they'd left in New York.

"Scientists and educators, writers and big business types, too," she added. "You have to have money, brains—and it probably doesn't hurt to have connections—to get in the door."

Peabody took a deep breath. "I know it's fresh mulch and plantings, but it actually smells rich."

"First time I've heard that rich smells like dirt. There's our escort."

Eve watched a woman—early forties—come out of the massive doors, walk down the white steps in black needle heels. The suit, slim, precisely knee-length, had a high collar and military cut.

She walked like a soldier, Eve thought, crisply, straight-backed. Her hair, also black, slicked back snugly into a knot and left her face with its almond eyes and dusky skin unframed.

She skirted the island, clipped along the bricked walkway.

"Lieutenant Dallas?"

"Yes."

"Ms. Mulray, assistant to the headmaster. I'll escort

you and Detective Peabody." She gestured toward the path. "Headmaster Grange is in a meeting, but has been informed of your arrival. She hopes not to keep you waiting long. I trust you had a pleasant trip from New York?"

It was rote rather than interest, so Eve answered in kind. "Uneventful."

Mulray opened one of the doors, held it open into a security station backed with thick glass. Eve glanced at the half dozen scanners, the two uniformed campus security.

"As weapons of any kind are banned on campus, you'll turn in your service weapons here."

Eve said, "No."

"I understand your reluctance, Lieutenant, but this is our policy."

"I'm going with NYPSD policy. We're police officers, your headmaster has been informed of our arrival and its purpose. The East Washington Police and Security Department has been so informed. Clearly you have armed campus security, as is protocol. We do not surrender our weapons.

"If this is a problem," Eve continued, "we can interview Headmaster Grange off campus. Say, Cop Central in New York. Detective Peabody, contact the prosecutor's office, request a warrant."

"If you'd wait here a moment." Stone-faced, Mulray stepped toward the glass. It opened for her, either signaled from a device on her person or through the security guards.

"Way to get in her face right off," Peabody said in a low voice.

"I'm betting Grange wanted to try a little power play."

"Should I really contact Reo?"

"Hold off until we see what she does next. If she wants to screw with us, we'll go talk to Hayward first, come back with a warrant."

Mulray walked back through the doors, and the doors remained open. "I apologize, Lieutenant, Detective. I misunderstood Headmaster Grange's directive. You are, of course, authorized to maintain your service weapons."

The words, clipped as her walk, didn't quite hide a simmering flash of temper. Grange had dumped responsibility and embarrassment on her assistant, Eve concluded.

And she bet it wasn't the first time.

"No problem."

Eve stepped through and into the spacious entrance hall. The founder's gold-framed portrait greeted them. Lester Hensen sat in judge's robes—looking, well, sober and judicious.

It didn't smell or feel like a school, Eve realized, and indeed she saw no signs of classrooms, or students. So administration only, she thought.

No mixing.

They passed another glass wall. Behind it a number of people worked at a number of stations. There a portrait of the founder, and one of the current headmaster, graced the walls.

Eve figured it would be like being spied on by the brass.

They moved past a number of offices, doors closed, then up a wide flight of stairs.

Light poured in from skylights, through graceful windows over the blue marble floor.

Eve wanted to ask Mulray just how much her feet and

legs ached after a day walking in heels on the unforgiving surface.

Grange's dominion also rated double doors. When Mulray opened them, pale gold carpet replaced the marble. A couple of drones who'd obviously been chatting got quickly busy at their desks.

Images of the campus graced the walls, along with another portrait of the headmistress. A waiting area held two sofas, four chairs. They kept going—and Eve saw the drones give each other a quick grin behind Mulray's back.

Through another door they entered the assistant's office. A single desk, fully ordered, a small wall screen, a couple of visitors' chairs, a recessed refreshment center.

Mulray used a swipe key to access the next door.

"The headmaster would like you to wait in her office," she began. "As I said, she hopes to be with you very shortly. In the meantime, is there anything I can get you? Some coffee perhaps?"

Eve let the question hang while she looked around the office.

About triple the size of her assistant's, it had walls done in a quiet green with a generous sitting area holding a sofa done in the same green with thin stripes that echoed the carpet. The facing chairs reversed the pattern.

On the wall, along with art of the school hung several photos of the headmistress with what Eve assumed were donors, luminaries, VIPs.

The desk with its mirror gloss angled so anyone sitting in the chair—high backed, dark gold leather—behind it had a full view of the door and the trio of graceful windows.

Mementos rather than books or work supplies on a set of floating shelves.

It had its own bath through a side door, tiled in marble with a shower and a long counter where the big-petaled lilies scenting the air sat in a crystal vase.

"Do you handle Ms. Grange's travel?"

"Dr. Grange," Mulray corrected. "Her professional travel, yes."

"Any recent trips to New York?"

"I— None that I recall."

"I'm going to need you to check on that. How long have you been Dr. Grange's assistant?"

"I wasn't aware you intended to interview me."

Eve just stared through her. "Do you need time to come up with the answer?"

"Five years." Mulray snapped it like a salute.

"You weren't assistant to the headmaster when she came to Lester Hensen?"

"I took the position in August of 2056, after my predecessor retired."

"Were you already on staff?"

"I was, as administrative assistant to the dean of students. I've been a part of Lester Hensen for nine years."

"Then you were here when Stephen Whitt was a student. He would have graduated in '53."

"We have between nine hundred and nine hundred and twenty students in this school every year. I'm afraid I couldn't possibly remember every one of them."

"Even the son of a major donor?" Eve walked over to a framed photo on the walls. "That's daddy right there."

"I'm sorry I can't help you."

"Me, too." Eve checked her wrist unit. "Why don't you see how much longer Dr. Grange intends to keep the NYPSD waiting?"

"Please have a seat." Back straight, Mulray walked out.

"I wonder how she walks around without wincing, given how stiff her neck is."

Eve smiled. "Practice. Somebody, I'm betting, was in the military before she got into administration. And somebody wasn't telling us the truth, was she, Peabody?"

"No, sir. She knew Whitt's name. You know what else?"

"Do I want to?"

"I think you'd find it interesting that the fabric on that couch, those chairs? That's going to go for about six hundred a yard."

Eve gave them another look. "That's a lot, I assume, not being updated on fabric prices."

"Figuring about fourteen yards—maybe fifteen—for the sofa, another twelve to fourteen for the chairs . . . Add some more yardage for the piping. You can do the math."

"No," Eve said, "I really can't."

"Well, you're going to hit over twenty-couple thousand, and that's before labor, before the fancy custom pillows, before the fricking sofa and chair bases you're covering. Before, because look around, the fancy interior decorator fee. Just the sofa and chairs? I'm betting forty large."

"For a sitting area in a headmaster's office? Seems . . . excessive."

"Oh yeah." Warming to the theme, Peabody gestured with both hands. "Add that desk? That's cherry-wood, the real deal, and so are those shelves. Plus, it looks custom. That's going to go for a good ten large right there."

"You can be handy, Peabody."

"I know my wood and fabric. You put it all together, with the tables, the lamps, those custom valances over the windows—and yeah, add the custom cherry frames on all the photos . . ." She poked her head in the bath. "Jesus, the Egyptian cotton towels and all that? You're cruising toward a couple hundred grand, Dallas."

"That's some decorating budget. You know what else, Peabody?"

"I don't know if I can take any more. I have wood and fabric envy."

"There's not a single book, not in here, in the assistant's area, not in the assistants to the assistant's area. Not a single file or disc on the desk, the shelves. This office is all about her."

"Yeah, it is. And even though I admire her taste, I don't like her already."

"Just channel that into looking intimidated. To start, anyway."

Eve turned as the door opened. She'd studied Grange's photo a number of times already, but she had to admit the woman was impressive. She wore her deep brown hair in short, fashionable waves, masterfully highlighted. Though she stood on the soft side of seventy, her skin glowed smooth, telling Eve she'd had masterful work there, too.

With the heels, she hit a statuesque five-eleven, with a curvy body shown to perfection in a tailored suit of blazing red.

Her eyes, a green as pale as the walls, studied Eve as coolly as she was studied.

"Lieutenant Dallas, Detective Peabody, I'm Dr. Grange. I'm sorry to keep you waiting. Teesha should have offered you coffee. Let me order some."

"We're fine. Since we're running behind schedule, we'd like to get started."

"Of course. Please have a seat."

She took the sofa, waited while Eve and Peabody took the chairs. Peabody cleared her throat.

"Dr. Grange, I'd just like to say your office is really lovely."

Grange offered Peabody a cool smile, and a flick of a glance at the pink boots. "Thank you. I find attractive and ordered surroundings conducive to focus and concentration. The responsibilities of headmaster at a school of Lester Hensen's import and reputation are many."

She crossed long legs.

"But I believe you're here to speak to me about my tenure at Theresa A. Gold Academy, in New York. I was very sorry to hear about the death of Dr. Rufty's partner."

"Husband," Eve corrected.

"Yes, of course. I believe I met Dr. Abner very briefly during the transition period. But given so much time has passed, I don't remember him well."

"Dr. Rufty replaced you at Gold."

Grange arched her eyebrows at the term *replaced*. "Dr. Rufty accepted the position of headmaster after I resigned."

"Right. And why did you resign?"

"I was offered the position as headmaster here. While Gold Academy is a very fine school, the board of trustees made me an excellent offer and opportunity here. We are a prep school for grades nine through twelve rather than an academy for kindergarten through twelve. I wanted to focus my skills on those vital years before college."

"So the move to East Washington didn't have anything to do with your divorce?"

Her eyes went steely. "I don't base my professional decisions on relationships. Reginald and I agreed our marriage had run its course, and parted without acrimony."

"Really? I got the sense he had some acrimony left over from the pile of it when he learned you were having an extramarital affair."

Now the jaw tightened. "My private business can't be relevant to the murder of the partner—husband," she corrected, "of the person who serves as headmaster of a school I left eight years ago."

"You'd be wrong about that."

"I find you very flippant, Lieutenant."

"I find you very evasive, Headmaster. Untangling your private affairs—make that business—while you lived and worked in New York is a key component of this investigation. And when you were headmaster at Gold, there was a teacher on staff, a Jay Duran. I'm sure you remember him, as Professor Duran filed complaints against you, along with some other members of the faculty."

Grange tapped a finger, tipped as red as her suit, against her thigh. "I remember Mr. Duran. He and I didn't see eye-to-eye on my methods, my policies. The fact remained, I was in charge; he was not."

"Elise Duran, Professor Duran's wife, was killed two days after Dr. Abner, and by the same method." Eve nodded slowly. "This isn't news to you."

"When the board insisted I take this meeting, I, of course, did my research. I'm sorry about Mr. Duran's wife, and for him, for his children. But he was no more than a slight irritation from years ago. I believe he left the academy in any case, not long after I did. Perhaps he also disagreed with Dr. Rufty's methods."

"He got his doctorate," Peabody said, very quietly. "He teaches at Columbia."

"How nice for him. And still, nothing to do with me."

"As primary investigator into these murders, I disagree. Both murders connect to the Gold Academy, and to you. Both victims were married to individuals who had issues with your methods and policies and sought to change them. Why don't we start with your whereabouts on the dates and times in question?"

Fury sparked, stiffening Grange's already rigid posture. "You're insulting."

"Oh, no, ma'am." Peabody played the wide-eyed conciliator. "That's not our intention. We—"

"You would come here and accuse me of murder?" Grange snapped back. "And claim you're not insulting?"

"No one's accusing you of anything yet." Eve put the emphasis on the last word to draw Grange's attention back to her. "Determining your whereabouts, corroborating same is routine. Now—"

"You will not impugn my reputation with your ridiculous *routines*." She sprang up, marched to the door. Flung it open. "Teesha, pull up my calendar and tell these women where I would have been on . . ."

Enjoying herself now, Eve somehow survived the molten stare and reeled off the dates and times.

"Yes, Dr. Grange. On the evening of April twenty-sixth you attended a dinner party at Congresswoman Delaney's home, with an arrival time of seven-thirty, a departure scheduled for ten-thirty. Mr. Lionel Kramer escorted you. On the evening of April twenty-seventh, you attended a performance of *Swan Lake* at the Kennedy Center with Mr. Gregor Finski. Curtain at eight."

"There. Satisfied?"

"I will be when we verify that data. As our investigation leads back to the period where you and Dr. Rufty transitioned, we need the name of the staff member with whom you had an affair while serving as headmaster."

"Teesha, I want Kyle Jenner from legal here asap." Grange slammed the door. "How dare you?"

"It's really easy. It's called doing my job."

"It's just we were given information," Peabody began, pulling off intimidated like a champ. "And we have to follow up."

"Gossip isn't information."

"Statements given to investigating police officers aren't gossip," Eve corrected. "Are you going to deny you engaged in sexual relationships outside your marriage to Mr. Greenwald? Think first," Eve warned, "as we have statements from Mr. Greenwald as well as others regarding this. It was part of Mr. Greenwald's statement," Eve continued, "that your marriage included a mutual agreement that either or both of you could engage in sexual relationships outside the marriage as long as you maintained discretion. Do you dispute that?"

"I do not. Why would I?" Haughty, not bothering to hide contempt, Grange took her seat again.

"A few months before you left Gold, your ex-husband received compromising photographs of you with an unknown . . . partner. Which shoots discretion all to hell. In addition, you were engaged in sexual activities with a teacher at Gold, inside the school, when another teacher walked in. Oops."

"I was fending off an advance, and the incident was misinterpreted."

"Fine. I need names."

Now Grange sat back, sent Eve a look simmering

with that contempt, and with smugness. "If you can recall the name of everyone you've had a sexual encounter
with, I'm sorry for you."

"If you judge your worth by the number of people
who've banged you, I'm sorry for you. But I don't need
all the names. Start with the name of the teacher—the
one you were 'fending off.' I'm sure you remember that
name, just as you remember the name of the one who
walked in."

She let out a sigh. "It was a misunderstanding on the
part of both instructors. The first who misread my interest
in his work as something more personal, and the second
who jumped to erroneous conclusions."

"Names."

"Van Pierson who taught history, middle grades. I
believe he resigned shortly after I left. I'm afraid I don't
know where he went or his position or location at this
time. Wyatt Yin, who was young, excitable, and problematic. I believe I heard he decided the rigors of private
education weren't for him after all, and opted to move
into public education."

"Decided that all on his own?"

"That is my recollection. Now, if that's all."

"Any other names you can remember? A discarded
lover often looks for payback."

"If you're intimating I'm in some sort of jeopardy—"

"I'm intimating nothing. I'm saying, very clearly,
two people are dead, loved ones of two people some
might see as responsible for you leaving Gold and New
York—and this lover. We've concluded that these murders spring from that."

"You conclude? Really?" Grange recrossed her legs,
twisted her lips into a sneer. "You conclude I'm somehow
indirectly responsible for two murders because I exercise

my sexual freedom? I take considerable issue with your conclusions, and the hypotheses upon which they're based. I left Gold eight years ago, cut all ties with the school, with New York. And you, somehow, believe that after eight years someone I may have slept with is punishing those who disagreed with my administrative methods."

Eve let the silence hang a moment. "In a nutshell."

On a look—very deliberate—of smug pity, Grange brushed at a wave of her hair. "You had a state-based education, correct, Lieutenant?"

"I did."

"Then you had, sadly, a bare-bones, limited education. It's an unfortunate foundation for true critical thinking."

"You think?" Eve said mildly.

"One rarely finds the brightest minds with such an educational disadvantage. And you, Detective? You were raised and educated by Free-Agers?"

"That's right."

"A pity, and a shame your parents didn't afford you a real education. Being raised in the foster system didn't allow Lieutenant Dallas much choice regarding her limitations, but your parents, Detective? How foolish and selfish of them to put their own odd lifestyle ahead of the welfare of their children. Still, considering your disadvantages, I suppose you've both made the best possible career choice by becoming police officers."

Eve started to speak, but Peabody jumped to her feet.

"You arrogant, entitled, condescending snob. You think your Ph.D. makes you better? I'll tell you what I learned in my Free-Ager education. Besides all you teach in a high-priced tomb like this, I learned to plant and harvest, to cook, to weave, to sew. I learned woodworking, mechanics. I learned about compassion and tolerance and kindness."

"You will watch your tone in my office."

"No, I won't. I'm not one of your students or underlings, I'm a New York City police detective, and a New York City cop knows a lying sack when she sees one. So don't think you're going to sit there and insult my family, my vocation, or my lieutenant. You aren't worthy to wipe the boots she'll kick your ass with."

When Grange pushed to her feet, so did Eve. And angled between them. "Peabody."

"I will have your badge!"

"Oh yeah." Now Peabody sneered. "Try it, sister."

"Detective Peabody!" Eve added a little elbow poke. "Take a walk. Take a walk, now, Detective."

With considerable effort, Peabody stepped back. "Yes, sir."

When Peabody stalked out, Grange turned on Eve. "If you can't control your subordinates any better than that—"

"Detective Peabody is my partner, and you're going to be careful, really careful, with what you say about my partner."

"I want you out of my office and off campus, immediately."

"No problem. I'll be sure to address your lack of cooperation in a murder investigation with your board of trustees. I'm sure they'll be interested," Eve said as she started for the door. "Like they're going to be interested in the fact I can and will confirm you were—what was it?—'engaging in your sexual freedom,' on school grounds, with subordinates. And quite possibly with parents—like, oh, Brent Whitt over there. Maybe students who struck your fancy when you weren't ignoring students who didn't strike your fancy when they were being bullied, threatened, and kicked around."

"You're no threat to me."

"Keep thinking that, because this state-educated cop also went to the NYPSD Academy, and once on the force was trained by the best damn investigator in the department. Here's a tip, Dr. Grange. You may want to consider retirement. Because I'm coming for you."

She opened the door, kept it open so her words would carry out. "Oh, one more tip? I wouldn't open any packages anytime soon. Discarded lovers can turn, and when they do, it gets ugly."

She stepped out, closed the door.

Mulray sat absolutely still, eyes straight ahead.

"Brent Whitt," she said, because Grange had gone just as still when Eve mentioned the name. "You think about that. Think about how you work for a liar who doesn't care about anybody—that would sure as hell include you—as long as she comes out on top."

Eve moved into the outer office, where both women sat with their mouths open and watched her cross to the door with wide, wide eyes.

As she continued, made the turn out, she watched a man stride briskly toward the headmaster's office in his dark suit and shiny shoes.

The lawyer, Eve thought as she kept going. Well, Grange would need one, but Eve doubted if she'd end up with one representing the school.

When she stepped out, she saw Peabody pacing the visitor's lot. Not clumping now, but stomping. And since every few seconds, Peabody waved her arms, shook a fist, Eve imagined her partner replayed the scene in Grange's office—and added fresh, pithy things she should have said.

Very much still pissed, Eve concluded as she went down the stairs, moved along the walkway.

"So," Eve began, "I think your intimidated pretense needs some work."

"I'm sorry, okay?"

She didn't sound the least bit sorry.

"I couldn't maintain, not when she's taking swipes at my family. Bad enough she started on you, but sure, you can handle yourself, but nobody gets away with saying shit like that about my parents, about the job, either. Nobody."

Eve leaned back against the hood of the car, let Peabody stomp and rant.

"I mean, I don't give a jumping *damn* if some asshole on the street calls me whatever, or some fucker in the box goes after me that way. But not my parents, making them sound like they, what, mistreated me or something. Like they're idiots. And like you're substandard because you didn't go to some fancy school like this. Bullshit on that. Just bullshit."

Eve waited a few seconds. "Are you done yet?"

"I guess."

"Okay. We're going to interview Hayward. While I'm driving, you can start the report of this interview for Whitney."

"Oh God, the commander." After squeezing her eyes shut, Peabody opened them toward heaven. "He's going to give me such a slap."

"Worry about that later. Once we're finished here, we'll complete the report on the shuttle home, send it to Whitney. So he can, in turn, notify the board of trustees that Headmaster Grange is a POI in our investigation, was not cooperative, and we have evidence that during her tenure at Gold she engaged in sexual congress, on

school grounds, with a subordinate. We have evidence
she routinely engaged in sexual activities outside her
marriage and so on."

"We're going to do that?"

"Oh yeah, we are. We're going to hit her board with
the statements on bullying, cheating, sex, the works."

"I'm starting to feel better."

"Good, get in, get started." Eve slid behind the wheel.
"Because I intend to kick her ass with the boots she's
not worthy to wipe."

Peabody gave a sheepish chuckle. "That was actually
a pretty good one."

"I liked it," Eve said, and drove out of the lot.

16

Kendel Hayward's showroom and offices were a pretty, peppy place with a pretty, peppy staff. It was, Eve thought, like being surrounded by a bunch of former cheerleaders.

Fortunately for Eve's mental health, the head cheerleader currently in charge told her Kendel had appointments at home until three, when she needed to be on-site to supervise a load-in.

Still she had to drag Peabody away from a display of sample napkins of various colors, sizes, patterns.

"It's a nice place," Peabody said as they got back into the car. "Cheerful, energetic."

"That kind of cheerful energy gives me a headache. Who goes into business to plan other people's parties anyway? And why can't you just get pizza and beer?"

"Sometimes you want the fancy."

"Not if you're sane. There was a whole deal in there for kids' parties. Jesus, buy a cake, some kid food, have alcoholic beverages for the adults. Done."

Since she was still thinking of her family, Peabody couldn't really disagree. She remembered her own kid parties. They didn't buy a cake. Somebody made it, and the kid food, and, yeah, even the adult beverages.

Good times.

Still . . .

"I think if you like parties—which definitely excludes you—planning them would be fun. Hayward's probably good at it—like I said, cheerful place."

"For all we know, Hayward lazes around her house, goes out to fancy lunches, gets her nails done or whatever while that bunch of obsessively peppy types do all the work."

"That could be true. So . . . I'm coming to the part of the report where I didn't maintain."

"We'll pick it up from there on the shuttle. This is Hayward's street."

Big, important houses stood well back from the road at the end of long drives—curved ones, circular ones, paved ones. Big, important trees with their leaves unfurled to a tender spring green spread or speared.

Ornamental shrubs showed hazes or open pops of color while lawns rolled, uniformly trimmed and green.

Eve turned into Hayward's drive, paved in earthy brown hexagons, circled around an island shrubbery centered by a small tree with fountaining branches already blooming snowy white.

The house itself stood two stories with generous and gleaming windows in quiet brown brick, with stone terraces graced with dark bronze railings. A single story, almost entirely glass, shot off the left side. A garage with reflective doors shot off the other.

Eve parked in front of the deep portico at the entrance.

As she got out, a dog about the size of a football covered in puffy white fur raced around the glass-walled side of the house to bark like a maniac.

Since Eve figured she could have drop-kicked the dog a solid twenty yards through the goalposts, she just gave it a cool stare.

Peabody, in contrast, went into gooey mode.

"Oh, aren't you cute? Aren't you the cutest little thing? It's okay, baby. What's your name, baby?"

"If it tells you, I'll strip naked and dance the hula right here."

"Jeez, then I really wish she would." Peabody crouched and made kissy noises.

The dog continued to bark, from a safe distance, but the ferocity eased. And it cocked its head as if considering its next move.

"You know, even dogs that size have teeth," Eve pointed out. "Sharp little teeth."

"She doesn't bite!" A woman ran around the house, long, lustrous ponytail swinging. "Quiet, Lulu!"

Lulu gave one last piping bark, then subsided. Kendel Hayward, looking like the picture-perfect upperclass suburbanite in black yoga pants, pink tennis shoes, and a thin white cardigan over a pink sports tank, scooped the dog up.

"We were just out back. She must've heard your car." Kendel gave Lulu a quick nuzzle. "She thinks she's a guard dog," she added with a smile. "Can I help you?"

"Lieutenant Dallas, Detective Peabody, New York City Police and Security Department." At the words, at the badge Eve held up, the smile on Kendel's face faded.

"Is something wrong?"

"We're investigating two homicides in New York

connected to Theresa A. Gold Academy. We'd like to ask you some questions."

"TAG? I don't understand."

"We'll explain. Can we come in?"

"I . . ." Kendel glanced at the house, clutched the dog a little tighter. "Yes, I guess so. I graduated from there, but that was eight years ago. I've lived in East Washington for nearly five years. I don't really know what I can tell you."

But she walked toward the house, up the two steps to the portico, used the palm plate to unlock the door.

The atrium entrance soared with a curve of staircase to the right, a small sitting room to the left. A trio of prints—Eve recognized Parisian street scenes—graced the wall over the plush little two-seater sofa.

A central table held a pale green vase of fresh spring flowers.

She led the way back, into a large great room, with conversation areas in shades of blue, green, gray. The wall of glass doors at the back stood open to the spring air.

"Actually, would you mind if we sat out on the patio? Lulu really needs some outdoor time, and even though we have the invisible fence, I like to keep an eye on her."

"That's fine."

"She's really adorable," Peabody commented.

"She's so sweet. My fiancé gave her to me for my birthday last summer."

When she put Lulu down on the smooth patio stones, the dog raced off for a little red ball. Came back, dropped it at Peabody's feet.

"Does she want me to throw it?"

"Yeah, but I warn you, she can keep it up for an hour."

"That's all right." Happy to oblige, Peabody tossed the ball.

"I was doing some work out here." Kendel picked up a tablet, a tall glass, a folder. "I'll just put this inside. I just made a pitcher of lemonade if you'd like some."

Give her a minute to settle, Eve thought, and said, "That'd be great."

The yard, where Peabody threw the ball, the dog chased the ball, held more important trees, more pretty shrubs and flowers, a couple of benches placed in strategic spots.

The patio boasted one of those outdoor kitchens under a vine-smothered pergola, another entertainment area with sofas most people would have been thrilled to place in their living rooms, deep chairs, tables.

Eve settled at the table where Kendel had worked, a kind of coffee in the morning, cocktails in the evening setup.

Kendel came back with a tray—glass pitcher with slices of actual lemon swimming in lemonade, a trio of tall glasses filled with ice. And a glass plate of what Eve thought of as girl cookies.

Small, thin, golden, and glossy.

After setting down the tray, Kendel smiled as the dog chased the ball. "Well, I did warn her. I'm nervous." She sat. "I think anyone would be when police come to the door, especially about murder."

"You graduated from Gold, but you haven't heard about the murders?"

"I've been buried in work the last couple weeks. And to tell you the truth—might as well start out that way—I've worked really hard to put my years at TAG behind me."

"Bad experience?"

"You could say that." Kendel poured out the drinks. Ice crackled in the glasses. "I brought most of it on myself. Can you tell me who was killed? I don't think I'd know any of the students—I didn't have much to do with the younger ones. But I might remember some of the teachers."

"Do you remember Dr. Rufty?"

Kendel let out a gasp, pressed a fist to her chest. "Oh no. No. He's dead?"

"Not him. His husband."

"Oh. I don't think I knew his husband. I might've, but . . . I'm so sorry. Dr. Rufty gave me a second chance. I didn't want it, didn't appreciate it—not then anyway—but he gave it."

"A chance for what?"

"Not to screw up my entire life," she said as Peabody came back. "I was doing a good job of it up until then."

Peabody picked up the dog, sat, ruffled white fur.

"She likes you."

"It's mutual."

"How were you screwing up your life?" Eve asked.

"Bad choices, bad behavior, illegals, drinking, doing whatever I could to make those less popular suffer. I just reveled in being mean, spiteful, disruptive, destructive. I had rich parents, friends who had rich parents, and we got away with—I was going to say murder. We didn't actually kill anyone, but we hurt plenty. When Dr. Rufty took over, it was come to Jesus."

"You resented it?"

"At the time? You bet I did. And my parents. I'd been able to get away with that metaphorical murder because they didn't know. My grades stayed reasonable—better than, as I pressured smarter kids to do the work. They thought my boyfriend at the time was great. Because he knew how to play the game. We all did."

"Headmaster Grange knew about your behavior?"

"Sure she did. And why should I have changed it when there were no consequences? Then she left, Dr. Rufty came in. And boy, there were consequences."

"Such as?"

"Detention, suspension—no more grading on a curve that had anything to do with how much my parents donated. In any case, once he had a conference with my parents, the hammer came down. I could straighten up, stay out of trouble, or I could be shipped off to a private girls' school in England. I hurt them, my parents, when they were going through a hard time of their own. Maybe because they were. Anyway, the mask got ripped off, and they saw I'd been a liar and a cheat, a bully and a brat. I was basically under house arrest for the rest of the year."

She stared into her glass. "God, I haven't thought of all that for so long. It's like another lifetime. I just don't know how that lifetime has anything to do with Dr. Rufty's husband."

"Do you remember Jay Duran?"

"I don't think so."

"He taught language arts," Peabody put in. "You had him in your junior and senior years."

"Oh, Mr. Duran—I don't think I ever knew his first name. Yes, I remember him, mostly because his were the only classes I actually liked." She added a quick, self-deprecating smile. "Of course, I couldn't let on I enjoyed them, got anything out of them, or I'd lose face. What happened?"

"His wife was murdered."

Her eyes, direct on Eve's, radiated distress, and bafflement. "I don't understand. I just don't understand. It's awful, it's terrible, but I don't understand."

"We're pursuing a line of inquiry. Who do you know from the transition period—Grange to Rufty—who would have carried a grudge for those consequences you spoke of?"

"God, probably half the school. No, not that much," she corrected. "But plenty. Not just students, but some of the teachers, too, and plenty of the parents, I think. He changed the status quo—do you know what I mean?"

"Yes."

"We were used to having our way, and that stopped. A lot of the upperclassmen planned to go on to Ivy Leagues, and Rufty's Rules—that's what we called them—could have screwed with that. They probably did for some, I don't know. Most of my group shattered—parents took their kids out, or did like mine and put the chains on."

"Do you, or did you, keep in touch with that group?"

"From school?" Kendel let out a short laugh. "No. At first because I couldn't. My parents took my 'link—can you imagine the horror of being a teenage girl without access to a 'link? It was hell. And they blocked communication from all my devices. Schoolwork only—which they checked. Constantly. I hated it, hated them. But I toed the line because they weren't bluffing about that boarding school. I've never seen my father so angry, or my mother so horrified. Not before, not since."

"After you got communication access again?"

"By then, I was done with it. I didn't like school—I was never a great student—but I liked the peace. I liked not having to constantly think of something outrageous to do. I liked getting a decent grade on a project I'd actually done myself."

Pausing, she studied her lemonade. "I owe my parents for that, and Dr. Rufty, and teachers like Mr. Duran. Second chances," she said, looking back at Eve before she looked around her pretty yard.

"I'm here because of them. Do you know what I mean when a situation or a time can feel like the end of your world, then somehow becomes the making of it, and you?"

"Yeah." Eve nodded. "I do. What did you do after you graduated?"

"I went off to college. I can't say I shined there, but it was a clean slate. I promised my parents I'd give it two years, and I did. Then I came home, started doing what I realized I really wanted to do. Work with my mom on the business. I'm good at parties, at planning them, at figuring out what the client wants and needs. It meant that I didn't look back on those years."

Eve turned another angle. "Your fiancé has political ambitions, and his mother may run for president—that's the rumor."

"It is." And now she showed Eve a damn good poker face.

"You were a teenager, true, but previous bad acts often get unearthed and used, politically."

"Tell me about it. I told Merritt the works when we got serious. And we sat down with his parents. Patience is a great woman, and she'll be an amazing president if she chooses to run. She knows it all, or all I could remember. She said she saw me as a case study in early redemption. That's who she is. I turned my life around. I'll hate if what I did at fifteen, sixteen, seventeen hurts

Merritt or Patience in any way. But I turned it around. I can't change what I did, only what I do."

"Do you remember Marshall Cosner?"

"Marsh?" On an exhale, Kendel shook her head. "Now, that's a ghost from the past. He was one of our gang—because a gang's what we were for a while. He got pulled out—or kicked out, I can't remember. I might not have known which. If I was a shaky student, Marsh was worse."

She smiled when she said it. "He was fun—the kind of fun I was looking for back then. Always good for a laugh. And a score. He could always come up with illegals, booze, an empty house to play in. What did we call him?" She closed her eyes a minute. "The Facilitator. God, we thought we were so clever."

"When's the last time you saw him, spoke to him?"

"Years. Ah, I remember a party at his place—his parents were out of town—right after Dr. Rufty came on as headmaster. We were all celebrating, all planning how we were going to slay him and his idiot rules. All drunk or stoned," she added. "I'm not sure I saw him after that. I must have, but I know it wasn't more than a couple days after the party, he was gone. That was right before my parents came in to talk to Rufty after I got suspended."

"Stephen Whitt."

"Steve? God, God, sexy Steve, another ghost. He was my guy back then. I was madly in love with him, the way you are in high school. He got pulled, too—maybe the same day as Marsh. I think it might've been. Before the hammer came down on me, we talked about taking off together. He would come into some of his trust fund when he turned eighteen, and he was nearly there. We'd just blow."

She closed her eyes. "So careless. So thoughtless, both of us. I might've done it, too, just run off with him, because teenage love, and it sounded exciting. But he got shipped off—I think to some school down south. I'm not sure. Everything was jumbled because, you know, my life was simply over. And I couldn't reach him because no 'link, no communications. I pined for a few weeks. And that was that."

"So you haven't communicated with him, either?"

"Not since the hammer dropped. Well—God, I'd forgotten—he tried to reach me once. Right after it all came down. Tagged a mutual friend, wanted me to use her 'link to talk, to make plans for that taking off."

"And?"

"I had to decide, then and there. If I got caught, boarding school. I wanted to talk to him, but . . . I told the friend—I can't remember her name—to tell him I couldn't. He called me—according to the friend . . . Annie, Allie? Doesn't matter."

She waved it away, took a sip of lemonade. Breathed out. "He called me a stupid, spineless cunt. Steve had a temper when denied. I cried myself to sleep over that."

"Did he ever contact you again?"

"Once Steve wrote you off, you were off. The end." She took a cookie, smiled a little before she nibbled at it. "Those days are long over, you know? For all of us. I mean, any of the people I hung with back then could've contacted me in the last few years. But none of them have."

"And you haven't contacted or tried to contact any of them."

"No. I put that whole era, you could say, behind me. I'm sure as hell not interested in a reunion. I'm going to get married in the fall to a man I love, a really good man. My parents are proud of me. I'm proud of myself. Why go back there?"

Eve tried a few more names, prodding at Kendel's memory. Some she remembered, some she didn't, or not well enough to add anything.

"We appreciate your time, Ms. Hayward, and your candor."

"Lie, and you have to keep lying. I'm living proof that you'll eventually get caught, and the lies make it worse. We were bad kids, Lieutenant Dallas, but we were kids. I honestly can't think of anyone who'd do something like this, not even back then when we looked for trouble. I don't know anyone who'd commit murder over something from high school."

I think you do, Eve mused as Kendel walked them back to the car. You just don't realize it.

Eve took a big gulp of New York after the shuttle landed. Once behind the wheel in a city that made sense, everything smoothed out.

"Let's jump into the big, fancy nest of lawyers," she decided, "and talk to Marshall Cosner."

"He sounds like he's still kind of a dick," Peabody commented as she programmed the address. "Hayward seems like she's gotten her life together, professionally, personally. But all the reports on Cosner point to him still cruising on his family name and money."

"Cruising isn't a motive for murder. Neither is being a dick," Eve added as she enthusiastically joined the traffic wars. "But you add those to possible continued illegals use, a simmering grudge over being yanked away from his gang of friends, a failure to reach family expectations, and maybe."

She did a quick bob-and-weave with a Rapid Cab and a sedan, then punched through the intersection. "And we could add one more. Both Rufty and Duran had built happy, satisfying lives, enjoyed long-term marital relationships, had a family that loved and admired them. It's the sort of thing that could stick in your craw if you remain an entitled, unaccomplished, addicted dick."

"Huh. I hadn't thought of that angle, but you're right. Both targets had accomplished a lot, going with personally and professionally again. Nothing on Cosner's data shows any on either level. So it could be envy, coupled with: Why should they have it all when they're part of the reason I don't?"

"We can poke at that, see how sore the spot is."

Eve hunted up parking, waited on the sidewalk for Peabody and the two-block walk.

"I can do a probability on the next target, factoring those elements in. There's bound to be another target."

Eve nodded. "Any staff member listed in the notes and records of lodging a complaint on Grange. The unidentified lover in the photos—as killer or target—the guy she was banging, if different from the one in the photos, when she got caught, and the one who caught her. All potentials."

Eve made the turn at the corner while a group of office types flowed by, nattering on their headsets.

She pushed through the doors of the steel-and-glass tower where Cosner's family headquartered their firm, crossed the green-and-white-marble checkerboard floor to the security sign-in. "NYPSD. Marshall Cosner."

Security gave her badge a look that said he didn't care either way. "Cosner is twenty-one through twenty-three. Marshall Cosner has his office on twenty-one."

Easy enough, she thought, and walked to the elevators in a lobby that struck her as fiercely dignified. No frills, no flowers, no moving maps or ornate statuary.

People streamed off the elevators, and she and Peabody streamed on with still others for the stop-and-go ride up.

When the elevator opened on twenty-one, they walked into another dignified lobby. The frills here, if they qualified, hit low-key. The wide, sternly black reception counter was manned by two bright-looking twenty-somethings who flanked a woman who might have held her station for decades.

Straight-backed, deep-cushioned chairs—more black—formed a waiting area where no one currently waited.

Eve opted for experience, and walked to the woman with a snowy cap of hair, deep red nails, and a dark suit relieved from austerity by a peacock pin on the lapel.

"Lieutenant Dallas, Detective Peabody, NYPSD. We need to speak with Marshall Cosner."

If the badge and request surprised her, Ms. Experience didn't show it. "Do you have an appointment with Mr. Cosner?"

"No. If he's not currently available, we can arrange one. At Cop Central."

She met Eve's eyes directly, and unless Eve missed the mark, she caught just a hint of amused disdain. "If you'd wait a moment, I'll check Mr. Cosner's availability."

Instead of using the inter-office 'link or her headset, the woman rose, walked to the side door, disappeared through it.

One moment became two, then three, but eventually

she came back out with a woman in a short, snug red suit that strained against generous breasts.

This one looked barely legal and had about a yard of tousled waves in guinea gold.

The older woman glided back to her station with the slightest of smirks while the blonde picked her way toward Eve and Peabody on towering red heels.

"I'm Mr. Cosner's assistant." Her voice sounded like a woman who'd just had energetic sex and was ready for a snuggle. "He'll see you now. You can come with me."

Eve followed, mildly amazed anyone could, well, mince along and still have hips that swayed like a pendulum. It had to be an innate talent.

They moved past cubes.

"Mr. Cosner is very busy this afternoon," the assistant added as they moved past a few small offices. "But he has a lot of respect for . . . civil servants," she finished, obviously digging up the term assigned to her.

The family might have stuck Cosner on the lowest rung of the law firm, but he still rated a corner office.

He had the door open so as to be seen behind his fancy desk, in front of his corner window, pretending to talk on his 'link.

The way he'd angled himself, Eve could actually see the blank display screen.

He had a smooth shock of deep blond hair, perfectly streaked as if the sun had threaded its fingers through it, and the warmly gilded tan of a man who might have spent his winter sailing a yacht in the South Seas.

His eyes, a bold blue, scowled below brows drawn sternly together. The disapproving mouth completed the image of an important man on an important call.

"I need that completed before the end of the business day. No excuses. I have another meeting."

He set the 'link down abruptly, and the scowl became a bright, charming smile as he rose.

"This is an honor!" He came around the desk, hand extended, a leanly built man in a perfectly tailored charcoal suit, crisp shirt the same blue as his eyes, a tie of muted stripes that added hints of burgundy.

"The famous Eve Dallas! Muffy, get us some cappuccinos while Lieutenant Dallas and her stalwart partner tell me what brings them here today. Please, please, have a seat."

Eve decided to let it play out, sat in one of the navy leather visitors' chairs.

She noted though he reigned in a corner office, it was still on the small side. The wall shelves held not law paraphernalia but awards and trophies—golf, tennis. He took a seat behind the desk that, while polished and important, held no sign of any work in progress.

No framed law degree because he didn't actually have one as yet.

"I followed the Icove case very closely, so of course, I read the book, saw the vid. Fascinating—horrifying, of course, but fascinating. More so as my family actually knew the Drs. Icove. Or I should say, thought they knew the Icoves. The masks people wear."

He shook his head as Muffy picked her way back with a tray.

Eve wondered if her parents had any idea when naming her she'd reflect the name as a walking cliché for a side piece.

"Thank you, Muffy. Be sure to shift my next appointment."

"You don't— Oh, yes, Mr. Cosner. Right away."

She picked her way back out, shut the door.

"Now." Cosner beamed another smile. "What can I do for you?"

"You can start by telling us where you were on the nights of April twenty-seventh and April twenty-ninth, between nine-thirty and eleven."

His smile didn't fade. It just froze. "I'm sorry, what?"

"We're investigating the murders of Kent Abner and Elise Duran. Your name has come up in the course of our investigation."

She took a moment, sampled the cappuccino. "Good coffee," she said, and waited.

17

"This is crazy. My name came up? I don't know the people you're talking about. How did my name come up?"

"You attended the Theresa A. Gold Academy?"

"Yes, years ago. What does that have to do with anything?"

"I take it you're not following this case closely, as you were the Icove investigation. The victims were both spouses of people I think you'd remember. Dr. Rufty, who replaced Headmaster Grange at Gold before your parents sent you to boarding school, and Jay Duran. He taught you language arts in your final term there, and creative writing the years before."

Nerves just poured off him.

"I hardly remember the names of all the teachers I've had in my life. And Rufty—he was only headmaster for a couple weeks before I left Gold. I simply don't remember them, or their spouses. Why should I?"

Lying, Eve thought. Lying badly over something inconsequential.

"Because they had a part in you being shipped off to Vermont, a boarding school, and away from the circle of—we'll call them friends—you'd formed for bullying, cheating, disrupting. Then there were the parties, with underage drinking, with illegals."

"That's absolute nonsense and exaggeration! My parents felt I would benefit from a finishing term at a very prestigious school out of state. This is ancient history, and it's insulting to have you come here accusing me of cheating or bullying or—"

"Miguel Rodriges."

"I have no idea who that is."

"Just one of the many you and your friends pressured, intimidated to do your schoolwork."

His eyes looked everywhere but at Eve. "That's absurd and untrue."

"That's documented, Mr. Cosner. Why don't we go back to your whereabouts on the nights in question?"

"I don't have to tell you a damn thing." He rose. "Now, you can leave on your own, or I'll have security escort you."

"If you don't want to answer, that's your right. You may want to engage an attorney—particularly since you've yet to earn your law degree—when we have you brought into Central for formal interview."

"You can't compel me to—"

Now Eve rose. "Watch me, and believe me when I tell you your old family friends the Icoves thought the same, and were proven wrong."

"Just wait. Just wait." He sat, gestured for her to do the same. "There's no need for this animosity. You simply took me by surprise. I'm not used to having the police accuse me of crimes."

"You've had some knocks, so you should be. You used and trafficked in illegals."

"I was young and foolish," he said stiffly. "Those days are over."

He reached in his inside pocket, drew out a memo book. "It's simple enough to check where I was on those dates. On the first," he continued as he scrolled through, "I attended a dinner party with a number of friends."

"Names," Eve said crisply. "Contacts."

"Oh for . . ." But as he reeled them off, Peabody noted them down.

"On the second evening I went to a club in the company of friends."

Peabody dutifully noted those names, and marked the considerable overlap.

"If that's all—"

"It's not," Eve interrupted. "We'll verify your alibis."

Jutting up his chin didn't stop the flood of nerves.

"I don't appreciate that term. I've done nothing, and therefore don't need an alibi."

"We'll verify," Eve said easily. "In the meantime, we're aware you and your circle caused considerable trouble during your years at Gold during Headmaster Grange's tenure. Dr. Rufty changed all that. Suddenly, there were consequences."

"He was a fucking tyrant," Cosner exploded. "Storming in there with his new rules, new agenda. He suspended a good third of the junior and senior classes, installed in-school detention, took the word of weasels there on *our* dime through scholarships over those of us whose families gave generously to keep that school running."

Button pushed, Eve thought.

"So you do remember him."

"I remember he walked in there like he owned the place. I know if my parents hadn't had the good sense to pull me out of there, I might not have gotten into law school because of his tyranny and arrogance. He actually accused me of cheating! And a handful of the substandard instructors, who begrudged the fact my family had wealth and prominence and they were nothing, made wild, baseless accusations."

"Such as Jay Duran. He made those accusations, he filed complaints against Headmaster Grange for allowing you and your friends a kind of free rein."

"Headmaster Grange understood a few . . . hijinks shouldn't affect a teenager's future."

"Hijinks? Is that your word for drinking and using illegals on school property, for cheating, for physical assault, for using intimidation tactics to coerce other students to help you cheat?"

Though he flicked his fingers dismissively, Eve saw the faintest line of sweat over his top lip. "I'd like to see the teen who doesn't occasionally sneak alcohol or experiment with illegals."

"So in your opinion, breaking the law is just teenage hijinks. Good to know. It sounds as if you hold a grudge against Rufty and those 'substandard' instructors."

"They mean nothing to me. Not then, not now. I'm a wealthy man from a prominent and respected family. I'm part of a prominent and respected law firm, one of the top firms in the city."

"I don't see a law degree on your wall, Mr. Cosner."

He flushed, a combination of temper and embarrassment. "I'm taking a gap year to gain practical experience. Not that it's any of your business."

"You learned how to cook illegals, had your own setup. It seems you did better there than you had in school—chemistry-wise."

"Those charges were dropped."

"You had to be taught by someone, had to get the supplies and equipment from somewhere. You can help yourself by giving us those names."

"Those charges were dropped," he repeated. "I have nothing more to say about them."

"You may want to rethink that." Eve rose again. "Because we're digging in, and we'll find the answers we need with or without your cooperation. Thanks for the coffee."

With Peabody, she started for the door. "Oh, and the next time you want to pretend to be on the 'link, being important?" She glanced back. "At least turn it on."

When they got into the elevator for the ride down, Peabody turned to Eve. "I know one thing for certain about Cosner."

"What one thing would that be?"

"He's a lying SOS."

"Oh yeah. He is that. And for somebody who's been a lying SOS most if not all of his life, he really sucks at it."

"Right, that makes two things I know for certain about him."

Eve shifted when the elevator stopped to let more people on. "The lying's autopilot with him, and not very skilled. He lies about the obvious and inconsequential, so by the time he gets to the big stuff it's just red-faced blather."

A woman in a business suit and sunshades glanced at Eve. "Sounds like my ex-husband. Some people plan a lie. Others?" she continued as the doors opened to let yet more people on. "It's involuntary instinct, like breathing."

"Tell me about it," someone else piped up. "I dated this guy once who'd lie if you asked him his name. He just couldn't help himself."

One of the new passengers let out a snort. "It's worse when they believe the lie—convince themselves it's true, keep beating you over the head with it until you start wondering if you're the one who's crazy."

"They all sound like my ex," the first woman commented as the doors opened on the lobby level.

"He gets around," Eve said, and heard the woman laugh as she and Peabody strode to the doors.

"That was interesting," Peabody decided as they walked back to the car. "Lying liars unite strangers in elevator. Dateline New York."

"Everyone knows at least one lying sack."

"That's really true. I'll check his alibis to see if they were a crock, too. Being such a crappy liar, he's never going to be even a halfway decent lawyer."

"Add deeply stupid. He's sitting at a fancy desk with a slew of lawyers all around—plus he has the family name—and he doesn't stop the interview, pull in a lawyer to run interference?"

"That makes three. A lying sack who can't lie worth crap, and a complete schmuck."

"I'll give you all three," Eve agreed. "The fact is, he'd have been better off agreeing to meet at Central, with his legal rep. Take time to prepare," Eve continued when they reached the car. "Have a seasoned mouthpiece with him. So a deeply stupid, terminally arrogant lying SOS schmuck."

Peabody settled into the passenger seat. "A killer?"

"Yet to be determined. Plug in Whitt's location, and

let's finish this up. Cosner's got the grudge going." Eve
watched for an opening in traffic, zipped out. "Rufty
equals tyrant because he laid down rules, enacted consequences. Any kids at Gold on scholarships? Just didn't
belong and deserved whatever they got. Cooking and
trafficking in illegals, pounding on some other kids?
Youthful indiscretions. Killing people responsible, in
his twisted, fucked-up mind, could be justified payback."

"You like him for it?"

"I like his arrogance for it, and the strong possibility he has some knowledge and skill with chemicals,
very likely has connections who have more. He is not,
remotely, rehabilitated when it comes to illegals."

"You think he's still using?"

"Why would he stop? He's entitled to do whatever the
hell he wants, isn't he? Fuck the law, the law's for suck-
ers and poor people. You run down the names he gave
you as alibis, and I'll bet you a month's pay the bulk of
them will have illegals busts and/or rehab experience."

"No bet. But . . ."

"Keep going."

"I don't think he's cagey enough—that's the word,
cagey—to have planned all this out. Lifting credit data,
the shipping, the timing, the research. Or the patience to
wait years for the payback. He hits me as more I want it
now. The kind who might see Rufty crossing the street
and try to mow him down—and any innocent bystanders in the way—with his shiny car."

"Got it in one, but there are actually two. No, he's
not cagey enough to have planned this out. And he also
lacks the ugly instinct to destroy what the enemy loves
rather than the enemy. Mowing down the target with his
car—just his style. And then it's all, the vehicle had a

glitch, or he stepped in front of me, or I saw a tall, dark stranger push him in front of me and couldn't stop."

"So you don't like him for it?"

"Can't say yet. But if he's a part of it, someone else is running the show. He's a follower," Eve decided. "He couldn't lead himself out of a room made of doors."

The hunt for parking netted zero, so she settled on an overpriced lot—which reminded her she *still* hadn't hit a machine for cash. Being overpriced and in the Financial District, the lot had one near its gate.

She dealt with it, stuffed the cash in her pocket, then caught the eye of the guy eyeing her.

She showed her teeth first as he made a move toward her. Then flipped open the topper, the suit jacket, showed her weapon.

"Still want to try for it?"

He turned on his heel, beat feet in his airboots.

"Some muggers like to hang around the machines," Peabody commented as they walked. "He sees a couple of helpless female types in their mag coats, and thinks easy score."

"Yeah. If I didn't want to get this done, I'd've let him try to mug me, then he'd be thinking about the error of his ways in a cell. Maybe next time."

They hiked to another steel-and-glass tower, this one pale blue in the afternoon sun. The lobby here spread wide and deep, offering cafés, boutiques, trendy markets along with its moving maps, a large screen displaying the financial news in various languages.

They crossed the dark blue tiles to the security station.

"Stephen Whitt, the Whitt Group." Eve held up her badge. "Lieutenant Dallas, Detective Peabody, NYPSD."

"How's it going, LT? I was on the job at Central when you came on as a rook."

She judged him as teetering on eighty, and fit. He had a close-cropped cap of gray, a dark face lined like a creased map, steady brown eyes that had plenty of cop in them.

"Detective Swanson. It's good to see you."

That lined face creased deeper with a grin. "You got a good memory, if you can pull my name out of your hat."

"Detective Peabody, the department lost a good cop when Detective Swanson turned in his papers. About ten years ago, wasn't it?"

"Nine. Got tired of fishing, and my wife got tired of me poking around the house, so I keep out of her hair this way. You want the fifty-second floor."

"Do you miss the job, Detective?" Peabody asked him.

"Every day. On a hot one, Loo?"

"Might be." She leaned in. "Do you know Stephen Whitt?"

"Fancy-pants, and snooty with it. Comes by it natural, from what I see. I've been on the desk here six years, and the father hasn't said so much as kiss my ass to me. If you're looking at him for something, I can keep a closer eye out."

"It wouldn't hurt. I appreciate it, Detective."

"Not a problem. I'm gonna clear you right up to fifty-two. You give Feeney my best, will you?"

"I will."

"Take the second bank. That'll express you to twenty."

"It meant something that you remembered him," Peabody commented as they walked to the bank of elevators.

"I remember a good cop who used to sit at his desk making those—what are they—you catch fish with?"

"Lures?"

"Yeah. He said it helped him think. He helped close a lot of cases." They stepped on the elevator. "If we get a buzz here, it won't hurt to have him on that desk."

Unlike the law firm, the financial one didn't go for subdued.

Pale gold carpet spread over their lobby area with a wide semicircle reception counter in gold—darker, shinier. Six people worked busily at their stations.

It held two waiting areas on either side, both done in chocolates and gold, with all seating fitted with individual screens and comm devices. Flanking the wall of glass with its bird's-eye view of New York, two ornamental trees speared out of huge gold urns.

Behind the reception counter, the company's logo showed a bull—again gold—with its hoof on the throat of a brown bear.

No, Eve thought, no sign of subdued here.

Despite the variance of race and gender, those manning the counter struck Eve as the same. Mid-twenties, attractive, sharp-eyed, and pissy.

Still, maybe Roarke had a point about the topper—the whole outfit—as every one of them gave her a look, then a practiced smile. She could almost see dollar signs dancing in their heads.

She walked to the center, and the Asian male.

"Stephen Whitt."

"Good afternoon. Do you have an appointment, Ms. . . . ?"

"Lieutenant." She wiped the practiced smile off his face when she held up her badge. "Dallas. Detective

Peabody. NYPSD. We need to speak to Mr. Whitt on police business."

"I'll need to check with his administrative assistant to see if he's available. If you'd like to have a seat—"

"We're fine right here. When you check," she continued, making sure her voice carried to those in the waiting areas, "be sure to tell the admin we're here investigating two homicides, and are prepared to wait until Mr. Whitt becomes available."

"Yes, ma'am, of course."

"Lieutenant." She tapped her badge, then put it away.

Rather than use the headset, the receptionist swiveled to his comp, used a keyboard.

Texting the admin, Eve thought, and gave him points for finding a way to keep her from hearing the conversation. After a couple minutes of back-and-forth, the receptionist cleared his throat.

"Mr. Lauder, Mr. Whitt's admin, will be with you shortly."

"Great."

It didn't take long. Eve figured they didn't want a couple of murder cops despoiling their gilded lobby area.

The man who came through the double frosted glass doors on the right had about two decades on the receptionist. His well-cut suit fit over a compact body. He wore his nut-brown hair brushed back from a sternly handsome face—and didn't bother with the practiced smile.

"If you'd come with me."

He led them through the doors—no cubes here. More gold carpet, art framed in gold on the walls, offices with their chocolate-brown doors closed.

Lauder approached an open one.

Two women worked at opposite sides behind glass panels—cubes by another name, Eve thought. Lauder's desk held the center.

He closed the door, walked to the desk, sat. Gestured, rather imperiously, for Eve and Peabody to take chairs.

They stood.

"I'm Ernest Lauder, Mr. Whitt's administrative assistant. I'll need more information regarding the purpose of your visit."

"As we informed the receptionist, who no doubt informed you, we're investigating two murders."

"Yes, and?"

Eve gave him an imperious look right back. "Two dead people aren't enough for you?"

"It fails to tell me why you'd wish to speak to Mr. Whitt."

"We have no intention of giving you that information, or any additional information about an ongoing investigation."

He spread his hands. "Then I'm afraid Mr. Whitt is unavailable."

"Fine. Detective, contact APA Reo and request a warrant to bring Mr. Stephen Whitt into Central for questioning in regard to two homicides."

"Don't be absurd."

"Mr.—Lauder, is it? Two people are dead. We will have a conversation with your boss in his house, or in mine. It's completely up to him. The more you stonewall, the more unpleasant that conversation will be."

"Wait here."

He rose, walked to the inner door, slipped inside.

"Should I go ahead and call Reo?"

"No. It won't be necessary. Whitt just wanted to flex his muscles."

"Sometimes admins—"

"Nope. This one follows orders."

Lauder stepped back out. "Mr. Whitt will see you now. Briefly."

Like Cosner, Whitt sat at his desk—a semicircle of dark gold, a smaller version of the reception counter. He didn't pretend to be on his 'link, and his workstation showed signs he actually worked.

His hair, nearly the same color as the workstation, streamed back thickly. He had the polished look of a vid star, the perfect profile, tawny eyes, the perfect two-day scruff.

He rose as they entered, and though he skimmed just under six feet, gave the appearance of more height with disciplined posture, lifted chin.

Whether for effect or comfort, he'd taken off the jacket of his midnight-blue suit and stood in shirtsleeves and tie.

"I apologize for keeping you waiting. Ernest is very protective."

Though he didn't extend a hand or come around the station, he gestured to the pair of chairs—chocolate again—before taking his seat.

Unlike his schoolmate, Whitt had diplomas gracing the wall. On another a screen ran the financial news from around the world, all holding on mute.

"Can we offer you something?"

"No, thanks."

"Thank you, Ernest. That's all for now."

"Yes, sir."

Lauder stepped back, closed the door.

"I'm in the dark here," Whitt began. "You want to talk to me about someone who's been murdered?"

"Kent Abner. Elise Duran."

"Still in the dark."

"Kent Abner was married to Dr. Martin Rufty and Elise Duran to Professor Jay Duran. Maybe that sheds some light."

"Not really, no."

"You did attend Theresa A. Gold Academy here in New York, correct?"

"Now, that's a name from long ago. Yes, I did, but I don't understand what . . ." Eyes narrowing, he sat back. "Rufty, yes, of course. He came in as headmaster right before I transferred. I finished my senior year and graduated from Lester Hensen Prep in East Washington, so we barely crossed paths."

"Our information is crossing paths is the reason you didn't graduate from Gold."

"True enough. My parents didn't like Rufty's administrative style, and over my considerable objections at the time, enrolled me at Lester Hensen, where Headmaster Grange had also transferred."

"You objected?"

"Objected, sulked, raged." He smiled as he said it. "I was seventeen, and considered my life essentially over. All my friends were here, the girl I loved was here. In the pecking order at TAG, I considered myself high up, and now my parents were sending me to another school in another city, where I'd also board? Life." He waved his hands. "Over."

"You must have blamed Dr. Rufty."

"Absolutely. The son of a bitch came in, took over what I considered my turf, threw his weight around, alienated my parents so completely I paid the price. Of course, as is often the case, it turned out to be the best thing for me."

"How's that?"

"Without the friends, the girl, the familiar, I focused on my studies to get through. In any case, my life didn't end. I don't see how my crisis, as I saw it, at seventeen has anything to do with these murders."

"Did you also blame Jay Duran for the transfer?" Peabody wondered.

"I don't think I know anyone by that name."

"You were in several of his classes when you attended the academy," Peabody pointed out. "language arts, creative writing, literature."

"Sorry." Whitt added a small, dismissive shrug. "I can't say I remember many of the teachers from back then."

"This particular one wrote you up multiple times. You and your friends," Eve added. "The records show he cited you for participating in a cheating ring, for bullying, for physical assault, underage drinking. It's quite an array. He issued formal complaints about you, about Headmaster Grange among others."

His eyes stayed even, direct. Empty. "One would assume if any of those accusations were true, Headmaster Grange would have taken appropriate disciplinary action."

"We don't assume, Mr. Whitt, as evidence shows Headmaster Grange overlooked accusations, statements, complaints in return for generous monetary donations to the academy."

"That wouldn't be on me, would it? Now, will I sit here and claim I never behaved badly as an adolescent or teenager? Of course not. Anyone who does so claim is either a liar or had a very boring childhood. In point of fact, the crowd I ran with while at TAG might have leaned toward the wild side."

He shrugged that off as well. "But we were harmless, and doing what most of that age do. Exploring boundaries, stretching them, experimenting."

"Illegals?"

He smiled, slyly. "I'm going to take the Fifth on that. Look, we had parties. A lot of our parents traveled, and we'd have parties. I won't deny we found ways to get our hands on alcohol. I hope, when and if I have kids of my own, to do a better job of supervising such things, but it's all really just a rite of passage. And while it's been amusing to take this little trip back to my youth, I really have work to get to."

"Then we'll jump forward to the now. Can you give us your whereabouts on the nights of April twenty-seventh and twenty-ninth, from nine-thirty to eleven?"

"Are you serious?"

"Yes, Mr. Whitt. We consider murder investigations very serious."

"You actually consider me a suspect because of some teacher and administrator from high school? You must be really reaching." Shaking his head, he scrolled through an appointment device.

"April twenty-seventh, I took a client and her husband to dinner at Le Jardin. We had eight o'clock reservations. I'd estimate we left around midnight. I escorted them back to their hotel—they were in New York from Belgium—then had the limo take me home. Again, I can't tell you precisely, but I should've been home before twelve-thirty, and didn't go out again."

"We'll need the names of your clients to verify."

"No." His jaw set; his eyes hardened. "I won't have you contacting important clients and questioning them. If you have to verify, talk to the restaurant. The maître d' knows me, as I often take clients there. The servers will certainly remember."

"We'll start there," Eve agreed. "And the second night?"

"I went to a club to meet a friend. I'm not sure of the time again, but it would have been nine or nine-thirty when I got there. Marsh was already there."

"That would be Marshall Cosner."

"That's right. Obviously you know we went to school together—but for that last semester. Our families are friendly, and Marsh and I remain friends. We get together when our schedules allow."

"Funny." Peabody took out her PPC as if checking data. "Mr. Cosner didn't mention your name among those he gave us when he told us about his club night."

"Probably thinking he'd keep me out of all this nonsense." He waved that off. "No need. We had a couple of drinks, a few laughs, caught up, scoped out the ladies. Neither of us brought a date. I left about midnight, I think, caught a cab home."

"Alone?" Eve asked.

"Unfortunately, yes."

"Have you stayed in touch with Kendel Hayward?"

"Ah, still a stab to the heart." He made a mock wince. "No. We were madly in love, of course, at sixteen, seventeen. Then cruelly—I felt at the time—separated. Her parents lowered the boom, it was all so fast. I couldn't even contact her, as they'd taken her 'link, locked down her comms, and I pined for . . . two or three weeks?"

He smiled again. "Such is the depth of love at seventeen."

"You did try to contact her once." Eve noted the faintest tightening around his jaw. "But she wouldn't talk to you. You didn't take that well."

"Seventeen," he said again. "She broke my heart. Then there were other girls to ease the pain, then college—

and other women, and Kendel became a sweet, vague memory. But she's not in New York, is she? I know I read she got engaged, some political type in East Washington. I admit I felt a twinge. First loves are potent."

"But not potent enough for you to contact her, or try to, after you graduated. Or since."

"One must move on. And that's exactly what I must do now. I can't help you with your situation. I'm sure this is a tragedy for Dr. Rufty and Mr. Durbin."

"Duran," Eve corrected.

"Right. It simply has nothing to do with me, and I can't spare any more time. If you have any more questions, you can take them up with my lawyer. That would be Lowell Cosner—Marsh's father."

He rose. "Best of luck to you."

"Thanks for your time."

She could all but hear his smirk as they walked out.

Peabody started to speak when they got in the elevator, but Eve just shook her head. So they rode down in silence with corporate suits and well-heeled clients.

"Now," Eve said when they stepped outside. "Because he's the type that might put an underling on the ride to report any chatter."

"I didn't think of that, and yeah, he's the type. I was going to say we now have two lying SOSs."

"We surely do, Peabody. We surely do."

"Still, if the alibis check out—"

"I've got an idea there. Check the addresses for the club, the restaurant, and the dinner party," Eve said as they walked back to the lot. "Then compare them with the drop points for both packages. Let's see what we have."

"Sure." Peabody pulled out her PPC.

"Cosner tagged him, you can bet on it, the minute we

left his office. He knew we were coming, had the admin set to try to block us. Knew the names we'd bring up, but had to act like, gee, who remembers? Stupid, really. But there's always some stupid in there, no matter how smart they are. Or think they are."

"And here's more stupid. The address for the dinner party, that's a solid twenty blocks from the first drop, but the restaurant where Whitt took his clients? Under two. And the club where Cosner and Whitt hooked up? Three blocks."

"They each did a drop. They cover for each other. They never thought we'd get this far, but they think they've covered it. Whitt thinks—Cosner's a follower."

Eve got behind the wheel. "Let's go by the restaurant—we've got time. I'm going to have Rodriges come in, give a statement. We'll hit the restaurant, check out the club, see if we can put some more holes in the lying SOSs."

"I'm for that."

Eve paid at the gate, drove on. "Whitt didn't even bother to ask why we'd question him about the spouses being killed. Because that's his whole point. That's the reason."

"And he'd hold on to blaming Rufty, Duran because he got pulled from a school—by his parents."

"There's more to it. First loves are potent, right? Not love, not really. He's a sociopath and he doesn't genuinely feel. But he lost the girl, his hierarchy, and more—there's more. The girl got engaged—and that got media play, a lot of talk in his social circle, too, believe it. It pisses him off. And Grange, she comes into it. Somehow. Whitt's parents are divorced, right? Check when."

"Just a second. Huh." Peabody pursed her lips at her

PPC screen. "Finalized the same summer Whitt graduated from Lester Hensen."

"The wife filed, right?"

"Yeah. Right after the first of the year."

"What do you want to bet Whitt's daddy's the one in that blurred photo?"

Peabody considered. "I think I'll save my money."

18

The hostess at the uppity upscale French restaurant obviously approved of Eve's topper, as she greeted her and Peabody with a warm and welcoming smile.

"Good afternoon! Under what name will I find your reservation?"

"Under no name, but you'll find this badge under Dallas, Lieutenant Eve."

Warm welcome turned to quick alarm. "Oh! Please, will you be discreet? Is there a problem?"

"Depends. I want you to check back for a reservation under Stephen Whitt for April twenty-seventh. Dinner. Eight o'clock."

"Mr. Whitt, of course. Party of three. Mr. Whitt often dines and lunches here."

"You were working?"

"Yes."

"How about you step away from your station a minute?"

"Oh, but . . . Henry? Would you take over for me for just a moment? Could we step outside?" she asked Eve in a whisper—discreetly.

"Sure."

Once they did, the woman let out a long breath. "I'm sorry, but we wouldn't want any of our guests disturbed or upset."

"Right. What time did Mr. Whitt arrive?"

"He brought his guests in just a minute or two before eight. He's always timely. Jordan, the evening maître d', escorted them to their table himself."

"Okay." Eve played a hunch. "What time did Mr. Whitt step out, maybe to use his 'link?"

"Oh. I think it was—I'm not sure exactly—but about ten? He's very considerate that way, and will step outside if he needs to make or take a call. We discourage 'link usage while dining."

"Sure you do. How long was he out?"

"A few minutes. Five, six. No more than ten. Less, certainly, than ten. He wouldn't have left his guests for more than a few minutes."

"You saw him go out and come back?"

"Yes. I'm sorry, I don't understand."

"I do. I need your name."

"Grace Levin."

"Does Mr. Whitt have an upcoming reservation?"

"I don't believe so. He often makes one for lunch the day of."

"If he does, if he comes in, it's important you don't mention this conversation."

"But—"

Eve took out her badge again, pointed to it. "Do you understand important? And discreet, Ms. Levin?"

"Yes."

"Good. Do you know the names of his servers from that night?"

"Yes."

Once she gave them, Eve sent her back inside.

"He thinks he's covered himself." Eve rocked back on her heels. "First, he doesn't really expect to be brought into it, but you need cover. He has the limo, the clients, a restaurant where he's known and respected. He fakes the need to use his 'link. Certainly has the limo waiting—just a matter of timing. Gets the package out of the limo because it's probably quicker to walk. Plus, he doesn't want to be seen making the drop, using the jammer. It only takes a few minutes. Go back in, apologize for the interruption. Let's have some frigging brandy or whatever."

"Slick," Peabody agreed as they got back into the car. "But the holes? The servers, the hostess, maître d', the driver. The clients—and we could get the names if we needed them. Somebody's going to notice he's gone out for a few minutes. The car service guy's going to know he called for the limo, got something out of it."

"He's used to doing what the hell he wants. Even the getting yanked out of school? Not because of his behavior. Because Rufty changed the rules, and his parents weren't going to let some headmaster claim they had a bad seed.

"He may sweat it a little now. But even so he's thinking he's covered. He'll convince, or try to convince Cosner they're both covered. Let's check the club."

They got nothing additional from the club, but for the club itself.

Eve got back into the car after a brief conversation with a couple of women who'd been mopping the floors.

"No door cam," she said. "No man on the door. A single-level club with a single bar, a dingy atmosphere. Not a dive, but closer to that than a trendy place like you'd expect a couple of rich guys to hang in."

"But location and lack of security equal a plus if you're a couple of rich guys planning a murder. Circumstantial," Peabody added, "but it's building."

"Let's put a damn roof on it before they send another package."

"You think they will?" Peabody shifted to Eve as they streamed through traffic. "Now that they know, have to know, we're looking at them?"

"Cosner, maybe not. But Whitt?" Eve powered through a light, switched lanes, and took the next right at the tail end of the pedestrian flood across the intersection. "He's made of arrogance. If anything he'd push up his schedule now."

"I can see that," Peabody realized. "Those bitches think they scare me? Shit, Dallas."

"We issued the warnings, Peabody, and that's all we can do there. We build it up. If it's just the two of them, one of them—likely Cosner—has the equipment, the supplies where he lives. They both live alone. Possibly they have a separate workspace, and we're going to look there."

"Also possibly they have that mad scientist on the payroll."

"So we look there." Eve pulled into the garage at Central. "Known associates, old friends—maybe from Gold—employees. Possibly it's a dealer connection of Cosner's, so we look there, too."

"A lover, maybe? Another addict." As they got on the elevator, Peabody played with the angle. "They get him or her a decent place to stay, keep her supplied with her drug of choice, and she cooks the agent in exchange."

"Not bad. We haven't found a romantic or sexual relationship with either of them, nothing that sticks. So maybe one they've kept buried. We'll take a closer look at their finances, looking for regular outlays. See if we can find any property they—or either of them—rent or own other than where they live. Investment properties. Who'd look twice normally?"

She ditched the elevator for the glides. "Let's get more hands in this. Check and see if EDD can spare McNab or Callendar. If not, we'll cull somebody from the bull-pen."

"You really think they'll hit another target?"

"In Whitt's place, with his mind-set? It's just what I'd do. Tag EDD," she said as they walked into the bullpen. "I want to write this up before Rodriges gets here."

Eve went straight into her office, straight for coffee. After updating her board, her book, she wrote her report, added a list of questions for Mira.

Since she expected Rodriges shortly, she'd dig into finances later. For now, she put her boots on the desk, angled toward the board to study and think.

Whitt's father's photo on the wall of Grange's office. The timing of the divorce. Maybe try to talk to the wife, see if they could convince her to confirm the affair.

Because there'd been one. Maybe still was.

If Whitt knew Grange had been at least partially responsible for his parents' divorce, why not strike at her? Didn't care, she mused. It didn't really impact his life.

What had—because she believed him there—was the transfer of schools and cities. He'd lost his base, his standing, his easy road, and had instead been demoted to the new kid.

Still, Grange might have covered for him, at least partially. Another reason not to strike out. But he'd had the brains as well as the money to make a top-ranked school, and do well.

So possibly he had focused on his studies. Success could be a form of revenge.

He'd hooked back up with Cosner, and probably had never completely lost touch. But the girl? He'd definitely lost the girl.

No contact, not even after they'd both graduated.

Her eyes narrowed on his ID shot. "How did you know her parents had taken her 'link, locked down her comms? Maybe somebody else from your circle of assholes told you. Maybe. But then she cut you off, too. Chose to follow the line instead of hook back with you. Hmm."

Setting the coffee aside, she rose, paced to her skinny window. "You're not going to contact that bitch after she dumped you like that. Screw her. She didn't mean that much to you anyway. Just an easy lay, right? Sure, sure. Plenty of easy lays out there for a good-looking rich boy."

She paced away, paced back. "Smart girls, too. Girls with more brains than tits who'd be grateful for the attention. Who'd help with college papers."

She went back to her desk, checked the date of Hayward's engagement announcement.

"Yeah, yeah, you'd read about it. First loves are potent—that's what you said, and that was pure truth for you, especially when you add first loves who kick you to the curb.

"Then what does she do? What does she do?" Eve asked herself as she picked up her coffee again. "She goes and hooks another rich guy. An important rich guy from an important family. Fuck me, her future mother-in-law might just be president. That's a kick in the balls.

She gets to flaunt it around the White House? And who's responsible, who ruined your life so you're a junior exec at daddy's firm and the girl who belonged to *you* gets to marry into political royalty?

"Rufty, Duran, and the rest of the sons of bitches who screwed up a good thing."

She walked to the ID shot. "That's the trigger. That's the goddamn trigger. I'd bet my ass on it."

She turned, intending to contact Mira's office and push her way into a quick consult. As she did, her machine signaled an incoming, and Peabody's clomp came down the hall.

She glanced at the incoming, gave a quick grunt. She'd been expecting it.

"Dallas," Peabody said from the doorway. "Rodriges is here."

"Set him up in the lounge. I'll be right there."

She waited until Peabody clomped away before answering the commander's office.

Detective Peabody and I are about to interview an individual regarding the current investigation. We will report to Commander Whitney's office immediately after the interview.

Grange, Eve thought as she headed out. She hadn't expected the headmaster to let Peabody's insults go. So they'd deal with it.

In the lounge, Rodriges sat at a table, one battered sneaker tapping nervously. He was a skinny little guy with his black hair tied back in a short, curly tail. A pair of soulful dark eyes looked out of a youthful face as Peabody brought him a fizzy.

He wore a T-shirt displaying the formula for pi, with the caption:

THERE'S ALWAYS AN EXTRA SLICE OF PI!

Eve imagined a personality like Whitt's had delighted in bullying him.

"Here's Lieutenant Dallas. Lieutenant," Peabody continued, and handed Eve a tube of Pepsi, "Miguel Rodriges."

"Thanks for coming in, Mr. Rodriges."

"That's okay." His smile flitted off and on, never reached those soulful eyes. "My, ah, supervisor said I kind of had to. That you had to talk to me about Dr. Rufty's husband and Mr. Duran's wife. It's . . . it's awful."

"You remember Dr. Rufty and Professor Duran?"

"Oh yeah, sure. I should've said professor. He wasn't when he was at TAG, but . . . I went to the memorial before work this morning. I didn't really know Dr. Abner, but I wanted to go, just for a few minutes. I'm going to go to Ms. Duran's memorial, too. It's important to pay your respects."

He took a gulp of fizzy. "I'm pretty nervous because I don't know why you want to talk to me."

"You liked Rufty and Duran."

"Sure. I knew Mr. Duran a lot better because he was there longer. I mean when I went there. English wasn't my best subject. I was better at math and science, but he really helped me, helped me keep my grades up there. I even joined the Shakespeare Club my senior year because he helped me, you know, get it. I don't know what that has to do with—"

"Miguel." Eve interrupted him, waited for his eyes

to meet hers. "Relax. We're just looking for some background."

"Okay. It's just when the big boss says go talk to the cops like now, it's a little scary."

"Nothing to be scared of," Peabody assured him. "You were good at chemistry."

"Yeah, well, I liked it. Chem, biology, physics, calculus, programming, comp science." This time his smile reached his eyes. "All the nerdy stuff. But I had to keep up with the rest, maintain, right? I was on scholarship. Mr. Duran, Ms. Chelsic, Mr. Flint, they really helped me with my weak spots."

"You liked the school," Peabody prompted.

"I'd never have gotten into MIT, never been able to land a job at Roarke Industries without the chance I got at TAG."

"You had some problems with some of the other students," Eve put in, and he looked down, shrugged.

"I mostly hung with the other nerds."

"Miguel, you were physically assaulted, taken to the hospital for medical treatment."

"We work with Detective Callendar," Peabody added. "You know her."

"Sure, sure. We hung a lot back in the day. Still do sometimes, but—"

"She remembers when you got beat up."

Miguel stared hard at his fizzy. "It was awhile ago."

"She's not the only one who remembers," Eve added. "Mr. Rosalind, your chemistry teacher at Gold, believes you were threatened, assaulted, because you refused to cheat. Dr. Rufty added what he learned of the incident in his records."

Looking up, obviously surprised, Miguel blinked. "He did?"

"He did. It would help us now if you told us what happened."

"It was a long time ago."

"You remember the names of teachers who helped you," Peabody reminded him. "I bet you remember Dr. Rufty, and went to the memorial for his husband this morning because things changed, for the better, when he took over as headmaster. You remember what happened."

"We're gathering information, and information from your last year or so at Gold could help us find the person responsible for two murders."

Alarm flashed over his face. His nervous foot tapped faster. "I don't see how."

"It's our job to see. Tell us what happened."

"I don't want to get anyone in trouble after all this time. I mean, you have to let go, right?"

"They're not going to get in trouble, with us, for what they did back then. But we need the information."

"Okay, well . . . Some of the kids liked to pick on the ones who were at TAG on scholarships. Best thing was to try to stay out of their way. It didn't always work. Some who got picked on did what they had to do. Wrote papers, did homework or projects, um, let somebody copy their work, or even . . . Okay, so they had somebody they bullied into hacking into some of the teacher networks for exams, even for changing grades. Everybody knew it."

"Including Headmaster Grange?"

"She knew. I can't prove it, and I don't want to. But everybody knew she knew. I got some pressure, got pushed around some. I was pretty puny. Some of the teachers—like Mr. Duran, Mr. Rosalind—they tried to look out for me, for the ones like me. But they can't be everywhere, you know?"

"Did they ambush you, Miguel?"

He looked at Eve. "I wasn't going to cheat. I don't cheat. I said I'd help them prep, help them study, but that wasn't good enough. They beat the crap out of me one day. Jesus, I was scared. But I wouldn't cheat, I wouldn't dishonor myself, my family that way. When they finished, they said if I told who did it, nobody would believe me. And if I didn't do what they wanted, they'd go after my brother, my sister. I was the oldest."

"You can tell us now. Nobody's going to hurt your family."

"Stephen Whitt and Marshall Cosner. They jumped me. I was stupid, okay? Just stupid. They said okay, help us prep for this lab work that was coming up, and to come to Stephen's house that night. So I did because I was stupid. They jumped me outside. I guess his parents weren't home because nobody came out when I yelled. They beat me pretty bad—I don't remember a lot of it after the first couple minutes. Then they dragged me into a car. I thought they were going to take me somewhere and kill me, because Marshall said how they could, maybe should. Stephen said if I knew what was good for me, I'd copy my work, send it to him, and how my brother and sister would get worse if I said anything. Then they dumped me out way downtown, near the piers. I passed out, I think. I tried to walk home, but I passed out. I woke up in the ambulance."

"Just the two of them?" Eve asked.

"That time, yeah. In school, there were more of them who'd shove you or trip you, or threaten you, whatever. But it was just those two who beat on me that night."

"You told your parents, the police."

"I was afraid for my brother and sister, my family. So I wouldn't say who did it. Not then. So the police couldn't do anything. My parents went to Headmaster Grange because they kept on me until I said it was some kids from school. But she wouldn't do anything. They wanted to take me out of TAG, but I begged them not to. It was my chance to get into MIT, my chance to do what I wanted, to get a good education, work in the career I wanted, for a good company. It was my chance."

"That was brave," Peabody said.

"I nearly wet my pants the first day back. I'm all banged up, kids are staring, pointing. And I knew they'd come after me because I wasn't going to cheat."

He took a deep gulp of his fizzy. "Man, I was scared. But this guy? Big guy, a year behind us? He wasn't a nerd, and he wasn't with them. A jock guy. Quint Yanger. He decided to look out for me. We barely knew each other, and he just decided he wasn't going to let them hassle me anymore. Word had gotten around with the kids—Marshall could never keep his mouth shut, and he got high and bragged about it. Quint went right up to Stephen, because he knew he ran things, and he told Stephen if I got hit, he'd get hit twice and harder. If I got shoved, he'd shove him out the nearest window. Like that?"

For the first time Miguel grinned. "They left me alone. Then Grange left, Rufty came on, and everything changed. Well, except Quint and I are still friends. Best friend I ever had. Anyway, things changed, and I got through high school just fine after that."

"Quint Yanger, defensive tackle? First draft choice a couple years back for the Giants?"

"Yeah, that's Quint. Big guy. Big heart. I like to think of it this way. If it hadn't happened, if they hadn't come after me, Quint and I probably wouldn't have become friends. Not like we are anyway. And I healed up okay."

"You're an interesting man, Miguel," Eve decided.

"Ah, thanks, I guess. I want to say, when Dr. Rufty took over, he called me in, talked to me about that night. I felt, maybe because of Quint, and because, well, they were already gone, I could say who. I guess it felt better to say who."

"Did any of this help?"

"It did."

He nodded, looked away. "You probably can't tell me if you think Stephen or Marshall are involved in the murders." He paused, then blew out a breath when neither Eve nor Peabody spoke. "I've got this far, so I'm going to go all the way. I'm going to say, I don't know them anymore, and people change. I haven't seen them since they left TAG right after the winter break. But . . . I thought they'd kill me that night. It wasn't just because I was hurt and scared. It was also . . . they wanted to. I could see it, hear it, feel it. They wanted to, and maybe if they'd been sure they could get away with it, like they did all the other stuff they did, they would have."

He pushed what was left of the fizzy away. "But people change, and I don't know who they are now."

"All right, Miguel. We appreciate you coming in like this. We'll have you taken back to work."

"Oh, that's okay. I'll take the subway. The big boss said I didn't have to come back after, but I'm into something I want to finish."

"The big boss is lucky to have you."

Eve leaned back when Miguel walked out. "Sometimes people change. But mostly they don't." She glanced at her wrist unit. "We're wanted in Whitney's office."

"For a report?"

"That'll be part of it. Let's go."

As she rose, Peabody paled a bit. "This is about my little episode with Grange, isn't it?"

"That'll be part of it."

"Crap, shit, fuck. I knew it. It's my slap, Dallas. You weren't in on it."

"I seem to remember not so long ago when similarly summoned someone talking about asses together in the pan."

"Yeah, but—"

"Butts, asses, same thing. I'm also your LT, so move your butt-ass and let's get this done."

"I can take it," Peabody muttered as they walked to the glides, since Eve saw a small horde pushing onto the nearest elevator. "I just don't want it to bog down the investigation. You can feel it heating up. You know, like the pan our asses are in."

"Funny."

"Feeney freed up Callendar to do some of the property search. McNab's on something else, but can get into it when he's done."

"That works. After Whitney I'm swinging by the morgue just to check in with Morris. Then I'm working from home. I'm going to pull our expert consultant, civilian, in on the finances. I'll start on them, but he'll finish before I could get halfway there."

"Yeah, he would. No offense."

"None taken." She paused outside the commander's office, got the wait signal from his admin.

"Lieutenant Dallas and Detective Peabody are here, sir. Go right in," he told them.

Whitney sat at his desk, his broad back to the city spread behind him. His face, wide and dark, remained impassive as he gestured them forward.

Then he leaned back in his chair, folded his hands, said, "So."

Eve, recognizing the silence as technique, kept her own. But she all but heard Peabody brace to spill, and knocked her right boot against her partner's left to stop her.

Whitney quirked an eyebrow, gave the most subtle of nods.

"We'll clear the decks first," Whitney continued. "Detective Peabody, I have a complaint from Headmaster Lotte Grange of Lester Hensen Preparatory in East Washington that during her voluntary interview with you and Lieutenant Dallas this morning, you became abusive toward her in your language and tone, threatened to do physical harm, and had to be ejected from her office. Would this be accurate?"

Don't be stupid, don't be stupid, don't be stupid, Eve thought as loudly as she possibly could.

Peabody took a breath, steadied herself. "No, sir, that would not be accurate."

"In part or in total?"

"While I don't consider my language or tone abusive, it was strong in response to the insults Headmaster Grange heaped on my family, my coworkers, my profession, and my lieutenant in her attempt to deflect the line of questioning. I did not threaten her with physical violence. I believe I told her, and stand by the statement, she wasn't worthy to polish the boot my lieutenant would use to kick her ass. Sir."

"So you threatened your lieutenant would use physical violence."

"Metaphorically, Commander."

"I see. Lieutenant?"

"Detective Peabody's statement is accurate, Commander. Grange became insulting, which I saw as a deliberate attempt to distract, and simply her nature. Peabody used the opportunity to reset the interview."

"'Reset'?"

"Yes, sir. Instead of good cop/bad cop, we played hot cop/cold cop. By suggesting Peabody take a walk, leave me alone with Grange, I allowed Grange to believe she had the upper hand. Temporarily. I was able to shift the balance, and take control of the interview, with the results that are outlined in our report.

"She's in this, Commander. Inadvertently or deliberately, but she's in this. I don't believe we acted inappropriately given the circumstances and the hostility of this individual. If you disagree, well, you're the boss."

Whitney took a moment. "Well played. All around."

"Thank you, sir. We've just completed an interview with Miguel Rodriges. He attended Gold when Grange was headmaster there, and graduated under Headmaster Rufty. During Grange's tenure he was bullied, threatened, and assaulted to the point of hospitalization. Grange was aware of this, did nothing. I believe she was also aware of the identities of the assailants. Stephen Whitt and Marshall Cosner."

She laid out her theory, compactly, and Whitney leaned back in his chair again as he listened.

"You believe these men held on to grudges since high school, and now acting on them have killed twice?"

"And will again. I believe Whitt's father had an affair with Grange and that, at least in part, led to divorce. Whitt was separated from his friends, his girlfriend, was shifted out of his pecking order. Now that girlfriend is engaged to a wealthy and successful man whose mother is a contender for president. She states she's had no contact with him, and I believe her. Cosner, the only friend he's held on to, is an addict, is weak. A follower."

"Why not target Grange?"

"It was Rufty who changed the map for him. I suspect her relationship with his father continued. They may still be involved. It's likely she blocked for Whitt during his time at the prep school. They ruined his life, took away what he wanted most. Now he's doing the same to them, those he sees as responsible."

"The timing and locations of the drops are good circumstantial."

"But we need more," Eve finished. "We'll get it. Cosner is the weak spot. We'll put more pressure on him. I want to bring him in. He didn't call lawyer the first round, and that might be because he didn't want word to get to his family he had trouble. He'll likely lawyer up the second round. But he'll break."

"Make it happen," Whitney ordered. "I don't want another spouse on a slab."

"Yes, sir."

As they started out, Whitney called to Peabody. "Detective?"

"Yes, sir."

"That was a good line about the boot. Best use it sparingly."

"Yes, sir."

"And be glad he didn't use his to kick your ass," Eve added when they headed for the glides.

"Believe me, I am."

"While you're glad, contact Cosner's firm. Go through reception, ask for Lowell Cosner."

"The father."

"Yeah, oops. If you get the father, identify yourself,

remind him you spoke earlier about the homicide investigation. Realize your mistake, apologize. You misread your notes, and are trying to contact Marshall Cosner."

"So we make sure that word gets up the chain."

"Yeah. Try to arrange for Cosner to come in tomorrow for a follow-up interview."

"And if he balks?"

"We'll speak to his attorney, blah blah. Do the drill. Get the PA on board, and let's turn up the heat on the weak link. And one more. Let Morris know I'm heading over. If he can't be there, maybe he could have somebody else give me the rundown."

19

Morris made time, of course. Though she'd have done the same for him, Eve still appreciated it.

When she walked in, his music sounded like sunshine as he methodically stitched up a Y-cut on a corpse.

"Nearly done here," he said without looking up.

"Take your time. I appreciate you making it for me."

"Never a problem. This young man thought to rob a store in the Diamond District, using the homemade boomer in his pocket as incentive."

Since she'd seen the case on the board in the bullpen—Carmichael and Santiago had caught it—she moved closer. And observed the large, jagged chunk missing from the DB's right side.

"Went off in his pocket."

"That it did. Fortunately for the bystanders, it wasn't very powerful. Unfortunately for our guest here, it was powerful enough to blow a hole in him. There now, all done."

He stepped back, blinked. "Well, look at you."

"What?" Thrown off, Eve glanced down at herself.

"You look gorgeous."

She'd have been less shocked if he'd stabbed her with his scalpel. "I— What?"

"Like a perfect spring day," he added as he walked over to clean his hands. "I calls 'em as I sees 'em."

"Huh." Weird, she thought, but . . . "Thanks."

"I suspect you simply wanted another look at Elise Duran, as I can't add anything of value to my report."

He walked to the wall of drawers, opened one. The cool fog puffed out.

"A woman who took care of herself until her death. Good muscle tone, lovely skin. COD, the same as our first victim. Unlike our first, I see no sign she knew what was happening, attempted to get to a window or door for air, for help. She dropped where she stood. Death came quickly, but painfully."

"Has the family been to see her?"

"The husband. He's arranged to have her taken to a funeral home tomorrow. The family will hold a private memorial before cremation, then they'll have an open one for friends and extended family in a few days."

Morris touched a hand, briefly, gently, to the top of Elise's head. "Her husband sat with her for some time, asked if he could just sit with her. And so he did, and talked to her, assuring her he'd take good care of their boys. He'd look out for her parents, and so on."

Morris sighed. "There are times, no matter how many you open and close, there are times it breaks the heart."

"Yeah. That's what he wants. Broken hearts, broken lives. He's already forgotten her. Duran, too. That's done, crossed off the list like a chore. Next? Fucker's not going to get a next."

Morris narrowed his eyes on Eve's face. "You know who it is."

"Yeah. I looked him in the eye today. You know what I saw in there, Morris?"

"What?"

"Not a damn thing. Behind the pretext they put on to mix with humanity, this kind is dead inside. She has more life in her than he does. It's not even real revenge, not the kind you'd get bloody for. It's more . . . It's a fuck-you," she realized. "Somebody cuts you off in traffic, you give them the finger, move on. Not this guy. Cut him off, he'll run you over. That's his fuck-you."

Eve stepped back. "Yeah, I guess I just needed to see her again. Thanks for that."

"Anything I can do that helps you take him down."

Eve had barely gotten back in her car when Peabody tagged her 'link. She took it on the dash, headed toward home. "Dallas."

"Wanted to update you asap," Peabody began. "Good call, damn good call about the oops with Cosner Senior. He hadn't gotten wind of our earlier visit. I say that with certainty because this took him by surprise. I know the angry to disappointed to exhausted dad look, and he ran the gamut while trying not to show it."

"How much did you tell him?"

"Here's the thing, after he got that the NYPSD had interviewed his son once, and wanted a follow-up, he stepped into his lawyer shoes. As his son's legal counsel, he demanded to know, etc. I kept it close, but gave him enough to worry him. Added that we'd have the PA's office there. He wants to speak to the prosecutor, made it clear he'd speak for his son, questions to be addressed to legal counsel, and all that. Ten tomorrow."

"Good work, Peabody."

"I know the dad look, right? He's pissed, and a little scared."

"Murder will do that. Tag Reo, tell her—"

"Already did. She's talking to her boss now. She'll tag you back."

"Okay. I'll get back to you."

She ran through it in her head as she drove. She needed more on Whitt, needed to build a solid case. Cosner could be key. The right pressure, she mused, he'd crack. Loyalty only went so far, and if they could convince the father they had enough to tie his son up in a murder investigation, convince him they believed Whitt had called the shots . . .

He'd make a deal to keep his kid on-planet. Maybe cut it to twenty per count, served concurrently. She could live with that—if it helped put Whitt away for life.

Her 'link signaled again as she drove through her home gates. "Dallas."

"Reo here. I just finished meeting with the boss. There's a lot of it depends here, Dallas."

"Whitt and Cosner, together, killed two people. No it depends about it."

"You say it, I believe it." Eve watched Reo with her stylishly curly blond mop and crisp white shirt program coffee from her office AC. "Proving it's different."

"He'll break, Reo. Cosner will break. He's weak, he's lazy, he's an addict. His family's propping him up. Eventually that breaks, too."

"His family's firm isn't peanuts. They're top-of-the-line, and we don't have enough to charge him."

"We have enough to sweat him."

"Maybe, but even if we loosen him up with enough sweat, there's no way his father or whatever criminal attorneys they bring in will let him talk without a deal."

Eve didn't mention she'd already worked out a deal in her head. "For fuck's sake, Reo." She parked, slammed out of the car for show. "We don't even have him in the box and you're talking deal."

"I'm talking reality," Reo snapped back. "First one to flip gets the prize. It's a classic for a reason. You believe Whitt's the one running things, so figure out how much you want him."

"I want them both." Eve shoved open the front door.

"So let's try to get them both. We start offering Cosner on-planet."

Summerset's eyebrows rose as Eve stormed down the foyer to the stairs.

"Maybe we should offer him some nice spa treatments while we're at it, some freaking canapés."

As she stomped up the steps, still bitching, Summerset smiled at her back. Then looked down at the cat. "The lieutenant's in a much better frame of mind this evening."

As if in agreement, Galahad trotted upstairs after her.

Satisfied Reo's outline of a potential deal aligned with hers, Eve headed to the bedroom. She wanted out of the suit.

From his perch on the bed, Galahad watched her dig out a sweatshirt—black—trousers—black—ancient high-tops—black.

"It's, what, monochromatic, right?"

She sat on the side of the bed a moment to give the cat a rub. "It's turning, pal, I can feel it turning. We just have to lock it down before he kills somebody else. The snotty, smug son of a bitch."

After giving Galahad one last pat, she rose, started

for the office. The cat beat her there, whizzed through the door, and leaped on her sleep chair.

And Roarke stepped out of his adjoining office.

"Hey. You're here."

"I am." He walked to her, kissed her. "As are you. I thought as much when I heard the thunder of cat feet."

"Not exactly light on them, is he? You're working from home?"

"Just finished, actually, and the timing's rather exquisite." He strolled over, opened the wall panel, chose wine, two glasses.

"I'm not finished working," she began, but he handed her a glass, took her free hand.

"No doubt, but, again, timing. We need to take advantage of it."

"Where are we going?" she asked as he drew her out of the room.

"For a bit of a walk before the sun goes down and takes the warmth of the day with it. And how was your day, Lieutenant?"

She could spare time for a walk, she decided, especially since he seemed seriously pleased about something. It was probably part of the Marriage Rules not to stomp on your spouse's seriously pleased before you even found out what it was.

"Productive," she told him. "I was going to tap you, if you have room for it, to make the rest of my day even more productive."

"Sounds interesting." He went out a door on the second floor, crossed over a terrace where somebody had placed pots of sassy-looking flowers, down stone steps.

To another terrace with tables, chairs, benches, big urns with exotic-looking viny things spilling out.

Who thought of all that? she wondered. The viny things, the sassy things, the happy pink and white and yellow and purple things poking up out of the ground as if they'd just decided to bloom there?

She supposed Roarke had final say on all of it.

And it felt good to be outside, she had to admit it. The air definitely felt like spring—a stroke instead of a bite. Smelled like it, too, sort of green and fresh and promising.

Trees and shrubs had begun to bud or unfurl. She heard birdsong instead of traffic. It didn't take her long to relax, or to figure out where he was headed.

"Did they finish the pond?"

He smiled. "You'll soon see. We'll supply the finishing touch ourselves."

They wandered through a grove of fruit trees—she remembered the peaches from the previous summer, how they'd smelled, tasted. How they'd looked out and discussed adding a pond, a bench for them to sit on.

And there it was, tranquil and lovely through the greening trees. Naturally, being Roarke's, the reality leaped well over her initial mental image.

"Jeez, you got a waterfall."

"A small one. It adds to it, doesn't it?" He drew her along to that music of water striking water as it spilled over stone rises into a pool where water lilies floated serenely.

Around the stone walls of the pool danced budding shrubs and little trees, lush grasses. She could smell them, and the water, the rich, thick mulch that gave way to pavers in that same natural stone gray. Pavers, she noted, that had been etched with the same Celtic design as their wedding rings.

Jesus, the man knew how to get to her.

The bench stood on the pavers, the perfect spot to look over the pond, its magical little falls of water, the castle of a house in the distance, the grove of budding trees.

"I thought it was going to be a hole in the ground filled with water."

"We wanted to do a bit better than that."

"It's . . ." She could only shake her head. "It's great. It's like it was always here."

"We wanted organic as well."

"Well, it works. I can't say I ever pictured myself sitting beside a pond drinking wine, but this works." She frowned, pointed. "What's all that?"

"The finishing touch."

He led her around behind and to the side of the bench where a small tree, its trailing branches fat with pink buds, waited beside a hole in the ground. With it, a couple of shovels leaned against a wheelbarrow full of mulch, another filled with rich brown soil. A bucket held work gloves, small spades.

"They didn't get to plant this?"

"They're not planting this. We are."

She shot him a look that fell between shocked and amused. "We are?"

"That we are." He set his glass, the bottle on the bench, took her glass and did the same. "Think of the satisfaction as we watch it grow over the years, bloom every spring."

"Think of the guilt when it dies because we killed it."

"We won't be killing it." He took gloves out of the bucket, handed her a pair. "I have very specific instructions on the process. The landscape crew dug the hole as, though I've dug a few holes in my time, literally and metaphorically, the head landscaper didn't trust me on it. And made that one clear."

She had to laugh. "He's still employed?"

"He is, as I have to respect a man who stands his ground. So." Roarke pulled on his gloves. "Into the hole with it, Lieutenant."

"Just . . . put it in there?"

"That would be the first step."

She looked at him as they maneuvered the tree to the hole. "This is why you changed out of your suit."

"And how handy it is you did the same. There now, you hold it up there, let's keep it straight, while I shovel some dirt around the root ball."

"Okay. How do I know it's straight?"

"You've eyes in your head, don't you? They've mixed peat in with the soil—I did have a bit of a go at that, under supervision."

It smelled, well, earthy, she supposed, as he shoveled the mix from the barrow into the hole. It was a pretty good look for him, too, she thought, the shoveling.

"She'll hold now. Do your share."

"I thought I was."

"Get your shovel."

Fully amused now, she did. Maybe she did get some satisfaction out of dumping dirt in a hole. Who knew? But the air, the scents, the light, the physicality all worked. Until, well, son of a gun, they had a tree in the ground.

"Now, we're to take the small spades, tamp the dirt down. Lightly, I'm cautioned, against the roots."

That required hands and knees, which was surprisingly okay. She wouldn't want to make a living at it, or even a habit, but as that finishing touch, it was really okay.

"How do we know if it's enough?" she wondered.

"It feels like it is, so we'll go with that." He pushed up, picked up a large silver container with a spout.

"What's that?"

"Haven't you ever seen a watering can?"

"Probably. Sure. It's big."

"It's got some weight." He planted his feet, poured water around the tree. "We put in underground irrigation, but I'm told we water it well at planting."

She sat back on her heels a moment, then pushed up herself. "I'll do this side."

Into it now, she thought as she let the water flow. Christ, next thing she'd want to name the damn tree.

"Is that it? Did we do it?"

"Mulch," he said, jerked a thumb toward the wheelbarrow.

She traded the watering can for the shovel. "How much?"

"A good couple inches all around, I'm told."

So they dumped mulch, smoothed, dumped and smoothed.

Then they stepped back, studied.

"We planted a tree."

"And a lovely one at that. Wait." He dug out his 'link, shifted her, slid an arm around her. "We'll document it."

"You never do that. You don't take 'link shots."

"How often do we plant a tree in the yard?"

"That would be . . . once."

"There you have it. Smile."

How could she help it?

He took the shot, pocketed the 'link. "We've earned that wine." He unfolded one of his tools, used the corkscrew to open the bottle. Eve held the glasses while he poured.

Then they sat hip-to-hip on the bench with the young tree beside them and looked over the pond.

"So." He kissed the top of her head. "Tell me what I can do to make the evening productive."

"Not yet," she decided. She put murder aside, tipped her head to his shoulder. "Let's just be here for a few minutes."

So they sat, drank wine while the water spilled, the lilies floated, and the shadows lengthened toward dusk.

By the time they went back inside, her mind felt sharp and clear and ready to reengage. Plus, she realized she wanted food.

"I'll get dinner," she began, but he trailed a finger down the dent in her chin.

"Update your board, as your mind's back on it. I'll get the meal."

Well, the man knew her. Even though it meant pizza was off the menu, she did want to update her board, and have her thoughts lined up for when they sat down together.

Not pizza, but whatever he brought out as she worked smelled really good.

"How was your meeting with Grange?"

"I'll start there, work my way through." She walked to the table. Some sort of chicken with the herby rice she preferred to the white stuff, and a pile of mixed-up veggies. She could live with it.

"Grange," she said, and began.

At one point, Roarke had to stop her. "Peabody? Our Peabody went at her?"

"Like a jungle cat on a snake. I had to stop her because I really think she was just getting started. Clearly, Grange isn't used to someone saying fuck you. Or if they do, she's used to crushing them like a bug."

Enjoying the replay, Eve scooped up some of the herby stuff. "She also, clearly, expected me to take the polite and apologetic route, since I told Peabody to take a walk. Oh, and the suit, the outfit." Eve ate more chicken, enjoyed the subtle bite of whatever it had been cooked in. "You were right about that."

"Good."

"So she wasn't prepared for me to go at her—or to point out the photo of Whitt's daddy and her on her wall. They've definitely tangoed."

"Is that right?"

"Bank on it. From there we got a completely different vibe from Kendel Hayward."

Roarke listened, shared bread with her, filled her water glass, as she'd go back to work.

"So the bad girl from high school found her way," he concluded. "Most do."

"She credits her parents for stepping in—stepping on her, and hard. They're divorced, and he's running some tropical dive shop, but she spoke of them as a unit."

"To her, they are. Her parents."

"Yeah, it seemed . . . healthy. Of everyone we talked to today, there are two I felt were honest, didn't hold back. That would be Hayward, and your Rodriges."

"I'm glad to hear it."

"Move to Marshall Cosner and Stephen Whitt? Good thing they can afford lots of pants because the ones they had on were on fire before we were done."

As she ran through the interviews, Roarke thought it a kind of expert play-by-play, the sort that put the listener into the game so clearly he could hear the tones, see the movements.

He nodded, and sat back with his wine.

"So Whitt's your man."

"I didn't say that."

"You didn't have to. I could hear it. How much of a dupe do you figure Cosner is?".

"I figure he looks to Whitt—and has for years—to lead the way. He gets off on the violence, no question, but he's no planner. Miguel said he thought they'd kill him, and I think, even then, if Whitt had said to Cosner, 'Hey, pal, pick up that rock over there and bash this asshole's head in with it,' that's just what Cosner would have done."

She nudged her plate aside. "He'd have felt a little queasy about it when the high wore off, when he was alone, but he'd have justified it. Guy deserved it; besides, Steve told me to. Miguel also said he thought Grange knew. She knew who'd tuned him up, and she covered. It's how she operates."

"You'll take her down as well."

"It's going to be a pleasure." Picking up her water glass, she toasted. "A really serious pleasure. I may not be able to put her in a cage, but when all this comes out, she won't be able to get a job cleaning toilets in a school much less running one."

"It sounds like the punishment you're aiming for fits the crime."

There she shook her head. "I wish it could be more, because she and Whitt, they're the same. Power over the weak and vulnerable is what fuels them. She may not be involved, directly, in the murders, but she helped create them."

"What will I do to help you take them down?"

"I'm doing a follow-up with Cosner—with his legal team headed, most likely, by his father—in the morning. We made sure Daddy got wind of the cops looking at his boy."

"Forewarned?"

"Not exactly. I think in this case, Peabody and I called it right. The father knows the son is a fuckup. They've been through the cycle, covered for him, given him busywork to try to keep him straight. This? Murder? It's going to be a bridge too far. What does that mean?"

Frowning, she stopped herself. "How can a bridge be too far? Too far from what? It has to go from here to there. Why did I even say that when it makes no sense?"

"I have no comment," Roarke said, wisely.

"Anyway, I'm going to break young Cosner, and offer a deal. He flips on his pal, he doesn't spend the rest of his life in a concrete cage off-planet. Meanwhile . . ."

"Will I have fun?"

She grinned back at him. "It's going to be your favorite thing. I want to drill down deep, into Cosner's finances, but more into Whitt's."

"That is my favorite thing—nearly. You're so good to me."

"I figured maybe Cosner figured out how to cook the agent, but now, after talking to him, I don't see him stumbling into that on his own. They had to have somebody—maybe Peabody's mad scientist. They had to pay somebody. At least until they had the formula. That means payments, equipment, ingredients, safety precautions. It wouldn't be cheap."

Rising, she walked back to the board, circled. "They're rich, but Whitt's smart, and he's a money guy. You wouldn't want the payments to show, to be tracked back to you. Not that he believes we'd ever actually try to hang this on him. He sees himself as above—just like Grange. But he'd be careful. He'd instruct Cosner to be careful."

"I'll enjoy this."

"Figured. You should start looking during the time Hayward got engaged and forward. I think that's the trigger. Whitt, he doesn't love, he's not capable, but in his mind she belonged to him. She—or her parents—cut him off."

"And the reason for that stems back, for him, to Rufty, to Duran."

"That's right. It might be he decided back then, well fuck her, I never really wanted her anyway. Or figured if he ever wanted her again, he could just pick up where they left off. But the engagement, and the splash, the prominence of the fiancé's family? Slap in the face."

"I see, yes. She doesn't just do well without him." Roarke studied Hayward's ID shot. "She doesn't give him a thought. She's successful in her own right, but then, to add insult, she's suddenly a media darling, engaged to the successful in his own right, son of a political powerhouse."

"Big-ass wedding to follow, you can bet," Eve added, "and more media attention."

"Which all should have been his," Roarke added, nodding. "The golden egg makes perfect sense. Gold Academy," Roarke continued. "He had everything he wanted his way there, and envisioned it would only continue. But Rufty and those like him killed the goose."

She frowned. "There's that goose again."

"The one that laid the golden egg, darling. Kill the goose, end the supply of golden eggs."

"Yeah, right, right." She circled around it, hit the point. "Okay, yeah, that's his little smart-ass symbolism."

"It only makes the delivery system uglier."

"I guarantee he's had some good laughs over his goddamn cleverness. But he'd need somebody, Roarke, somebody to cook up the agent, to figure out how to—distill it or whatever it's called. That had to cost."

"I'll look into it. And what will you do?"

"I'm going to see if I can dig up more teachers, more students who'll talk to me. Especially the one who walked in on a fellow teacher bumping uglies with Grange on school property. The one who banged her died in a car accident."

"Suspicious?" Roarke asked.

"No. Five years ago last winter. Michigan, icy roads, multicar wreck with two fatalities." She shook her head. "So I have to hope others I talk to remember. Then I'm going to start digging into Whitt, the college years. There may be some threads to pull there."

"Then we should both be well entertained for the evening."

"Nice how that works, huh?" Since he'd gotten dinner, she walked over to clear the table. "You know what else? I actually liked planting that tree."

"So did I."

"Not that I want to take up gardening."

"I think, though we did well, we've both chosen the right career path."

She couldn't argue with that, and carted plates into the kitchen.

20

Using Rufty's notes of meetings with staff during the transition, and Peabody's notes from her first pass, Eve compiled a list. She arranged it by priority for face-to-face interviews the next day. After that, she culled out the handful who'd transferred out of state, and opted to try to contact them before digging into Whitt.

She considered the forty minutes or so that took time well spent. Expanding her own notes, she combed through the prevarications, the Grange cheerleaders, the hesitations, the Grange blasters.

Darcie Finn-Powell, an elementary-level teacher who now worked in the public school system upstate, hesitated, lowballed, then spewed.

And became Eve's favorite.

"She hit on my husband!"

While inwardly, Eve did a quick happy dance, she responded with a carefully neutral, "I see. Can you explain that?"

"Thad's a firefighter, and he came in to talk to my

class. Third graders. They just love firefighters. He came in with his turnout gear, helmet, the works. It was great. Headmaster Grange observed part of the presentation, and then she asked Thad to come to her office. She said she wanted to talk to him about other visits, a field trip, and that sort of thing."

"Okay."

"Then she *moved* on him. Got, you know, handsy, suggested they should meet for drinks, discuss how to start a fire. He was mortified."

"I assume he told you all this."

"That same night. He said at first he thought she was sort of joking, saying things like she found risk takers so attractive, how he must be able to tolerate a lot of heat. I mean, really? And you know what else? I was pregnant with our first. She knew it!"

"Can you tell me how you handled it?"

"Yes, why not? I'll say up to that point I tried to keep my head down. I taught third graders, and did what I could to stay out of school politics and drama. I knew some of the other teachers had issues with the headmaster, especially in the upper grades, but I just wanted to teach. It was a good position, and we had a baby coming."

She paused, blew out a breath. "But I wasn't going to look the other way when she went after my husband. I went to her office the next morning, and laid into her. And you know what she did?"

Oh yeah, still pissed, Eve thought, and added some high kicks to that internal happy dance. Pissed enough she'd likely give a written statement.

"What did she do?"

"She laughed at me! Laughed right in my face. She said since my husband had obviously misconstrued her remarks, he must be dissatisfied at home. She claimed he'd flirted with her, which she considered harmless enough. And if I wanted to keep my job, I'd keep my marital issues out of the school. She was lying about Thad flirting with her. You have to understand—"

"I believe you."

"Good." Darcie drew air in through her nose, visibly relaxed on the exhale. "Okay, good. In any case, I stopped keeping my head down. I just couldn't. I signed complaints with the others who went to the board. I stuck it out, even though it got stressful. It got better, so much better, when Headmaster Rufty came on to replace her. But I was only there, with him in charge, for a short time, as I went on parental leave to have our first. Thad and I decided to move, to get out of the city, so I never went back."

"Let me ask you this. Do you know of any other instances where Headmaster Grange acted inappropriately, with another spouse, a parent, another teacher?"

Darcie went back into hesitation mode. "I'd rather only speak about what I know, personally."

"I get that. You're an educator. As an educator, given your knowledge of and experience with Lotte Grange, do you consider her qualified to serve as headmaster of an educational facility?"

"No, I don't. At all."

Eve let the silence hang.

"Damn it. Damn it." Darcie shut her eyes a moment. "I can only tell you what I heard or was told. I can't absolutely swear to it even though I believe it."

"We're not in court. I'm not going to hold you to anything."

Blowing out air, Darcie dragged a hand through short, nut-brown hair. "Boy, this is bringing it all back. I'm pouring myself a glass of wine. Okay?"

"It's okay with me."

Eve caught glimpses of a kitchen—a friggie covered with kid art, a kind of bulletin board holding photos and notes.

Darcie poured straw-colored wine, took one bracing sip.

"She was caught having sex, at school, with Van Pierson. He taught history, middle grades. Wyatt—Wyatt Yin, computer science, also middle grades, walked right in on them. Van was the last, I think, before she left. He wasn't the first, not according to others."

"Do you have names?"

Eve noted them down.

"Parents?"

"Oh boy, oh boy." She paused, blew out a long breath. "The only one I have personal knowledge of is Grant Farlow—and that's because I taught his little boy, and knew his mother. He wasn't in my class when this happened, but in fourth grade."

On another sip of wine, Darcie stopped pacing around her cheerful, kid-friendly kitchen, and sat.

"They pulled him out of TAG, and I spoke to his mother because Deke was such a good student. She told me Grant had confessed to having a fling with the headmaster. It was over, they were going to counseling, but she wouldn't have her son in the school."

"You were friendly with the mother?"

"Yes. They ended up moving to Philadelphia— fresh start. We've lost touch except for the occasional e-mail, but I know the marriage didn't make it. Grant's not blameless, but this woman is a predator."

"So there were others?"

"You hear, or heard. But again, I don't have personal knowledge."

"What can you tell me about Stephen Whitt?"

"I remember the name because it came up a lot when the group of us who'd formed got together. Bully, cheat, ringleader, and headmaster's pet."

"Her pet?"

"He could do no wrong, and he knew it. I didn't interact with him, but others in the group did. His parents were big contributors—the money flowed in. And . . ."

"And?"

"Well, crap." She took another drink. "I can't confirm. It's really speculation that the headmaster had a relationship with Stephen Whitt's father. He wasn't the only one, but that was the name in big lights before she transferred. And since the boy also transferred, a lot of us thought that capped it. But it's really no better than gossip."

Gossip added up, Eve thought as she expanded her notes.

And the name Whitt wouldn't keep filling in blanks if it meant nothing.

She managed to contact Wyatt Yin in his home in Colorado. He looked at her with dark, soulful eyes.

"Yes, I heard the terrible news. I still keep in touch with some of the friends I made at TAG."

"You left the academy about a year after Dr. Rufty came on as headmaster."

"Yes, but not because of Dr. Rufty. He was a fine headmaster, dedicated, fair. It was . . . I never felt quite at home, not in New York, not at TAG. It was all too big, and at the same time, confining. I spent a summer here in Colorado teaching underprivileged kids, and found my place. I met my wife." He smiled now. "It was meant. Here I am home."

"Tell me about Lotte Grange."

The smile faded. "TAG was my first experience with such an elevated private institution. She was my first experience with a headmaster."

"Would you describe her as a fine headmaster, Mr. Yin? As dedicated and fair?"

"I would not. Again, I was very new, and only had the experience with her for some eighteen months. And again, I was not a good fit."

"Tell me about Van Pierson."

He sighed. "It was not his fault. You have, obviously, heard what happened all those years ago. I want you to understand, he wasn't at fault."

"Why is that?"

"We came on at the same time. Both very young, very new. Van and I taught the same grades and often spoke about our mutual students. He was a good teacher. I was working late, tutoring one of my students. This wasn't encouraged, so I . . . you could say I did this on the down low?"

"All right."

"After I sent the student off, I did some work. As I was leaving, I stopped by the break room. I thought to get some coffee for the walk to my apartment. And I walked in on the headmaster and Van. I was shocked, of course, embarrassed, left very quickly. A couple hours later, Van came to my apartment, shaken, distraught. First he begged me to say nothing. I don't know what I would have done, but it came out—and I believed him—that she had pressured and demanded. She had insinuated that if he wanted to keep his position, he would allow her to . . . be intimate. He was new, like me. Young, like me. So he did as she wanted."

"You didn't say nothing."

"No. We talked, for some time, Van and I. And I

convinced him we had to report this. She'd used her power and authority to coerce him into sex, and that couldn't stand."

He sighed again. "But you see, we were young and new, and she was power. She countered this, claimed he had assaulted her, and that I had taken his part against her. He was dismissed. I was reprimanded. I needed the work, so I stayed, and I knew by then she was leaving at the start of the year, so I stayed.

"Van left New York, and with this black mark was unable to teach anywhere. There was a car accident five years ago. He was killed. And I think, if I had said nothing, he would have continued at TAG—where he was a good fit. He wouldn't have been in that car in Michigan on icy roads. So how much is my fault?"

"None of it. It begins and ends with Grange, Mr. Yin. Besides Van, do you know of others Grange either pressured or just had sexual encounters with?"

"There were rumors. I only know, conclusively, about Van."

"Brent Whitt. Stephen Whitt's father."

"At the time of all this, the strongest rumors aimed there. But I don't understand how this information helps in your investigation into the tragedies."

"That's for me to figure out."

And, Eve thought, she damn well would. She began digging down through the layers on Stephen Whitt.

Academically, there hadn't been so much as a blip with his transfer. Probability of that, she mused, dead low. She believed him when he'd told her he'd been pissed, upset, argumentative.

Added to it, he'd bullied and cheated his way, apparently with Grange's blessing, at Gold. So, logical assumption? She'd smoothed over that period.

Family legacy and money would have helped get him into Northwestern, but he'd needed the grades, too. And he'd needed to maintain them once he didn't have Grange running interference.

Not stupid, though. Highly intelligent. And savvy enough to know he had to buckle down enough if he wanted that big corner office.

He liked money—playing with it was a game to some. Didn't she know it, she thought with a glance toward Roarke's office.

Money was power, and power was the goal. Power and prestige and lifestyle.

She scanned through articles. Society pages, financial pages, gossip pages. Oh yeah, he was an up-and-comer, a young gun. Lots of fancy dos with him with a woman on his arm. Never the same more than twice, she noted, and wasn't it interesting how many of them bore at least a surface resemblance to Hayward?

She hung you up, didn't she, Steve? The one who got away.

She kept digging.

She barely glanced up when Roarke came in, when he eased around her to use her command center's Auto-Chef.

"I've got more on Grange. One way or another she's going down. If it comes to it, I might be able to leverage her against Whitt. Or use them against each other. Plus, he's still hung up on Hayward, so . . ."

She caught the scent before he set the little plate on the counter. Cookie. Big, fat, chunky cookie.

She picked it up—still warm—and shifted when he sat at her auxiliary. "Either you got something that meant cookie reward, or you bombed out and wanted the cookie consolation."

"The first." He bit into his own. "You'll want to run Lucas Sanchez, aka Loco, though I already did. He's dead, killed about a month ago in what appeared to be an illegals deal gone south. Stabbed multiple times in an alley in Alphabet City. Jenkinson and Reineke caught it."

"It's still open." She pulled the bullpen's board into her head. "Open and going cold." She had to push back, pull reports and quick conversations back into her head. "An illegals cook, an addict."

"That's correct. If one goes back about a decade, it appears young Lucas had one semester, on a science scholarship, at Gold Academy before that scholarship was rescinded when he was arrested for possession."

"Son of a bitch! In a really good way," Eve added.

"I thought you'd see it that way. Some of the possession was already inside his system when he attempted to mug a couple of tourists in Times Square. Females. One of whom kicked him in the balls while the other called the police."

"He knew Cosner and Whitt."

"Almost assuredly. I also believe he qualifies as Peabody's mad scientist. He showed flashes of brilliance with chemistry, earned that scholarship."

She shoved up. "They bullied scholarship students—not one of them. But he'd have had a leg up if he could cook illegals, supply them. Cosner, another addict—The Facilitator, according to Hayward. Loco might've been his supplier, and that may have led to using him to cook up the agent."

She turned back to Roarke. "How'd you get that out of the financial search?"

"Roundabout. Cosner isn't so clever as Whitt. They both use casual gambling, purchases to cover payments."

Eve felt another happy dance coming on. "What payments?"

"I'll get to it. Cosner, however, slipped twice, and has a transfer of ten thousand to Lucas Sanchez. As Whitt ostensibly had gambling losses of the same amount at the same time, I thought it expedient to look at Sanchez."

"I know it insults you for me to say you think like a cop, so I won't say it."

"Appreciated. There are other similar losses or outlays—such as Whitt listing a painting he claims he bought from a street artist in Paris for twenty thousand—cash—which remains uninsured. There are various and classic laundering schemes, and the outlay was regular, twenty thousand between them, twice a month from last September until January. In January until near the end of March, it doubled to twenty apiece, then nothing. Late March coordinates with Loco's sudden and violent demise."

"They had what they needed from him. Enough of the agent, or the formula. Doubled the initial payments—maybe he demanded still more. He got greedy or mouthy, or they just didn't want to risk keeping an addict in the loop."

"Agreed."

She buzzed up more coffee for both of them to go with the cookie. "Hold on, let me tag Jenkinson, see if he can add anything."

"I've more myself, but I'll just finish my cookie while you do that."

She tagged Jenkinson, who answered with a distracted, "Loo?"

She could hear chatter in the background, and somebody said, "That's a full-of-shit bluff."

Feeney?

"I'll see that full-of-shit bluff and raise it ten."

Definitely Feeney.

"Is Reineke in the game?" she asked.

"Yeah, him, Feeney, Callendar, Harvo."

"Harvo?"

"She's a killer. Something up?"

"That's right. I need your attention."

"You got it. I already folded." She heard his chair scrape back as he got up, moved away from the table. "I'm losing my shirt to a girl with green hair and the captain of the geeks. It's humiliating. What you got?"

"Lucas Sanchez. Loco."

"Yeah, dead cook, addict. Stabbed a couple blocks from the flop he used. Hadn't been seen around the neighborhood for months, according to every-damn-body. And that same every-damn-body didn't see anything, hear anything, know anything."

Scooping a handful of chips out of a bowl, he munched as he talked. "And every-damn-body said he was an asshole, but could cook good shit. Genius shit. No product on him, no cash. Took his shoes, too. Live by the junk, die by the junk. Or that's how it's looking."

"Not anymore."

Jenkinson's eyes changed. "How's it look now?"

"He's linked to the nerve gas, to my two prime suspects."

"Son of a bitch. Okay, shit. He had a rep for what you'd call innovation. Not your average cook. Coming up with new recipes, blending chems, ah, personalizing product. Couldn't keep profits in his pocket because he blew it on LCs, his own product, or the horses. Couldn't keep a legit job for the same reasons. Had a real knack and a brain with it, but no legit lab or research place would touch him. He had a sheet, went in and out because he was a screwup. Always getting caught, doing some time, bouncing out, then back again. I'm remembering the ME said he'd have been dead in ten anyway if he kept living and using the way he was."

Roarke, cookie finished, worked on her auxiliary. Eve ignored him.

"I want you and Reineke to go over it again, reinterview. I'm going to send you pictures of the suspects. Stephen Whitt and Marshall Cosner. They went to school together for a while. Cosner is an addict, and he'd likely have used Loco as a supplier."

"They rich guys?"

"They are."

"We had a couple of LCs he liked to use. They said he'd brag about how much the rich guys paid for his work. He told one he was cooking up something special that'd make him a rich guy. But she said, and others confirmed, he was always talking big like that."

"Doesn't look like it was just talk this time."

"Ah," Roarke said from the auxiliary, "there it is." He swiveled to her. "Would you like an address?"

"An address for what?"

"Well, I can't say, not for certain, but it's a property Marshall Cosner has behind a shell company he established last fall. It appears to be a small warehouse downtown. Loco had to live and work somewhere, didn't he?"

"Roarke's sending you an address," she said to Jenkinson. "Get Reineke and meet me there."

Once he had, Roarke followed Eve's long-legged stride out of the room.

"I need to change, need my weapon. How'd you find the building?"

"Persistence, and process. They needed somewhere to

set up the lab, to keep their cook happy. And Whitt funnels money to Cosner every month. Like you would for a loan or a share of an investment expense. The property's only in Cosner's name—Whitt's careful. The shell company only shows Cosner's fingerprints. They call it The Golden Goose."

"Smug fuckers." Eve pulled on boots. "But not for much longer."

About the time Eve briefed Jenkinson, Marshall Cosner paced the elaborately furnished living space in the converted warehouse.

He wore a hooded sweatshirt, dark jeans, black hightops—all designer label though he believed they helped him blend into the neighborhood.

Stephen Whitt, on the other hand, wore a fresh business suit, one he'd changed into for his dinner speech at a financial event at a Midtown hotel.

He knew he'd timed it well—he was good at timing. He'd made certain he'd mixed, mingled, made conversation before he'd jammed the cameras on a service entrance to slip out.

He'd had the scooter he'd "borrowed" from a cousin parked in another hotel lot a block away, and had made it downtown in ten minutes. Ten minutes back, he thought, ten minutes or so here, and he'd simply blend back into the post-dinner dancing and bar scene with no one the wiser.

Despite his panic, good old Marsh had delivered the next package to the drop. But he'd never hold up to the pressure that was coming. Steps had to be taken, Whitt thought, so he'd taken them.

Time to cut ties. Old school ties.

"Dad doesn't believe me." Cosner paced, paced. "He practically grilled me like a fish."

"You denied everything."

"Of course I did. I'm not an idiot, Steve, but he doesn't really believe me."

"You're going in with a platoon of lawyers, Marsh. You'll be fine."

"Easy for you to say."

Yeah, Whitt thought. It really was.

"I can't figure out why she's zeroed in on me. We did everything right, didn't we? We've got alibis. We did everything right."

"She's bluffing, trying to get to you. We're good as gold. Look, I've got to get back before somebody misses me. You just need to relax."

"Jesus, you try to relax when you've got cops on your ass." Pacing, Cosner wrung his hands. "Maybe I should take off. Head to Europe."

"We don't run. Come on, Marsh, take a dose. You're jonesing."

"Why's she looking at us? We barely knew Rufty, TAG was years ago. She shouldn't have looked at us. You said the cops would never look at us."

Calmly, Whitt walked to the tacky mirrored bar Loco had demanded, picked up a vial, poured it into a lowball glass, added a good two fingers of unblended scotch.

"She's got nothing. She's fishing. Loco's dead and cold, and that hasn't come back on us, right? We've got the formula now. When we're done here, we'll do just what we talked about."

"Take it overseas, sell it for billions."

"That's right." And all mine, Whitt thought as he handed his oldest friend the glass. "Drink up."

Cosner knocked it back, sighed.

Just enough, Whitt thought, to make him happy, and a little sloppy.

"Did you get the last egg ready?"

"Yeah. I'm glad we decided it's the last, Steve. I thought this would be more fun, but it's been a lot of work. What say when we're done, you and me, we take a little vacay? Hit the tropics."

"Sounds good. Why don't you show me the egg, Marsh, just to make sure. Then you can come back with me. We'll hit the bar, pick up a couple live ones."

"Now there's a plan."

He was already cruising as Whitt steered him out of the living area and up the iron steps to the lab. Across from the white counters, the burners, the refrigeration, the scopes, computers, containers, ranged an organized shipping and packing area.

Three golden eggs remained on shelves, one in a clear, airtight container—and Whitt regretted he wouldn't be able to have the other two filled and all three delivered. A fourth sat in another clear container waiting to be packed.

"Looks good. You know, why don't we pack it up, drop it off tonight. A twofer. Then we'd be done."

"Done." Glassy-eyed, Cosner smiled. "I'd really like to be done."

"Yeah, shit, why wait? We'll take that vacay," he added, and made Cosner grin.

"Real ready for that."

"Pack it up, drop it off, hit the tropics. Pack it up, Marsh."

"Pack it up, get it done. Naked women on the beach. Whoo!"

Whitt stepped back, well back, drew on the air mask.

And when Cosner opened the airtight container, the egg, with its seal already broken, released the agent.

Staggering, Cosner dropped it so it shattered on the floor. He clawed at his throat as he stumbled, fell, stared up at Whitt.

"What?"

"Sorry, bro." Whitt's voice rumbled through the mask. "I gotta do what I gotta. I'll miss the hell out of you."

As Cosner's system revolted, as he tried to crawl, Whitt checked the time. "Wow, I have to book."

He jogged down the stairs, tossed the mask back in a storage room.

Ten minutes back, he thought as he let himself out, as he took some solution out of his pocket to clean the sealant off his hands.

He zipped uptown without a care in the world.

Since it made no sense for her suspects to take risks when one of them had a date in the box the following morning, Eve expected to find an empty building.

She had a search warrant—thanks to Reo and the sheer stupidity of naming the shell company The Golden Goose—and had figured to enter, go through, possibly turn a more comprehensive search over to her detectives.

But when they pulled up, she saw lights shining behind privacy screens.

"Could be on timers," she mused as she and Roarke got out of the car. "Could just be careless about turning them off."

"Could."

"Or we could have the extra-special bonus of finding one or both of those assholes in there."

"Possibly along with a supply of deadly nerve agent."

"Yeah, yeah." She'd thought of that, too, which was why she contacted Peabody, told her to log out masks from Central and meet her.

Now she paced the sidewalk.

"There's only one reason I can think of for one of them, or both of them, to be in there."

"Preparing the next shipment."

"And make the drop tonight. That's just the sort of thing the smug sons of bitches would do. We need to spread out, cover any possible exits. Box them in."

Roarke studied the building as the thief he'd been might have. Considering security, best ways in, best ways out, vehicular and pedestrian traffic flow.

"They'd be idiots to work with that substance without protection of their own."

Couldn't argue with that, she thought. "So we'll be even. Except there'll be more of us, with badges and weapons."

She recognized Jenkinson's car as it rolled up, then saw Feeney's roll up behind it.

Couldn't hurt, she thought, then watched, surprised, as her two detectives, the EDD captain, Callendar—Jesus—Harvo, Peabody, and McNab all piled out of the two vehicles.

"What the hell is this?"

"More cops the merrier." Jenkinson grinned as he walked up, and she was baffled enough not to notice he didn't have a tie.

"Harvo's not a cop."

"Aw, come on." Obviously revved, the queen of hair and fiber lifted her arms. "I never get to have the fun. I bet there's hair and fiber in there, and I'll be right on the scene."

"There may also be one or two very dangerous men in there along with a supply of a deadly nerve agent."

Harvo shook back her green hair. "So, you go first."

Feeney lumbered up, his topcoat over a wrinkled beige shirt with a telltale salsa stain. "Figured EDD should get in on it. I told McNab to get some toys and we'd swing by and pick him up."

"Good. Wait. Think."

She took a few paces away to do just that. Paced back.

"Heat sensors in the toys, McNab?"

"You bet."

"Check the building. Peabody, pass out the masks. Whatever the status, no one enters without a mask. Feeney, how about you and Roarke deal with any alarms and/or locks. Reineke, you and Jenkinson make the circuit. Let's mark all exits, then we'll cover them."

"What about me?"

"You wait," she told Harvo.

"Bogus. Roarke's not a cop, either, and I'm an expert consultant, too. Plus, I work with the cops totally."

"Are you authorized to carry a weapon?"

"No, but—"

"Then you wait."

Reineke jogged back. "Back and front, first level, south side and back, fire escapes on the second level."

"No heat sources," Callendar called out.

"If there aren't bad guys—"

"You still wait," Eve interrupted Harvo's next pitch.

"We'll still take it front and back. Reineke, Jenkinson, Callendar, McNab on the rear. Peabody, we'll take the front with Roarke and Feeney. We've got a damn army taking an empty building," she muttered.

She marched up to Roarke. "It's empty."

"It's bypassed anyway, alarms and locks."

"Then this'll be easy." Empty or not, she drew her weapon, went through the door low.

The lights on full illuminated the gaudy tackiness of a living area with enormous gel sofas—a trio—done in dizzying patterns of red and black. Giant entertainment screens dominated two opposing walls. All the tables shined in mirrored gold, which was picked up by a bar fronted by a couple of stools designed to resemble the female form wearing only high heels.

She pointed Feeney and Roarke in one direction, Peabody in the other, and moved straight ahead.

On her sweep she noted a game system, posters—more naked women—bottles of high-end booze, a jar of Zoner, a bowl holding a variety of pills.

She added her call of "Clear" to the others as Roarke, Feeney, and Peabody moved back from the sides, the other team from the rear.

"Kitchen, storage for cleaning droids and supplies," Peabody said.

"Bedroom and bath," Roarke added, "designed to fulfill a teenage boy's wet dream. Complete with currently deactivated sex droid."

"Another john, and a game room," Feeney added. "Refreshment area."

"Let's clear upstairs. They outfitted this for Loco. Neither rich guy's taste runs to sex-starved tacky. Lab's going to be upstairs."

She started up the metal stairs, had gotten no more than a quarter of the way when she smelled it.

"Fuck!" She threw up a hand to stop the rest of her team, then jogged until she could see the second floor. "We've got a body. Back out. Everybody, back out, masks or not. Peabody, call in the hazmat unit."

She took a sweep not only for the visual but so her

lapel recorder could capture the scene. Then she followed her team back outside.

She yanked off her mask. "Jenkinson, go around and seal the back entrance. Reineke, let's get some uniforms for backup, to canvass. Callendar, tag Morris, see if he can come on scene."

She dragged a hand through her hair. "Son of a bitch."

"Do you know the DB?" Feeney asked.

"Yeah. It's Cosner, Marshall Cosner. It looks like he was packing up another poison egg, and had a little lab accident." Her eyes narrowed. "That's how it's supposed to look."

"Very handy he'd have that accident the night before you'd have him in the box," Roarke commented.

"Yeah, isn't it? He went whining to Whitt, that's what he did, and Whitt found a way to cut his losses. The thing is, he wouldn't expect us to find Cosner so fast. Wouldn't expect us to find this place. There were more eggs up there, a whole lab set up, a shipping prep area. Boxes, packing stuff. But he's not stupid enough to come back here."

Thinking, thinking, she paced the sidewalk. "No, he's done here. Maybe he took some of it with him. Maybe he really is cutting his losses. He'll let it end with Cosner. Can't continue the fun with Cosner dead and have us pile the blame on Cosner."

"He'll figure he has plenty of time and room now," Feeney added. "You were taking the DB in the box tomorrow."

"Yeah, we had that set."

"So when he doesn't show, we go looking. We find something that clicks to this place, find it, find him. And there's your dead guy, piles of evidence, killed by the same method he used to kill, which has a nice clang to it." Feeney nodded as he studied the building. "Asshole figures case closed."

"Yeah, and he'll have a cover for tonight. But it'll have a hole somewhere. Cosner was a follower. No way he came here tonight, all wound up about the interview tomorrow, and decided, on his own, to pack up another egg."

"And without precautions," Roarke added. "Would you, knowing what's inside the egg, handle it without a suit? Or the very least gloves and a mask?"

"No, and good point."

Harvo, who perched on the hood of Jenkinson's ride, ticked a finger in the air. "You have to figure, right, the other bad guy was here—sometime or the other. Right?"

Eve glanced back. "Had to. He runs the show."

"On average, a human sheds between fifty and a hundred hairs a day. Some experts say up to two hundred, but I lean more toward a hundred. Average." She smiled. "We'd only need one."

"It's a big place, Harvo, with cleaning droids, and without any way—at this point—to confirm when the suspect was last inside."

Tonight, Eve thought. She'd make book on it, but . . .

Harvo angled her head, spread her fingers to examine glossy blue nail polish. "Do you doubt the queen?"

She'd be a fool to, Eve admitted. "Okay, Harvo, once the specialty team clears the building, you can go in, take a look."

"Mag-o!" She hopped down from the hood. "Will you hold off the sweepers, let me have first pass?"

"I can do that."

"Even more mag-o. Can I get a lift to the lab and back? I need some stuff."

"McNab," Feeney said. "Take my ride."

When the uniforms arrived, Eve had them set up barricades, start the canvass. Then she waited as the specialty team donned their protective suits.

When Junta came out a few minutes later, she walked straight to Eve. "The air's clear, but I need you and your team to stay out. There's another egg loaded, and there are hazardous chemicals. We need to secure and remove before I can clear you in."

"How long?"

"I'll let you know. And I'll tell you something, Dallas. Whoever was living in that place, in the same place we've already found and identified sarin, chlorine gas, sulfur trioxide, fricking anthrax? They're a fucking lunatic."

"Were," Eve said.

"Yeah. Well, let's all stay alive." She replaced her hood, started back.

21

It took nearly an hour, but that gave Morris time to arrive on scene. He wore a jacket over a light sweater and jeans, and had his hair in a loose tail rather than a complex braid.

Which told Eve he'd been at home, relaxing.

"I appreciate you coming."

"The job's the job." He glanced around. "You've quite the team already assembled."

"Just worked out that way. The building's just been cleared." She glanced over to where Harvo tucked her green hair into a cap. Not a white one, but like her suit and booties, a hot candy pink.

Harvo was never boring.

"Harvo, you can take the first floor. DB's on the second. Morris and I will take the body, Peabody, Jenkinson, Reineke, standard search. E-team, security and electronics, including droids."

She carried her field kit, Morris his medical bag, and,

ignoring the people gathered at the barricades, they headed inside.

"It could be even less tasteful," Morris commented. "It would take effort, but it could be less tasteful."

"It could and is," Roarke told him. "You haven't seen the bedroom."

Leaving the team to spread out, Eve went up the metal steps with Morris. He studied the body.

"Some would call it just deserts."

"I call it damned inconvenient. I'd have broken him in the box. I'd have this wrapped, he'd be alive to spend many sad decades in a cage."

She walked to the body, crouched, took out her pad for official ID while Morris began his exam.

"Body is identified as Marshall Cosner."

"TOD," Morris announced, "twenty-one-twenty."

"Victim is a Caucasian male, age twenty-six, and owner of this building through a shell company."

"Severe burning of the eyes, the dermis, inside the mouth," Morris continued as he used a penlight, "the nostrils. Loss of blood and other bodily fluids through the mouth, ears, eyes, nose. Anus to be confirmed in-house."

"No visible defensive or offensive wounds," Eve added. "The victim is wearing a gold wrist unit . . ." She emptied pockets. "A 'link, a wallet—cash and plastic—and there are numerous valuables in the building, so no evidence of an altercation or robbery."

"We'll confirm in autopsy, but from this on-site, it appears Mr. Cosner's COD is the same as the two previous victims. He was exposed to the nerve agent, inhaled same, and would have succumbed within minutes."

Leaving him to the body, Eve rose, recorded the room as she studied it.

"There was a single glass on the table downstairs. So he had a drink—we'll test it to see if he had alcohol, any illegals. Was he alone? I just don't think so. He's not a loner. More eggs."

She walked over to the cabinet that held them. "Two here, and one more already loaded and secured. So they planned at least four more. The one he was packing, the one loaded, the other two. Maybe they had extra in case. The fake wood boxes, with sealant and interior padding. Shipping boxes here—standard, strapping tape, packing. Organized well."

She turned. "Lab area over here."

"Quite a nice one, too," Morris commented.

"There were chemicals and solutions, whatever, stored in these temp-controlled units. So they could make more if they wanted. Or had the nerve. Masks, suits, gloves. But he's not wearing any protective gear."

"Which is why he's dead. There's some burning here, on the palms, between the thumb and forefinger."

She looked back. "Didn't the other vics have burns on the hands?"

"Fingers, burning on the fingers."

"More on the fingers," she mumbled and walked back, took one of the empty eggs from a cabinet. "Because they opened this little hinge here—with their fingers, pulled the top up, broke the seal."

"That was my conclusion."

"But if you take the egg out of the container—airtight container—you hold it like this, carefully if you're not a complete idiot, because it's loaded. You think it's sealed, but it's not. Or not all the way? It burns, the fumes strike, you drop the egg."

She got out her microgoggles to examine the broken pieces. "You're essentially dead when it hits the ground, but it takes another minute. It's designed to be contained to a small area. The one who's killing you has to judge the distance, but he's not going to risk it. He'd put on protection.

"Why didn't you?"

She walked to the steps. "Peabody!"

"Yo!"

"Bag that glass on the table. Flag it priority for the lab. I want to know what Cosner drank."

"He's very freshly dead," Morris said. "I can run a tox when I get him home. I should be able to identify the contents—or if not, put a second flag on it."

"Good. Say he had enough of something to impair his judgment. Or he's just stupid anyway, and he's doing what he's told. I'm standing back here, safe distance. 'Pack it up, Marsh. Let's get one more delivery.' And Cosner is turned away, getting the egg. You put on the mask, and you just wait. It doesn't take long."

"No," Morris agreed, "it wouldn't take long."

"How did he feel, I wonder? His oldest friend—and the first he'd seen die. Did he feel anything?" She shook her head. "Probably not, or not much."

She turned back to Morris. "You got this?"

"I do. I'll take him in, see to him."

She walked over for her kit, crouched again to meet Morris's eyes. "He's the last one, I swear to Christ, this bastard puts on a slab."

Morris put a hand over hers. Even through the seals, she felt the warmth. "This one, God knows, inflicted misery and was ready to inflict more. And yet, he's ours now. We'll both do what we have to do."

"Fucking A," she said, and taking her kit, headed downstairs.

Peabody intercepted her. "I had a uniform take the

glass straight to the lab. We might have better luck that way. Harvo's doing stuff with weird little lights and whirly-humming things—plus, she took both cleaning droids apart already. I guess that's okay."

"Leave her to it. Put sweepers on standby, but let her do what she does."

"Hey, boss." Reineke came in. "Kitchen and game room ACs stocked with junk food and addict munchies."

"Makes sense."

"Fancy duds—look new—in the bedroom, shoes never been worn, some of them. And a lot of porn on the entertainment units. Games and porn, porn games."

"Also plays."

"We're still at it, but wanted to pass on we haven't found any 'links or tablets, and no comm devices. Roarke, he said there was a setup for a data and comm center, and Feeney checks that, but the unit's not here."

"There's a comp upstairs, but no comm. DB had a 'link on him. I'll have one of the geeks get on it."

She spotted a geek as McNab came in from the back.

"Security's tight, Dallas," he told her, "with the notable exception of cams. Not a single one."

"They didn't want any record of them coming and going."

"Right, but there were some cams—interior."

"Were?"

"We found a couple hookups."

"Okay. Take the upstairs e's," she told him. "There's a comp, password protected, and the vic's personal 'link. No communications on it after business hours today. You can check if you think there were cams up there."

"He and Whitt probably have drop 'links."

She nodded at Peabody. "Bet on it. I need you to stick

here, finish up, seal it up. I'm going to notify next of kin and take a pass at the vic's residence. Harvo's cleared to do her thing upstairs after the body's transported."

"Got it. On it."

"Where's Roarke?"

"Back." McNab jerked a thumb. "He and Feeney are trying to figure the missing cams."

She walked back to what she took as the game room—as floridly decorated as everything else—where Roarke stood on a stepladder in a closet while Feeney frowned and watched.

"Mounted from in here. And the mount itself is still in place. This one appears to have been hastily yanked out. Fingertip hole for the lens."

She saw Roarke's fingertip press against a tiny hole above the frame of the closet.

"They wanted to watch the mad scientist."

Feeney glanced back as Eve spoke.

"Sure. Make sure he wasn't fucking up, didn't bring people in, didn't start plotting against them. Not a lot of trust."

"Since Whitt's killed both of them, from where I'm standing, not a lot of call for it. I've got to do the notification and hit the vic's apartment."

She watched for another minute. "Hell, nearly forgot. I saw Detective Swanson earlier. He's security at Whitt's office building."

"Well, no shit." Hands in pockets, Feeney nodded. "Good cop."

"He said to give you his best."

"He always did."

"Do you need the civilian?"

"I can manage."

"Then, Roarke, with me."

"All right then." He came down the ladder, dusted off his hands.

"Did you seal up?"

"I know the bloody rules."

She gave him a nod, started out. "Peabody, make sure the sweepers check any and all previous cam locations. You'd be careful what you touched, wouldn't you?" she continued as they went out. "You'd probably wipe down surfaces if you weren't sure, or even seal up. But would you think of it when you're pulling out cams from inside closets, behind a wall?"

"Me personally?"

"Not you, you think of everything, but the fact is these two are amateurs. Sure, Whitt's smart, he's careful, he's patient, and he plans. But maybe. Just like he'd have been careful to create a solid alibi for tonight. But there's got to be a hole, even a fingertip hole. I'm going to find it."

"You're so sure he was there?"

"It doesn't work otherwise." While Roarke got behind the wheel, she plugged Lowell Cosner's address into the in-dash. "Cosner would need Whitt to reassure him about tomorrow. He'd need Whitt to tell him what to do, how to act, what to say. Morris found burns on the palms—different from the other vics. I think Whitt tampered with the seal on the egg, protected himself, then when Cosner took it out of the airtight to pack it, dead."

"You said from the beginning it was both cold and personal. That would be both."

"He had to be there. Cosner's 'link was in his pocket, and showed no communications since about sixteen hundred—and none today with Whitt. They would have used drop 'links to discuss anything to do with this. Otherwise, it's done face-to-face so there's no trail."

"And your estimation of Cosner is he wouldn't act on his own."

"He's been following Whitt's lead most of his life." And she could see it, as if she'd been there. "He'd have been anxious about tomorrow, dealing with his father, those questions and demands. He'd have needed his old pal's support."

"And by staging all this, Whitt not only eliminates his old pal, but heaps evidence against him. It's efficient."

They pulled up in front of the luxury tower, which boasted two doormen.

"Since you don't own the place—I checked," Eve added, "I'll handle the doormen."

She got out, flashed her badge as the one on the right started toward her. "NYPSD, and this is an official vehicle, which will stay where I put it."

He looked both displeased and resigned. "How about maybe you pull it down about ten feet, keep my neck off the block?"

"We can do that." As Roarke obliged, she turned back to the doorman. "Lowell Cosner."

"Yeah, he came in a couple hours ago. What's up?"

"Marshall Cosner."

"Okay, yeah, he lives here, but I haven't seen him tonight."

Eve pulled out her PPC, brought up Whitt's ID shot. "Do you recognize him?"

"Sure, that's Mr. Whitt. He's a friend of Cosner Junior."

"When's the last time you saw him here?"

"I don't know. Couple of days."

The other doorman—female—wandered over, peered at the image on-screen. "That's Mr. Whitt. He came by earlier."

"I didn't see him."

"You were helping Ms. Troski with all her bags. He breezed in about five, I guess. He breezed out again, maybe five-thirty."

"Was he carrying anything?"

"Ah . . ." She screwed up her face in thought. "Sure, a briefcase, good-sized one. And, yeah, a fancy messenger bag."

"Thanks."

She walked into the lobby, quiet as a church. The green marble floor gleamed. Spring flowers in cylindrical vases scented the air. A woman in a pale pink suit sat at a desk with a D and C unit, more flowers, and a gracious smile.

"Good evening. How can I assist you?"

The gracious smile turned professionally blank when Eve flashed her badge. "Is Lowell Cosner at home?"

"I believe so."

"We'll need to be cleared up to his apartment. We'll also require access to Marshall Cosner's residence."

"I don't believe Marshall Cosner is currently at home."

"No, and he won't be back. Homicide," Eve said, tapping her badge. "We're here to notify Mr. Lowell Cosner his son is dead."

"Oh my—my God."

"Clear us up, and make sure we're cleared to access Marshall Cosner's level and apartment."

"Yes, of course. If I could just verify your identification." She took an ID scanner out of a drawer, ran it over Eve's badge. "Mr. Lowell Cosner is Penthouse Level

Two. Mr. Marshall Cosner is—was—3610, thirty-sixth floor. Is there anything more I can do?"

"What time did you come on the desk?"

"Eight."

Too late to have seen Whitt. "I'll need the name and contact of whoever was on the desk at five."

"Of course."

When she gave it without hesitation, Eve noted it down. "Thanks. We'll also need the security feed from the front door, the lobby, the elevators, and Marshall Cosner's floor. From, let's say, four-thirty to six this evening."

"I can arrange that."

"Do. We'll take it from here."

She walked with Roarke to the elevator, waited until they were inside before speaking again. "He came to get rid of anything Cosner might have had in his place to tie him to this. Possibly to plant something that laid the guilt more directly on Cosner. He was always going to kill him."

"Always?"

"Addict, weak sister, loose end. He used Loco until they had what they wanted, disposed of him. He needed Cosner until he'd finished, but with the pressure building, opted to deal with it, cut things short.

"Breezed in," she repeated. "I bet that's accurate. Just breezing in, breezing out again."

"Shortsighted not to calculate you'd ask or check security feeds."

She shook her head. "He figures he has at least a couple of days if not more before we find the building and the body. By then the feed's overwritten, and the memories of the doormen questionable. Added to it, the evidence would be so strong against Cosner, he feels he'd be clear."

"The building's in Cosner's name." Roarke nodded as they stepped off the elevator. "Valuable property, but he didn't take any part of legal ownership. Yes, you're right. He always meant to do for his mate."

"People like Whitt don't have mates in any definition of the word."

She stopped outside the pure white double doors of the Cosner penthouse. Pressed the buzzer.

Seconds later the security comp responded.

Mr. and Ms. Cosner have retired for the evening.

"NYPSD." Eve held up her badge to the scanner. "Dallas, Lieutenant Eve, and civilian consultant. We need to speak to Mr. Lowell Cosner on official police business."

One moment while this information is relayed.

When the door opened, Eve expected a housekeeper or butler type, maybe a droid, but Lowell answered personally.

He'd shed the business suit she imagined he'd worn through the day, exchanged it for trim pants, a sweater, and had the faintest whiff of alcohol and tobacco around him.

His face, already sternly handsome with its thick crown of silver-dusted gold hair, showed fury.

"How dare you? How dare you come to my home? This kind of harassment won't be tolerated. Do you think barging into my home with your badge and your"—he waved a dismissive hand at Roarke—"*consultant* will intimidate me?"

"Mr. Cosner, we're sorry to disturb you, but we have difficult news. Can we come in for a moment?"

"No, you cannot. And if you've found some petty way to attempt to arrest my son or further attempt to implicate him, I'll deal with you in the morning, as agreed."

"Mr. Cosner." Before he could shut the door in her face, Eve braced a hand against it. His eyes, bright against his rich man's tan, went molten.

"That will cost you your badge."

"Mr. Cosner, I regret to inform you your son, Marshall Cosner, is dead. We're sorry for your loss."

He reared back. The fury only increased with disbelief whipped across it. "You lie!"

"No, sir. I examined and identified his body myself, along with the chief medical examiner of New York. Your son died at approximately nine-twenty this evening."

"Lowell." Roarke used his first name when he saw something shatter in those bright eyes. "It would be better if we came inside."

"How? You tell me how."

"He was exposed to the same nerve agent that killed two other individuals," Eve told him. "Do you want to hear the rest in the doorway?"

Lowell simply turned away, walked through the entrance foyer into a living area done in quiet colors and quiet patterns. He sat heavily in a chair where soft sage merged in tiny diamonds with soft cream.

"He was murdered, like the others. You tried to say he was part of the killing. You—"

"Mr. Cosner, he was." Eve decided not to wait for an invitation and sat directly across from him. "Were you aware your son owned a building on Pitt Street downtown, one he set up through a shell company?"

"No, that's ridiculous. Marshall wouldn't begin to know how to create a shell company."

"I imagine he had help," Eve said simply. "He purchased the building, set it up as a residence and workspace for Lucas Sanchez. You know that name," she said as she saw the knowledge on Lowell's face.

"Yes. My son has an . . . addictive personality. He has a weakness for certain chemical enhancements. Sanchez exploited that weakness. Marshall assured me, his mother, his family that he had cut ties with Sanchez. After Marshall's accident, after he recovered from his injuries, he assured us . . ."

You didn't believe him, Eve realized. But you hoped. You had to hope.

"I'm sorry, he didn't. Moreover, evidence indicates, strongly, Sanchez was paid to create the nerve agent."

"You expect me to believe my son was some sort of terrorist?"

"Your son was part of a conspiracy to murder certain individuals over a long-held grudge. Sanchez and the nerve agent were tools, and when Sanchez had created the agent, he was killed. Mr. Cosner, your son was packing the agent in its receptacle for shipment when he was exposed."

Lowell shook his head, just kept shaking it. "He wouldn't know how. He wouldn't know."

"Lowell," Roarke interrupted. "Let me get you a drink."

His eyes glittered with tears as he turned to Roarke. "I have . . ." He gestured vaguely. "I was reading, having some bourbon, unwinding when . . ."

"I'll find it," Roarke told him, and left Eve to continue.

"You took your son out of Theresa A. Gold Academy after Headmaster Rufty took over for Headmaster Grange."

"That was years ago."

"Why did you take him out?"

Lowell dropped his head in his hands, sat like that for several moments. "We came to understand Marshall was using, that he was drinking, that his grades had been . . . inflated. We came to understand his friends weren't . . . appropriate. We believed the best solution was to send him to boarding school, to have my wife's parents help supervise him, to remove him from the situation. We did what we thought best. We tried rehab. He's my son. I did what I thought best."

"I'm sure you did."

Roarke came back, put a glass in Lowell's hand.

"His mother—she was so upset about the accusation, the police, the interview, she finally took a tranq and went to bed. How will I tell her our boy's gone? Why didn't we find the way to save him?"

"Did he give any indication he was angry with Dr. Rufty, any of his teachers?"

"At the time, of course. He was mad at the world. At us, at the school, but he was so young. He seemed to do a little better. Off and on he did better, but . . . He was always good at hiding things, at pretense. It was often easier just to believe him rather than deal with the drama and disappointment. But I can't believe, won't believe he'd do the things you're saying."

"And as I said, he had help."

Lowell took a slow pull on the bourbon. "Stephen."

"Are you referring to Stephen Whitt, Mr. Cosner?"

"I am. After it became clear what Marshall had been a part of at TAG, we did what we could to separate him from those influences. Against my better judgment Marshall and Stephen remained friends. Oh, he's another who's good at hiding things, at pretense. I don't believe Marshall lied when he finally broke down and told us Stephen had devised most of the schemes, had served as ringleader. Marshall looked up to him, always had. My wife never liked the boy, always said there was something missing in him. I dismissed that, but agreed we should do what we could to cut the bond."

He looked down into his drink, set it aside. "We didn't, even though they went to different schools in different states, then different colleges, we never broke that bond. Marshall's a grown man. We can't forbid him his friendships, even when they're destructive."

Lowell swiped at his eyes.

"If Marshall had any part in this, you can be sure Stephen was behind it. Marshall would have followed him into hell." He picked his glass up again. "And now he has."

"You know the Whitts," Eve prompted.

"We were friendly when the boys were in school together. Now we're polite. My wife dislikes Brent—Stephen's father—and has for some time."

"Because?"

"Primarily because he lied to and cheated on his wife, whom my wife was fond of. And more, I suppose, since she learned he carried on an affair with the headmaster of our son's school."

"Lotte Grange."

"Correct. My wife happened to be meeting an out-of-town friend, waiting for her in the lobby of her hotel. And she saw the headmaster and Brent come in, check in, and share, we'll say, a public display of affection on their way to the elevator. It was particularly upsetting, as she had a friendship with Brent's wife."

"Okay."

"Neither here nor there now," Lowell mumbled. "Nothing is now."

"Mr. Cosner, are you Stephen Whitt's attorney?"

Cosner's brows shot up in surprise. "No. I would hardly share such information, even under the circumstances, if I represented Stephen."

Another lie, Eve thought. Another unnecessary lie.

"We need to see our son."

"I'll arrange that as soon as possible." Eve rose. "We need to go into and through your son's apartment at this time."

"We thought having him live in the same building would help. But it didn't. I need to tell my wife our boy is gone. I need to tell her our boy helped kill people. How do I do that?"

22

Eve stood outside Marshall Cosner's apartment door—pure white again, but a single. Since it had layers of security, she let Roarke work his way through.

"This kind of lock and alarm system's overkill in a building like this," she said.

"Not if you have something to hide. His father loved him. Didn't respect him, trust him, but still, loved him."

"He didn't do anything to earn the respect or trust. I guess love just comes with the package for most parents."

"Most," Roarke agreed, "and there we are. After you, Lieutenant."

Cosner's apartment didn't boast a foyer, and its living area was about half the size of his father's. Still, it wasn't exactly a dump.

No terrace beyond the windows, but plenty of city lights. Bolder, more sleekly modern furnishings than his parents'. A lot of hard color against shiny chrome.

Eve wandered through. "Okay, mostly open—dining area, kitchen over there. That would put the bedroom area on the other side. Let's start there."

She found the master, and a smaller second bedroom that served as a home office. "Take the office, I'll take the bedroom. If they used drop 'links, Whitt might have missed one, or a notebook, a file on the comp, some communication on the house 'link. I'm going to check in with Peabody first."

While she did, Roarke sat at the steel-and-leather desk. It took him less than two minutes to melt through the password on the computer. And hardly more to find Whitt's work.

"Darling? Spare a minute?"

She came back, her 'link pressed, screen down, to her chest. And hissed, "Don't call me darling when I'm talking to cops."

"Sorry, Lieutenant Darling."

She rolled her eyes. "What?"

"At seventeen-oh-eight, a number of files on this unit were deleted."

"Son of a bitch!" She strode over, scowled over his shoulder. "Can you get any of them back?"

He merely shifted his gaze up to hers. "Such insults don't deserve a darling."

"Just . . ." She waved at him, lifted the 'link. "Yeah, tell the e-geeks to contact that science nerd in the lab. Ah, Siler. Once they get the rest unencrypted, he can verify whatever the hell it is."

"Dallas," Peabody said, "it's after midnight."

"It's— Shit. Get some rack time, everybody. Tag the science nerd at eight hundred. I want somebody to sit on Whitt. I don't think he's going to rabbit—not when he thinks he's free and clear. But I don't want to risk it."

"Got it. Harvo found twelve hundred and sixteen human hairs."

"Are you fucking with me?"

"I am not fucking with you. She was revved up, and since it took her for-nearly-ever, the sweepers are really just getting going."

"Have them seal up. Rack time." She clicked off. "Do what you can with that," she told Roarke. "I'm going to go through the place. We can take the unit with us, log it out. I can get the e-team to finish the recovery in the morning."

"No darling for you, she of little faith," he replied, and kept working.

She went through the bedroom—the well-situated single man's motif with deep colors, straight lines, no fuss but a lot of status.

The goodie drawer by the bed told her he at least had the occasional sex partner. Wardrobe told her he liked to spend money on his duds. All designer, right down to the socks and underwear.

She found his stash of illegals, noted some of them were hand-labeled just as the ones at the warehouse had been.

Probably cooked up there, she mused, bagged them, sealed them.

In the second, smaller closet, she found his sports equipment. The golf clubs, tennis rackets, golf shoes, tennis shoes, and the wardrobe deemed stylish for same. She also found his old uniforms—summer and winter— from Gold Academy.

And found that oddly sad.

Even as she thought it, she glanced up. Frowning, she stepped back, rose on her toes, and just caught the edge of a box—dark blue, on the high shelf.

She had to hunt up a chair, drag it in, climb up to reach. The fine layer of dust told her it hadn't been opened in some time.

She climbed down, opened the lid.

Photos—a lot of them. Photos of Cosner, Whitt, Hayward, others in their younger days. Mugging photos, obviously stoned photos, photos from sporting events. Clippings from same. School bulletins and announcements for dances, events. Bits of memorabilia.

Sad, she thought again, and dug through.

Found the thick notebook on the bottom. Not electronic, but the kind you wrote in. And, she realized as she flipped through, Cosner had written quite a bit in his very poor, cramped printing.

"Eve."

"Listen to this," she said without looking over. "'We beat the hot shit out of that faggot Rodriges last night. Jerkwad actually believed we wanted him to tutor us, but me and Steve tutored the hell out of him. Talked about finishing him—who'd miss the little fucker? But we decided just to dump his sorry ass, then go have a few brews.'"

She flipped pages. "There's more, a whole lot more. Enough to bring Whitt in for a serious conversation."

"Eve," Roarke repeated. "I've restored some files. One in particular you need to have a look at."

"Okay." She glanced up, saw his face. "What is it?"

"A target list, detailed."

She took the notebook with her to the home office, then looked over Roarke's shoulder.

"I'm still restoring files. I'd say Whitt—as he's quite obviously your man—knows little about how comps actually work. His delete was standard, and easily countermanded."

"Jesus, Cosner actually titled it Payback Time, like they're still in high school."

"And as you see, the targets of that payback are listed in alpha order, with the intended victims attached. There's more following the list. It's schedules for the targets, optimum times to schedule delivery for the intended victims, selected drop points and delivery services, even the names chosen for the bogus shop listed as sender."

"He wrote it all down," Eve said as Roarke scrolled through. "The alibis, cover stories. Who made the drops. And he's dead. It piles on the circumstantial, but he's not alive to confirm it. But it's more than enough to get Whitt in the box.

"Go back to the target list."

When he did, Eve ran them through. "Duran, then Flint—Rodriges mentioned him—he's retired in South Carolina now. Rosalind, the chem teacher. Rufty, then Stuben, art teacher, Woskinski, and Zweck, school nurse now doing private care. That's seven designated targets, Cosner himself makes three victims. There were only three undamaged eggs left on scene. Either Whitt has the seventh, or it's already been shipped."

"If Whitt always planned to kill his friend—"

"Not like this. Even an idiot like Cosner could add. Seven targets, seven eggs. You eliminate Cosner the easy way—feed him an OD. This was necessity, do it quick, move on. We can't risk it."

She yanked out her 'link, tagged Peabody.

"Contact Rosalind and Zweck from the academy's list," she snapped. "We need to know if they received any deliveries, we need to know their status. Is McNab with you?"

"Yeah, but—"

"Have him contact Stuben from the academy. I'll take Woskinski and Flint. They're all on the kill list Cosner had on his comp."

"Well, Jesus. We're right on it. Wait—that doesn't add up."

"Exactly. There's very likely another egg out there, very likely loaded. We need to find it. Confirm status first. These individuals' safety is first priority. Report back when it's done."

"Give me Woskinski's contact," Roarke told her. "You take the last. Quicker that way."

Once she'd confirmed all remaining targets safe and secure, she shifted to the next priority.

"We have to find that goddamn egg. How much time do you need for a full restore?"

"I've about got it. As I said, he doesn't know much. He didn't even throw in a virus."

"Keep at it. Copy that file to my PPC for now. I need to wake up Reo."

While he worked, Roarke listened to her with a combination of admiration and amusement.

Reo, video blocked, said hoarsely, "I hate you, Dallas."

"Marshall Cosner is dead, poisoned by the nerve agent. We have reason to believe another shipment has already been dropped."

"What? Wait. God, why isn't there coffee right here?" There was rustling and thumping. "Details."

"We hit the converted warehouse Cosner bought," Eve began, and filled in those details up to and past the time Reo unblocked video while standing in her kitchen with a giant mug of coffee.

"We established Whitt came to Cosner's apartment building—when Cosner was not in residence—tonight.

One of the doormen ID'd him, and we have security footage we'll pick up on the way out. Though files were deleted from Cosner's home office comp—and other devices that should be here are missing—Roarke was able to restore. We found a kill list. There are seven names on it, with details. Three eggs have been used to kill, three have been taken into evidence. One's missing."

"Any mention of Whitt in those files?"

"Yes—coordination of cover stories."

"That'll help. But with Cosner dead, won't ring the bell."

Fire flashed, in Eve's eyes, in her voice. "I'll ring the damn bell. Right now I need warrants. We have to find that shipment. We have a list of preferred delivery services and drop points. I need warrants for all of them."

Reo took a big gulp of coffee. "Send them to me. I'll get them."

"I want a search and seizure on Whitt's residence and office, and a warrant for his arrest. On tap," she added. "We find the package first."

"I'm going to need more coffee. I'll work on it. Get me what you've got."

"Sending now," Roarke told Eve.

"Thanks," Eve said to Roarke. "Get back to me," she said to Reo.

Then woke up CI Michaela Junta. "You're going to need to put teams together," Eve began.

"Fully restored and copied," Roarke announced when she'd finished.

"Good. I'll have EDD pick it up. We'll work better at home. And I want to see the security feed."

"I haven't met this Whitt, but I'm going to make a deduction. He's not nearly as smart as he thinks he is."

"You'd be right about that." Eve bagged the note-book, sealed and labeled it. "What he is? Smug, self-important, a sociopath who's been protected by privilege and money all his life. That's about to end."

She locked and sealed the apartment. "I'm going to review the security feed in the car, save time. Junta won't let me near the drops or the search for the nerve agent. Which is a pisser and understandable, as I'd do the same damn thing in her place."

In the elevator she rocked back on her heels, wanting to move, to move. Once she had the security disc, she plugged it into her PPC even as they walked out to the car.

She scanned through while Roarke drove.

"Doorman had the time right. There he is. Walks right by the desk guy, who greets him. Obviously he comes by often enough nobody questions him."

She switched to the elevator cam when he got on. "Okay, there he is. Checks his wrist unit. Checking the time. Taking out a 'link—drop 'link. Yeah, yeah, answer-ing a tag from Cosner, you bet your ass. We can get a lip reader on this if we need. Quick convo, puts the 'link away—one he'll ditch later. Smirks. Oh yeah, that's a smug fucking smirk."

She switched to the corridor cam, which showed him strolling straight to Cosner's apartment, using his own swipe and palm print to gain entrance.

"Doesn't he realize you'd check the security?"

"Cosner wasn't killed there—that's how he sees it. Why would we bother? And again, by the time we found the body, the feed's overwritten. And here he is, heading back out. He spent thirty-two minutes in-side. Whatever he removed—say, spare drop 'links, any other electronics—are inside the briefcase and messenger bag. I need to know where he was tonight, what his cover is."

"He'd need time to slip away, get to the warehouse, deal with Cosner, get back." Roarke drove through the gates of home. "So it's most likely something more public than private. He'd need a crowd, wouldn't he?"

"Another club, maybe, or a concert, a sporting event, a banquet—business but not a client dinner. This took too long to fake taking a tag."

"Let me see what I can find out." Roarke smiled as he opened the door. "I still have my ways."

"Good. You can use your ways while I check in with Junta, with Reo. I figure to give Feeney a few hours of downtime, then we're going to hit Whitt with the search. Bright and early."

"He thinks he's home free, and is feeling very good about himself right now. Likely sleeping like a baby."

"Babies are always crying."

Roarke stopped on the way up the stairs with her. "That's quite true, isn't it? I'll give you that one. He's sleeping like a sociopath. And he's bound to have the formula for the nerve agent."

She turned to him as they walked into her office. "What would you do if you were a sociopathic bad guy and had the formula for a chemical weapon that can kill in a kind of pinpoint way, in minutes, before it dissipates?"

"Sell it. If I wasn't a complete berk as well as a sociopathic bad guy, I'd wait several months first. A year, maybe two."

"He won't wait a year or two, but he'll wait awhile. I'm betting he's already doing some due diligence on where to sell for the best return."

She went straight for coffee.

"You won't give him the opportunity. Let me see what I can find out."

He stopped by her board. "Will you update this tonight?"

"It's routine for a reason."

"He had everything going for him," Roarke said as he studied Marshall Cosner's ID. "Wealth, privilege, education, opportunities. All wasted."

"Now he's in the morgue." She sat at her command center, got to work.

She touched base with Junta, with Reo, wrote up her report, then yes, updated her board. As she finished, Roarke came back.

"The Whitt Group had a major client seminar, dinner, with entertainment following tonight at the New York Grand Hotel. Whitt was a featured speaker."

"Where is it? What time did he speak?"

"He was the dinner speaker, scheduled for eight. As for where, let's do this."

He leaned over her, did a few keystrokes to bring a map of New York onto the wall screen. "Here's the Grand." He highlighted it. "And the warehouse."

"Too far to walk, not enough time for that. Or to run even if you were a speedy naked marathoner."

"A what?"

"Later," she said. "He had to have transpo."

"Agreed. Even with that it would take several minutes."

"Wouldn't get a cab." She got up to pace. "Wouldn't risk that, certainly wouldn't risk the subway. He'd have his own—not a driver because that adds another person in. Does the Grand have parking?"

"It does, but valet only."

"That won't work. So he needs to park somewhere close, where he can get out then back in easy, fast. What've we got within a block?"

More keystrokes. "You'd have the Hubble Hotel, which has an accessible parking garage, a block away. The next closest parking would be three blocks more."

"We need the security cams for both hotels."

He turned to her. Fired up, yes, he thought, but running on fumes nonetheless.

"And I imagine there are cops capable of doing that who are actually on duty at near to two in the morning. You need to get some sleep."

"I don't . . ." She realized she was revved by the movement in the case, and that it wouldn't last. She needed to be sharp to go up against Whitt in the morning. "You're right. He's not going anywhere, the rest of the targets are secure, and Junta's team will find the package. I'll get someone to handle the hotels."

Roarke brushed a hand over her hair. "Well now, that was easy."

"Because it's either some rack time or I have to take a booster before I take Whitt down. I hate those things."

She made the arrangements, then tried to turn her brain off as they walked to the bedroom.

"I wonder who he'd targeted next?" she said as she undressed.

"Whoever it was, they're safe."

"You had a big part in seeing they are."

"We can both rest easy for a few hours knowing we did our part."

She slid into bed where the cat already stretched out, tried again to let the long day go as Roarke drew her back against him. She took Roarke's hand.

"They had everything we didn't. Now one's in the

morgue, and the other will spend the rest of his life in a cage."

He kissed the back of her head. "And here we are. Sleep now." Knowing it lulled her, Roarke rubbed her back. "Morning comes soon enough."

Morning came at five-twelve when her communicator signaled. "Block video," she mumbled as she groped for it.

Already up, Roarke ordered the lights on at ten percent.

"Dallas."

"Junta. We've got the package. It's secured."

She shoved a hand through her hair as she rolled out of bed. "Where?"

"They went Allied again, made the drop at nineteen-forty. Kiosk's just a couple blocks from the warehouse. We tracked it to the shipping port, confiscated it. They got cute with the bogus sender. Duck, Duck, Goose. It was addressed to Lilliana Rosalind."

"The chemistry teacher's wife. Good work, Junta."

"All around. Finish him off, Dallas."

"That's the plan. I'll get back to you."

When she clicked off, Roarke handed her coffee. "Thanks. You were already up. Mostly dressed."

"'Link conference shortly." He stood in black suit pants, a dove-gray shirt while he flawlessly knotted a tie that blended those tones with a sharp red in tiny checks. "What's next, Lieutenant?"

"Check in, get teams together, set things up. I want Mira observing my interview with Whitt. I can coordinate most of that from here. I'll grab a shower and get moving."

"I'm in my office if you need anything. It was good

work, all around," he added before picking up his suit
jacket.

So far, she thought as she headed to the shower, and
he went out.

With Cosner disposed of, evidence removed, Whitt
considered himself in the clear, she calculated as the hot
jets pummeled her system awake. Wouldn't it be satisfying to disabuse him? Still, she had to take care on where
and how to apply the pressure.

Debating her options, she hopped in the drying tube.

More coffee, she decided, and grabbed that before
going into her closet. She started to grab whatever at
random, thinking how much easier that chore had been
when she'd had maybe six choices. She didn't have time
to think about stupid style and horseshit image.

Giving a passing thought to spring weather, she
opted for a vest rather than a jacket, grabbed sturdy
ankle boots, and walked out to strap on her weapon harness. As she grabbed her 'link, her communicator, she
caught sight of herself in the mirror. Stopped. Thought:
Hmm.

Maybe she hadn't realized she'd given it any thought,
but she'd managed to pair black leather pants with the
black leather vest over a straight-lined black shirt and
the thick-soled black boots.

Good for running after bad guys, and kicking asses.

All in all, she came off just a little mean. Which she
considered perfect.

She went straight to her office, her command center,
and her third cup of coffee.

She tagged Peabody first, gave her partner the update
and instructions while she checked for any incoming reports from Harvo, Morris, the sweepers.

Nothing yet, but she had to consider it was still shy of six hundred.

From Peabody to Jenkinson, from Jenkinson to Feeney, from Feeney to Reo. Rather than wake up Mira and Whitney, she sent memos.

Forty minutes after her comm sounded, she had her teams set, her plan in place, and was ready to roll.

When she walked over to Roarke's office door, he held up a finger for her to wait. She saw a group of people at a conference table on-screen, and . . . yeah, that was Big Ben outside the glass wall.

"Once we receive those changes, we'll look over the paperwork. We should be able to have this done by the end of your business day. Thank you."

Once he'd finished, he turned to Eve. "It only lacks a whip, and since I expect you want the hard-ass image today, well done."

"He's going to get more than the image. I've got a no-knock warrant coming through and a whole bunch of no-bullshit cops ready to go through the door."

"Hard-ass playing hardball." He rose, walked over to set his hands on her hips, kiss her. "Eat something. Coffee and adrenaline aren't actual fuel, and you'll need it," he added when she rolled her eyes.

"I'll pull up something in the car."

"Good enough. You should wear your long black coat—finish off the look. He's a bad one, Lieutenant." He kissed her again. "So you take care of my cop."

"I'm a lot badder than he is."

Trusting she was, he watched her go, then sat down to take the next conference.

At oh-six-thirty, Eve stood outside the uptown townhouse. She'd have pegged Whitt the type for a fancy penthouse in a building chock-full of fancy amenities. But she realized this made sense.

No real neighbors, fewer people who might notice his comings and goings, no one in charge of security but himself.

As ordered, Peabody had pulled in four uniforms, Jenkinson had drafted Baxter and Trueheart, and Feeney added on McNab and Callendar.

Overkill, sure, but she wanted the show.

"One heat source," Callendar announced. "Second floor. He's still beddy-bye, Dallas."

"Then this should fulfill my quota of waking people up this morning. Can you get through the locks and alarms, Feeney?"

"We're getting it," he muttered as he and McNab worked. "You wanted this quick, you should've brought Roarke."

"I've got the battering ram for quick."

"Couple minutes," Feeney griped.

"We're starting to draw some early-morning attention. Officers?"

The uniforms snapped to, moving people along as Feeney and McNab exchanged fist bumps. "You're clear."

"On my lead then. We announce as we enter. Keep announcing as we move through as outlined."

She drew her weapon—considered that mostly show as well—nodded to Peabody. Went through the door.

"This is the police! NYPSD. We have a warrant to enter. This is the police," she repeated and aimed for the stairs. "We have a warrant. We are armed. Stephen Whitt, you're ordered to come out, to show yourself. Show your hands."

He came out of a bedroom, and since he was naked, showed more than his hands.

"What the fuck do you think you're doing?"

"Stephen Witt, we have a warrant to enter and search these premises. We have an additional warrant for your arrest on suspicion of conspiracy to murder, two counts, possession and distribution of chemical weapons, suspicion of murder, one count."

"You've lost your goddamn mind."

"You have the right to remain silent. You also have the right to put on pants before I cuff you and have you taken into Central."

"You keep your hands off me, keep them off my things. I'm contacting my lawyer."

"Also your right, and we'll get to the rest of your rights and obligations. But really, Steve? Pants. Baxter! Come on up here and assist Mr. Whitt in getting dressed. Mirandize him while you're at it."

Inside those empty eyes Eve saw flickers of a dark, deadly heat. "You're going to pay for this."

"I'm standing here looking at you naked, with bed hair and a bad disposition. I've already paid."

23

Whitt contacted his lawyer. Eve imagined he'd have a fleet of them when they got down to business at Central. But for now, she had two burly, hard-eyed uniforms escort him out to the waiting black-and-white.

"You're finished." While his eyes stayed cold, empty, his cuffed hands balled into fists. "You don't know who you're dealing with. I'll finish you."

She only smiled as the uniforms perp-walked him out.

"No smirk," she commented. "Not so smug. Pissed more than scared, but not so smug."

She looked around the perfectly ordered living area, more showroom than home to her eye, with its navy gel sofa, its white accent chairs, polished steel tables, and splashy modern art.

"We're going to find something," she mumbled. "Something he thinks he's stashed away where we won't find it, but didn't think he needed to get rid of or hide somewhere else."

"He didn't even ask about the charges," Peabody pointed out. "Especially the last one. The third murder."

"That's right. He's trying to work out how we found Cosner so fast. He thinks he's covered on that. He'll have a safe, at least one. We'll get into that. But he's got some hidey-hole, something a little trickier. Let's find it."

She started in the bedroom, as she found people generally considered that their safe space. She found the safe, spent several tense and sweaty minutes bypassing the locks, only to find nothing of particular interest inside. Man jewelry, some cash, his passport.

Feeney walked into the closet. "That's a decent safe. You bypass?"

"Yeah."

"You're picking things up, kid. And speaking of Roarke, you said how he said Whitt didn't know much about comps? I'm here to tell you, he don't know dick. Had the unit in his home office passcoded so weak Mavis's toddler could've gotten through. A couple of basic filters you can poof just giving them a hard stare."

"I take it you're in."

"Oh, we're in." Feeney took a bag of candied almonds from his baggy pocket, offered some. "Mostly business on it. Financial gobbledygook for clients. Roarke could figure it, or we'll bring in a forensic accountant, but it looks legit. Here's what's not on there. Any of his personal finances."

"Roarke looked at those. Suspects some money laundering. Cash outlays that don't make sense." Frowning, she sat back on her heels. "You're saying he doesn't have any personal stuff on there?"

"Not money-wise. I'm guessing he didn't know enough to keep two sets of books."

"Add arrogance. Hidey-hole." She scanned the closet.
"There has to be one. Maybe a false wall. Let's—"

"I've got it! Woot!"

At Peabody's call, Eve scrambled up, and found her
partner on her hands and knees at the foot of Whitt's
bed.

Obviously pleased, Peabody actually wiggled her
butt. "That rug was over it. I thought, well, you never
know, took a peek under, and hey, I did know. Secret
compartment in the floor. It's really well done, custom
work. With a thumbprint lock."

Eve calculated how much time it would take to bypass, walked to the door, shouted, "I need a crowbar."

Pleased shifted to seriously distressed as Peabody
pressed a hand to her heart. "Aw, Dallas, the flooring's
gorgeous."

"Suck it up."

And she rolled her shoulders, imagining the pleasure
of prying up floorboards.

By nine Eve sat in her office with Reo, going over the
evidence gathered. Reo sat back in Eve's desk chair, enjoyed the very fine coffee.

"I don't believe the PA's office will be inclined to offer
any sort of deal to Mr. Whitt, and in fact will push, and
push hard, for the maximum on all charges."

"I should fucking hope so."

Reo only smiled. "He's got three high-powered criminal attorneys just waiting to tear the arrest to shreds.
They've already filed to have the charges dismissed,
and filed for false arrest. They'll be pulling strings
while we're in Interview. That'll be Kobast, Broward
Kobast, in Interview. I'm going to join you and Peabody, and I'm going to enjoy— No," she corrected.

"Let me say I'm going to relish being part of knocking them down, several pegs."

"Gone up against them before?"

"Two of the three. You win some, you lose some." Reo shrugged. "This one's a win."

Peabody came to the door. "Whitt and his attorney are in Interview A. His other attorney's up with the commander. I don't know where number three is."

"She's probably arguing for the dismissal." Reo rose, faked dusting off her navy suit. "Let's go disappoint all of them."

Eve hauled the evidence box off her desk and led the way.

Peabody opened the door to Interview A.

"Record on. Dallas, Lieutenant Eve, Peabody, Detective Delia, Reo, APA Cher, entering Interview with Stephen Whitt and his designated legal representative Broward Kobast. This interview is re charges against Mr. Whitt stemming from case numbers H-4945-1, H-4952-1, H-4963-1."

"My client will exercise his right to silence, so you will speak to me. He also, of course, disputes all of these injurious charges. We've filed for their immediate dismissal, and have filed charges of harassment and false arrest against the NYPSD and you personally, Lieutenant."

Kobast looked like an elder statesman, with his shock of white hair, his trim white beard, the contrasting slash of black brows over crystal blue eyes.

Eve said, "Okay," and took her seat. "Maybe your client would like to state his whereabouts last night from eight to ten P.M."

"He doesn't have to, as I can verify them myself, as I attended the same event. The Whitt Group dinner at the New York Grand Hotel. Stephen was the dinner speaker."

Eve nodded as if that was news to her. "And at what time did he speak?"

"It would have been about eight." With a small, smug smile, Kobast nodded back. "He was quite informative and entertaining."

"I bet. And how long did he speak?"

"Perhaps twenty minutes."

"Until about eight-twenty. That doesn't cover the full time period in question."

Now Kobast sighed. "Lieutenant, dozens of people will verify Stephen was at the Grand, in their main ballroom. If one of your ludicrous charges hinges on this—"

"It does. Yes, it does, as Marshall Cosner's time of death was twenty after nine."

"Marsh?" Whitt sucked in his breath, jerked as if slapped. He did both well, but couldn't quite bring the horror into his eyes. It couldn't penetrate the slight sneer. "Marsh is—is dead? How— What happened to him?"

"He succumbed to the same nerve agent you and he hired Lucas Sanchez to cook up so you could punish some old enemies."

Making an effort to look shaken, Whitt turned to his attorney, gripped Kobast's arm. "I don't know what she's talking about, Broward. My God, Marsh was one of my oldest friends."

"Quiet now, Stephen. My client couldn't be in two places at once."

"He didn't have to be. Peabody."

Peabody opened the evidence box, took out a disc. "This is a copy of the security feed from the Grand, the Fifty-third Street service door, followed by the security feed from the Hubble Hotel garage on Fifty-second. Note the time," Peabody added as she cued it up.

"You missed the cam on the gift shop, Steve," Eve said as at twenty-thirty-two he strode quickly past. "Further note the feed on the exit door skips eighteen seconds. Our EDD confirms this skip was caused by a jammer."

"So I walked by the gift shop. Is it against the law to hunt up a bathroom now?"

At the outburst, Kobast signaled Whitt to silence.

"Switching to the garage cam at the Hubble," Peabody announced. "Time stamp twenty-thirty-five. Freezing at twenty-thirty-eight."

It froze on the image of a man in a suit on a black scooter. The helmet and visor hid his face.

"Are you kidding? That's not me. You can't see his face, for God's sake. I don't own a scooter."

"Ms. Reo." Kobast turned to her, and his voice dripped pity and derision. "This is hardly identifying evidence. I expect better of you."

"Oh, I've got better. First, unless you've suddenly lost the power of sight, Mr. Kobast, you can clearly see the man on the scooter is wearing the same suit, same tie, same shoes as Mr. Whitt wore in the Grand Hotel feed. Added to it, while he doesn't own a scooter, his cousin James Cutter does. In fact, that very scooter with that plate is registered to Mr. Cutter. Mr. Cutter confirms that your client has the codes to the garage where said scooter is kept, and the codes to said scooter."

"It's not me." Whitt folded his arms over his chest. "I never left the Grand. I was there from seven until after eleven."

"No, you weren't," Eve countered, "but let's skip that

for now and go back in time. How about five that same evening? Five yesterday."

Whitt merely shrugged. Kobast folded his hands. "Was another crime committed? Another murder you'll try to hang on my client?"

"Not a murder, but a crime. How about if we rephrase and ask your client what he was doing entering Marshall Cosner's apartment—when Mr. Cosner wasn't in residence—at five last evening? And before he works up a denial, we also have that security feed."

Peabody took another disc out of the evidence box.

"This is ridiculous. Marsh was my *friend*. He borrowed a set of my earbuds to try out, and I wanted them back. He told me to go on by and get them, so I did."

"Did you take anything else out of Mr. Cosner's apartment?"

"Of course not. It's all right, Broward," he said before his attorney could interrupt. "It's simply a mistake."

"It's not a mistake that several items were missing from Mr. Cosner's apartment."

"How would you know?"

"Stephen—"

"Well, how would she know?" The arrogance was back, in full. "She's just throwing things against the wall, desperate for something to stick."

"Okay, let's throw this." Eve rose, took a tablet, a mini-comp, and a drop 'link out of the evidence box. "These items belonged to Mr. Cosner and were retrieved by me and my partner from the hidey-hole in the floor at the foot of your bed. We know this drop 'link, not yet activated, was Mr. Cosner's, as he left his fingerprints on it. These other two." She took them out. "Those are yours. Now, what's an upstanding financial adviser doing with drop 'links, and his dead friend's devices in a hidden area under his bedroom floor?"

Whitt turned to his lawyer. "She's lying, of course. They obviously planted those. For some reason she's got it in for me."

"Mr. Kobast." Reo spoke up. "You're aware that, by law and regulation, Lieutenant Dallas and all police officers who entered Mr. Whitt's residence, fully warranted to enter and search, wore body recorders. The entire search is on record, which we can provide for you here if you require it."

"A safe, concealed area isn't against the law," Kobast returned. "Neither is holding some electronics for a friend, or acquiring a drop 'link."

"Got me there." Eve enjoyed Whitt's smirk as she reached into the box again. "And neither is possessing five hundred thousand in cash." She set the stack of bagged, banded bills on the table. "Though, boy, a money guy ought to know keeping cash under a metaphorical mattress doesn't earn dividends. But what is illegal?" She tossed the jammer, a bagged passport, driver's license, ID card on the table. "Acquiring a jammer, acquiring false ID."

"This is bullshit! They're trying to railroad me. I don't have to sit here and listen to this."

"Sit down!" Eve snapped as Whitt started to rise. "You're under arrest. It's sit down or sit in a cell." Deliberately, she angled her head. "I bet this feels as frustrating to you as being yanked out of Gold, pulled away from your sycophants and girlfriend."

"That's enough, Lieutenant." Kobast maintained his calm, but Eve had seen the surprise when she'd tossed down the fake IDs. "I want to speak with my client."

"Sure." She repacked the evidence box. "We've got a few more surprises in here." She winked at Whitt. "You know what they are. Dallas, Peabody, Reo exiting Interview. Record off."

"Well, Kobast knows he's got a liar for a client," Reo said cheerfully once the door closed behind them. "And he's wondering if he's got worse. So . . . cold drinks? I'm buying."

"Tube of Pepsi," Eve said.

"Diet of same, thanks."

Reo started toward Vending, met Mira as the doctor stepped out of Observation. After a quick word, Mira continued toward Eve and Peabody on canary-yellow heels that matched her slim dress and jacket.

"His lies aren't holding." Mira glanced toward the interview room door. "So he'll shift them. I suspect he'll shift any blame to Cosner. After all, Cosner can't contradict him."

"Yeah, I'm with you there."

"He feels entitled to lie, as he was entitled to punish those who offended or betrayed him—or who simply became inconvenient. He doesn't fully recognize, certainly doesn't respect, your authority over him. And it infuriates him. He has no feelings of guilt or remorse, even doubt, to trip him up. It's his anger that will."

"Piss him off. That's a win-win for us, right, Peabody?"

"Like winning the lottery and having crazy sex with Tiger Bellows."

"Who the hell is Tiger Bellows?"

"He's a vid star," Mira supplied, smiling. "And he is dreamy."

"Oh, did you see him in *Surrender*?" Carting tubes, Reo sighed.

"Those eyes." Peabody closed her own. "You just want to melt."

"Great, good to know." Eve snatched her tube. "Maybe we could, I don't know, segue back to nailing this murdering bastard."

"I can tell you the IDs threw Kobast off his stride, and he's pushing Whitt to explain." Reo passed out the rest of the tubes, including Mira's cold tea.

"He won't tell his lawyer the truth," Mira said.

"Oh, we're used to being lied to. Kobast is a vet."

"And Whitt's a lying, murdering, homicidal sociopath," Eve added. "He's also the spoiled, pampered, rich son of an important family. People are supposed to clean up his messes."

Eve pulled out her signaling 'link. "I've got some incomings." She stepped away to take them, paced as she read. Walking back into a discussion on where Mira got the canary-yellow shoes didn't dim her smile.

"Did you win the lottery?" Peabody wondered.

"The forensic lottery, yeah. Here's what we've got, and how we're going to use it."

The twenty minutes Kobast spent conferring with his client gave Eve plenty of time to outline the strategy. She walked back into Interview, restarted the record, set down the evidence box.

"My client," Kobast began, "in a mistaken yet understandable attempt to protect his oldest friend, one he's just learned has died, has shaded the truth on certain matters."

"Lied?" Eve supplied, and Kobast ignored her.

"He will make a brief statement, explaining how certain items in evidence came into his possession."

"Well, we're all ears."

"I noticed Marsh was acting strange," Whitt began.

"Nervous, excited, angry, all over the map. I thought . . . well, it's no secret Marsh had an illegals issue. I suspected he was using again, even tried to talk to him about it. He blew me off. When I found out he had some sort of deal going with Sanchez, I tried to talk to him again. Sanchez had been supplying Marsh with illegals since high school."

"Only Marsh?"

Whitt cast his eyes down. "I'm not going to deny I experimented a little in high school, but I don't use. But Marsh . . ."

He broke off as if overcome. Breathed out as if to gather himself.

"When I met Marsh at the club the other night, he was really whacked-out. He was talking about TAG, and how he got a raw deal, shipped off to boarding school, hounded by his grandparents. How smooth everything had been until some of the teachers started pushing in, pushing at the headmaster, how everything went to shit after Rufty came in. And . . ."

Whitt looked down again, folded his hands together. "How he'd found a way to pay them back, pay them all back."

He looked up then. Eve imagined he believed he'd worked horror into his eyes, but he didn't have the skills. They stayed ice-cold. "I didn't know—I never imagined he meant to hurt anyone. I thought it was just bullshitting. I even got into it some, just joking around. When you came to my office and told me . . . I never put it together. I never even considered it was Marsh.

"Could I have some water?"

Without a word, Peabody rose, started out.

"Peabody exiting Interview," Eve said for the record.

"Then he tagged me. We had drop 'links. It was just a kind of gag since school. Just our thing. But he tagged me, and in a real panic. He told me the cops were closing in. I didn't know what he was talking about, thought he was high. But he begged me to go by his place, get his tablet, his mini, his drop 'links, the jammer. He said he had something to finish, and wouldn't tell me what. I finally said I'd do it to calm him down. It's the last time I talked to him. The last thing he said was 'You're my best friend, Steve. I'm doing this for both of us.'"

If he tried to work up tears, he failed, but he did manage to make his voice crack a bit at the end.

Eve let the silence hang for a couple of beats. "You stated you've been to Mr. Cosner's apartment many times. In fact, had his codes, and your palm print was programmed for access."

"Yes. We were close friends."

"I expect you knew where to find the items he asked you to remove—or he told you where to find them."

"Yes, sure."

"It wouldn't take long, a few minutes, to locate the items, place them in your briefcase and messenger bag. So why did you spend more than thirty minutes inside Mr. Cosner's apartment?"

Hadn't thought it through, Eve concluded as Whitt hesitated, calculated.

"Peabody entering Interview."

Peabody set the water in front of Whitt. He drank deep.

"Keep going," Eve urged.

"I had the event to attend, didn't see the point in going home first . . . And, to be truthful—"

"Yes, let's."

"I was worried about Marsh. I looked through his place for illegals. I was going to try to do an intervention, get him back in rehab."

"Just thinking about your friend. Your best friend, who obviously trusted you. Did you find the illegals?"

"No."

"Funny, we found his stash in the top left-hand drawer of the master bathroom vanity in about three minutes."

"My client is not the police," Kobast began.

"In the bathroom drawer," Eve repeated, let that hang a moment. "You didn't explain the false identification, Steve."

"I found it when I was looking for the illegals. I—I didn't know what to think. I just grabbed it, stuffed it in my bag. I put everything in the floor safe when I got home, and planned to talk to Marsh about it all today. But he's . . . he's gone."

"He sure is. So during your thirty-minute search, where you failed to find quite the stash of illegals in a bathroom drawer, you stumbled across false identification that your friend had made for you?"

"Yes, I was baffled. Shocked."

"But you didn't find any for him? No fake IDs for Marsh?"

"No, I didn't." Whitt stared through her. "Did you?"

"We did not, which means you actually expect us to believe your dead friend, out of his own pocket—a considerable expense—out of the goodness of his heart, purchased false identification for you, but not himself. And you have no idea he'd done so, or why he'd done so."

"That's right. I'm telling you all I know."

Eve leaned forward, locked eyes. "You're not nearly as good a liar when you don't have time to plan it out."

"Lieutenant!" Kobast objected.

She flicked him a glance. "You're not buying this any more than I am. But let's move on. Were you aware Mr. Cosner owned a building downtown, a converted warehouse?"

"No he didn't." Whitt let out a laugh. "I helped Marsh with investments. He didn't own any real estate."

"Well, gee." Peabody knitted her eyebrows, pursed her lips. "You helped him with investments, communicated with him on drop 'links, had the codes to his really well-secured apartment. Your palm print was registered on the same. All that, and you didn't know where he kept his stash, didn't know he'd laid out considerable money for a false ID—for you. Didn't know he owned a building downtown."

She sent Eve a wide-eyed, incredulous look. "It doesn't sound like a balanced relationship."

"You're right. Maybe Marsh didn't trust Steve as much as Steve thought." From the evidence box, Eve took the paperwork on the building, laid it on the table.

"I don't understand this. He would have told me."

In a snap, Peabody switched from incredulous to sympathetic. "I guess it's hard to find out all this, but addiction can make you do strange and destructive things," said Sympathetic Peabody. "If he'd been thinking straight, he would have told you—a friend, a financial adviser. He'd have wanted you to see the property, and yeah, advise him."

"Of course he would."

"But he didn't." Eve slid the paperwork toward Kobast so he could study it. "So you never knew about it. Never went there."

"No, never. What in the world was he doing with a warehouse? And in that neighborhood."

"He set up a place for Sanchez to live, set up a lab for Sanchez to work. That is until Sanchez created the formula, the agent—and was murdered."

"Loco's dead?"

"You didn't know?"

"No, why would I? I haven't seen Loco in years. I know he supplied Marsh, but I didn't associate with him. This, all this, had to have been Loco's idea. Marsh would never have done something like this on his own. He had to have Marsh whacked on illegals."

"Lieutenant, Ms. Reo, as your evidence—and my client's cooperation in this matter—clearly points to Mr. Cosner's culpability, we demand the charges against Mr. Whitt be dropped."

"Mmm, there's just a little hitch with that. Well, a few really," Eve amended. "Did you know a human being sheds between fifty and a hundred hairs every day?"

"What nonsense is this?" Kobast demanded.

"Just a fun fact. A fun forensic fact. Since you're a criminal defense attorney, I imagine you've had an occasion to cross-examine our hair and fiber expert, Ms. Harvo."

Carefully, Kobast kept his face blank. "Please get to the point."

"Harvo's the point. You'd know just how good she is. So good, in fact, she found, identified, and matched DNA with two hundred and twenty-three hairs Mr. Whitt left in Mr. Cosner's converted warehouse. The one he's just stated, for the record, he knew nothing about, had never seen, had never been to. And one of them—bonus point—was found caught in the strap of the air mask he used to protect himself when he killed his old pal, Marsh.

"How'd your hair end up there, Steve?"

"This is more bullshit. Broward, they're still trying to screw me. I've had enough."

"Quiet." Kobast put a hand on Whitt's arm. "Be quiet."

"You're probably going to ask for another little confab with your lying sack of a client, but you might as well have more forensics before you do. Like the thumbprint you left behind the shelves when you removed the spy camera you'd placed in the lab where Sanchez cooked up the nerve agent that killed three people."

"I was never there. You're the liar."

"Two hundred and twenty-three hairs and a thumb-print," Eve said. "Oh, and you haven't seen Loco for years, didn't know he was recently deceased? Murder by stabbing. Our sweepers are really good, too."

Eve took a bagged steak knife out of the evidence box. "And yet this knife, found in your kitchen drawer, has traces of blood still on it. People think they clean it all over, but almost never do. Our ME—he's a genius, as your attorney knows, I'm sure—matches this knife with the stab wounds on Lucas Sanchez's body."

"Marsh must have used it. Taken it, used it, put it back."

"Not a balanced relationship," Peabody repeated with a sad shake of her head. "Poor old Marsh."

"Yeah, poor old Marsh," Eve agreed. "You should have walked a few more blocks before catching the cab when you left Cosner's apartment, Steve. You only gave it a block, then took said cab to your cousin's garage. You left fingerprints on the keypad, on the door, on the scooter. We actually check these things."

"You think you're so smart."

"Yeah. I think you're not as smart as you think—but a hell of a lot smarter than your dead school pal."

She slapped a hand on the table mostly for the satisfaction of seeing him jolt. "You were the brains behind this. He went along with you, the way he always did. Like when you beat Miguel Rodriges, put him in the hospital."

"Who?"

"I don't doubt you don't remember him. He remembers you, and your pal documented the beating—and the consideration of just killing the kid—in this book."

She took it out of the box. "You missed this when you went through Cosner's place."

"That's not proof of anything."

"It starts adding up, as your attorney knows."

"Be quiet, Stephen. Put your cards on the table, Lieutenant."

"It goes back to Gold Academy, to Grange. Your father had a sexual relationship with her. It didn't bother you she had sex with some of the teachers, some of the other fathers. But yours?"

She took a photo of Whitt's father and Grange out of the box. "You didn't send this one to Greenwald because you didn't, at least then, want your father ID'd. But, like the one you sent, you took this—kept it in your hidey-hole. But I'm guessing Cosner took this one."

And pulled out another, one of Lotte Grange with Stephen Whitt.

"My client was a minor, and this woman an adult, and the headmistress of his school."

"Agreed, and that will be addressed, take my word. You wanted to punish her for doing your father, your own father, while she was doing you, didn't you, Steve? You made sure you got one of Grange with your father's face turned away, obscured."

Pausing, she pulled a copy of what she described out

of the evidence box. "You sent it to Grange's husband. The divorces, your parents, Grange, that was just fine. But you didn't expect Grange to leave the school. She was your shield, plus sex. Seriously teacher's pet, right?"

"As a minor—"

Eve cut Kobast off with a vicious look that jolted him as much as her slap on the table had Whitt. "This is where it started." She jabbed a finger on the photo of Grange with Whitt—a teenager, a student.

"Right here. But it didn't end until today. Grange cut her losses, took another position in another city. Then the next thing you know, Rufty's in there laying down new rules. That son of a bitch. You're getting pulled out, but at least you'll still be with Grange, still have that shield, probably the sex. But you lose the girl."

Eve rose, walked around the table. "You didn't love the girl, you're not capable of it. But she belonged to you, she did what you said, what you wanted. She was nearly beautiful and obliging enough to be worthy of you. And all of a sudden, she moves on. She just let you go. You can blame her parents at first, but Jesus, she doesn't even try."

She leaned down, close to his ear, whispered, "That stupid, spineless cunt."

Eve watched his hands fist as she eased back.

"Then what does she do? She gets tight with the mother who separated you, she goes off and starts a business. Then, the final blow." Eve reached into the box, took out the bagged clippings from the evidence box. "She gets engaged, and not to just anyone, but to someone important, to the son of someone really important. She had no right."

Eve rapped a fist on the table, whipped out the words.

"Isn't that how you saw it? Nobody walks away from
you like that. And whose fault was it?"

She took the printout of the kill list, tossed it on the
table. "Theirs. It's just not as simple as hitting delete,
Steve. You didn't want to kill them, not the ones responsible. You wanted them to suffer, to lose, to never forget. The academy had been your golden goose, and they
killed it. So you killed Rufty's husband, Duran's wife.
You killed Sanchez when you didn't need him anymore,
and you killed your partner in this, your best friend, so
you could shovel all the blame on him and walk away.

"But." She leaned over his shoulder again, turned her
voice into a verbal sneer. "You weren't smart enough to
pull it off. Every time you thought you covered your
tracks, you left bread crumbs. You kept the knife you
used to kill because you're arrogant, and too stupid to
throw it away."

"Shut the fuck up," Whitt snarled at her.

"Lieutenant," Kobast began, but she pushed over
him.

"Cards on the table. You kept a record of your enemies, the targets, their schedules on a tablet in the hole
in the floor because you felt smug when you looked at it."

To back up the words, Peabody pulled the tablet out
of the evidence box, and a printout of the kill list taken
from it.

"You spent a half hour inside your friend's apartment before you murdered him because you're such a
moron it never occurred to you we'd check the damn
security feed.

"You didn't destroy Cosner's tablet and couldn't get
by his passcode because you're stupid. He kept up his
habit of documenting, like a journal. Only he went from
a book to a tablet. It's all on there."

Shifting, she pushed her face into his, filled her voice with derision.

"You're an idiot who couldn't get through high school without cheating. You cheated on your girlfriend with a woman old enough to be your grandmother. You preyed on the weaker, the defenseless because it made you feel like a big man. But you're not, never were. You're still a small, selfish, stupid boy."

"Fuck you!"

She shifted again so the elbow he tried to jab brushed her hip. Now she could add assaulting an officer if she wanted to pile it on.

She wanted to pile it on.

"Stephen, you need to be quiet."

"Fuck quiet. Stupid?"

She saw emotion in him now. Saw the ugly rage.

"If I'm so stupid, how come Rufty's fag husband's dead? And that asshole Duran's bitch? How does stupid get some loser junkie to focus in, to do the work to make something the military would pay *billions* for? If you're so goddamn smart," he shouted over Kobast's orders to stop talking, "how come you didn't figure it out sooner? Before Marsh got high and took out the egg?"

"You gave him the illegal in the scotch. You tampered with the seal of the egg."

"So the fuck what? He still did it himself. And if you're so much smarter than I am, why is that pontificating excuse for a chemistry teacher's older-than-dirt wife dead?"

"You mean Lilliana Rosalind? She's fine. We intercepted that shipment because you're an idiot."

"Enough, enough. This interview is over." Kobast lurched to his feet.

Eve nodded. "You know it is, Counselor. Your client

has confessed, on the record, to four murders and an attempted murder. The other assorted charges are mixed in there, too. And all because somebody said he couldn't have everything he wanted when he wanted it."

She looked back at Whitt. "Now you'll spend the rest of your life in a cage being told every day what you can't have."

"I won't go to prison." His lips curled. "Do you understand who I am? Who my family is?"

"I absolutely do."

"Stephen, be quiet. I don't want to hear another word. This interview is over. Stephen, you'll need to go back to your cell and wait for me. Ms. Reo, we need to talk."

"You better fix this, Broward, do you fucking hear me? You better fix this if you know what's good for you. You've got a wife, too."

Kobast jerked at the shock of the threat, said nothing.

"Peabody, get a uniform to assist you in taking Mr. Whitt back to his cell."

"I'll come after you," Whitt mumbled, his eyes dead and fixed on Eve.

"Stephen, for God's sake."

"I'll come after all of you."

"Keep believing that," Eve suggested. "It may help you through the first decade or so. Interview end. Record off."

Epilogue

In her office near end of shift, Eve drifted off with her head on her desk. She'd sent Peabody home, written the reports, filled out the forms, turned the lock.

She'd had her meetings with Reo, with Mira, added them to her notes.

And closed the book, cleared the board.

When she'd realized she couldn't take another cup of coffee, she put her head down, closed her eyes.

Roarke woke her with a stroke on the back, a kiss on the head.

"I'm just . . . resting."

"Out for the count, Lieutenant, but I thought you'd object to me carrying you out of your office."

"Yeah, I would." She rubbed her eyes clear. "I appreciate you coming down."

"I'm happy to be a part of this, and you can tell me how you worked it all on the way."

"Okay."

"Your board's clear."

She glanced back at it as she rose. "For now."

She started the saga on the way to the garage, wound through it as Roarke drove.

"His counsel pushed for a deal. Reo stuck firm. They'll order their own shrink, try to work something there, but it won't fly. He knew right from wrong, he just didn't give a rat's ass."

"Will you tell the ex-girlfriend?"

"I've already talked to her. I thought she should know before this hits because the media will dig up her name and the connection. And I spoke with Rosalind, let him know there's nothing to worry about. Same with the others on the list. I figure I owe Harvo a big bottle of something, even though she's feeling pretty good without it."

"She seems like a champagne sort."

"Maybe. Okay. The son of a bitch killed his only real friend because it was convenient. He didn't have a scrap of remorse over it. There was a time Mavis was my only friend—not that I wanted one. Well, and Feeney, but that was different, because boss. But after Mavis wore me down into friendship, I'd have stood for her no matter what. Now I've got all these damn people, and it's the same. I'd stand for them."

"He has nothing inside him. And no one who means more than he means to himself. What about Grange?"

"She's done, or will be. I only wish I could put her in a cage. But I had a discussion with the powers that be at the prep school, gave them documentation, which includes her naked with a then student—minor. She's done."

"It did start with her, didn't it?"

"People like Whitt, I think they're born empty. But yeah, she nurtured it, planted the seeds for it, perpetuated it. So, done," she said when he pulled up at Rufty's house.

Charles and Louise waited on the sidewalk.

"We wanted to walk awhile," Louise said as Eve got out of the car. "So we walked down to wait for you." She took Eve's hands. "Thank you."

"It's the job, Louise."

"I know it, but this is personal."

"It's not the job to take this time, to know he'd need a friend," Charles put in, "when you tell him. It won't bring Kent back, but it will give Martin some peace."

She hoped it would, as she hoped it would bring some peace to Jay Duran when she told him.

She walked to the door and, taking Roarke's hand, rang the bell.

Later, sometime later when the day was finally done, she sat with Roarke by the pond, beside the tree they'd planted, with the scent of spring in the air, the stars blooming overhead, and the lights of the house glowing.

She'd done the job, and would hold on to her own peace while it lasted.

Read on for an excerpt from

SHADOWS IN DEATH

by J. D. Robb

Available in 2020 in hardcover from
St. Martin's Press

1

As it often did since he'd married a cop, murder inter-rupted more pleasant activities. Then again, Roarke supposed, the woman lying in a pool of her own blood a few steps inside the arch in Washington Square Park had a heftier complaint.

After all, he'd known what he, a former criminal (no convictions), was getting into when he fell for the cop. He doubted the woman in fashionable athletic wear expected to end the pretty spring night with her belly sliced open.

He and his cop might have missed the last scene of an entertaining play, but the woman missed the rest of her life.

And here, on a balmy May night, in the blooming spring of 2061, he watched another kind of play.

His cop and the victim held center stage under the hard crime scene lights. Together they made a sad sil-houette against the thin curtain meant to shield the dead from the prying eyes of onlookers.

Uniforms had barriers up to separate the rest of the audience. The vendors, the lovers, the strollers and tourists, the buskers and dog walkers goggled at death.

He kept out of the way as the lead—Lieutenant Eve Dallas—performed her duties in this tale of morality and mortality.

She crouched beside the body, lean and tough in her leather jacket and boots, her field kit open beside her, her short brown hair shining under the lights.

"Victim is identified as Galla Modesto, age thirty-three, residence on Prince."

"Galla Modesto."

When Roarke spoke, Eve lifted her head, narrowed those whiskey-colored cop's eyes. "You know her?"

"No. Her brother a bit. Modesto Wine and Spirits. She'd be one of the heirs—third generation, I'd think. International, family-owned company, with their home base in Tuscany."

"Interesting. Married—Jorge Tween—six years. One offspring, a son, age four." She took out a gauge. "TOD, twenty-two-eighteen. COD, from on-site observation, would be the eight-inch vertical slice through her abdomen."

Now with microgoggles in place, she leaned closer to the gaping wound. "It looks like a deep stab into her lower abdomen, with an upward thrust to open her up. ME to confirm."

Still crouched, she shifted a little. "No visible defensive or other offensive wounds. No handbag recovered, but the vic's dressed for a run or the gym. She's wearing a good-sized diamond and diamond-crusted ring on her left hand, what look like diamond stud earrings—two in the left, one in the right. And a sport-style wrist unit.

"No evidence this was a mugging."

Eve opened the zippered pocket of the woman's warm-up jacket. "'Link." She bagged it, then reached into the pocket in the running pants. "ID."

Rising, she moved around to the other side of the body, opened the other pocket. "Panic button. Obviously didn't panic in time."

"Here's our Peabody," Roarke told her, "with McNab."

Eve's partner hurried toward the barricades with her main man, EDD detective Ian McNab.

Since Peabody wore a dress—one covered with pink tulips under her pink coat—and McNab wore his version of party wear in pink baggies, airboots so violently green they glowed, and a shirt with jags and jigs of both colors, Roarke deduced they'd been out when the call came through.

They both badged the uniforms, moved into the cordoned-off area. Peabody, still sporting red streaks in the dark hair she'd styled in festive curls, went straight to Eve and the body.

"Sorry, Dallas, we were at a club on the East Side, got delayed getting here."

Eve gave Peabody's outfit—including the skinny-heeled party shoes—a flick of a glance. "Officers Frist and Nadir first on scene. Talk to them, start interviewing any potential wits." She glanced back. "McNab can see about any security feed since he's here."

"Got it."

"Seal up and help me turn her first. Vic's Galla Modesto," she began, and gave Peabody the main points as they worked.

With the body turned, Eve saw no more wounds or marks—and found another small pocket in the back of the running pants. "Key swipe," she said for the recording. "Body and Mind Fitness Center," she read, then bagged it into evidence.

She closed her field kit, took out her comm to contact the sweepers and the morgue.

When she turned, Roarke held out a go-cup of black coffee.

"Where'd you get this?"

"An enterprising vendor. I suspect it's somewhere between cop coffee and palatable."

She drank, shrugged. "Somewhere between. Thanks. You should head out. I need to talk to witnesses, talk to her husband, go by the gym she used."

"I'm having your car sent down—and arranged my own transportation."

She drank more—barely—palatable coffee, and looked at him.

That face, that face. One of life's serious miracles, and sure as hell one of hers. Eyes, boldly blue with lashes as silky as the black hair that fell nearly to his shoulders, looked into hers. He had a mouth creative angels sculpted on a particularly generous day. The planes, the angles combined in a result somewhere between the romance of a poet and the sexuality of one of those angels defiantly taking the fall.

Add the music of Ireland in his voice, and you had an exceptional package.

"Always handy."

And that perfect mouth curved. "We all do our part. I'll just stay handy until the transpo gets here." Absently, he scanned the crowd behind the barricades. "McNab should be back shortly with the security feed so . . ."

She saw his eyes narrow, saw something dark come into them.

"What?" She shifted instantly to look in the same direction. "What did you see?"

"Someone I used to know."

Before she could speak again, he walked away, quick and smooth.

"Well, shit." She gestured a uniform over to stay with the body, started to go after him when Peabody hurried back.

"We've got a few witnesses who saw her go down, and we have one who didn't but claims she was coming here to meet him. He's wrecked, so I'm thinking there might have been some hanky in the panky."

"Let's take him first."

What the hell was Roarke doing? she wondered.

He cut through the crowd. He knew how to move fast, sliding through. Once upon a time he'd have come out the other side with pockets full from pockets he'd picked.

But though he moved fast, eyes scanning, instincts alert, he didn't see the face again.

That bloody shadow from his past, Roarke thought as he looked beyond the lights, the crowds, the sparkle of the fountain, the empty benches, had shown himself deliberately.

A taunt. A kind of flipped middle finger, as he'd been—again deliberately—far enough away to easily melt out of sight and vanish again.

Well then, if the fecking bastard wanted to come out and play, he'd be more than willing for the game.

"We're a long way from the alleys of Dublin now, boyo," he muttered, and made his way back again.

Since the wit, Marlon Stowe, was shaking, with tears streaming, Eve took him to one of the benches.

Mid-thirties, she judged, about five-ten, a lot of thick, sandy hair, brown eyes, and a stubbly goatee.

"You were meeting Ms. Modesto here?"

"By the fountain. She said she'd try to be here about ten-fifteen, no later than ten-thirty."

Since he wore black pants, a thin black sweater, black boots, she understood they hadn't planned to take a run together.

"Why were you meeting?"

He swiped at his face. He had a smear of blue paint on the side of his thumb. "We were involved. We met last summer. Galla bought one of my paintings. I had a sidewalk display, and she liked one I'd done in Tuscany. She—her family—they're from Tuscany, and she said it reminded her. And she came by a few times, and to this gallery, and . . . we fell in love."

"You had a romantic and intimate relationship with Ms. Modesto."

"We fell in love," he repeated. "Sometimes we'd meet here, and just sit and talk. Sometimes we'd go to my loft. I knew she was married, she told me. We never lied to each other. She has a little boy. She wanted to leave her husband, but she has a little boy. She wanted to leave him, even talked to her lawyer. But . . ."

Now he covered his face with his hands. "She told me, the last time we were together had to be the last time. We both knew . . . Right from the start we both knew it couldn't last. She had to think of her son first. She had to try to fix her marriage, fix her family."

"But she agreed to meet you here tonight."

"I asked if she would. Not to be together. Just to really say goodbye. I had something I wanted to give her."

"What's that?"

He opened the bag he carried, took out a package

wrapped in thick brown paper. "It's a painting. Like a companion piece to the one she first bought. I thought, it's the first and it's the last."

"You must've been hurt and angry."

As he shook his head, his eyes welled again. "I loved her. I knew she was married, had a child. She never lied. She never promised. And . . ." He drew a long breath. "I knew she loved me. She couldn't be with me, but she loved me. If I hadn't asked her to come here to-night . . ."

He fell apart then, so Eve looked to Peabody, the soother.

"Marlon." Peabody sat beside him. "You can't blame yourself, but you may be able to help. Did anyone else know you and Galla were meeting here tonight?"

"No. We were careful—our relationship. It was private. It was . . ." He used the heels of his hands to scrub his face dry. "It was just for us. She said she'd tell her husband she was going to get some time at the gym. Just a quick solo workout. She did that, so it wouldn't be unusual. She wouldn't have told anyone she was coming here. I didn't tell anyone."

"How did you communicate?"

"Just texts."

"When were you last together, when she ended it?"

"Just last week. She came to the loft, and told me. We made love one last time. And today, the painting was ready, so I texted her and asked if she'd come here, so I could give her a gift. That it would help me say good-bye."

"When you met here, did you ever notice anyone paying particular attention to her, to the two of you?"

"No. It's such a good space. It always felt safe here."

"When she came to your loft?" Eve drew his attention

back to her. "Did you ever notice anyone outside, any-one who made you feel uncomfortable?"

"No. I have a small loft right in the Village, over the gallery. I work there, show there, do some teaching. She could only come once a week, sometimes twice, but usually once a week when she could get away, when her son was out with his nanny or on a playdate. We'd only have an hour, maybe two. We loved a lifetime's worth. We knew we only had that little bit of time."

"Did she ever tell you she felt threatened or had been threatened?"

"No, no. God no."

"Did she fight with her husband?"

Almost absently now, he swiped his fingers over his eyes. "Not really, she never said so. He was more in-terested in the business, and the show, you know? How they looked together, going to events. She wanted to go back to Tuscany, to take her boy. For us to live there. We dreamed about that, even knowing it was just a dream."

He thrust the painting to Eve. "Will you take this? I can't look at it. I don't want it. It's too painful."

"Peabody, give Mr. Stowe a receipt for the painting. We'll need to take it into evidence for now."

"I don't want it." He began to cry again. "I can't sell it. Just keep it."

"We're not allowed to do that. But we'll work some-thing out. Detective Peabody will give you a receipt, and take your contact information."

Eve spotted Roarke, passed the painting to Peabody. "Then you're free to go. Do you need transportation?"

"No, no. I can walk. I'll walk."

"We're sorry for your loss, Mr. Stowe. Please contact me or Detective Peabody if you think of anything that may help our investigation."

She got up, moved quickly to Roarke. "What's going on?" she demanded. "You're pissed. Scary Roarke pissed."

He took her arm. "Let's walk."

"I can't just—"

"With me." He tightened his grip to lead her away from the crime scene. "Lorcan Cobbe," he began. "You'll want to do a run there. From Dublin, and he'd be three or four—maybe five—years older than me."

"One of your old friends?"

"Not remotely." He moved away from the lights so they stood in shadows. "He worked for my father, and as he had no talent for thievery and considerable for viciousness, he did enforcement, intimidation, helped with the protection racket. We can get into all of that at another time, but you'll want to run him. And you'll want to take care."

He put his hands on her shoulders. "A great deal of care, Eve."

"Why?"

"He'd do me in a heartbeat if he could manage it, but he'd kill what matters to me and enjoy it all the more. A killer is what is he, and always has been."

"And you saw him, at my crime scene."

"I saw him. He made sure I did. Aye, he made certain of that, bloody bastard."

He scanned the park again, but knew he wouldn't see that face again. Not tonight.

"I'm telling you, I didn't have to see him put the knife in that woman to know he did. He'll be your man on this."

"Why her? He couldn't know you'd be here."

"That's just a nice twist of fate for him. Killing's what he does, Eve, for pleasure and profit. He does his work primarily in Europe, but this wouldn't be his first job in the States, I'd think. I don't know of him coming, for business at least, to New York before, and I think I would. But he's here now."

She took it in. It was rare to see him agitated—more than angry—so she took it in, and took it seriously. "Describe him—as you saw him tonight."

"About six feet, a strong build, wide in the shoulders, light brown hair worn in what you'd call a topknot. Light complected, clean-shaven. Black pants and shirt, a red jacket. He stepped clear so I'd see him, looked right at me. Smiled."

He ran his hands down her arms, back again. "He'll know what you are to me. Or if he doesn't, he'll now make it his business to find out."

"Why does he hate you, particularly?"

"Particularly? He claimed to be Patrick Roarke's bastard, and as senior to me, his oldest son."

"Was he?"

"Unlikely, but not impossible, I suppose. Unlikely, as the old man liked him considerably more than me, and if he'd been his blood, would have taken him in. That's not important at the moment. He bloody well didn't just happen to be in the park when a woman—a wealthy one—ends up gutted. And gutting, throat slitting, disemboweling are favorite pastimes of Lorcan Cobbe."

"All right, I'll run him. I'll put out a BOLO."

Now he framed her face with his hands before she could object. "And you'll take care. Take very good care."

"Yes," she said because he needed her to. "And same goes."

"He won't try for me right off—what's the fun in that? I have to contact some people."

"We're going to need to talk about this, in more detail."

"And we will. Your car's here." He gestured toward the arch. "I'll see you at home."

As she watched him stride away, she realized she was worried because he was worried.

Marriage, she thought. It could fuck you up.

"LT." McNab pranced over in his airboots, long tail of blond hair swinging. "Got your security discs. I already looked at the footage of the kill."

"We have the kill on the feed?"

"Yes and no. I'm going to say the killer knew the cam angles, and kept his face clear. What we've got is the vic coming in, then what appears to be a male, about six feet, probably about one-ninety, black pants, black hoodie worn up, cutting across her path. We got him from the back, so no way to tell age or race or make a firm determination of gender."

McNab glanced back as the morgue team bagged the body. A line of colorful hoops glittered on his earlobe. "He had his hands in his jacket pockets, his head down, moving right along, then cuts in front of her. She stops. You can see his right arm jerk up, then pull back. He keeps right on walking, and she staggers a couple steps. A lot of blood even before she goes down. Then you've got a couple of people running over to her. One of them turns her over. And the screaming starts. He's already out of cam view by then."

"Take them in, run through them. I need copies. All feed, all angles."

"You got it. He had to be waiting for her, Dallas. The way he moved on her. It was purposeful, you know? Not random, it just didn't feel random."

He might dress like a circus act, but she knew his cop instincts hit solid.

"No, I don't think random. Peabody," she said when her partner joined them.

"I talked to a handful of people, and to a couple of the uniforms who talked to people. Most didn't see or notice anything until she went down, but I have two who stated they saw a man in a black hoodie walking away as she fell. No solid description beyond the hoodie, worn up, and the assumption of male."

"That coordinates with the security feed. McNab, when you're going over the discs, look for a male—the height and build you described. Caucasian, late thirties to early forties, light brown hair—man bun deal—red jacket. Flag anything you find with a view of him."

"Okay. Is he a suspect?"

"Odds are. His name's Lorcan Cobbe, out of Dublin. Roarke saw him in the crowd, recognized him. He's a pro."

"I can start reviewing on my portable if I stick with you for now," McNab told her.

"Fine. Let's move. Peabody, start a run on the vic's husband, Jorge Tween, and let's go notify him."

"If this was a hired hit," Peabody began.

"The spouse is number one," Eve finished.

Her car waited at the curb, as advertised. She got in, sat a moment. "We'll run Cobbe, too, put out a BOLO, but let's see who we're about to talk to first."

Peabody got in the passenger seat, not so discreetly slipped her feet out of her party shoes as McNab climbed in the back. "Tween is forty-two, a VP in distribution at Modesto. He's worked for them for sixteen years. No criminal coming up. Married Galla Modesto six years ago—first and only marriage for both. Son, Angelo, age four."

Eve pulled out, started the short drive to the Modesto/
Tween residence.

"They purchased their New York residence five years
ago. Tween works out of the NY headquarters. Got his
net worth here at just under nine million."

"Hers is more than ten times that," Eve remembered.
"There's a fine motive added to her having an affair."

"She broke it off," Peabody pointed out, but Eve just
shook her head.

"She had an affair, and more, if Stowe's not full of
it, fell in love. It takes a little time to arrange a hit, so
there's that. Then do you call it off because she called
off the affair? Are you sure she did? Did she confess all?
Doubtful. Either way, what's to stop her from changing
her mind, going back to her artist lover, taking her big
mountain of money and moving to Italy?"

Reluctantly as Eve squeezed into a spot at the curb
near the address, Peabody pushed her feet back into her
shoes.

"I'll stick here with this," McNab said from the back.
"Especially if I can get a fizzy from the AC."

"Do that."

He added a winsome smile. "Maybe you got some
chips in here."

"I don't know what the hell's in the AutoChef." Leaving him to find out, Eve got out.

Peabody didn't quite hide the wince when they
started the half-block walk, crosstown.

"Why are you wearing those idiot shoes?"

"They're pretty shoes! We went out dancing—date-
night dancing. You need pretty shoes for date-night
dancing. I didn't know they were going to be work-a-
case shoes."

She moaned a little. "And they're killing me."

"Suck it up."

"This is sucking it up. So Roarke knew this Cobbe back in Ireland?"

"Dublin, when he was a kid. I'll get more details, but Cobbe let Roarke spot him. Wanted him to. Roarke says he's a killer by nature and profession. I'll get more details," she said again, and stopped in front of the house to get a sense of it.

Three stories of whitewashed brick had an elegance, a quiet charm. The security light glowed pale green, but no glow came from the lights at either side of the front door.

The lights that would have welcomed someone home.

Windows stayed dark, so no one waited up for the woman who'd never come home again. Flowers spilled out of painted boxes on the windows flanking the door.

She caught the scent of something soft and sweet as she stepped up, pressed the buzzer.

The household has retired for the night. Please leave your name and contact information. If this is an emergency—

"NYPSD." Eve cut off the computer, held up her badge. "Inform Jorge Tween the police need to speak with him."

Please state the nature of your emergency.

"Your circuits are going to have an emergency unless Mr. Tween is informed the NYPSD is at the door. Scan the damn badge, and get it done."

The scanner light swept her badge.

Your identity is verified, Dallas, Lieutenant Eve. Please wait.

"I hate those damn things."

"You actually have those damn things. You know, on the gates, and on—"

"Doesn't mean I can't hate them. Not a light on inside," Eve commented. "Your wife goes out to the gym, doesn't come back in, say, an hour. Do you just turn off the lights and go to bed?"

"Doesn't seem right," Peabody agreed. "Even if you're pissed at each other, it feels off. At least the lights here should be on if someone's out. Who doesn't do that?"

"Someone who's not expecting anyone. It's a little thing. It's a petty little thing."

Lights came on inside, flooding the windows with their cheerful flowers. Locks clicked.

The door opened for a woman of about fifty in a dark blue robe. Her dark hair tumbled around her face. Her eyes, gypsy brown, held fear and worry.

"You're the police."

"Yes, ma'am." Once again, Eve held up her badge. "We need to speak to Mr. Tween."

"Yes? The system alerted me. I'm the housekeeper. Please, excuse me, come in."

She had an Italian accent and bare feet with toenails painted bold red.

Narrow tables stood on either side of the entrance. They held slender purple flowers in long, thin vases, reflected back by tall mirrors. The tile floor spread in the color of gold sand.

"Please, here in the parlor you can sit." She gestured as she led the way. "You would like coffee? Tea?"

"We're good. Could we have your name?"

"Of course. I am Elena Rinaldi. I am the housekeeper. Please sit. I will alert Mr. Tween. He and Ms. Modesto are sleeping. It is very late."

"Ms. Rinaldi, when did you last see or speak with Mr. Tween or Ms. Modesto?"

"Ah . . . I think about nine this evening. Yes, about nine before I retired to my quarters for the night. Please sit," she repeated, and went out.

"Before Modesto went out," Peabody murmured.

"Yeah." Eve looked around what she imagined they called the front parlor.

More flowers—someone had a fondness for them. And a formal sort of feel with cream-colored sofas, peacock-blue chairs, tables with a slight sheen of gold. More gold in the ornate frame of the big oval mirror over a white marble fireplace filled with flowers and candles now for spring.

The art went for Italian scenes. Red tile roofs on stucco houses and great cathedral domes. Rolling hills and farmhouses. She recognized Tuscany—because she'd been there. As well as a painting of the Spanish Steps in Rome.

She walked to the one of Tuscany—those hills, those tall, slim trees, vineyards with purple grapes climbing, a winding path leading to a house of pale rose stucco with flowers rioting at its feet.

And in the corner, the artist's signature.

M. Stowe.

"It's good work," Peabody commented. "I sent the other one in, still wrapped. You've been there, right?"

"Yeah."

"Does it really look like that?"

"Yeah, it does. It's her room. This is her room."

"Why do you say that?"

"It's formal and elegant. The flowers, the paintings— especially that one. The couple of photographs?" Eve gestured. "The kid, her and the kid, but not the husband.

Her family, most likely, but not with him. The dust catchers all feel female."

Frowning, Peabody looked around. "You're right about that. It all feels female. Not frilly, but female."

Eve gestured. "The tablet on the table by the chair that faces Stowe's painting? She could sit there, read or work or whatever, look up and see the painting. Think about her lover. Think about home.

"A company room," Eve added. "But otherwise hers."

She turned when she heard footsteps, and waited to meet Jorge Tween.

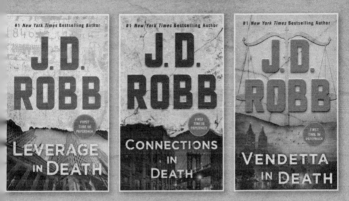